PRAISE FOR LISA EDMONDS

"An action-packed debut with a strong, compelling heroine. Heart of Malice is sure to cast a spell on urban fantasy readers and leave them clamoring for more adventures with Alice Worth."

—JENNIFER ESTEP, NEW YORK TIMES BESTSELLING AUTHOR OF THE ELEMENTAL ASSASSIN URBAN FANTASY SERIES

"The complex magic system throughout Heart of Malice is a genuine joy to read and there's danger and intrigue through-out. The characters leap off the page and the secrets which Alice Worth carries make her a wonderful character. I can't wait to read more of this thrilling series!"

—HELEN HARPER, AUTHOR OF THE BLOOD DESTINY AND LAZY GIRL'S GUIDE TO MAGIC URBAN FANTASY SERIES

"Heart of Malice hits the ground running with the perfect blend of magic action, compelling characters, and sizzling romance. Snarky and cynical Alice Worth is a complex and flawed woman who is not simply kickass but refreshingly intelligent. Lisa Edmonds conducts the twists and turns of the plot like a maestro conductor, spellbinding the reader with her original and innovative worldbuilding, solid magic system, and a compelling backstory that haunts the main story in surprising ways. It's an absolutely delightful, one-sitting, devour it now read."

— DEBORAH WILDE, AUTHOR OF THE UNLIKEABLE DEMON HUNTER AND MAGIC AFTER MIDLIFE URBAN FANTASY SERIES

"Fast-paced and action-packed, the story created by this author is both intriguing and addictive, as is the world she builds. Her prose is lively and entertaining and laced with just the right amount of humor. [. . .] This suspenseful urban fantasy pulls the reader into an imaginative world—one that seamlessly marries reality with the supernatural—through the author's outstanding storytelling skills."

— IND'TALE MAGAZINE

"Edmonds has an eye for both detail and entertaining characters, and her story is fun and energetic. Readers will enjoy this installment and look forward to more in the continuing saga of Alice Worth."

— PUBLISHER'S WEEKLY

"It's no secret that this is one of my favorite series and that Alice is my girl. The author shook me with this book. From the story to the action to the characters, it left me with a huge book hangover. [. . .] I. Loved. Every. Minute. Of. It."

— THE LITERARY VIXEN

Heart of Ice

Alice Worth Series
Book Three

Lisa Edmonds

STORYBOOK House

To Jennifer White, friend and boxer, who is a real, honest-to-goodness superhero;

To Amy Hopper, who makes magic with ink and paint;

To my father, who loved gardening;

And to Bill, for all the love and laughs.

ALSO BY LISA EDMONDS

The Alice Worth Series

Heart of Malice

Heart of Fire

Heart of Ice

Heart of Stone

Heart of Shadows

Heart of Vengeance

Heart of Lies

Heart of the Pack

Heart of the Damned

Short Stories and Novellas

From the Ashes

Just For One Night

Blood Money

Ghosting 101 (included with *Blood Money*)

Perfectly Magical

Alice Worth and the Elite Death Machine

The Alice Worth World Novels

Mortal Heart

THE PLAYLIST

Judas Priest, "Some Heads are Gonna Roll"
Eddie Money, "Two Tickets to Paradise"
Hall and Oates, "Maneater"
The Guess Who, "No Sugar Tonight"
Golden Earring, "Twilight Zone"
The Runaways, "Cherry Bomb"
Electric Light Orchestra, "Strange Magic"
Quiet Riot, "Mama Weer All Crazee Now"
The Rolling Stones, "Sympathy for the Devil"
Rick Astley, "Never Gonna Give You Up"
Alice Merton, "No Roots"
Survivor, "Eye of the Tiger"
The Cars, "Magic"
Marshall Tucker Band, "Can't You See"
Stevie Nicks, "Edge of Seventeen"
The Eagles, "Heartache Tonight"
Scorpions, "Rock You Like a Hurricane"
Whitney Houston, "I Have Nothing"

David Lee Roth, "Just Like Paradise"
The Beach Boys, "Kokomo"

CHAPTER 1

As a private investigator, I'd pretended to be a lot of different people: a sex worker, a door-to-door doughnut salesperson, a tarot card reader. Hell, I'd once posed as a member of the Russian mob. This role, however, was by far the most difficult I'd ever had to play.

"It's not just the fangheads who have to die, you know." Mike Robinson, aspiring terrorist, leaned forward in eagerness. "It's mages and shifters too, and everyone who stands with them. If we're ever going to be free, we have to exterminate them all. This world was meant for humans, not creatures like that."

"I couldn't agree more," I said.

We eyed each other across his living room. Robinson was the leader of the group and the host for this meeting. The manager of a quarry thirty miles from the city, he was in his late forties and heavy-set, a widower with no children and a lot of pent-up rage. He and I sat opposite each other in armchairs.

I crossed my legs and settled back. "We all want a human future, but it won't be easy and it won't happen overnight. We have to plan five steps ahead and think big-picture. That's why groups like the one I represent are always on the lookout for the kind of people who are truly committed to not just winning one battle here or there, but to winning the war."

"We are committed," Robinson assured me.

I studied the faces of the others in the room. On the sofa sat Andrew Davis and his kid brother Corey. Andrew, an A/V installation tech by day, was the group's self-described "gadget guy." He'd met Robinson in a support group for people who'd lost a loved one to a vampire attack. Unlike Robinson's wife Samantha, who'd died after being drained by a vamp, Andrew and Corey's brother Luke had *become* a vampire. Drinking blood was worse than being dead, according to his human brothers. Corey, a mechanic, had tagged along to the meeting but been quiet. While Andrew was angry about his brother's recent transition to vampire, Corey seemed to be grieving.

The fourth member of the group stood off to the side, arms crossed, biceps bulging. He'd been standing for almost an hour without moving, expressionless and silent. Kent Stevens was a former Marine who worked at the quarry with Robinson. He'd shaken my hand when I arrived and then stationed himself near the doorway as a very large and ominous sentry. His brother had been killed by a vampire while Stevens was serving overseas in Afghanistan. If Mike Robinson and Andrew Davis's anger was visible and red-hot, Stevens's was ice-cold. For all Robinson's talk of genocide, I was pretty sure Stevens was the real menace in this room.

No doubt my driver-slash-bodyguard agreed. He stood behind me, a silent sentinel in a suit. Though Robinson and the Davis brothers glanced at my companion constantly, Stevens watched me, as if sensing I was the bigger threat, despite the size of the man standing behind me and the fact I appeared to be unarmed. It was this perceptiveness as much as anything that made me wary of him.

"We're ready to act," Robinson said. "Give us a target, or we'll find one on our own, but we want to do something. This city is the place where it starts, Ms. Day. This is where the revolution begins. People are angry after the harnad murders. They hate mages; they hate shifters. They've always hated fangheads. I heard local membership in Human rights organizations like yours is up by three hundred percent in the past two or three months. It's the perfect time to declare war."

I held up my hand. "I appreciate your enthusiasm, Mike, but as I said before, Human Future is cautious about making new affiliations. That's what has kept this side of our organization under the radar for so long, while the public front supports laws and political candidates who share our vision of a supe-free future. After this meeting, I'll go back and make my recommendations, and then we'll decide whether to bring you into the network."

Robinson drummed his fingers on the arm of his chair. "When can we expect a decision?"

"When the background checks are complete and we've had a chance to evaluate your prospects." I regarded him. "You're enthusiastic and driven. You have good leadership instincts, and I believe you have the potential to do well in an organization like ours."

Robinson preened at my praise.

I glanced at the others. "The rest of you each bring skills to the table that would be useful, but so far, all I've heard is the same kind of big talk I read in the comments section on our website, or in the online forum where we first made contact with Andrew." I raised my hands, palms up. "You claimed responsibility for quote, 'the biggest attack on the fangheads,' unquote, during the protests a month ago, but several groups have made that assertion. There were a half-dozen cases of arson, but none of them were what I'd call major attacks. For a city you argue is on the front line in the war, there doesn't seem to be much going on."

"We didn't set any of those fires." Robinson looked smug. "We bombed a business belonging to a member of the Vampire Court."

Stevens's eyes flicked to Robinson. I wondered if he was unhappy Robinson had told me that. Andrew crossed his arms, as if daring me to contradict their leader. Even Corey raised his chin defiantly.

I narrowed my eyes. "You're the third person who has told me they were responsible for that bombing."

"Bullshit," Robinson snapped, his face reddening as he pointed to the others. "Corey obtained the van we used, Stevens built the pipe bomb, and Andrew made the detonator."

"And what did you do?" I asked, my tone skeptical.

"I chose the target and did the recon." He crossed his arms. "The bar was closed, but the building was destroyed."

I glanced at Stevens. "Why did you put ball bearings in the bomb?"

He remained impassive. "I didn't. I used silver flechettes."

That particular detail had certainly never been released to the public, but that question had tripped up others who had claimed responsibility. It would appear they were telling the truth.

I nodded slowly. "Perhaps we can find a place for you with our organization. Let me ask you this: if you had access to better weapons and better resources, what would your next target be?"

Robinson didn't hesitate. "Northbourne Manor, the headquarters of the Vampire Court."

My eyebrows went up. "That's a big target."

He smiled. "With the right people and the right weapons, it could be done. I want to be the one to do it."

"I," not "we," I noticed. Interesting.

I rose. Robinson and the Davis brothers followed suit. I extended my hand to Robinson and he shook it. His palms were damp. "I'll be in touch," I told him. "Keep a low profile for now, until you hear from me. There are a lot of feds in town, thanks to the protests and the attacks on Darius Bell's cabal. It's a lot of heat. Not a good time to be careless."

"We're never careless," Stevens said, with a note of finality in his voice that I didn't particularly care for.

I picked up my briefcase and headed for the door, with my driver in front of me and Robinson right behind us.

The meeting had gone well—better than I'd hoped, really. I

wasn't home free yet, but thanks to the recording device in my brief-case, we had what we needed.

My escort reached for the doorknob.

And that's when it all went to hell.

SEVERAL THINGS HAPPENED PRETTY MUCH SIMULTANEOUSLY.

My escort stiffened and turned toward the living room just as the lights went out.

"What the—" I began.

Someone brushed past me, knocking me aside. An explosion went off behind me and the blast felt like a punch to the side of my head. Disoriented, I staggered as the world went blindingly white for a millisecond, then pitch-black.

Blinded, confused, and unable to hear over the ringing in my ears, I stumbled and reached toward where I thought my driver was standing, but my fingers encountered nothing but air.

Somewhere in the darkness there were indistinct voices and muffled pops like distant firecrackers that some part of my brain recognized as gunshots. Without warning, a white-hot fist punched me in the upper back near my shoulder. The impact spun me around and I went down with a shriek I couldn't hear.

At first my left shoulder and arm were numb, and I wondered if someone had hit me with a pipe or a bat. Then the pain arrived and stole my breath. I curled up on my side and clutched the wound as hot blood pumped through my fingers. Apparently I'd been shot, but by whom?

I still couldn't make sense of anything, but some of my vision was coming back. Indistinct shapes moved around me in the dim light. The sounds of gunshots had ceased. I heard voices from beyond the buzzing in my ears, but they sounded like *mwaaaa mwaa mwaaa mwaaaa-mwaaa mwaaa.*

A very large shadow appeared above me. I tried to scramble away, but whoever it was had an iron grip on my leg. My earth magic spiraled out of my hand and I lashed out instinctively with my cold-fire whip.

I heard a grunt but the hand on my leg didn't let go. A face swam in and out of focus above me and I felt a jolt of recognition, but what I thought I saw didn't make any sense. Maybe I was concussed; my brain definitely felt muddled and I still couldn't string together a coherent thought.

Then another face appeared. Bright silver vampire eyes met mine and I heard Charles Vaughan's familiar voice in my head: *Alice, let us help you.*

The larger of the two shadows said something I couldn't hear, pried my fingers away from my shoulder, and ripped my suit jacket and blouse apart. He tore off his own shirt and wadded it up against the hole in my shoulder, while he lifted me and used what was left of my jacket and blouse as a bandage on the wound on my back. When he compressed my shoulder between his hands like a vise, the wave of pain made me convulse and struggle to get away, but Charles held me down. The room did a weird kaleidoscope spin and the ringing in my ears drowned out all other noises as I started to fade out.

A cool hand brushed my forehead. *Alice, look at me.* Charles's words cut through the fog of pain and dizziness and I was compelled to obey.

I opened my eyes—which was odd, since I didn't remember closing them—and met the vampire's gaze as everything else faded to background noise. My world shrank until all I could see or think about was how beautiful his eyes were. They glowed with a soft silver light as if lit with moonlight from within. The pain faded to a distant ache. I exhaled in a long sigh.

Dimly, I realized Charles had used suggestion to ease my pain. Normally I would have resisted or refused simply on principle, but the wound was bad and the agony was worse. Despite Charles's command, my eyelids were heavy and unconsciousness pulled at me.

Bryan Smith, Charles's head enforcer, said something else I couldn't understand. His tone was urgent and it galvanized the vampire into action.

Charles caressed my cheek. Bryan lifted the makeshift bandage away from my shoulder. A blade flashed and cool fingertips pushed into the gunshot wound.

Even vampire suggestion had its limits. I bit back a scream and retched. I'd experienced a lot of torture, but having someone stick their fingers into a bullet wound was pretty close to the top of my personal pain scale.

A nexus of soothing warmth and comfort formed in my shoulder, taking away the pain like a tide going out. I recognized the healing effects of vampire blood, but instead of offering me his wrist to drink from, Charles had apparently slashed his own fingers and stuck them directly into my wound. How bad was the injury if the vampire had decided drinking his blood might not heal me fast enough?

Charles withdrew his fingers from my shoulder and pulled me against his body until I was half-sitting. He tore back his sleeve, bit savagely into his wrist, and pressed his arm to my mouth. Cool blood ran down my chin. *Drink,* he told me.

I blinked slowly up at him, torn between my reluctance to put myself under his influence again and the knowledge that though the blood from his fingers had begun the healing process, my wound could kill me or leave me incapacitated in the middle of whatever was happening here. My head buzzed like it was full of bees.

Alice, drink, the vampire repeated, more forcefully. *You are losing consciousness.*

Reluctantly, I obeyed.

As I drank, the waves of pleasure and warmth that rolled through me were frighteningly intense. Things began moving in my shoulder. I moaned and struggled in Charles's arms. When he gently started to pull away, I licked his wrist to clean off the blood. The vampire made a sound low in his throat that was definitely not pain.

He held me as my bones and flesh healed and the ringing in my ears faded. It took a long time. Finally, the strange sensations subsided and my other senses returned as the blood healed the damage to my vision and inner ears.

When I opened my eyes, I discovered someone had turned on a few lights but left the house in semi-darkness, probably in deference to those of us who were still suffering the aftereffects of what I now realized had been a flash-bang grenade.

When the lights went out, I'd been almost at the front door, but now I was lying in the living room with no memory of how I'd made it there. I stared around the room, trying to process what I saw and make sense of it.

Robinson's living room was in a shambles. The large windows facing the backyard were gone, the curtains were torn down, and broken glass was everywhere. Bullet holes in the walls indicated a gun battle. The furniture was overturned and smashed as if a big fight had taken place. A half-dozen Vampire Court enforcers in black stood guard around us. Through the missing window, I saw several more in the backyard.

Charles sat on the floor with me in his lap, in a distressingly large puddle of blood that had apparently come from me. Bryan was on one knee next to us, shirtless, our blood-soaked clothes in a pile beside him. I was covered in my own blood, my jacket and shirt were gone, and my bra was held on by a few threads, but I was sitting in the middle of what looked like a war zone and that seemed more important at the moment.

Three men lay face-down and unmoving on the living room floor, their hands cuffed behind their backs. I recognized them as Robinson and the Davis brothers. They were alive but unconscious.

"Where's the other guy?" My voice sounded funny; my hearing was still messed up, or maybe it was shock and blood loss.

Bryan shook his head grimly. "Escaped."

He had a welt across his chest where my cold-fire whip had struck him. I grimaced. "Sorry," I said, gesturing at the wound.

"Don't worry about it," he rumbled, waving off my apology. "You were confused and blinded, and it will heal."

Someone crouched beside me. "Miss Alice."

I looked up at my oversized Vampire Court-assigned bodyguard. "Hey, Fortune. Oh, crap, were you hit?" His suit jacket was bloody near his right shoulder, as was his right pant leg, and he was pale.

"They're just flesh wounds. I'll be fine." He looked at Charles, his expression grim. "Sir, I failed to protect her. I offer you my blood and my resignation."

"Wait. Back up. What the hell happened?" I started to sit up but thought better of it when a wave of dizziness reminded me that my shoulder might be healed, but I'd lost a lot of blood.

Charles looked like he'd bitten into something rancid. "We intended to arrest Robinson and the others once you had obtained their confession."

His arm was still around my middle, holding me against him. I pushed at it, but he tightened his grip. "Let go."

"Don't try to stand up," Bryan advised. "You'll pass out."

As much as I hated to admit it, he was probably right. I stayed on the floor and glared at them. "Somebody needs to explain this to me," I snapped. "We had a plan, Charles. I go in, get the confession, hand it over to the feds, and they make the arrest. Why are you here?"

Charles's eyes flashed. "The Court was concerned the bombers would suspect they had been deceived and flee before the federal agents acted on our evidence."

I might have known the vamps would change the play at the last minute. I scowled. "So you decided to toss in a flash-bang and get us shot?"

"They planned to wait until we were clear of the house before coming in," Fortune told me. "Stevens cut the lights and threw the flash-bang."

So Fortune had been in on the Court's plan all along and hadn't told me. What a surprise.

"Why did he do that?" I remembered seeing Fortune turn toward the former Marine right before all hell broke loose. "What happened when the lights went out?"

Fortune looked mad enough to chew up rocks and spit out gravel. "Stevens got some kind of alert. I heard something buzz twice, like a signal. He put his hand in his pocket and the lights went out. The flash-bang was hidden in the couch next to him. He threw it before I could get to him."

Which meant he'd been close to the grenade when it went off. I winced. As much as the flash-bang had left me deaf, blind, and disoriented, it had to have hurt Fortune far worse. The enforcer's hearing and eyesight were enhanced from drinking vampire blood regularly, which meant he healed faster, but the initial detonation would have left him virtually incapacitated long enough for Stevens and the others to grab weapons.

"We came in when the banger went off," Bryan said. "In the confusion, Stevens and Robinson got a couple of shots off before we could gain control of the situation."

"Looks like it was more than a couple, unless some of those are yours," I said, gesturing at the bullet holes in the walls. "Stevens probably had some kind of perimeter alarm set up and you guys tripped it as you were making your approach."

He nodded grimly. "It would appear so."

Well, I'd have some words for Charles about being left out of the change in plans, but that could wait until we were in private. "Did you call in the feds?"

"We did," Bryan told me. "The neighbors called the police about the gunshots. There are officers outside. Agents from the ATF are on their way to take them into custody." He gestured at Robinson and the Davis brothers.

"How did Stevens get away?"

"He went out a window on the other side of the house and made it to a vehicle." Bryan's eyes blazed. He was obviously furious Stevens had escaped their net. "We have people looking for him. He won't get far."

"Good." I looked at the blood on the floor and sighed. "I can't leave that here. Get me up."

Bryan looked at Charles doubtfully.

"This amount of blood loss will be debilitating," the vampire told me, as if I hadn't already figured that out.

"I have a job to do. Just get me on my feet and I'll do the rest."

Charles stood and lifted me in one smooth motion, then held me upright when my knees tried to give out and my ears rang. Fortune stood beside us, guilt written on his features as I trembled from blood loss and the feeling of cold air on my bare skin.

Fortune took off his suit jacket and draped it over my shoulders. It was bloodstained and hung almost to my knees, but at least I was no longer standing in front of a room full of people in what was left of my bra.

I pulled out of Charles's grip and crouched carefully, putting my fingertips in the blood on the floor. "I'm going to burn this," I said.

Charles gave Bryan a nod. "Do it," the enforcer told me as some of the other enforcers moved back. Their caution was understandable but unnecessary; the burner spell would only remove traces of my blood without touching anything or anyone else.

I took a deep breath. "*Burn.*"

The spell flared, knocking me back. Charles caught me before I could land on my butt. White fire rushed across the floor and across our clothes, consuming my blood and leaving behind a thin layer of fine ash. The vampire helped me stand and held me up as ash floated down to the hardwood floor.

In the meantime, Mike Robinson was coming around. He struggled, pulling at his cuffs and swearing, his words slurred. He rolled onto his side and tried to rise, flopping like a fish.

Bryan put a hand the size of a baseball glove on Robinson's

shoulder, pinning him to the floor without noticeable effort. "Stay down," he rumbled.

"Screw you," Robinson spat. He craned his neck and spotted me, standing with Charles's arm around my middle. His face twisted in rage and disgust. "*You.* You c—"

"If you wish to keep your tongue, you will be silent." Charles's voice was pure menace. A slight lisp told me the vampire's fangs were out and he was angry enough to not enunciate carefully.

Robinson made the wise choice and shut up, but hate radiated off him in almost visible waves. Unfazed, I stared back at him.

You don't need to protect me from words, Charles, I told the vampire. *Sticks and stones and large-caliber bullets may break my bones, but words will never hurt me.*

No one speaks to you in such a way in my presence, was his curt reply. His arm tightened around me.

Adri Smith, another of Charles's enforcers, came in through the front door. "Sir, the ATF agents are two minutes away."

Charles addressed Robinson. "I am Charles Vaughan, the vampire whose bar you bombed. It gives me great pleasure to see you in handcuffs. You will be handed over to federal agents momentarily."

It occurred to me rather belatedly that Charles had a second motivation for arresting Robinson and the others in person tonight, rather than simply letting the feds handle it: he'd wanted the satisfaction of putting on the cuffs himself. I couldn't say I blamed him; I'd been a part of the investigation for much the same reason. I'd almost died when they bombed Hawthorne's. If I'd been a second slower in my reaction when the bomb was thrown through the window, I'd be dead. It was worth the bullet wound to see Robinson on the floor in cuffs, his eyes widening as the reality of the situation began to sink in.

"You murdered my wife," Robinson ground out.

"I had no involvement in her death," Charles countered. "Nor did anyone of my line or any of my employees. The Court investigated your wife's murder. The vampire who killed her was unfamiliar to us and not sired by anyone on the Court. Your target had no bearing on your wife's case."

"I don't care. You all deserve to burn in hell." Robinson turned to me. "I did it for my wife. I did it for Samantha."

"No you didn't," I told him as the front door opened and four federal agents came in. "You did it for yourself."

With Charles's arm around my waist, we slowly made our way toward the front door as the feds took over.

One agent, an African-American man in a suit and ATF windbreaker, stopped us in the foyer. "Ma'am, are you injured?"

"No, just disoriented from the flash-bang," I told him, speaking too loudly, as if I was still a little deaf. Charles shook slightly. If I didn't know better, I'd have thought he was laughing silently.

The agent handed me a card and I tucked it into the pocket of my borrowed jacket. "I'm Special Agent Marshall. You'll need to come to our office to give your statement." He glanced at my attire and raised his eyebrows. "Once you're had a chance to change, of course."

"Of course," Charles interjected smoothly. "Three hours from now, at your office?" When Marshall frowned, Charles added, "She can hardly be expected to give a statement before she has recovered, Agent Marshall. Her testimony would be compromised."

I did my best to look shaky and unfocused. With the blood loss, it didn't take much acting.

Marshall relented. "Three hours," he agreed, then headed into the living room, where the other agents were conferring with each other and ignoring Robinson, who was loudly demanding a lawyer and that we be arrested for assault and false imprisonment.

Three hours is time enough to see to your medical needs and discuss your statement, Charles told me as he ushered me out the door. An SUV waited at the curb with Adri behind the wheel and Fortune at the rear passenger door, ready to open it for us.

With each step, the buzzing in my head got louder and I could no longer feel my own feet. I stumbled and almost went down. I gritted my teeth. Unless I wanted to collapse on the sidewalk in front of a dozen feds, I needed help. *Charles, I'm not going to make it to the car.*

He picked me up and moved vamp-fast to the waiting SUV. Fortune opened the door and climbed into the back seat much quicker than I would have thought possible for a man of his size. Charles handed me off to the enforcer, who laid me on the seat as his boss climbed in and shut the door.

"Ride in front," Charles told Fortune, who quickly exited through the other door and hurried around to the passenger side. He jumped in and Adri pulled away from the curb, accelerating down the street in a roar of horsepower.

Charles arranged me so my feet were propped up against the opposite door and my head was in his lap. The increased blood flow helped clear the cobwebs and the ringing faded.

He met Adri's eyes in the rearview mirror. "Call ahead to the house and have a doctor and blood transfusions waiting."

"Already done." Adri glanced at me in the mirror. "How are you doing, Alice?"

"Never better," I muttered.

Charles brushed hair back from my face. *I am sorry our change of plans led to this*, he said in my head.

I understand why you did it, but you should have included me in your plans instead of dropping me into the middle of a shooting gallery. I've earned that much.

He twitched, as if my statement had startled him. *Yes, you have. I apologize.*

An apology from a member of the Vampire Court. As if the day hadn't already been strange enough.

CHAPTER 2

I woke up just after noon to the feeling of a large, warm body curled up behind me and a heavy weight pinning my legs.

"Hey," Sean murmured, his lips on the back of my neck.

"Hey," I echoed, my voice thick with sleep. "How long have you been here?"

"Since about ten. I didn't want to wake up you up, but I couldn't stay away once I knew you were back." He wrapped his arms around me.

"I'm awake, sort of." I yawned and smiled at the black-and-white dog lying on my feet. "Hey, Rogue."

The dog woofed and laid his head back on the bed, closing his eyes.

"When did you get home?" Sean asked.

I rubbed my eyes. "A little after dawn."

"So you've only been asleep for a few hours. Go back to sleep. We'll go downstairs." He kissed my cheek and started to pull away.

I held him back. "No, stay."

He settled back in and nestled me against his body. I was bone-tired, but it had been too long since I'd seen Sean or my dog and I couldn't have gone back to sleep now if I'd wanted to.

"You want to tell me about it?" Sean asked after a few minutes.

His werewolf nose had no doubt alerted him immediately that things had gone sideways. I was surprised he'd waited until I woke on my own to ask what had happened. The Sean I'd first known would have demanded an explanation for why I smelled like blood that was not my own, and that earlier version of me would have been annoyed and angry at being questioned. I realized neither of us were the people we'd been when we first met and was surprised that I liked the change in myself.

"Alice?" he prodded.

"Hang on," I said with a note of irritation in my voice. "I'm having a revelation."

Sean chuckled. "Isn't it a little early in your day for that? You haven't even had coffee yet."

I elbowed him in his hard stomach. He made an exaggerated *oof* sound and nuzzled my neck. "So, do you need a minute to process this revelation, or...?"

I sighed. "No, you ruined the moment."

"Sorry." He pressed a kiss into my hair. "So, things did not go well last night, I take it."

"Actually, overall, things *did* go well. We got the bombers in custody." Most of them, anyway. I wondered if they'd caught Kent Stevens yet. I'd have to text Adri and ask.

"Good, then we won't have to leave the house today." He settled in more comfortably.

"Don't you have to go to work?"

He snorted. "I haven't seen you in more than a week, Alice. I took the day off." He rubbed my arms, his hands wonderfully warm. "So, how did you end up needing vampire blood *and* a blood transfusion?"

"I can't go into details because of my contract with the Court," I reminded him. "All I can say is not everything worked like it was supposed to at the end, but I'm all right now."

He stopped rubbing my arms and just held me. "It was close, though, wasn't it?"

The old Alice would have denied it, but I was trying not to lie to Sean—at least, not unless I absolutely had to—and I'd sort of made an agreement not to tell him I was fine when I wasn't.

"Yeah, it was," I admitted.

Sean's anger prickled on my skin. He might not have demanded an explanation for my injuries, but that didn't mean he didn't want to find the person who'd hurt me and tear them apart. "I know you probably had no choice, but I don't like that you had to drink Vaughan's blood again. It gives him some influence over you and that son of a bitch is always plotting and scheming."

"I didn't have a choice about drinking his blood, but I *do* have a choice about whether I let him manipulate me afterward. If that's what he's hoping for, he's going to be sorely disappointed."

He squeezed me and kissed my temple. "So, what's on the agenda for today?"

"I planned on taking it easy and just doing some things around the house. Thanks for picking up some groceries; let me know what I owe you for that."

"You can get dinner for us later and we'll call it even." He paused. "Have you given any more thought about what you're going to do for an office?"

A month ago, I'd been evicted from my office during the height of violent anti-vamp and anti-magic protests that swept the city after it was discovered a group of mages was responsible for dozens of murders. The building's owners cited safety concerns, since several mage-owned businesses were targeted for arson and vandalism. I was having a difficult time finding anyone willing to rent me office space. The contents of my office were in storage while I figured out how I was going to deal with the situation.

Sean had offered to lease me space in the Maclin Security building, but I'd declined. It felt too much like a commitment and like I'd be mixing my professional and personal lives in a way I wasn't comfortable with.

"I don't know," I said. "Something will become available soon, I'm sure."

"There's still space available in our building if you want it," he said mildly. "Decent-size office on the first floor, with its own bathroom and a great view of the loading dock."

"Thanks. I'll keep it in mind."

He let go long enough to lean back and grab something off the nightstand and hand it to me, then pulled me back into his arms.

It was a travel brochure for a resort in the Bahamas, featuring isolated cabanas with private beaches.

I looked over the brochure. "Still wanting to take a beach vacation with me?"

Sean had wanted to go on a trip after we'd put the West-Addison harnad in jail, but within days of closing that case, the Court had hired me to help catch the bombers. I'd decided to take the job instead of the vacation and Sean had not been happy.

"Look at that sand," he murmured in my ear. "And that crystal-blue Caribbean water. Tell me you don't want to spend a week away from everything, swimming in the ocean, drinking rum punch, and lying in a hammock under the palm trees."

"It does look pretty fantastic," I admitted, folding the brochure. "Let me think about it."

He raised up on his elbow. "Let's stop thinking about it and just do it. You and I, we think too much. My pack, my company, your ghost, your work...it will all be fine while we're gone." He kissed my forehead. "Pack a bag and let's just go, Alice. Whatever we need that we don't have already, we'll buy when we get there."

"I can't go to the Bahamas; it's too far away. If something happened here, it would take too long to get back."

"What do you think might happen?"

I rubbed my face. "Anything could happen. I just...I can't go to the Bahamas. Maybe we could go to a beach somewhere closer, somewhere we could get to and from quickly, if we had to."

He sat up and leaned against the headboard. "I'd really like to know what you think might happen if you leave town. If you're worried about your house, between Malcolm and your wards and my security company, it's safer than Fort Knox. Malcolm is protected inside the house. The Court can do without you for a week; they have other people who work for them and two new full-time investigators. What are you worried about? Explain it to me so I can understand."

How could I explain how vulnerable I'd feel so far from my home and its wards? My home was my security, the first and only thing that was every truly *mine*, after twenty-four years of being a prisoner in my grandfather's cabal compound. If my grandfather ever tracked me down and I had to run, that would be one thing, but even the thought of being away for a week made my stomach churn.

"I'm not sure I can explain it," I told him finally, rolling onto my back and staring up at the ceiling. "Maybe it's irrational."

"You're never going to let me forget that, are you?" he asked wryly.

During an earlier fight over my refusal to let him buy me new furniture, I'd called him a bully and he'd called me irrational. "I wasn't referring to that," I told him, running my fingers through his hair. "Really, it *is* probably irrational of me to be afraid of going out of town."

"Is that something we can work on together?"

I took a deep breath. "Maybe we could start with something not so far away. When that goes okay, maybe something a little farther. Then, maybe the Bahamas, assuming you're not sick of me and my bullshit by then."

"I'm kind of fond of you and your bullshit." He kissed me again, more purposefully this time.

I ran my hands up under his T-shirt and over his chest, scratching him lightly with my nails. He growled low and slid a hand across my stomach where my tank top had hiked up while I slept. I shivered at his touch and pulled him half on top of me, suddenly no longer sleepy. His kiss grew hungry and his hand slipped under my top. I moaned.

Rogue raised his head and barked at us.

I laughed. "Butt out, fur-face. Sean and I need some private time."

Sean growled. Unimpressed, Rogue tilted his head, his tongue hanging out.

I threw back the covers and swung my legs over the side of the bed. "Hold that thought. I'll let him out in the backyard, and then we can—"

"Don't let him into the backyard," Sean interrupted. "There's something...weird going on back there."

I blinked at him. "In my backyard? What—?"

I didn't get to finish my question. I sensed a surge of power and a wave of magic rolled over the house. Rogue went berserk, jumping off the bed and barking. I staggered and almost fell. Despite my shields, the wave of magic left me disoriented.

Sean was off the bed and at my side in a heartbeat. "Alice!" He sat me down on the bed, his hands on my face as he stared into my eyes. "Are you all right?"

"Magic attack," I mumbled, trying to clear my head and focus.

"What do you mean, a magic attack?"

Suddenly, Malcolm was in my room. "What the hell was that?" the ghost asked.

"Did someone attack the house?" Sean demanded.

"No," Malcolm told him, floating over to me. "It feels like something big just happened, but somewhere else. Alice, you okay?"

The disorientation faded. "I'm okay. That was a massive wave of magic. Malcolm's right; something big just happened. I don't think I've ever felt anything like that."

"Let's go see if the news has anything about it," Sean suggested.

We headed downstairs. Sean turned on my new television and I went to the kitchen to make coffee. While the pot was brewing, I joined Sean, Malcolm, and Rogue in the living room. Sean had found a local station with a breaking news alert.

The anchor addressed the camera. "We have no official statements yet from either local law enforcement or federal authorities, but we are receiving reports that the magic pulse that has caused widespread disruption and minor injuries was some sort of shockwave that seems to have originated from the northeast part of the city. We have crews en route to the scene now, and will bring you more information as we receive it."

Sean turned the TV volume down as a commercial came on. "A magic shockwave? Is that possible?"

"It's possible. All magic produces energy, but to create a pulse that powerful..." I shook my head. "It had to have been a *massive* coordinated attack."

"An attack on what, though?" Sean asked. "The northeast side is mainly residential. What was the target?"

I heard the coffee pot gurgling and headed back to the kitchen. "You want a cup?"

"Definitely," Sean said.

I poured two cups of coffee, added cream and sugar to mine, and returned to the living room just as Sean was turning up the volume again.

The television showed live aerial footage of a sprawling mansion —or what was left of it. Most of the building had collapsed and it looked like the doors and windows were gone on the section that still stood. People were running from the rubble, some helping others who had been injured. A caravan of vehicles was on its way down the driveway, heading away from the ruin toward a half-dozen ambulances, fire trucks, and police vehicles parked outside an enormous gate.

The news anchor spoke. "Channel Five has learned that the epicenter of the magic pulse is a residence believed to belong to local businessman Darius Bell. As you can see from our live footage, there appears to be significant damage to the home and surrounding buildings. We have been told that emergency personnel are not being allowed to enter the property at this time. We do not yet have any information about casualties or the cause of the disaster."

I stared at the screen, dumbfounded. I could think of only one possible explanation for the devastation: after months of small-scale attacks on Bell's operation, Moses Murphy, my grandfather, had decided to declare open war by breaching Bell's wards and destroying his cabal headquarters. No wonder the shockwave had been so powerful; the blast that had broken the wards and demolished most of the building had to have been enormous.

I tried to estimate how many mages would have had to work together to create an attack on this scale. It would have to be dozens, and half or more of them would probably be incapacitated or dead after breaking the wards. I had no doubt Bell would have had land-mines and cascades embedded in his wards designed to kill anyone who tried to break them. Moses had sent those mages to their deaths.

"Alice?"

I realized Sean was talking to me, and judging by his tone, it wasn't the first time he'd tried to get my attention. I tore my gaze away from the television and looked at him.

I don't know what my face looked like, but he took the coffee cups from my hands. "What's wrong?" he asked. "You're as white as a sheet. Sit down."

I remained standing, too horrified by what my grandfather had done to really process what Sean said. He set the coffee down on the floor, since I still had no other furniture other than the couch, and made me sit.

I had to say something to explain my reaction. "The wards around Bell's compound were powerful and deadly. Breaking them would have killed the mages who did it."

"What kind of magic could do that?" he asked.

"Earth magic; destabilize the ground, destroy the building. With that much power, I'm surprised any part of the house is still standing, but breaking the wards probably killed half the mages they brought in for the attack. Maybe they didn't have enough firepower left alive to finish the job."

"It had to have been the Murphy cabal." He rubbed my back. "They've been hitting Bell a lot lately. I've never seen anything like this, though." He jerked his head at the screen.

"No one has." Malcolm stared at the television. "Mages and cabals have always wondered if this kind of coordinated attack could be done, but no one's ever pulled it off until now."

"Maybe because no one was ever willing to sacrifice so many lives for one single strike." My voice was harsh.

I felt a spike of awe, horror, and anger that wasn't mine. Malcolm's emotions were leaking over to me. He floated back and forth, a sign of how unsettled he was. "Hey, you okay?" I asked him.

"I used to live there," he said quietly. "They had me in the east wing of the house for the last year I belonged to the cabal."

We watched the news for the next hour. Sean and I sat on the couch with Rogue curled up at our feet while Malcolm floated around the room, obviously upset but not wanting to talk.

It didn't take long for the national news networks to pick up the story, so Sean switched back and forth between several channels as we tried to find out what was happening. There was a lot of speculation but no real answers, other than what we could see occurring live at Bell's compound.

I wondered how long Bell's people were going to be able to keep police and federal agents from entering the property. There were dozens of them camped out on the road in front of the gate; I saw members of the ATF, FBI, SPEMA, and local and state law enforcement personnel. I supposed it was a question of how long it would take to find a judge willing to sign a warrant.

Just how much Bell did not want law enforcement poking around in his compound became evident when aerial footage of the scene showed all of Bell's people moving away from what was left of the house and heading for the gate.

I stood up and walked toward the television, Sean right behind me. "What's going on?" he asked.

"They're going to blow it up," I said.

The camp of waiting law enforcement must have come to the same conclusion, because it suddenly became a hive of activity. Men and women representing various agencies began running or taking cover behind their vehicles as the last remaining cabal personnel left the compound. The news helicopters moved to a safe distance.

Rather than the massive explosion law enforcement feared—and the news media no doubt hoped for—it was a controlled demolition that began in the center of the C-shaped building with a fireball that spread toward the ends in a series of smaller detonations. In about fifteen seconds, the entire main building was a burning ruin. Three smaller buildings went up after that, reduced quickly to smoking rubble.

"I guess they really didn't want the cops to get in there," I said when the explosions stopped.

"So, what now?" Sean asked.

"Bell will regroup and strike back at Murphy, back in Baltimore and wherever he can find anyone affiliated with the Murphy cabal. Meanwhile, Murphy's probably already on to phase two of the plan. It wouldn't surprise me if there's another attack on Bell before the day is out."

"The city's about to become a war zone," Malcolm said grimly.

I watched the burning remains of Bell's compound. "And we're all going to be caught in the middle."

SEAN WAS HUNGRY, so I ordered Chinese food. While we waited for it to arrive, Malcolm disappeared into the basement to deal with his complicated feelings about watching his former prison blow up, and I took a shower and got dressed.

I got back downstairs just as Sean returned from taking Rogue for a walk. "Hey, that reminds me," I said.

He unclipped the leash from Rogue's collar. "We need to talk about your backyard."

I went to the back door with Sean and Rogue behind me. As I unlocked the door, the dog growled, which surprised me. Rogue rarely growled.

When I stepped out onto the porch, I stopped and stared. "What the heck? Why is there a jungle in my backyard?"

A week ago, I'd had two large, empty flowerbeds I'd planned on filling when I got a chance. Both flowerbeds were now overflowing with plants no less than four feet tall, and some were even bigger. When I looked closer, I realized they were impossibly giant-sized versions of the flowers and plants I'd intended to grow.

And they were *moving*.

"So, I wanted to surprise you," Sean began.

I gaped at the swaying mass of vaguely menacing greenery. "Well, you nailed it."

He sighed. "You worked so hard getting these flowerbeds built and then you were too busy to plant anything, so a couple of days ago I went and bought the plants you had on your list and put them in. When I came back the next day to water the plants, they seemed bigger already, but I decided it had to be my imagination. The day before yesterday, they were huge and I realized it *wasn't* my imagination. I decided I needed to do something before the situation got any more out of hand. I tried to pull one out of the ground and it bit me."

My eyebrows shot up. "The *plant* bit you?"

He showed me his forearm. There, a few inches above his wrist, was a semi-circular scar.

I touched the scar as if to convince myself it was real. Despite all the fights he'd been in, Sean had few scars thanks to his shifter healing abilities and the ones he did have were from particularly severe injuries. And yet, somehow, a plant had wounded him badly enough to leave a scar.

While I was processing my shock, he continued, "It also made me sick for a couple of hours. It felt like I had a bad case of the flu, and I almost never get sick because of my shifter immune system. Meanwhile, the plants just kept growing and growing. Also, they eat birds. At this point, they could probably eat the dog if he got too close, or any strays that happened to get into the yard."

I headed down the porch steps and crossed my backyard with Sean at my side. As I approached, I felt a caress of dark magic and the plants leaned toward me, their leaves shivering in excitement.

"Hungry, are you?" I said dryly.

"Do you know what the hell is going on?" Sean asked.

"Oh, yes. I suppose this is my fault—well, part of it—but I didn't think you'd be doing any gardening back here. I should have warned you not to. I'm sorry you got hurt."

I reached out and one of the plants bent down toward my hand. Sean grabbed my arm. "Watch out."

"It's okay. I'm going to let them know who's boss."

Reluctantly, he let go. Wisps of black, red, and purple blood magic danced on my fingers. The plant bent down and rubbed gently against my hand like a cat.

He gaped. "What the hell?"

"This was going to be my blood garden," I said as the plant caressed my hand. "Well, I guess it still is, but it looks like my magic wasn't the only magic that got into the flowerbeds."

"Your *what* garden?"

"A garden is full of life energy. My plan was to plant a garden to help feed energy into my house wards and that I could draw from if I needed to, in case trouble came knocking at my door again. I infused the soil with my blood magic."

"When you say you 'infused' your blood magic into the soil, you mean...?"

"I mixed my blood, full of magic, with the soil. My blood and magic is in these plants."

He stared at me for a full five seconds. "So, who the hell else's magic got in here?" he asked finally.

"Whose blood did we spill back here, right before I put in the flowerbeds?"

His mouth became a grim line. "Scott Grierson's demon father, Ravan."

"Yup. Demon blood, demon magic. I burned up his blood but there must have been some residual magic left behind."

"So, now we've got demon plants." He frowned at my garden. "What are you going to do with a backyard full of bloodthirsty little Audrey Twos?"

"Audrey Twos?"

"*Little Shop of Horrors*?"

"Oh yeah, the man-eating plant. Very funny. Can I get a drop of blood?"

He eyed me.

"I need them to know that you're not food," I said.

He produced a pocketknife and cut the pad of his thumb. I smeared his blood on my fingers, then let the plant caress my hand. When I moved back, my fingers were clean. The plants made a sound like a sigh.

Sean shook his head. "Of all the weird shit I have seen in my life, this is by far the weirdest. What about the dog?"

"Don't worry; I'll make sure he's safe too. Hold out your hand."

He crossed his arms defiantly.

"Come on, you can trust me," I wheedled.

"It's not *you* I don't trust." He grudgingly let me take his hand and reach out toward the garden.

The plant leaned down and brushed against his skin. Sean held perfectly still as it ran its leaves over our entwined hands. The garden rustled.

"See? That wasn't so bad, was it?" I asked him.

He kissed my forehead. "So, you're going to keep your demon garden, huh?"

"I think so. There's a lot of power in it, and if I put wards up, no one will accidentally get eaten. Plus, it might come in handy. You never know when we might need to get rid of a body."

He stared at me.

"I'm kidding," I added.

"I kinda feel like you aren't," he said.

The wards tingled and Rogue barked inside the house. "Oh, hey, I think the food's here," I said. "Maybe the garden would like some sweet and sour chicken."

Sean snorted as we headed toward the back porch. "Better that than werewolf, mage, or dog. If there are any leftovers, the garden is welcome to them, I guess."

Behind us, the plants rustled and sighed.

CHAPTER 3

AFTER WE ATE, SEAN AND I SPENT THE REMAINDER OF THE AFTERNOON AND early evening watching the news and waiting for the other shoe to drop, but it never did.

I had no doubt Moses was planning another attack on Bell, but for whatever reason, he didn't strike again immediately, either because he'd lost more mages in the first attack than he'd planned to and didn't have the manpower, or because he didn't have the right target. Either way, I figured it was only a matter of time.

We found the news channel with the best coverage and turned the volume down to a murmur. Live footage of the smoldering ruins of Bell's compound—now surrounded by emergency vehicles and being doused by fire trucks—alternated with announcers recapping the events and interviewing a series of law enforcement and civilian experts on cabals and magic who offered various theories about how the attack had been planned and carried out. No one wanted to guess at how many mages had died breaking the wards, or how many were needed to destroy the compound. It didn't escape my notice that no one explicitly called out Moses as orchestrating the attack.

I took some solace from the fact my grandfather was not in the city; the news showed him making himself conspicuously visible in Baltimore while his people attacked Bell on the other side of the country. No doubt he'd sent one of his lieutenants to run things in his stead. I wondered how many of the lieutenants I'd known five years ago were still alive. Moses tended to go through them fairly quickly, and when he terminated someone's employment, it wasn't with two weeks' notice and severance pay.

I was concerned about Malcolm, who hadn't come back up from the basement, but I gave him space. He'd talk when he was ready.

As the evening wore on, I went from sitting next to Sean on the couch to lying down with my head in his lap while he rubbed my back. I was fighting sleep, but it was a losing battle, thanks to the stress of the last few weeks, getting very little rest, and being short on blood by a pint or so.

Then Sean's hand slid under my top and suddenly I was a whole lot less tired.

I rolled onto my back and looked up at him. It had gotten dark and we'd left the lights off, so the only illumination was from the TV. His eyes glowed softly. "You feel like going upstairs?" he asked.

"I dunno...I'm really comfortable," I said, feigning indifference.

He grinned and my heart skipped a beat. "Let me see if I can pique your interest," he murmured.

His hand moved under my top and stroked my stomach, making it flutter, before moving to my breast. I couldn't stop my sharp intake of breath, or the instant reaction low in my belly that made his nostrils flare and his eyes go golden.

I rolled to my feet and returned to the couch to straddle his lap, running my fingers through his hair as I kissed him deeply. He gripped my butt tightly and pulled me close, then slid his hands up my back toward my bra.

I broke our kiss and leaned back. "We should go upstairs. I don't want to scandalize Malcolm if he comes up from the basement."

"We may scandalize him anyway," he warned me, his eyes glittering. "I hope you don't expect to stay quiet. I intend to be a *very* bad wolf."

Before I could respond, Sean's phone rang from somewhere in the couch. He swore and dug in between the cushions until he found it. The screen said *Jack Hastings*.

"My beta," he said. He answered the call. "This is Sean."

I heard the growly voice on the other end say, "It's Caleb again."

I climbed off Sean's lap. He stood and paced in front of the couch as he listened. Finally, he asked, "Is he back at his apartment or with you?"

A terse response.

"Let's meet over there, then. We have to talk to him, find out what the hell is going on. I'm on the east side, so it'll take me about a half-hour to get there. Go easy on him until we find out how it started. I'm on my way." He disconnected.

I went over to him. "Pack troubles?"

"I'm sorry," he said, putting his phone in his pocket. "Caleb's a nineteen-year-old kid who got bitten while he was out running a couple of months ago and is having a hard time adjusting. We took him into our pack hoping to help him adapt, but we're not having much luck keeping him out of trouble. He keeps getting into fights and shifting in public."

I grimaced. Shifting in public was a quick way to get shot by law enforcement or an armed citizen, and behavior like that would bring a lot of trouble to Sean's pack. "Go take care of your people."

"It will probably take a while." He rubbed his face. "Damn it."

"It's okay. I'm going to turn in early and try to get a full night's sleep. Will you have to work tomorrow?"

"I have some meetings in the morning, but I'll probably be free in the afternoon," he said. "I'll text you and let you know what my schedule looks like."

"Okay. Be careful."

"You too." He kissed me thoroughly. "I'm glad you're home."

"I'm glad to *be* home." I walked him to the door, then waved from the front porch as he backed down my driveway.

I took Rogue to the front yard to do his business, then fed him in the kitchen and left him to eat dinner while I went out to the backyard and spent a half-hour putting wards around the flowerbeds to keep the dog from getting eaten. The aversion spells would keep both people and animals away while I figured out how to address my garden's dietary needs.

When the wards flared, the garden rustled. It sounded disgruntled. "No dog for you," I told the plants firmly. "And no trying to eat the werewolf either. He may be delicious, but he's mine." More unhappy rustling.

When I got back inside, I found Rogue sitting expectantly by the back door. I turned off the television and all the lights except for the one in the kitchen.

After a moment's hesitation, I opened the door to the basement and called out, "Good night, Malcolm."

"Good night," he replied. He sounded better than before, which was a relief.

I shut the door and Rogue and I went upstairs. The dog settled onto his bed by the window while I changed into pajamas.

It wasn't even ten o'clock, but I was exhausted. I brushed my teeth, turned off the lamp, and crawled into bed. In minutes, I was sound asleep.

ALICE, *let us in.* The sharp command cut through my deep, dreamless sleep like a scythe.

I was on my feet and halfway to my bedroom door before I was awake enough to realize what I was doing.

Charles? I asked in my head, groggy and confused. The clock on my nightstand said it was a little after three.

We are outside your residence and must speak to you. Charles's voice in my head vibrated with urgency.

I threw a cardigan on over my tank top and hurried downstairs with Rogue on my heels.

Malcolm waited in the foyer. "That creepy vamp is outside. You want me to go tell Sean that he's here?"

"Not yet. Let me find out what's going on. Please stay in the basement for now."

Malcolm shimmered as he passed through the closed basement door and the wards that protected it. Just to be on the safe side, I shut Rogue in the downstairs bathroom. I dropped my house wards and opened the front door.

A black SUV was parked in my driveway. The driver's door opened and a Vampire Court enforcer I didn't know emerged. As he opened the rear door for Charles, the front passenger door opened and a tall blonde woman stepped out.

At first, I thought she was another enforcer, but she didn't come around the vehicle to stand beside Charles. Instead, she scanned the yard, then looked over the house. When her gaze finally met mine, her brow arched. In her black leather jacket and tall boots, she looked like she'd just stepped off the cover of *Badass Weekly*, and I was suddenly aware that I was wearing pajamas with sheep on them.

I didn't have a chance to worry about what my choice of sleepwear was doing to my street cred because Charles was suddenly on my porch in a puff of air. I gasped.

The front of his suit was soaked with blood and his hands and face were streaked with it. He looked livid. He was also extremely pale, even by vampire standards.

"We must get inside." His voice was flat.

I stepped back and they all filed into the house. I shut the door and locked it, then raised my wards.

When I reached for the light switch, the male enforcer snapped, "Leave the lights off." He went into the living room and yanked the curtains closed. The blonde woman took up a position near the door.

Whatever the hell was going on, I wasn't accustomed to being given orders in my own home. My eyes narrowed as I turned to the blonde woman. "Who are you?"

"Arkady Woodall, Vampire Court investigator."

So this was one of the new full-time investigators the Court had hired after I turned the job down. She looked to be about my age and was a little taller than me, with the grace and lean muscle of a fighter.

We shook hands. "Arkady?" I asked.

The corners of her mouth turned up. "Arkady."

I jerked a thumb at the enforcer looming in the living room doorway. "And who's Mr. Sunshine?"

He made a noise like truck gears grinding. "Matthias."

I turned my attention back to Charles. "What happened? Are you hurt? Where's Bryan?"

"This is not my blood. Bryan Smith has been shot and Fortune is dead," Charles said.

The words hit me like a punch in the gut. "*What?*"

"Kent Stevens ambushed our vehicle as we arrived home an hour ago." Charles shook with anger as he paced around my foyer. "We were coming from a meeting at one of my businesses. Fortune was driving and Bryan and I were in the back. When we got to the gate, it jammed instead of opening. Fortune began to retreat when Stevens opened fire with an automatic weapon. Bryan was shot six times; five bullets in his torso, and one grazed his head. Fortune was shot twice in the head. I could do nothing to save him."

I made a choked sound.

Charles stopped pacing and turned to me. His eyes were black and his fangs were out. "I was able to heal Bryan's injuries and he is resting now. Adri is with him."

Rage built inside me like a tidal wave and I struggled to rein it in. "What happened to Stevens? Tell me he's dead."

He shook his head. "He deployed countermeasures and evaded my enforcers. I had to choose between saving Bryan's life or pursuing our attacker. I chose to stay. By the time Bryan was stabilized, Stevens was gone."

"Bryan's life was more important." I took a shaky breath and tried to make sense of what Charles was telling me, but it wasn't computing. How could Fortune be dead? I'd spoken with him less than twenty-four hours ago. He'd driven me home after I was done giving my statement to Agent Marshall. He'd sat in my driveway and watched to make sure I got safely into my house before he drove away. I hadn't known him long, but I'd liked him.

Bryan, on the other hand, I had known for years. Things hadn't always been amicable between us because his loyalty was to Charles and the Court, which meant I'd been furious at him more than once, but he'd ripped off his own shirt to keep me from bleeding out on Mike Robinson's living room floor. I took a deep, shuddering breath.

"My enforcers who gave chase tell me Stevens was unusually fast and strong for a human," Charles said. "They suspect Stevens may have been drinking vampire blood."

At first, I was startled; Stevens had made no secret of his hatred of vamps, but that didn't mean he wouldn't use their blood to enhance his strength and speed. It would certainly help explain how he managed to evade capture twice. I'd credited adrenaline and training for the first escape, but two successful getaways meant the enforcers' assessment was probably accurate. I wondered if he'd been drinking expensive black-market bottled vampire blood or if he'd been draining and killing vamps we didn't know about. No doubt Charles had people already looking into that possibility.

He started pacing again. I'd never seen him so agitated. "I can find no trace of Stevens. His trail ended by the side of the road. He may have had a vehicle parked or been picked up by a confederate. The Court has dispatched Hunters to locate him. He will not be at liberty for long, and when he is found he will certainly suffer greatly for everything he has done."

I went into the kitchen and ran a towel under hot water. I brought it back to Charles, who accepted it and began cleaning the blood off his face.

"You are in danger. Stevens tried to kill you once already," he said as he scrubbed dried blood off his pale skin.

"He doesn't know who I am," I reminded him. "He only knows me as Julie Day from Denver. I assume you've got people combing the city looking for him, in addition to the feds who are looking."

"We have deployed surveillance teams to Stevens's home, the quarry where he and Michael Robinson worked, and the homes of his immediate family members and friends, as well as your home and mine. The Court has committed its resources to finding him."

"Then you've done all you can until he turns up. With so many people looking for him, he won't get far."

Charles hissed. He dropped the towel, spun, and put his fist through the wall with a force that demolished the drywall, splintered the stud behind it, and punched through to the other side. Rogue started barking and scratching at the bathroom door.

I was too startled by his uncharacteristic outburst to object before he spoke. "It is my fault," Charles snarled, his back to me. "We should not have allowed him to escape us at Robinson's house. We should have anticipated he would have an exit strategy in place and been more prepared for him to attack. I should—" He cut himself off.

I wondered if he'd been about to say that he should have left Bryan to die and chased Stevens down instead of staying behind to save his enforcer. No doubt other vampires would have done so. I wondered if he would face criticism from the Court for his decision.

Saving Bryan was the right choice, I told him through our telepathic link. Out loud, I said, "Charles, this not your fault. You can't expect to foresee every eventuality."

"There is a man dead because of me," he ground out.

"There is a man dead because of *Kent Stevens*. There is a man *alive* because of you," I corrected him as I picked up the wet towel. His hand was already healing, the cuts closing and bones knitting back together as I watched.

I took his hand and cleaned off the fresh blood. "I know you feel like you have to blame yourself and maybe I would too in your position, but we both know it's not going to help. All that matters now is catching the bastard. Put your anger into that instead of remodeling my house."

He stared at the hole in my wall as if he didn't remember making it. "I apologize for my outburst. I will have this repaired immediately."

"I know you'll take care of it."

Charles let me finish cleaning his hands. I wiped the towel down the front of his suit, but it didn't seem to make much of a difference. There was so much blood.

"Bryan will be all right." I wasn't sure if I was reassuring him or myself.

"Yes," he said firmly. "Bryan is far stronger than a normal human. He has healed and received transfusions. He will be on his feet later today and on duty by tonight."

"What about you? You're pale. You didn't even stop to change or have a meal to regain your strength before you came over here." I was surprised he hadn't brought someone in the vehicle he could drink from on the way to my house. Strange that Arkady Woodall hadn't supplied him with a meal, but perhaps that was outside the scope of her job description.

"I needed to warn you immediately that Stevens had attacked us and escaped."

"You could have sent someone else to do that, or called," I pointed out.

"Perhaps I needed to see for myself that you were safe." Charles's eyes searched my face. "Come with me until he is captured."

My stomach knotted at the thought. "No way. I'm not letting you lock me away."

"I must protect you, Alice."

"I don't need protection," I countered. "I'll be fine. Stevens has no idea who I am. He knows who *you* are. You need to stay somewhere that's well-protected until he's caught. You shouldn't even be here."

"He has proven himself to be highly resourceful. He has access to weapons and other equipment, including whatever he used to sabotage my gate. I have the ability to heal, but you do not. My home is secure; yours is not. Stevens took the time to shoot you before he escaped Robinson's house. At least permit me to give you bodyguards."

"I won't take any of your people away from protecting you. Bryan won't be back to one hundred percent for at least a couple of days. You need your guards and I'm not defenseless."

"Stevens is a killer. Refusing protection would be foolhardy. I do not think you are foolish."

I understood his desire to safeguard a Court asset from the threat Stevens represented, but I didn't need a protector, least of all one sent by the Court to stick their nose into my life, and his insistence grated on my nerves. "I can't do my job if I have a babysitter. More to the point, I'm not going to give up my freedom and my job on the off chance he's out there gunning for me."

"Based on his record and psych profile, I think it's more than an off chance he'll come looking for you," Arkady interjected.

"Even so, I'm a private investigator. I can't work if I have an entourage."

"Adri Smith has a PI license. She could accompany you," Charles said. "I would find that acceptable."

I gritted my teeth. "Adri's place is with her brother while he recovers. With Bryan injured, she's even more essential for your safety."

Charles looked stubborn. I'd have to come up with an answer to the problem before he decided to insist on doing things his way and I had to insist that he get the hell out of my house.

As much as I despised the situation, there might be an option I could live with that didn't involve having a Vampire Court enforcer dogging my every step. Dealing with this type of scenario was Maclin Security's bread and butter. Sean and I worked well together. He'd be an asset in the field, if his schedule allowed for him to take me as a client. Considering the antagonism between them, Charles might not like my idea, but it wasn't his decision to make.

"I'll ask Sean to provide security, if he has the manpower available," I told them. "You want me to have protection until Stevens is in custody, fine, but it's on my terms."

I was right; Charles plainly didn't like the idea of Sean as my bodyguard. His frown was thunderous.

"To be clear, I'm not asking your permission," I said. "This is my decision. I'm safe behind my wards for tonight. I'll call Sean in the morning and tell him the situation. If he's unavailable, I'll contact Adri and let her know what my backup plan is."

"I do not like this arrangement," Charles stated.

"Duly noted. But whatever else you may think of Sean, you can rest assured my safety will be his number-one priority." I was not happy to be forced into this, but at least it was me making the decisions and not Charles. "Please keep me updated on the manhunt."

"We will," the vampire said.

"Be safe," Arkady added.

I doubted Stevens would be able to connect "Julie Day" to me, but there was a chance. I hoped the vamps would deal with him before the former Marine could find me.

"Just catch the bastard," I told them.

"We will. He has much to answer for." Charles's eyes flashed silver.

I thought of Fortune and Bryan. Magic sparked on my fingers and a cold breeze blew over us. "Yes, he does."

IT WAS ALMOST four by the time Charles, Arkady, and Matthias finally left. I told Malcolm what had happened and asked him to strengthen the wards on the house and yard.

I let Rogue out into the backyard to go to the bathroom and watched him growl at the garden while it rustled ominously, then went back to bed and stared up at the ceiling, wide awake and thinking about Charles, Fortune, Bryan, and Kent Stevens. Though I tried to sleep, I was haunted by visions of Bryan, his body riddled with bullets, bleeding out on the side of the road while Stevens vanished into the night.

I thought about the fact that somewhere out there, right now, the former Marine was on the loose. Would he go after Charles? Continue with his mission to take out as many vampires as he could? Try to find me? Or would he run, knowing he was at the top of the vampires' Most Wanted list? There was nothing about Stevens that made me think he would skip town. No, he would probably find a place to hole up and then go on the offensive. As much as I didn't want to dwell on it, there was a good chance Charles and I were at the top of his hit list. As long as Charles stayed in a Vamp Court fortress, he would be virtually inaccessible. That left me.

The only people who knew Julie Day's real identity were Charles, Bryan, and Adri, and Valas and Niara of the Vampire Court. I felt reasonably certain Stevens would not be able to find me, but nagging doubt made my stomach churn.

Around five, I gave up trying to sleep and got up. I showered, dried my hair, and got dressed in a T-shirt and an old pair of jeans. I dug out a broom and dustpan and cleaned up the drywall and pieces of wood on the floor in my foyer and started a load of laundry. Rogue followed me around the house for a while, then settled into his bed in the living room and dozed.

Malcolm had been hard at work since Charles and the others left; the house wards felt supercharged and prickled on my skin. I made sure all the curtains were closed and stayed away from the windows. The knot of worry in my stomach was giving way to anger. I was already starting to feel like a prisoner in my home. I resolved to go furniture shopping today, Kent Stevens be damned.

Sean had stocked my refrigerator for me, so I actually had food to eat. I was drinking orange juice and scrambling some eggs for an early breakfast when Malcolm came up from the basement.

"Hey," he said somberly.

"Hey yourself. Nice job on the house wards."

"Nobody's getting in here. Anyone who tries is going to need a hospital or the morgue." I felt a surge of anger and magic from my ghost.

I stirred my eggs and threw in some chopped ham. "You doing okay?"

He sighed. "Yeah. Sorry I've been hiding out."

"Don't worry about it. If you need space, I understand. I know this has got to be weird for you."

"Do you know how many times I've fantasized about seeing that place destroyed?" he blurted out.

I thought about my own fantasies of watching my grandfather's cabal compound burn to the ground. "I can guess."

"I feel like I shouldn't be glad about it, but I am."

"Of course you are. They held you prisoner, tortured you to make you hurt other people, and killed you. You're entirely justified in how you feel. The only thing that could have made it better was if Bell himself died in the attack."

"How do you know he didn't?"

"Nobody panicked afterward. The evacuation was controlled, the security force didn't let anyone into the property, and the demolition went like clockwork. That says Bell is still alive and calling the shots. He's in a bunker somewhere, planning a counterstrike and waiting to see what Murphy will do next."

After a few moments, Malcolm said, "So, are you going back to work?"

"Yes. I'm not going to cower in the house. I doubt Stevens will be able to find me—there's really no way for him to connect 'Julie Day' to me. I can't be scared of him, Malcolm." I dumped the eggs on a plate.

"You're not scared of much."

Heh. It was nice that he thought so.

Malcolm went back to the basement to work. I ground some fancy coffee beans and brewed what had to be the single best-smelling pot of coffee I'd ever made in my life.

While the coffeemaker gurgled happily, I went upstairs and got my laptop. I took my coffee mug and breakfast to the couch and prepared my invoice for the Vampire Court while Rogue snoozed by the back door, lying on his back and snoring.

When I added everything up, I blinked at the total and double-checked the math to make sure I had the decimal in the right place. When the numbers added up, I sent the invoice to the Court's Accounts Payable clerk—yes, the vampires had accountants—and received a confirmation that it would be processed immediately.

By the time I put the clothes in the dryer, made my bed, and tidied the kitchen, it was after six and the sun was up. I took my phone to the living room.

I sat on the couch as I drank another cup of coffee and fumed. I didn't like having to mix my personal and professional lives yet again, but I couldn't see any better option. Finally, I decided to bite the bullet and called Sean's cell.

He answered on the second ring. "Hey, babe." His early-morning voice had a hint of growl and it made my pulse speed up.

"Hey," I said, aiming for casual. "Sorry to call while you're getting ready for work."

"What's wrong?" Sean's tone changed immediately. Evidently my voice wasn't as neutral as I'd hoped.

I sighed. No matter how I downplayed the danger, this was going to bring the overprotective alpha werewolf out in him.

"Alice, what's going on?" His voice was sharp.

"I have a...situation," I said slowly. "What's your schedule looking like today?"

CHAPTER 4

An hour later, Sean stood in my foyer looking decidedly grim, a heavy, oversized black duffel bag in each hand and a matching backpack on his shoulder.

"It's not that big of a deal," I said for the umpteenth time as I closed the door and locked it. "This is purely a precautionary measure." I adjusted the curtain in the front window.

"Stay away from the windows," he said automatically. He noticed the hole in my wall. "What the hell happened there?"

"Charles was pretty upset. He's going to fix it."

"I should hope so." He carried his bags into the living room, where he put them down carefully on the hardwood floor. "Where's Rogue?"

"In the backyard. Don't worry; I've got wards around the garden." I went to the back door and opened it. The dog galloped inside and jumped up on Sean.

"No," Sean said firmly and pointed to the floor. "Sit."

Rogue sat, his tongue hanging out.

Sean chuckled and scratched the dog's head. He looked around the living room and sighed. "We have to get you a coffee table and some chairs. The *dog* has more furniture than you do."

Rogue went to his bed and plopped down with a heavy thump.

"I was actually planning on going furniture shopping today."

"You're not going out, not for that," Sean stated. "We can shop online and have everything delivered."

I frowned at him. "Sean Maclin, you are not going to tell me what I can and cannot do. You are not going to take over my life, and I am not buying furniture *online* without trying it out first."

He crossed his arms, straining the shoulders of his polo shirt as it stretched over his muscles. "I had a feeling you weren't giving me the straight story on this Kent Stevens, so I called Adri Smith on my way over here and she sent me his file. This is serious, Alice. Stevens is a highly trained Marine. He got the drop on two enforcers and nearly killed both of them, and he's already shot you once."

I scowled.

Sean's gaze was intense. "You cannot hold back key information like that. I can't protect you if I don't know what I'm up against."

I had to admit he was right, but that didn't mean I had to like it. "Fine."

He cupped my cheek. "I know you hate needing help. You hate when people worry about you and you hate feeling vulnerable. I don't want to make this any harder on you than it already is, but you can't keep things back from me. You call the shots on your cases, but when it comes to keeping you safe, you're going to have to let me do my job—which I'm actually pretty good at, by the way."

The corner of my mouth turned up in a wry half-smile. "Can I get you some coffee?"

"That would be great. Then I want to hear everything you know about this guy. Adri said to tell you the Vampire Court has amended the confidentiality agreement you signed so that you can read me in on the entire operation. They're sending the paperwork over by courier for you to sign."

"Okay." I went into the kitchen and came back with two cups of coffee.

Sean was unzipping the duffel bags when I returned. My jaw fell open. "What is all that?"

"Sensors for the doors, windows, and yard. I know you have wards, but I'm going to take extra precautions. There's also a couple of panic buttons and some other goodies."

"What about the backpack?"

He unzipped it and pulled out a bulletproof vest. "It's the latest technology. It's as light as they can make them, and it will go under your clothes. They're actually pretty comfortable."

I rubbed my forehead.

"Alice." He stood, his eyes serious. "Please wear it when we go out."

At least I would be allowed to leave the house. Fantastic.

A COURIER ARRIVED while Sean was bringing in the rest of his stuff. After I signed the updated confidentiality agreement, Sean and I settled on the couch with our coffee. He took out his laptop to take notes and look at the files Adri had sent.

I took a deep breath. "So, here's the story. In the days following the bombing, it became obvious that SPEMA, the FBI, and the ATF had bigger and more serious cases that needed their attention. There were riots and fires and people were getting hurt. The bombing was basically a property crime and no one was injured as far as the feds knew, so it got back-burnered in favor of more pressing cases, ones that were getting more public pressure because they involved injuries to humans."

"And so the vamps decided to solve it themselves," he guessed.

"Bingo. The only evidence besides what was left of the bomb

itself was the van the bombers used, but it was stolen and burned, so other than some traffic cam footage of it leaving the crime scene, that didn't give us much. One thing the ATF did determine was the bomb's design didn't match anything in the federal database. The silver flechettes used as shrapnel were unusual, but the bomb's components were too generic to be of any help. Without physical evidence, we had to look elsewhere for leads, so we turned to the online forums."

"Whose idea was that?"

"Kim Dade, the Vamp Court data analyst who helped us catch the West-Addison harnad."

Kim and I had spent nearly two weeks combing through discussion threads looking for posts about the bombing. We ended up reading thousands of hate-filled, disturbing posts, many of which either advocated violence against vamps, mages, and supes, or boasted about actual crimes. The worst were those directed toward potential female victims. Those gave me nightmares.

It had been a rough time for Sean, as my anger mounted along with his frustration that I couldn't tell him what I was working on for the Court. I did talk to Malcolm and Adri, but the case was like a wall between Sean and me. He weathered my moodiness with the patience of a man used to dealing with a pack full of volatile werewolves.

On the plus side, we'd both enjoyed blowing off steam in the bedroom—or wherever else we happened to be when the mood struck us—so it wasn't all bad. Some mornings we'd both had to drag ourselves to work looking a little worse for wear, but it was hard to be mad about it.

Malcolm had complained about us "going at it like rabbits" until I reminded him that he'd wanted me back with Sean, so he shouldn't grumble about werewolf libido. Truth be told, I initiated sex as much as Sean, but he certainly never turned me down and I always wore out before he did.

Sean and I had installed a heavy bag in my guest room so I could take up kickboxing again. It helped me work off the lingering effects of being exposed to a meth-like drug called Black Fire. Lately, I'd needed it more to take out my fury at what Kim and I had to read in the discussion forums.

To deal with the stress, Kim had doubled up on her yoga classes. I tried that too, but there was too little punching involved for me to find it very helpful.

"You need to go punch the bag for a while?" Sean's tone was teasing, but his eyes were dark with concern.

I gave him a wry smile. "No, I'm good. Anyway, Kim and I spent a good week or so slogging through posts by bottom-feeding bigots before we found someone who claimed responsibility for the bombing. That suspect we quickly eliminated with a couple of questions. Same with the next several people who claimed responsibility. Then we found Andrew's post bragging about the bombing and I had a feeling we were onto something. He wouldn't give details, but the few he did reveal matched what we knew. We needed to make direct contact, but I couldn't do that as myself. I needed an alter ego and a plausible reason for seeking them out. So Julie Day was born, in a manner of speaking."

I described how the Vamp Court had supplied me with a complete fake identity. Julie Day supposedly worked for Human Future, a real anti-supe Human rights organization. She'd come to the city from her base of operations in Denver to meet with local activists willing to fight for the cause. It had taken some careful persuading, but Andrew finally put me in touch with Mike Robinson.

The group leader's ego made him laughably easy to manipulate with a classic "Mr. Big" sting. The operation involved baiting the alleged bombers with the possibility of joining Human Future, in hopes they'd confess to the bombing in an effort to impress me and my superiors at Human Future. It all went like clockwork, right up until it didn't.

"So, what went wrong?" Sean asked.

I explained the failed attempt to arrest the bombers. When I told him how Stevens had incapacitated us with a flash-bang and shot me, Sean's eyes blazed. "Let me see your shoulder," he said, his voice growly.

"You saw it already yesterday," I reminded him.

"Show me again."

I pulled my T-shirt off over my head. He lowered his head and ran his lips across my bare skin where I'd been shot. I shivered and moved my bra strap aside so he had unobstructed access to my shoulder, and his kisses became more insistent. He always managed to smell so good to me, that unmistakable scent of forest that made me forget everything else.

His hand slid between my thighs and rubbed along the seam of my jeans. He inhaled deeply and growled. I was suddenly acutely aware of how long it had been since we'd had sex and how much I'd missed the feeling of his hands on me.

I climbed into his lap and took his face in my hands. I kissed his mouth, then moved slowly across his jaw, enjoying the scratchiness of his stubble against my lips and chin. Sean nuzzled against me, breathing deeply. The feeling of his fingertips on my bare flesh made sparks run all the way to my toes. I moaned a little and nipped his ear. The forest scent intensified and I shivered again.

Just as I decided the rest of this conversation could wait until we ended our drought, Sean kissed me one last time and held me against his chest. "You know I want to tear your clothes off and finish what we just started, but I need to hear the rest of the story."

Clearly, I needed to work on my make-out skills if I wasn't able to distract a werewolf with sex. I sighed and moved off his lap, pulling the T-shirt back on and rearranging my clothes. "That's really all there is to tell. The Vamp Court enforcers came into the house and took out Robinson and the Davis brothers, but Stevens escaped out a back window to a vehicle he had waiting. Charles healed my wound and the feds arrived to take the others into custody. I gave the feds my statement and Fortune drove me home. That was the last time I saw him alive."

He tucked me under his arm and I rested my head on his chest. "I'm sorry about Fortune. I know you liked him. What else is bothering you about this case?"

I picked at my jeans. "Now that it's over, I expected to feel better, or at least have some satisfaction at a job well done. Instead, it feels like a completely Pyrrhic victory. Fortune is dead and Bryan almost was too. Robinson's wife is dead and so is Kent's brother. The Court is still looking into those murders but they may never know who was responsible. That's not right. It doesn't excuse what they did or what Stevens is doing, but he and Robinson have a right to be angry."

"Do you feel sorry for them?"

"For Robinson, a little. By all accounts, Samantha Robinson was a good person who was in the wrong place at the wrong time. Whatever else you can say about him, he loved her. I don't feel sorry for Andrew and Corey; their brother isn't dead or a victim of vampires, and if they can't accept him for who he is, then that's their choice and their loss. But as for Stevens..." Blood magic sizzled on my skin. Sean didn't let go, even though it had to hurt. "If the vamps get to him before the feds do, he'll never be found. I can't bring myself to feel sorry about that."

Sean growled low in his throat. "I'm pretty thoroughly disgusted with the vamps for letting Stevens get loose a second time. His training, combined with his access to military-grade weapons, means he's a very real threat. Everything points toward a very mission-oriented psychology. If he's gunning for you, we have to be concerned about that as much as his weapons ability and the fact he may have been drinking vampire blood."

I shook my head. "There's nothing linking me to Julie Day. I have no plans to go anywhere near Charles's house or any of his businesses. Stevens won't find me."

"Hopefully he won't, but we have to prepare in case he does. He's smart and resourceful, and he apparently has access to weapons and gadgets."

"That's what Charles said." I sighed and laid down on the couch, resting my head in Sean's lap.

He squeezed my hand. "Tell me what I can do to help."

"You're doing it." I closed my eyes. "It's been a rough couple of weeks."

"If you want to talk about what's on your mind, you know I'm here to listen."

"Thanks. That means a lot."

The radio on his belt beeped. "Mobile Team One to Alpha," a brisk male voice said.

Sean took the radio out. "Go ahead for Alpha."

"The temp team is gone and we're on duty."

"Ten-four." He set the radio on the arm of the couch.

"You have a mobile team outside?" I asked.

"Yes. This is a multi-person job. I need eyes watching for him while I'm protecting you up close. Vamp security will stay and watch your house while the mobile team shadows us." He read my expression. "We talked about this. You have to let me do my job."

"I understand why they're out there," I said quietly. "That's not what's bothering me. I feel crowded. I've lived alone for a long time, and all of a sudden there are people all around me, watching me."

He looked surprised, then thoughtful. "I hadn't thought of it like that, but I can see why you feel that way. I come from a big family and I'm a werewolf, so I'm used to being in a pack and I enjoy the feeling of closeness. I should have known you would be uncomfortable." He squeezed my hand.

My phone dinged. Sean dug it out of the couch cushions and handed it to me. I had a voicemail from my work number. I hit *Play* to listen to the message and heard a familiar male voice. "Hello, Alice. This is Aaron Riddell. One of my clients would like to meet with you. Please call me at your earliest convenience." He disconnected.

"Aaron Riddell of Riddell, Ives, and McAllen." Sean sounded surprised. "If not the best law firm in town, certainly the priciest. He didn't leave a number, though."

I sat up and stretched, feeling my back pop. "I've got his number; I've worked for a couple of his clients in the past."

At his expression, I added, "Don't look so astonished; some jobs are better suited for small-time MPIs than big firms. The people on Aaron's client list want small jobs handled quietly and it's hard to keep things confidential in a big firm. If he's calling me, someone's got a sticky situation they don't want anyone to know about."

He frowned. "I'm not sure how to feel about that."

"Well, *I* feel good about it. My fees are on a sliding scale and any referral I get from Aaron is automatically at the top of that scale. It will help offset the cost of the security you're providing."

He went still. "Alice, there is no way I would even think about charging you."

"And I'm not about to let you do all this for free," I countered. "This is a business arrangement. I didn't ask you to do this as a personal favor. I want invoices, time sheets, and so forth, the same as you would do for any client."

His eyes darkened. "We are keeping track of all that."

"Good."

"The Vampire Court is covering all expenses related to your security." The words were clipped.

I stood up and started to go to the window, then remembered I had to keep the curtains closed. I stopped in the middle of the room and stood with my back to him, my arms crossed.

He rose. "Are you angry because the Court is paying to provide personal security for you? Because that is ridiculous."

I spun around, but he cut me off. "Stevens escaped them not once but *twice* because they underestimated him. They feel responsible for putting you in danger and rightfully so. They may catch him an hour from now, or tomorrow, or next week, but in the meantime, they need their 'asset' kept safe." His eyes glowed softly golden. "But even if they weren't paying me a dime, I'd still be here because *I* need you to be safe. If the situation were reversed, you'd do the same."

"No, I wouldn't," I retorted. "I'd send you an invoice every single day and expect payment each Friday by noon."

We stared at each other. My lips twitched.

He chuckled and pulled me into his arms. "You are impossible," he said into my hair. "I am allowed to care about you, you know. The Court is protecting an asset. I am protecting my..." He hesitated. "My girlfriend."

I groaned. "'Girlfriend'? That makes us sound like we're in high school."

"What would you say, then?" He eyed me. "And don't say 'colleague.'"

I gave him a look. "You're not still holding a grudge about me calling you my colleague back when we first met, are you?"

"It's more like a running joke now, don't you think?"

I rolled my eyes. "I need to call Aaron back."

He sighed. "Fine, call the lawyer, but we're going to finish this conversation at some point soon."

I took my phone into the kitchen. He would be able to hear every word I said, but I could focus on the call without being distracted by my...whatever Sean was. Not boyfriend. Partner? Significant other? And what had he been about to call me, before he'd changed his mind?

I called Aaron's direct line and got his assistant, who transferred me.

When he came on the line, Aaron's voice was warm. "Alice, how are you?"

"Doing all right, Aaron. And you?"

"I'm on top of the world," the lawyer said. In the background, I could hear papers shuffling on his desk. "You busy this afternoon?"

"I just closed a big case, so I'm pretty open at the moment. What's the job?"

"I'll let my client discuss that with you. We are prepared to pay for a consultation. Same rate as before?"

"That's fine."

"I'll have a check waiting. Are you available to meet her at two?"

"Sure. At your office?"

"That would be ideal. As always, confidentiality and discretion are essential."

I hesitated. "I'll have someone with me."

"Who?" His voice sharpened.

"My personal security detail, Sean Maclin of Maclin Security."

"I know Maclin by reputation." Aaron pondered that. "I'll run it by the client, but I don't think it will be a deal-breaker as long as he agrees to the same terms of confidentiality."

"That will not be a problem."

"See you soon."

"Wait, who's the client?" I asked.

A pause. "Esther Aldridge."

My eyebrows went up. "Okay, I'll see you at two." We disconnected.

Sean came into the kitchen. "So, what's the job?"

"I don't know the details yet, but the potential client is Esther Aldridge."

"*The* Esther Aldridge?"

"Unless you know another one." I rinsed out my coffee mug and put it in the sink. "Aaron couldn't tell me what the case is about over the phone. In any case, I'll at least meet with Aldridge and get an idea of her situation before making a decision. If nothing else, it will keep me busy so I don't sit around wondering if Kent Stevens is going to pop up and shoot me again."

He jerked, his eyes shining gold. "Please don't joke about it." A muscle twitched in his jaw. "Every instinct in my body is telling me to keep you in this house until he's in custody. All I can think about is keeping you safe and how difficult it is going to be to protect you when the threat is a highly trained former Marine. My wolf is uneasy and that makes things difficult."

Though we'd only been seeing each other for a few months, Sean's wolf thought of me as his potential mate. As worried as Sean was, I could only imagine how much more displeasing the situation was for his furry half.

I put my hand on his arm and squeezed. "I'm sorry. I'm not trying to make this any harder on you than it already is."

He nuzzled my hair, which always seemed to soothe both him and his wolf. "I know you aren't. You say what you feel and you cope with everything the best way you know how."

"If I could stand to stay in my house to make this easier for you, I would, but I can't. Not after these last few weeks, and not after... everything else I've been through."

I'd been held a prisoner by my grandfather for twenty years. I'd never allow myself to be trapped again, not even if it meant Stevens might find me. Better that than give up my freedom. I couldn't explain any of that to Sean, so I shook my head to indicate that we'd run up against the part of my life that I had to keep hidden.

"It's okay. I don't need to know those secrets today." He kissed the top of my head. "If we're going out in a couple of hours, I'm going to get to work installing alarms on the windows and doors. When do we need to leave?"

"By one fifteen."

"Okay." He headed to the living room for his bag of gadgets.

I used an app on my phone to order a pizza and got my clean clothes out of the dryer. I took them upstairs and stayed out of Sean's way by puttering around cleaning for a while. When I came back down, he was finishing putting alarms on all the bottom-floor windows.

When the pizza arrived, we ate it sitting on the couch, curled up together. After the last slice was gone, I took the pile of dishes and trash to the kitchen.

I rinsed the plates, then put the trash in the can and wiped my hands on a towel. "I'm going downstairs to work on spellwork with Malcolm. I'll be back up in about an hour. Don't try to come down; if you need me, shoot me a text."

A pause. "Okay."

When we were first together, I'd given him access through my basement wards, but revoked it later and never restored his privileges. Right now, I needed a refuge, and with Sean in the house, the only place I could retreat to was the basement.

I could feel his gaze on me as I opened the basement door and the wards sizzled on my skin. "Coming down!" I called.

"Clear!" Malcolm's voice floated up to me.

I paused and looked back at Sean, where he was standing in the middle of my living room. "Hey, thank you for doing all this for me."

He smiled and some of the tension eased out of my shoulders. "Of course. Whatever you need, you know I'm here for you."

"I know." I headed down the stairs and gently closed the door behind me.

My basement was part library and part magic workshop. Like most mages, I had a collection of books on magic theory, history, and practice, Though more books were becoming available in e-reader format these days, most older and more esoteric titles were only available in hard copy. The large open space of the workshop contained several storage cabinets, a work table, and three concentric circles inlaid into the floor.

When I got to the bottom of the steps, Malcolm was in the spellwork area. "I got a call about a potential case," I told him. "Not sure what it's about yet, but I have a client meeting in a couple of hours and then I'll let you know what I find out."

"Sounds good." He met me halfway across the floor. "You doing okay?"

"I'm good. Do you have time to spar?"

"Sure. What do you want to work on?"

"It's been a while, so how about we warm up with some basic defense?"

"Okay. *En garde.*" Malcolm floated to the right. I shifted my weight and watched him closely.

Suddenly, he vanished. A flash of bright green to my left; I threw up a protective shield and Malcolm's bolt of earth magic crackled against it. I scowled and dropped the shield. "Faster, Malcolm. Don't hold ba—"

Zzzap! I yelped and staggered as his bolt hit me in the small of my back.

"Are you okay?" he asked from behind me.

I spun and lashed out with my cold fire whip. He vanished before it could touch him. Another zap to my left side. I stumbled, wincing, and reached out with my senses. I felt his presence to my right and threw up a shield just in time to intercept his magic bolt. I dropped the shield, sensed him behind me, spun, and lashed him with the whip.

"Better." Malcolm's disembodied voice seemed to be to my right. I lashed out, but the bolt hit me from the left, searing a welt across my side.

"Son of a bitch!" I yelled. I took a deep breath and grimaced, touching the burn. The pain felt good. "More," I ordered. "Faster."

"Are you sure?" He materialized in front of me, looking concerned.

"Yes. I have got to get better. My life may depend on it."

"Okay, it's on." He vanished.

I waited until I sensed him to my left, then manifested my whip again and lashed out, intercepting a bolt in midair.

"Yes!" he yelled.

I laughed. "Keep 'em coming, ghost." *Zzzap.* "Ow! Damn it! Again!"

CHAPTER 5

I opened the basement door and staggered out into the living room.

"I thought you were working on spellwork. What on earth have you been doing?" Sean was sitting on the couch, his phone in one hand and a small black key fob in the other. He stared disbelievingly at my tattered clothes and the dozens of small burns and welts all over my body. Rogue looked up from his dog bed, chuffed softly, and went back to sleep.

"Sparring practice with Malcolm," I said breathlessly, pulling the basement door closed and stumbling toward the stairs. "I really needed to blow off some steam and work on my magic defenses."

"Do you need help?"

"Nope, I'm good." I grabbed the banister and started dragging myself up the stairs. "I'm going to clean up and heal these burns, and then we'll be ready to go."

When I looked back, he was shaking his head, his attention back on his phone. I appreciated that he wasn't fussing over me. Maybe we were making progress with that.

I was back downstairs in thirty minutes, in my Armani suit and four-inch Louboutin heels, briefcase in hand. My wounds were healed, and I'd showered, put on makeup, and pulled my hair up in a neat French twist. Simple diamond earrings and my monogram pendant completed my outfit.

Sean was waiting for me in the kitchen, wearing a Maclin Security jacket over his shoulder rig. On the counter were the bulletproof vest and a couple of key fobs.

"You look lovely," he said, kissing me on the temple.

"Gotta look the part when you go to see Aaron Riddell or they won't let you past the front lobby. What's all this?"

He held up one of the key fobs. "Panic button with GPS locator, designed to look like a car remote. You can put one in your pocket, one on your keys, and stash the other two either in your house or your car." He handed me the fob. "What looks like the ignition button is actually a very loud alarm. The lock button dials my phone directly and transmits audio one-way from you to me and the unlock disconnects the call. The trunk release sends an alarm to my phone, and the car alarm is a silent all-hands-on-deck emergency distress call. I've got that one set up to go to my phone, my mobile team, and the vamps. They'll dispatch the closest pack of Hunters."

Hunters were dhampirs—half-vampires—with abnormally sharp senses of smell, sight, and hearing. They were also notoriously unstable, violent, and single-minded in pursuit of their targets and could go for a week or more without sleep or rest. If the vamps had committed multiple packs of Hunters, I doubted Stevens would be running around for very long unless he found a place to hole up and had someone to bring him food and supplies. All it would take is for one Hunter to catch his scent and they would likely be able to follow it directly to him. I would not want to be Stevens if and when the Hunters caught up to him. There was a very good chance he would be alive but not in one piece when they delivered him back to the vamps.

I looked over the panic button. It looked exactly like a car remote and even sported a Toyota insignia for additional camouflage. "Fancy," I said, tucking it into my jacket pocket. "I'll put one on my keys and figure out where to keep the others."

Sean picked up the bulletproof vest. I sighed. "I already have one."

"What kind?"

I took him to my storage room and showed him my vest, which he immediately deemed inadequate. "It's not designed to stop rifle rounds."

I poked at the vest he was holding. "This one is?"

"Yes. There are ballistic plates in the front and back."

"What about you?"

He pulled up his polo shirt and showed me his own vest. "Standard issue for everyone on the team."

Reluctantly, I took the vest from him. "Holy crap, this is heavy."

"Compared to the lightweight one you have, it is, but it's not nearly as heavy as it could be."

We went back to the kitchen and I took off my suit jacket and blouse. Sean unfastened one side of the vest and helped me put it on over my head. With practiced ease, he adjusted the Velcro fasteners on the sides and shoulders until the vest was snug. Without the ballistic plates, it might not have been too bad, but with them, it was far from comfortable. At least my posture would improve, I supposed.

I grimaced as I put my blouse and suit jacket back on. "Anything else?"

He kissed my forehead. "Not right now. Thank you for putting on the vest."

"If it makes you feel better, I suppose it's worth it."

He smiled and squeezed my hand. "I put Rogue out in the yard. Ready to go?"

"Yep." I picked up my briefcase and headed for the front door.

He pulled a small walkie-talkie radio from his belt. "Mobile team, we're heading out now. Are we clear? Over."

My stomach roiled. I wasn't sure why until I realized that on the rare occasions that I left Moses's compound in Baltimore, our security escort had gone through the same routine with the guards outside the gate. I pretended to check something inside my briefcase so Sean couldn't see my eyes.

A short pause, then the male voice replied, "Clear to go. Over."

"Ten-four." He stuck the radio back on his belt and moved to the door. "Stay between me and the house and let me open your car door for you. Once you're in, I'll go around to the driver's side."

"Okay. Ready when you are."

Sean opened the door, looked around, then stepped out onto the porch. I followed him, allowing him to shield my body with his as we stepped outside.

I didn't like the feeling of being guarded, for a lot of reasons, but my rational side knew that I would be safer with extra eyes watching my back. At least two of those eyes belonged to Sean, and that helped. It was the first time I'd seen him in professional bodyguard mode. As much as it rankled me to do so, I had to follow his instructions and let him do his job. I locked the door and hurried down the steps and over to his SUV, staying in his shadow. I felt furtive and jumpy, and I hated it.

Sean had the SUV unlocked and already running when we got to it. He opened the door, I climbed in, and he shut it firmly. As he was walking around to the driver's side, I closed my eyes and blew out a breath, feeling squashed inside the tight-fitting vest. I thought of the packs of Hunters combing the city for Stevens and wished they would hurry up. I hadn't been under Sean's protection for six hours and already I felt smothered.

Sean climbed into the SUV and buckled in. I followed suit and he backed out of my driveway. Another black SUV followed as we headed down the street. "That your mobile team?" I asked.

"Team One, the eight a.m. to four p.m. shift. Jack and Karen."

I remembered that he'd said some members of his pack worked

for him at the security company. "Is that the same Jack who's your beta?"

He glanced at me. "Yes."

"How many of your employees are members of your pack?"

"Just four in the field: Jack, Karen, Karen's brother Patrick, and Phillip. Ben Cooper is my installation manager."

We drove for a while in silence. Finally, Sean said, "Adri told me if you wanted to take a vacation, there's a jet waiting at the airport to take us anywhere you want to go. First-class travel and accommodations for two, courtesy of the Court."

"I'm not running. If I want to take a vacation, I'll take one, but it won't be because of Kent Stevens."

"I figured you'd say that," he said wryly. "I thought I'd ask anyway."

"We have work," I reminded him. "Esther Aldridge, namesake of the Aldridge Art Museum, the Aldridge Concert Hall, and a half-dozen other buildings in town, has a problem that needs fixing."

"Can't wait to find out what it is." Sean's eyes moved constantly, checking his mirrors and scanning around the vehicle as we drove toward downtown and the offices of Riddell, Ives, and McAllen.

I was relieved and eager to be back at work after being on the bombing case for so long. It felt like one more step toward normalcy, even if I had a security detail.

We arrived at the office building at one forty-five and turned into the parking garage. Mobile Team One—Jack and Karen—pulled in behind us as Sean headed up the ramp. He found two empty spots on the second level near the elevators. The mobile team parked next to us, on my side.

"Same drill as before, in reverse," Sean said. "I'll come around to open your door. Stay next to me. I'm going to introduce you to Jack and Karen and then Karen will stay here while Jack comes with us." He touched my hand. "Don't look Jack in the eye for more than a few seconds. His wolf is very dominant and aggressive. Karen's more submissive."

"Got it."

Sean got out of the vehicle and moved around to my side. When he opened the door, I stepped out with my briefcase.

The doors of the other SUV opened. The man who got out of the driver's seat was enormous, taller even than Sean, with a larger physique. His hair was blond, his eyes bright blue.

"Alice Worth, this is Jack Hastings," Sean said.

I shook hands with Sean's beta. "Nice to meet you," I said, my eyes fixed on his chin.

"Glad to meet you, Ms. Worth," Jack said gruffly. "We've all been anxious to meet the woman who's caught the eye of our alpha."

Was I imagining it, or was there a distinctive note of disapproval in his tone? I felt the weight of his appraising stare. I resisted the urge to meet his gaze, even though avoiding eye contact made me feel submissive and I didn't like it.

Jack's companion came around the back of the SUV. Karen was about my height and looked to be my age, with short dark hair and green eyes. I instinctively liked her.

Smiling, she held out her hand. "I'm Karen Williams. It's great to meet you, finally."

"Do we have any idea how long this meeting will last?" Jack asked.

I shrugged. "An initial client consultation usually takes forty-five minutes to an hour, but it's hard to say for sure. Once I talk with my client, I'll know more about what I'll need to do from there." I glanced at my phone. "We need to get moving."

"I'll keep an eye on our vehicles," Karen said. "See you in a bit."

Sean headed for the elevators and Jack gestured for me to walk between them. Having the beta at my back made me itch between my shoulder blades.

At the elevators, I hit the up button and we waited, Sean at my side as Jack guarded us. When the elevator arrived, we stepped inside and they maneuvered me to the back, blocking me in with four hundred pounds of werewolf.

"What floor?" Sean asked as the doors closed.

"Twenty."

Sean hit the button. As the elevator rose, he said, "Don't sit or stand near any windows. If I tell you to hit the floor or run, do it."

I blew out a breath. "Okay."

When the doors opened at the twentieth floor, we stepped out into the posh lobby of Riddell, Ives, and McAllen. I approached the reception desk, flanked by Sean and Jack.

The receptionist's gaze lingered on my entourage for a few extra beats before she looked at me. "Can I help you?"

I gave her a quick smile. "I have a two o'clock appointment with Aaron Riddell."

She checked her computer. "Ms. Worth and Mr. Maclin?"

"Yes."

"Follow me."

Jack took a seat in the reception area while Sean and I followed the receptionist down a long hallway. She stopped at a pair of doors and knocked twice.

"Come in," Aaron called.

The receptionist opened the door and ushered us inside, then closed the door behind us.

The conference room was enormous, with thick carpet, a long oval table ringed by eight leather chairs, a complete audio/visual system, and floor-to-ceiling windows overlooking downtown on two sides.

I could tell immediately that Sean did not like those windows. He moved slightly in front of me to block any shots from the building next to ours.

Three people rose as we entered the room: Aaron, his assistant, and a slim, gray-haired woman in a light blue designer pantsuit.

The woman and the assistant waited while Aaron came around the table to greet us with a smile. The tall African-American lawyer wore his usual tailored suit. He took my hand and kissed me lightly on the cheek. Next to me, Sean tensed.

"Alice, it's so good to see you," Aaron said. "You look lovely, as always."

"Good to see you, too, Aaron. It's been a while."

"Too long." Aaron and Sean shook hands. "Mr. Maclin, a pleasure to meet you. I've heard many good reports about your company."

"Call me Sean. It's good to meet you as well. Can we close these blinds?"

Aaron didn't hesitate. "Absolutely. Alex, if you would?"

Aaron's assistant did something on his tablet. The blinds closed with a quiet whir and the lights turned up.

Aaron gestured behind him. "I'd like to introduce my client, Ms. Esther Aldridge."

Esther was in her late sixties, with platinum hair in a neat twist and sharp blue eyes that raked me from head to foot as I approached her with my hand outstretched.

"Ms. Aldridge, it's an honor to meet you," I said. "The new exhibit hall in the museum is beautiful."

"I'm very proud of it," she said, shaking my hand with a surprisingly firm grip. "I've wanted to expand our collection of African art for years. I'm very pleased with our curator's work." She turned to Sean with narrowed eyes. "Mr. Maclin, I understand you're providing security for Ms. Worth."

"Yes, we are."

"Mr. Riddell has confidentiality agreements for both of you to sign, but I'm a bit old-fashioned. I would like your word as a gentleman that everything we discuss here today will remain confidential and that your employees will be required to maintain that same level of discretion."

"You have my word," Sean told her.

She studied him, then nodded briskly. "Fine. Let's get down to business."

We moved to the conference table. Esther sat on one side, with Aaron on her right and Alex next to him. Sean and I sat across from them.

Alex slid confidentiality agreements over to us. I scanned mine. It appeared identical to ones I had signed previously and I signed, initialed, and dated as required. Sean read his thoroughly, then signed and handed it back.

I took out a notepad and pen from my briefcase as Sean poured us each a glass of water from the pitcher on the table. Aaron's assistant poured water for his boss and Esther.

Aaron folded his hands on the table. "Ms. Aldridge has asked to meet you because she was recently the victim of a burglary that resulted in the theft of cash, jewelry, and several magical objects."

"When did the burglary take place?" I asked.

"Two nights ago, I believe," Esther said. "I was out of town for a few days and returned last night to discover I had been robbed. I called Mr. Riddell this morning and asked his advice on how to proceed. It was he who suggested I employ the services of a private investigator with experience in tracking magical objects—and whose discretion could be counted upon."

I nodded. "I understand. What can you tell me about the burglary itself?"

"My home has always had top-notch security and I've never had any problems. A few months ago, a friend told me he had recently added a different type of home security—one that utilized magic. I was skeptical, but wished to learn more."

Magic could certainly be used for home security; wards provided varying levels of protection and defense. While electronic systems could be circumvented or manipulated, wards were difficult to penetrate or break without causing serious harm to the interloper. I was somewhat surprised Esther had never considered their use before; her own art museum used wards to help protect its most valuable pieces.

Esther sipped her water and continued. "My friend showed me the protections at his home. It was a system of wards, 'anchored'—I believe that is the word—by a magical object provided by a mage. I saw for myself how effective the wards were and made an appointment to speak to the mage in question. He visited my home, assessed my needs, and recommended a similar system. I had it installed about six weeks ago and had no issues with its use. I believed my home to be secure until two nights ago, when someone, or perhaps a group of people, waltzed in right past the wards and my security system and robbed me blind."

"They broke the wards?"

"No, they simply passed through them, which I was led to believe was impossible."

I shook my head. "You were misled, unfortunately. The mage who set the wards could cross them. Also, there are 'passkey' spells that allow someone passage through a ward, but they have to be made by whoever created the wards in the first place."

"So this mage who set up the system has to be involved in the burglary?" Aaron interjected.

"More than likely. It's possible he had passkey spells on hand for some other reason, I suppose, and these thieves got hold of them, but the more likely scenario is that you were deliberately targeted and the mage who set your wards is in league with whoever burgled your house."

Esther's mouth compressed into an angry line. "I have attempted to call the mage several times and there was no answer."

"That's not a good sign," I said. "So, what is it you want me to do?"

"I doubt there's much chance of recovering any cash or the jewelry, but I want the magical objects recovered. I am willing to pay double your standard rate for your undivided attention and a fifty-percent bonus if all three objects are returned within the week."

"What about the wards the mage placed? Do you want me to remove them?"

Her eyes flashed. "I want those wards gone and replaced with a new security system." She turned to Sean. "I understand you own a security company, Mr. Maclin. How soon would your company be able to install a new system?"

"Let me look at our schedule." Sean pulled out his phone and checked a calendar. He looked up. "I can have our crew at your house by six o'clock."

"Do it," Esther said.

As he texted his staff to set up the installation, I turned to Esther. "Meanwhile, I'll need full access to your home and grounds, photos of the missing objects, and everything you have on the mage who set up the wards."

"Agreed," she said briskly.

Sean spoke up. "With your permission, I'll look into the breach of your security system, unless you would prefer that the company that installed it run the diagnostic?"

"The fewer people who know about the situation, the better, so I would prefer not to involve the other security company," she told him. "You have free access to the system. I'll see that you get the necessary codes."

"A question," I said. "Is it only the items you are interested in, or do you want the thieves found and arrested?"

"Only the items. I'm not interested in prosecuting the thieves or anyone else involved in the robbery; I want no part of any trial or publicity."

I'd expected as much. "Has your friend who recommended this mage also been a victim of a burglary?"

"I suppose it is possible, but I do not intend to ask, and nor should you."

I tilted my head. "Why is that?"

She set her water glass down. "Ms. Worth, there are good reasons I have called you and not the police to track down my missing items. First, I am a private person. Second, the missing objects are of questionable legal status. Third, they must be handled with care, by someone who understands magic. Fourth, I don't want anyone to know I was the victim of a burglary, and if my friends were also victims, they would feel the same way. If they *were* burgled, they may have hired someone like yourself to go after the thieves and their missing valuables. They are looking after their own interests; I must look after mine."

"I understand. Do you have the photos of the missing items?"

At Esther's nod, Aaron slid a folder over to me. I opened it.

The first magical object was a wide bronze or brass arm cuff. On the next page was a photo of a battered cup that looked to be made of pewter. The third item was a beautiful silver hand mirror.

I looked up at Esther. "What magical properties do these items have?"

She narrowed her eyes at me and said nothing.

I put down my pen. "I have to know what they do, Ms. Aldridge. Magic is volatile. Magical objects often have a mind of their own, sometimes quite literally. I'm not going to get killed because I don't know what I've got my hands on. I need full disclosure on this or I'm out. You can try to find someone else who's willing to go after magical objects without knowing what they do. Good luck with that."

We stared at each other across the table while the men were silent. Finally, she crossed her arms and spoke. "None of them are volatile. Drinking from the cup permits a vampire to walk in daylight for one hour. The mirror allows glimpses into one's forgotten memories. The cuff…" She coughed delicately. "The cuff belonged to my husband. It made him strong and quite virile."

Oh good Lord, I did *not* need any details. "Ms. Aldridge, just because their magic seems tame doesn't mean they aren't volatile." I was relieved, however, to hear that none of them contained the vengeful spirit of a five-hundred-year-old blood mage or the power to lay waste to a hundred square miles at a time. I could probably handle a cup, a mirror, and a magical Viagra bracelet, assuming I didn't break the damn mirror and net myself seven years of bad luck —or something much worse.

"Let's say I find one or more of these objects. There are a couple of possible scenarios for recovery." I ticked them off on my fingers. "One, someone is careless and leaves them lying around."

"Obviously, the ideal situation," Aaron said.

"Ideal, but unlikely. Two, they are available for purchase from someone who has acquired them."

"Safe to assume that said agent will not be willing to return them as stolen property." The lawyer exchanged a glance with his client. "Ms. Aldridge is willing to negotiate for the return of the items. Obviously, we want to limit both our expense and our exposure, so you are authorized to act as our agent if you believe the items can be bought for a reasonable amount."

"Define 'reasonable.'"

Esther spoke. "Six thousand for the mirror and cuff and ten thousand for the cup, to be paid in cash or bearer bonds. You will deliver the payment and collect the items yourself."

"The third possible scenario is that the items may be in a location that is very hard to get to. Before I or anyone else gets too deep in recovery efforts, I have to ask: what's special about these three items? Why not just buy new stuff? I get that the cuff belonged to your late husband, but—"

She interrupted me, her eyes flashing. "This is not about some sentimental attachment to a couple of knickknacks. Someone has stolen from me, and that cannot stand."

I raised my hands. "Okay, I can understand that. You want your stuff back, I'll get it back."

She gave me a nod. "Any special efforts required to reclaim the items will be justly compensated, as per our contract."

"Naturally, neither Ms. Aldridge nor I condone any actions that violate the law," Aaron said, his eyes twinkling.

"Naturally," I said dryly.

Esther leaned forward to pick up her glass of water. "So, how do we begin?"

"We need to sign a contract, and I need a retainer."

Alex produced paperwork and Aaron handed it to me. "I took the liberty of preparing a contract based on your standard terms and the special conditions we discussed here today."

I looked through it, then initialed, signed, and dated it and passed it back. He gave it to Esther, who signed and dated it as well.

Aaron slid an envelope across the table toward me. "Is this amount sufficient for a retainer?"

I opened the envelope, peeked at the check, and nodded. "Yes, that will work. I need all the information about the mage you hired to install the wards. Sean and I need to go to your house so he can see how they got past your security system and I can examine the wards and their anchor."

"Very well." Esther handed me a file. "This is my agreement with the mage who provided the wards. I'll let my assistant know you'll be by this afternoon. Her name is Christina Harris. If you need anything, she will provide it. I have meetings at the museum this afternoon and then dinner with friends, but I should be back home around seven."

I put the files and my notepad back into my briefcase and zipped it closed. We rose and shook hands. "Would you prefer that I call Aaron with updates?" I asked Esther.

She nodded. "Please. He will pass the information along to me."

We said our goodbyes. Alex escorted Sean and me back to the main lobby, where Jack sat leafing through a travel magazine.

He rose when we appeared. "Are we ready to go?"

Sean turned to me. "Where are we headed?"

"Home first so I can change, and then we'll head over to her house."

"By that point, it will be time for a shift change," Jack said as we entered the elevator and Sean hit the button for parking level two. "Should I have Team Two meet us at the nest?"

"Let's do that," Sean said. "I want to meet with both teams."

Jack pulled out his phone and sent a couple of texts as we descended in the elevator.

When we arrived on the parking deck, Karen waited by the SUVs. "Nothing to report," she said as we approached, giving me a smile. "All's quiet."

"Good. Let's head back to the nest, secondary route," Sean told Jack.

The blond man grunted assent and the mobile team got into their SUV as Sean loaded me into ours.

As we approached the exit of the parking garage, I said, "So, what have you been telling your pack about me?"

"Not as much as they would like," Sean said, turning onto the street. "I know you're a private person, so I really haven't said a lot. That's somewhat unusual; most werewolves bring their significant others around the pack so everyone can get used to each other."

"So, is keeping me away from them and not telling them about me causing friction?"

He hesitated. "Yes."

We drove in silence while I thought about that. On the one hand, I *was* a private person whose life depended on staying below the radar, but I didn't want to cause problems for Sean with his pack. If we were going to try to make this work, I would have to observe some shifter customs, including socializing, or at least interacting, with his pack.

"I guess I need to get to know your people," I said as we slowed and stopped at a traffic light.

Sean looked at me with a strange expression.

"What?" I asked, frowning.

"When we get home, I am going to kiss you," he said, his attention back on the traffic as we started to move again. "You don't know how happy I am to hear you say that, Alice."

"When we get home, I suppose I will permit you to kiss me," I said haughtily.

He gave me a wolfy grin that made me warm all the way down to my toes.

Things were changing between us. I'd once been so afraid of letting anyone in past the walls I'd built around myself that I'd driven him away. Now I realized that I very much liked the change he'd brought into my life, so much so that I was willing to put my fear aside and meet his pack. I'd been safe behind my walls, but I'd been very lonely too. I hadn't really been living then, only existing. In a way, it wasn't much different from my life with Moses.

Little by little, one step at a time, I was freeing myself from my past and the fortress I'd built for myself.

I smiled and gazed out the window as Sean drove us home.

CHAPTER 6

The closer we got to my house, the more tense Sean became.

By the time we parked in the driveway, he was on high alert, his face hard and eyes golden. He moved quickly, exiting the driver's side of the SUV and coming around to mine. As soon as I stepped out of the vehicle, he was practically wrapped around me, hustling me up the sidewalk and the steps to the front door so quickly that I almost tripped several times.

I unlocked the door and in a flash we were inside. He shut and locked the door behind us, leaving Jack and Karen in the SUV outside on watch.

I scowled as I set down my briefcase and removed my jacket and blouse. "Why don't you just carry me inside next time?" I took off the bulletproof vest with a sigh of relief.

Sean took the vest from me and kissed me very thoroughly. "I need my hands free."

I sniffed and headed upstairs to change, carrying my jacket and top. "You're lucky I like you. Anybody else who tried to herd me like that would still be smoking on the ground outside."

When I came down fifteen minutes later, wearing a button-up

shirt and khakis, Sean was in the living room with Jack, Karen, and two young men I took to be Team Two. Everyone was ominously silent.

The tension in the room went up a few notches as I reached the bottom of the stairs. Sean looked grim, Jack's expression was a combination of anger and annoyance, and none of the others looked at me. Fantastic. It wasn't hard to figure out what they'd been discussing before I came downstairs.

Sean spoke. "Alice, this is Team Two, Philip and Tom."

We exchanged subdued greetings.

"I've briefed them on who you're working for," Sean added. "Team One is going off duty, so Team Two will be accompanying us to the Aldridge home and standing watch while we work."

"Okay. I'm going to the basement while you guys wrap up your meeting. I'll be back up in a minute."

I headed for the basement door. Sean intercepted me and kissed my cheek. I felt the weight of Jack's stare as Sean squeezed my hand.

I opened the basement door, waited a moment in case Malcolm was in the middle of spellwork, then headed down the stairs, closing the door behind me. After a beat, I heard Jack's angry voice, but his words were indistinct.

Malcolm met me at the bottom of the stairs. He read my expression and asked, "You want me to go up there and find out what they're saying?"

I shook my head. "Shifters are more sensitive to the presence of ghosts, and I don't want them to know about you. I'll get the details from Sean later." And wouldn't that be a fun conversation?

I put that aside and focused on the task at hand. "Good news: we've got a case." I told Malcolm about Esther Aldridge's burglary and our mission to retrieve her stolen magical objects.

The ghost was even more excited than I was at the prospect of checking out the wards at Esther's house and going after the missing items. "A cup that lets vamps walk in daylight and a mirror that shows forgotten memories? Very cool."

"Very," I agreed. "I'm going to head there first and get a sense of what we're dealing with, but I might want help with the wards and the trace, if there is any. I'll summon you when I know the situation is secure."

"Sounds good. I'll hang out here until you're ready for me."

Back upstairs, I found Sean waiting alone in the foyer, holding my vest. "Team One left." His voice was tight with suppressed anger. "Philip and Tom are waiting in their SUV."

I took the vest from him and put it on. "You planning on telling me what's going on?"

"On the way, if that's okay."

"All right." I put on a blazer over the vest and checked my reflection in the mirror by the door. I made a face, picked up my shoulder bag, and sighed. "Ready."

Sean got the all-clear from the mobile team and we headed out.

We drove in silence for a while. Sean's jaw was so tight that it made mine ache.

"Let's hear it," I said finally.

He sighed. "I mentioned that my not being forthcoming about you has been causing some tension, but there's more to it than that. A few members of the pack would prefer I date a shifter. There's no rule saying an alpha has to have a werewolf mate, but it's traditional. It's only a couple of people causing problems; the rest have no issue with you being a human mage."

I said nothing.

"My relationship with you is not open to debate or contingent upon anyone's approval," Sean said flatly when I was quiet. "You have nothing to prove to them. All that matters is you and me."

"That's not exactly true, is it? If they don't like that you're dating someone who isn't a shifter—"

"Then they are more than welcome to take it up with me, in whatever manner they see fit," he broke in. "As I said, who I date is not subject to a vote. A pack is not a democracy. You don't need anyone's approval."

"Is Jack one of the people who wants you to have a werewolf mate?"

"Yes."

"Who else?"

"Jack's mate Delia. Eddie and his mate Thea. Caleb because he follows Jack's lead. A few others are concerned about it but haven't voiced objections."

"So, that's five or more out of how many total pack members?"

"Fifteen at the moment, not counting the kids or human spouses."

I stared out the window.

"What are you thinking?" Sean asked.

"Is this likely to cause someone to challenge you?"

He shook his head. "I doubt it. They may be angry, but they know it's not worth dying over. I'm sure once they get to know you, they'll come around."

"I don't think Jack is going to 'come around.' He seems to feel pretty strongly about it."

"Like I said, it doesn't matter," Sean stated. "If anyone has a problem, I'll deal with them."

In a werewolf pack, "dealing" with a problem almost always involved bloodshed. The question was, whose blood would be shed: Sean's, Jack's, or mine?

ACCORDING to the paperwork Esther gave me, the mage who had installed her wards was a man named Joseph Kendall. Like many self-employed mage security consultants, he had a small office downtown. His website was very professional and he clearly catered to wealthy clients. His photo showed a smiling, dark-haired man of about forty-five in a tailored suit.

As Sean drove, I called Caitlyn Morse, a freelance researcher who used to work for Mark Dunlap Investigations but had quit after Mark's murder, unwilling to put up with the new management. As usual, I felt a stab of grief when I thought of my former mentor.

Cait's cheery voice distracted me from unpleasant memories. "Alice! How are you?"

"Doing well, Cait. You looking for a project?"

"Always. What do you have?"

"I need a background check on a man named Joseph Kendall." I gave her the information I had for him.

Computer keys clicked rapidly. "How deep do I need to go? Vitals only, or do you need his first-grade teacher's name?"

"I need the works," I said. "Particular emphasis on any known criminal associates and any past history of shenanigans. I'm on a time crunch and my client's paying for express service, so when you invoice me, figure your fees appropriately."

"That's what I like to hear. I'll get right on it and e-mail you the files when I've got them. Anything else?"

"Not at the moment. Happy searching." We said our goodbyes and I disconnected just as Sean and I arrived at our destination.

Sean turned into a long, winding driveway that led to an imposing mansion hidden from the street by trees. He parked out front and the mobile team pulled in next to us.

As we exited the SUV, the house wards tingled on my skin. Sean and I walked to the front door as Tom emerged from the mobile team SUV and took up a position next to it, scanning the yard.

The front door opened as we approached, revealing a stern ash-blonde woman in heels and a dark green suit.

I held out my hand. "I'm Alice Worth. Are you Ms. Aldridge's assistant?"

"Yes. I'm Christina Harris." Her handshake was brisk. "Ms. Aldridge told me to expect you. Please come in."

As I walked inside, I sensed only deterrent wards, set to incapacitate anyone who tried to get through, and no deadly black wards.

Those were illegal, but some unscrupulous mages used them anyway if a client paid them enough. We stepped into an enormous entryway and Christina closed the door behind us.

As Sean examined the security system keypad by the door, I placed my hand against the wall and closed my eyes, assessing Kendall's magic.

He was an air mage. The wards were well-made but simplistic. That didn't necessarily mean he lacked skill, but considering the wealth and status of his client, they were woefully inadequate, even without taking into account the passkey spells. A loud sneeze could break them. The shoddy workmanship alone made me angry.

I sensed the trace linking the wards to their anchor. It was a pulsing white line leading somewhere in the house, to the item providing the wards' power. I followed that line to its source, expecting to find an object charged with Kendall's own magic, and instead found something else.

I sucked in a breath and yanked my hand off the wall.

"What's wrong?" Sean asked.

"I'm not sure," I lied. I turned to Christina. "Can you show me the anchor, please?"

"Of course. This way."

We followed her through the entryway, down a long hall, and around a corner. She opened a pair of doors and ushered us into a large office overlooking the garden behind the house.

Sean went to close the curtains immediately, but my attention was on a ceramic figure of a nude woman on a small table next to a wall of bookcases. It pulsed with magic.

The statue was about two feet tall and surprisingly heavy. I turned it around, then picked it up and checked the bottom.

I glanced at Christina. "Do you have something I can put down on the floor, like a drop cloth?"

Her eyebrows went up. "I can bring you something. One moment." She left the office. I listened to her heels clicking down the hallway.

"What's going on?" Sean asked in a low voice.

"We might have a problem. I need Malcolm." I closed my eyes, found the cool blue-green trace in my mind linking me to my ghost, and tugged. I felt a few seconds of dizziness, and then it faded.

About ten seconds later, I sensed Malcolm had jumped to a crystal on my bracelet. I touched the crystal with my other hand. "*Release.*"

Malcolm appeared next to me. "Hey, Alice. Hey, Sean." He glanced around in appreciation. "Nice digs."

"I need your help," I said. "Tell me what you sense in this statue."

He stared at the ceramic figure, then cursed and flitted back four feet in the blink of an eye.

"What's in the statue?" Sean asked.

Malcolm was swearing a blue streak, so I answered. "There's a ghost trapped in the statue. That's what Kendall's using to power the wards instead of his own magic."

Sean stared at the statue in horror. "There's a *person* in there?"

Footsteps approached. "Malcolm," I hissed. I didn't know if Esther's assistant had any ability to sense a ghost but I didn't want to take any chances.

Malcolm cut himself off in mid-curse and went invisible.

Christina reentered the office, carrying a folded piece of heavy cloth like the kind used to drape over furniture in storage. She handed it to me. "Will this work?"

"Perfect." I unfolded the cloth and spread it on the floor. I glanced at Sean. "Would you mind?"

"Not at all," he said, picking up the statue.

"Wait," Christina began.

Sean raised the statue and smashed it on the cloth. Esther's assistant stumbled back, shocked, as pieces of ceramic scattered across the floor. "What are you doing?" she demanded.

"Ms. Aldridge instructed me to break the wards," I told her, using the toe of my boot to nudge the debris. "I'm working on doing that.

You need to go into another part of the house while we work. We'll find you if we need anything."

Without a word, she spun on her heel and left.

Malcolm reappeared next to me. "Where's the crystal?"

I crouched and poked around carefully until I uncovered a marble-sized blue crystal embedded in a chunk of ceramic.

"How long do you think the ghost has been in there?" Malcolm asked me.

"I don't know. I can't tell how old this statue was. It could be months or years. Or decades."

We stared at the crystal.

"What do you want to do?" Malcolm asked.

"We have to release the ghost," I said. "We don't know what kind of shape it'll be in, so we need a circle to contain it. If it's gone wraith, I'll have to discorporate it." I looked at Sean. "You need to be outside the circle. Malcolm and I will handle this."

Reluctantly, he moved away. I took a piece of chalk from my bag and drew a circle around the drop cloth, closing myself and Malcolm inside.

"Charge the circle and hold it. Don't let the ghost break it," I told Malcolm. "Sean, stay out of the circle, no matter what."

The circle flared around us, its power tingling on my skin.

"What do you mean, no matter what?" Sean demanded.

"The ghost may be violent, but I won't let it hurt me." I crouched and picked up the piece of ceramic that contained the crystal. As I stood, the ghost's power buzzed on the edges of my senses. The question was: how stable would he or she be, after being trapped in the crystal for so long?

I pressed the crystal into the palm of my hand, and a jolt of power made my head jerk. I braced myself, focused on the crystal, and spooled my blood magic. With a single blow, I severed the binding spell holding the ghost in the crystal and released it.

A piercing scream filled the air as the ghost emerged in a wave of madness. The spirit wasn't a wraith yet, but it was only a matter of time. Like a poltergeist, she no longer looked human, but I saw two crazed eyes in a formless face a split second before she picked me up and slammed me against the barrier of the circle, my feet dangling eighteen inches from the floor.

Outside the circle, Sean growled and paced, but my attention was on the tormented spirit.

"You're all right," I told her, though she was too far gone to understand me. "You're free of the crystal now."

She made a heartbreaking keening sound. Sean couldn't hear it, but Malcolm and I could. A white ribbon of trace bound her to Kendall. She'd been his bound ghost and he'd trapped her in the crystal to use as a power source.

I felt a spike of fury and realized it was Malcolm's. "Discorporate her," my ghost pleaded. "Please. She's suffered enough. Do it before he realizes she's been released and summons her."

Malcolm was right; the moment Kendall sensed the ghost had been freed, he could pull her back to him and we might never find her again.

There was no time to be kind or gentle. "May you find rest," I whispered, and used my blood magic to pull her apart.

Her wail was excruciating. I dropped to the floor on my hands and knees as the ghost disintegrated. Kendall's binding broke with a sound like a snap.

A strange surge of familiar blue-green magic flared as Malcolm vanished. He was trying to follow the link back to Kendall.

"Malcolm, no!" I shouted. I grabbed my ghost and yanked him back. The hard ricochet of magic left me dazed.

I huddled on the floor, disoriented, trying to shake off the effects of the magic. Malcolm and Sean were shouting, but I couldn't understand what they were saying. Malcolm sounded angry with me and Sean was worried. I heard a female voice and Sean's angry reply, followed by the sound of a door slamming.

Malcolm broke the circle and Sean picked me up. "Alice, talk to me," he said urgently. He carried me over to a sofa and put me down.

I forced my eyes open and blinked slowly, focusing on Sean's face as he crouched next to me. "I'm okay," I told him, squeezing his hand.

Malcolm appeared in my line of sight. He was so furious he was flitting in place, flickering in and out. "Why didn't you let me go after him?" he shouted. "He had her trapped in there for years. Why did you pull me back?" His anger sizzled on my skin and I flinched.

Sean turned toward the sound of Malcolm's voice and snarled, "Back off, right now."

I pushed myself up until I was sitting. "He could have broken our binding," I told my ghost angrily. "He might have been able to take you from me, you idiot. What if he took you and put you in a crystal and I couldn't find you? You'd end up like her, or worse. Did you even think of that? I would never have forgiven myself!"

Malcolm disappeared. At first, I thought he'd jumped somewhere else, but I realized he was on the other side of the room, by the bookcases, his back to me.

I struggled to get to my feet. Sean helped me up and I stumbled across the room. "Malcolm, I'm sorry. I can't lose you like that. I can't."

The ghost turned around. He looked anguished. "She was suffering so much."

"I know. We did what we could to help her."

When he spoke again, it was in a tone of voice I'd never heard him use before. "We have to find this guy and make him pay for doing that to her."

"I agree, but for now we need to remove the house wards and Sean needs to figure out how the burglars got past the security system."

"Are you okay?" Sean asked me.

I took a deep breath and let it out. "I'm all right. Did Christina Harris come in here while we were dealing with the ghost?"

"She came running when we started yelling. I got her out of here."

"I'll have to go apologize for all the chaos. Malcolm, can you unweave the wards while I go find her?"

"I can do that. They're basic wards. It won't take me ten minutes."

"Thank you." I touched his hand. It was a strange feeling, like touching thick fog. "Be careful, you jerk."

He gave me a lopsided smile and turned to face the exterior wall, his fingers moving as he traced the wards.

Sean and I went in search of Christina Harris. We found her at a desk in a solarium down the hall, working on a laptop, a stack of papers at her side. She looked up as we entered and gave us a hard stare as Sean moved to stand between me and the windows.

"I apologize for all this," I told her sincerely. "We uncovered something very unpleasant in regard to the house wards and it was a difficult and dangerous situation to resolve."

She looked surprised. "I thought it would be a simple matter to deal with the wards."

"So did I, until we got in there," I said. "The mage who set up the wards was rather unethical in his methods. I'll report what we found to Ms. Aldridge."

"What can I help you with at this point?"

"Sean needs the information for the main security system, if you have that handy. Meanwhile, I'd like you to show me where the magical items were kept."

Christina rose and handed Sean a folder. "Those are the codes and the rest of the information about the security system."

"Thank you," Sean said. He squeezed my hand, then headed for the front door as I followed Esther's assistant back to the office.

Malcolm had gone invisible but I could sense his presence near the bookcases as he worked on unweaving Kendall's wards.

Christina led me to a corner of the room, where she slid a panel aside to reveal a large safe. She punched in an eight-digit code, turned the handle, and opened the door. The safe was empty.

"Was everything in the safe taken?" I asked.

She shook her head. "The only things taken were approximately five thousand dollars in cash, some heirloom jewelry, and the three magical objects. We cleaned everything else out and moved it to a different safe when this one was compromised."

The safe had no wards, which meant any mage who entered the house would probably be able to sense the magic trace emanating from the objects stored inside. I shook my head. This sort of thing happened often when people without magic dabbled in collecting magical objects as a hobby. They didn't really know what they had or how to keep the items safe and hidden.

I reached into the safe and closed my eyes so I could focus on what little magic trace was left behind by the missing items. The white air magic was undoubtedly an echo from the mirror, since memory spells were a form of air magic. The cup had left behind blood and earth magic, as I would have expected from an object designed for vampire use. The hint of fire magic was probably from the cuff. I committed the traces to memory so I could identify the objects when I found them.

The mirror seemed to be the strongest trace, so it had probably been in Esther's possession the longest. I wondered if she used it regularly, and if so, what memories it showed her. While the cup was intriguing and the cuff was maybe the oddest item I'd ever been hired to find, the mirror was certainly one magical object I wanted nothing to do with. My past had few good memories to offer. I had a hard enough time keeping the ones buried I remembered; I certainly didn't need to dredge up any of the ones I'd managed to forget.

When I opened my eyes, Christina Harris was sitting in a chair, leafing through an architecture magazine, and Malcolm had finished unweaving the house wards. I realized with a start that I'd been standing at the safe for almost fifteen minutes.

"I'm done with the safe for now," I said. "I think I'll go check on Sean."

As she closed up the safe, I headed down the hall, following the sound of voices. When I rounded the corner, I found Sean and a young, dark-haired man in a tool belt and a Maclin Security shirt by the security system keypad. The younger man had a small laptop.

Sean smiled as I approached. "Alice, this is Ben, head of our installation division and a member of the pack."

Ben shook my hand and gave me a cheery smile. "It's nice to meet you, Alice."

"Nice to meet you." I smiled back. "You guys getting to the bottom of the security system breach?"

"We're getting there," Sean said. "It looks like whoever got in here bypassed the system with some pretty advanced equipment. What did you find out?"

"The thieves cracked the safe to get to the missing items."

"What kind of safe? Biometric scanner? Fingerprint? Voice identification?"

"Eight-digit code."

Sean shook his head. "You're kidding me. Might as well have been keeping the stuff in a cardboard box labeled 'Valuables.'"

"I suppose if you've never had a break-in, you might get a little too complacent." I pulled the folder containing the pictures of the missing items from my bag. "I'm going to work in the office for a while and make some phone calls."

"I'll join you soon. The rest of the installation crew will be here any minute."

"Sounds good." I headed back to the office.

Christina had gone back to working in the solarium, so I sat down on one of the couches in the office.

Malcolm reappeared and floated over to me. "All done with the wards. They were a joke."

"I know. Thank you for unweaving them."

"You're welcome."

"You should probably jump back to the basement for now. I'll summon you if something comes up, or I'll see you when we get home later tonight."

"Okay." He hesitated. "I'm sorry I tried to follow the trace back to Kendall. That was stupid."

"It's okay. I understand why you did it. As awful as seeing her in that condition was for me, I'm sure it was ten times worse for you."

"That could have easily been me. If I'd ended up back at Bell's cabal as a bound ghost, that *would* have been me, trapped in a crystal until I went wraith. Remember what I told you when we first met, that I'd rather you discorporate me than let that happen to me?"

I nodded.

"Nothing's changed about that. If they ever come for me, send me on if you can, as long as it doesn't put you at risk."

"I will," I promised, though my stomach hurt to even think about doing to Malcolm what I'd just done to Kendall's bound ghost.

"Thanks, Alice. That lady's coming back. I'm out of here." He disappeared.

Christina appeared in the doorway. "I'm about to make some coffee. Would you like a cup?"

I sighed. "More than just about anything in the world. With cream and sugar, please and thank you."

As she headed back down the hall, I opened the folder Esther had given me and studied the pictures of the missing magical items. "Okay, my pretties. If I were a recently stolen magical object, where would I be?"

No answer from the photos, but it didn't take a rocket scientist to figure it out. I tapped my fingers on the arm of the sofa. "I'd be on my way to someone who could sell me, that's where I'd be."

This kind of hardware couldn't be fenced or sold very many places. If it was still in the city, there was a short list of possible buyers and sellers, and I knew a couple of them personally.

That was when I felt it: a distant surge of magic, not nearly as formidable as the one that had destroyed Darius Bell's cabal compound, but powerful and deadly nonetheless. It washed over the house like a gentle tide.

The other shoe had finally dropped.

"Oh, Moses, you old bastard," I whispered. "What have you done?"

CHAPTER 7

BELL INDUSTRIES WAS A METAL-FABRICATION COMPANY HEADQUARTERED next to the river. It was a major supplier of commercial construction materials in the city and one of Darius Bell's most profitable businesses—*was* being the operative word.

Earth mages had razed Bell's compound, but it was water mages who'd destroyed Bell Industries and a one-block radius around it. They pulled the river over its banks and into the company's facility, then used the force of the water to demolish all three main buildings.

Most of the employees had already left for the day, but early reports listed more than three dozen people missing and presumed dead. The damage was estimated to be in the tens of millions. The new police chief had already made a statement condemning both incidents and offering a substantial reward for information, a reward I was pretty sure would go unclaimed.

I doubted Bell had been there, so my grandfather's attack was probably designed to cripple Bell financially as well as send a message that any and all of Bell's assets and people were fair game.

Sean and I looked at news articles about the attack online. "These cabals are run by psychopaths," he said as we watched aerial footage of the widespread damage caused by the water mages. "They don't care about collateral damage or how many people they kill in their wars."

"No, they don't," I said bitterly. "Cabal leaders only care about money and power. People are expendable." I stopped before I gave anything away about my past involvement with cabals.

He squeezed my hand. "Are you going to be all right while I help with the security system installation?"

"I'm fine. Go help your people. I need to make some phone calls."

He kissed me and left the office in search of Ben's crew.

My first call was to Adri. The phone rang twice and then she answered. "Hello, Alice." Her cheerful tone seemed forced.

"Hey, Adri. How's Bryan?"

"I'll let him tell you himself. Hang on."

There was a rustle, as if Bryan was still recovering in bed. "Miss Alice." His voice was a shadow of its usual deep rumble.

"Hey, Bryan," I said, my throat tight with unexpected emotion. "It's really good to hear your voice."

"It's good to hear yours. The werewolf keeping you safe?"

"Yes, he is." I was so glad to talk to him that I didn't even chastise him for referring to Sean as "the werewolf." I cleared my throat. "I'm sorry I didn't call sooner."

"Don't worry about it. I hear you're back at work."

I blinked. "Wow, the vamp grapevine sure works fast."

"We're all very concerned about your safety, so of course we're keeping up with what's going on." A long pause. "I'm sorry I let him get away from me, Alice."

"Stop that right now," I snapped. I thought of the six bullets Stevens had put into him and couldn't stand to hear him blaming himself. "It wasn't your fault."

"Whose fault was it, then?" he retorted. "We should have captured him at the house. I shouldn't have let him get the drop on us last night. I underestimated him completely and now Fortune is dead because of it."

"We all underestimated him. There's a lot of blame to go around on this one, but I think you've more than paid your penance."

He did an impressive imitation of a werewolf growl. "Not until he's in a cell at the Vampire Court and facing justice for Fortune's murder and for shooting you."

"And for almost killing you," I said. "I hope you get him soon. I'm hip-deep in werewolves over here and they all think they're the boss of me."

Bryan snorted. "I'd pay real money to see them try to boss you, Alice. I appreciate you checking in on me. Was there something else you needed?"

"Yes, as a matter of fact. Could you ask Charles to call me when he's up and about?"

"Can I tell him what it's regarding?"

"Magical objects."

"Well, that will definitely intrigue him." I could hear the smile in his voice.

I sighed. "I guess I'll see you when this is all over. I doubt Charles will be leaving wherever you guys are holed up, unless he's thinking about trying to draw Stevens out?"

"There are several options on the table," Bryan said, demonstrating he hadn't lost his ability to be cagey.

"Well, whatever you decide to do, be careful."

"In the meantime, stay close to the werewolf. Let him do his job."

I huffed. "I do want to stay alive, you know."

"I know you do. I also know that sometimes you do what you think needs doing, and that's not always compatible with staying safe."

I started to protest and then had to admit he was right. "Well, with any luck, the Hunters will find Stevens soon and we can put all this behind us."

"You and I will raise a toast to that. Take care of yourself."

"You too."

Once we'd disconnected, I scrolled through my contacts and

called a number I hadn't used in some time. The call went to voice mail. There was no recorded message, only a beep.

My message was terse. "This is Alice. Call me back."

My phone rang less than thirty seconds later. "Alice Worth," I said briskly.

"Girl, why you callin' me this early?" It was a familiar scratchy male voice. "Sun ain't even down yet."

"Sorry if I interrupted your beauty sleep, Phil. I'm on the trail of some hot merchandise, and the faster I find it, the bigger my payday. Thought I'd give you a call and see what you knew."

"Answers cost money. Fast answers cost more." There was no trace of Phil's good-ol'-boy persona now.

"You know I'm good for it. Cash or a favor?"

"Favor. I got some folks bothering me and I need some wards that bite." Phil was a pawn-shop owner and a fence. I wasn't surprised that he needed wards for protection.

"Done. I'm going to send you a couple of pictures. If you hear about anyone trying to buy or sell them, will you tag me in?"

"You got it. How hot are they?"

"Like a sidewalk in the summer."

"I'll call you if and when I hear something."

"You're a decent human being, Phil."

"Don't tell nobody that." He ended the call.

I took quick photos of Esther's missing items and sent them to Phil the fence, and then I made calls to two of his competitors and made similar deals with them for information. I'd just hung up from the second call when Sean came into the office.

"How goes the installation?" I asked him as he dropped onto the sofa next to me.

"Smoothly. We'll be ready to go soon. You running down some leads?" He laced his fingers with mine and kissed my knuckles.

"Putting out some feelers with some of the city's more upstanding citizens and waiting on a call back from my best potential source of information." I glanced at the sliver of fading daylight visible through a gap in the curtains.

Sean saw me look, put two and two together, and frowned.

"He's a broker," I reminded my disapproving bodyguard. "If those objects come on the market in this city, he'll know about it."

"You'll be asking him for a favor," Sean reminded me. "Vampires never do anything for free."

"All things considered, I think I might have some favors coming my way." That hole in my shoulder had to be worth something.

He squeezed my hand. "Speaking of sundown, we've been invited to dinner with Karen and her husband Cole tomorrow evening at their house. They've also invited Felicia Lowell, her mother, and her brother. I told them it would depend on how things are going with the case, so we're not locked into accepting."

Felicia had been kidnapped by the West-Addison harnad, who had attempted to manufacture a new drug using werewolf blood. Luckily, we'd taken them down before they were successful and rescued Felicia.

"That sounds nice," I said.

"We don't have to go. You've got an important case right now. We can always take a rain check for another time."

"Your pack is important too, Sean." I bumped him with my shoulder. "If we're not running down a hot lead, we'll go. Tell them we'll be there."

He narrowed his eyes at me. "Who are you, and what have you done with my girlfriend?"

I lunged at him and he pulled me close, laughing. "That's better," he said, kissing my hair. "For a minute there, I was worried about you."

"Jerk." I tried to pull away but he kissed me quickly before letting go and scooting over a few inches.

The reason for his quick movement became evident a few seconds later when I heard two sets of heels clicking briskly toward us. We got to our feet just as Esther Aldridge entered the office, followed by her assistant.

"Do you lovebirds need a few more minutes alone?" Esther asked as she strode over to her desk.

At our startled expressions, the older woman waved her hand dismissively and sat down. "It was rather obvious from the moment you arrived in Aaron Riddell's office that you're not merely her personal security. Do give me some credit for not having been born yesterday." She looked at me with an arched eyebrow. "I can't say I blame you, dear. He's quite a catch."

Before I could reply, Sean spoke up. "It's me who's lucky. *She's* the catch."

Esther let out a very unladylike snort. "If you weren't a werewolf, I'd call you 'silver-tongued,' young man."

I was taken aback that she knew Sean was a werewolf, but to my surprise, he chuckled.

She settled back in her chair and appraised us. "I understand from the nice young man out front that your installers will be done shortly. I appreciate your quick response and excellent service. What do you know about how the thieves got past the old system?"

"They're professionals with cutting-edge equipment," Sean told her. "The existing system had a flaw they were able to exploit. I'm sorry to say that your safe in here is woefully inadequate for its purpose. I would strongly recommend replacing it with a more modern version. I can make some recommendations, if you would like."

"Send me a proposal," Esther said.

I spoke up. "If and when the magical items are found and returned, you should have wards set around the safe to obscure the magical trace. Otherwise, anyone with magic will be able to sense exactly where the items are in your house and get a good idea of what they are, even without seeing them. That might be how you got on the thieves' radar; Kendall would have been able to sense the trace."

"Thank you. I will certainly consider it." Esther glanced at the drop cloth and chalk circle on the floor. "Ms. Harris tells me there was some excitement regarding the anchor."

"Joseph Kendall is a poor example of a mage security consultant," I told her frankly. "His wards were insufficient, in my opinion, but worse than that, instead of using his own magic, he trapped a ghost inside that statue and used her to power them."

Christina gasped. Esther stared at me. "There was a ghost inside the statue?"

"Yes, ma'am, there was. He'd had her in there for years, probably, using her for various purposes, until he brought her here."

"Is this sort of thing common?" Esther demanded.

I shook my head. "No. Most mages consider it reprehensible. Cabals use ghosts like that, but they're not really known for their morality. Please don't judge all mages by what Kendall did."

"Where is the ghost now?" Christina asked, scanning the room as if looking for the spirit.

"Once I released her, she passed on," I said, opting for partial truth. "She's gone. I am sorry about the mess in here, but I had no choice."

"You did what had to be done." Esther looked shaken. I couldn't blame her. "Do you have everything you need to begin looking for the stolen items?"

I nodded. "I think I do."

Christina handed me a card with her name and a phone number. "If you have any questions, or need to return to the house, please give me a call."

I put her number into my phone, then tucked the card in my bag. "With your permission, we'll take off. I'll keep Aaron posted on our progress."

"Thank you." Esther rose from her desk to give us each a handshake. We said good night and headed for the front door.

"So, where to?" Sean asked as we walked. "Looking for Kendall?"

I shook my head. "The goal is the missing items. I don't want to tip him off that we're snooping around. I think we head home for now."

Out front, two Maclin Security installation vans were parked beside our SUVs. Ben stood next to one of them, phone in hand. He looked up as we exited the house. "I was just about to message you that we've tested the system and everything's green across the board."

"Good work." Sean clapped Ben on the shoulder. "I appreciate the people who stayed late. If any of them want to go out for beers after, the first round is on me."

Ben grinned. "I'll make the offer. I'm sure a couple of them will take me up on it. I bet you get that Boss of the Year mug you've been wanting."

"Been waiting on that for a while," Sean joked. "You got it from here?"

"Yep. We'll button things up and head out." He held out his hand and we shook. "It was great to meet you, Alice. You coming to the pack's cookout next week?"

My eyebrows went up. The werewolves were having a cookout?

Part of me was apprehensive at the thought of facing the entire pack at once, but I was curious as to how many hamburgers a werewolf pack could eat. I'd seen how many Sean could put away at one sitting. It might be worth it to go just to get an answer to that question.

"I'm not sure yet," I told Ben with a smile. "My schedule is pretty erratic, but I'll be there if I can."

Ben's smile widened. "Awesome. My girlfriend Casey is helping coordinate the food. If you think you can make it, let me know so she can put you down for something."

"Will do."

Sean and I headed for our SUV. Once I was inside, he stopped to talk to the mobile team and then got in beside me. The sun was disappearing behind the horizon.

I cleared my throat. "So, there's a cookout?"

He sighed as he turned the key in the ignition and headed down the driveway with the other SUV right behind us. "I was going to wait to ask you about that until you'd had a chance to get used to the idea of being around the pack. I thought if we went to dinner at Karen and Cole's tomorrow night and it went well, that would be a good time to float the idea, but Ben stole my thunder." He glanced at me as we paused at the end of Esther's driveway. "This is all too much too soon, isn't it?"

"Well, it's a lot for someone who's been on her own for a while, but Karen and Ben have been very friendly and from what you've said about Felicia and her mother and brother, they seem like a nice family. It might not be so bad." I picked at a loose thread on my khakis.

"And?" Sean prompted.

I scowled. Sean was getting increasingly attuned to my emotions. That wasn't uncommon for a shifter, but it felt intrusive sometimes. "My birthday is coming up in a couple of d—" I caught myself. "Months."

Sean nodded. "I had it on my calendar, but I wasn't sure if you celebrated birthdays. It's a milestone, though, huh?"

"The big 3-0."

He reached over and squeezed my hand. "Are you having an existential crisis?" he teased. He saw my face and his smile vanished. "What's wrong?"

When I didn't say anything right away, he didn't press me for an answer. A few minutes later, as we were approaching a stoplight, I said, "I guess I've been thinking about family lately, or my lack of one. It's probably a direct result of my impending birthday because usually I don't dwell on that sort of thing. When I see big, happy families, it's hard. Your pack is like a family. Part of me wants to stay away because it hurts, but there's a part of me that wants that for myself."

"That's understandable."

I shrugged and stared out the window. "I'm sure it's just a

temporary thing. Once this birthday is over, I'll go back to being my old solitary self."

"I don't think you will. You've changed since I met you. As rough as these last few months have been otherwise, look at all the connections you've made, the people you've gotten to know. You're not a loner anymore. You actually lit up at the idea of going to dinner at Karen's house tomorrow. When Ben mentioned the cookout, I thought you'd get that deer-in-the-headlights look. Instead, you looked like you were thinking about whether to bring potato salad or a dessert. I can tell you're intimidated by the thought of meeting the whole pack, but you didn't say no instantly like you would have done before."

"If I did volunteer to bring the potato salad, do they sell it in five-gallon buckets, and if so, how many are we talking?"

He laughed. I smiled and reached over the console to rest my hand on his thigh. It was something I'd never done before. There was something wonderful and comforting about such a casual intimacy.

When he didn't react, I started to pull my hand back, suddenly self-conscious.

"Leave it," Sean said. "Please."

I did.

WHEN WE GOT BACK to my house, we let Rogue in from the backyard and Sean fed him in the kitchen while I went upstairs to change into jeans and a T-shirt.

My phone rang as I was coming back downstairs. I glanced at the number, then answered. "Hello, Charles."

In the kitchen, Sean grumbled.

"Good evening, Alice." A shiver went down my spine at the sound of Charles's voice. I scowled. I was still feeling the effects of drinking his blood. "What a lovely surprise to hear you called. I can think of no better way to begin my day than by hearing your voice."

A low growl from the kitchen.

"My people tell me the werewolf is providing your protection detail," he continued. "If your security situation is not adequate, my invitation to join me remains open."

Another growl, much louder.

"My security is more than adequate," I assured him. "The reason I called is I'm looking for some magical objects that might be coming on the market and I wondered if you could keep an eye out for them."

"Intriguing." I could almost see his ears perk up. "What are these items?"

"I have photos I can send you, but briefly, there is a silver hand mirror, an antique pewter cup, and a fancy arm cuff."

"What do we know of their powers?"

"From what I've been told, the mirror supposedly lets you see forgotten memories. Drinking from the cup allows a vampire to walk in daylight for an hour. The cuff apparently increases male libido."

"Fascinating. I take it these objects are not being sold by their rightful owner?"

"They're not being sold by the person who had possession of them until a few nights ago. I'm not sure the term 'rightful owner' has much meaning when it comes to magical objects. I think the prevailing philosophy is more along the lines of 'possession is nine-tenths of the law.'"

He chuckled. "That is certainly true. Please send me the photos of the items in question and I will make discreet inquiries."

"Thank you. Any news on the manhunt?"

Rogue came into the living room and plopped down on his bed. In the kitchen, the coffee grinder fired up.

Charles made an odd sound that was almost a snarl. "Nothing substantial. Frankly, I expected to wake to the news he had been found and was quite dismayed to hear there are no leads thus far."

I sighed. "Well, it's only a matter of time. I doubt he's skipped town, so he's out there, somewhere. I'm assuming you're looking into weapons suppliers in town, in case he's in the market for more firepower?"

"That is one of the lines of inquiry Ms. Woodall is pursuing. Her work for us has thus far been exemplary."

"Excellent." I looked forward to teaming up with Arkady Woodall at some point for an investigation, assuming my sheep pajamas hadn't given her the wrong first impression. I grimaced. Maybe she'd forget about that.

"I will begin looking into the magical items you described." Charles sounded almost energized by the prospect. I wondered if he was already bored and stir-crazy. As antsy as I was surrounded by watchful werewolves, at least I wasn't trapped with him.

"Thanks, Charles. Call me anytime if you have news on either."

"Good night, my dear." We disconnected.

"You want a cup of coffee?" Sean called from the kitchen.

I snorted as I sent the pictures of the magical objects off to Charles. "You need to ask?"

He appeared carrying two cups of coffee. "It was pretty much a rhetorical question," he said, handing one to me and settling onto the couch. "No sign of Stevens, I take it?"

"None." I sipped my coffee. "In a way, it's surprising; with so many people looking for him, anyone else would probably already have been found. Then again, anyone else wouldn't have gotten away from the vamps in the first place."

My phone beeped with a text reply from Charles: *Photos received. I look forward to the hunt.*

"So, are we in for the evening?" he asked.

"I'm in a holding pattern until I hear back from either Cait with the background check or one of the people keeping an eye out for the magical objects." I yawned and took a couple of chugs of coffee. "I thought I'd look at some furniture options online, on the off-chance I get time to stop by the store tomorrow and make some purchases. If I knew what I wanted ahead of time, it wouldn't take long to make the final choices."

"That sounds like a plan. In the meantime, I'm going to see about getting us some food."

I reached for my bag. "We should try that new Italian place that delivers. I'm thinking lasagna. Let me give you my credit card."

"I've got this one. You got the pizza earlier."

I hesitated, then relented. "Okay, fair enough. Do we need to feed Philip and Tom?"

"I'll get something for them. A couple of meatball subs each should do it."

I laughed and shook my head. "Still getting used to werewolf appetites."

"We're pretty much always hungry, for all kinds of things," Sean said, his eyes gleaming. "Speaking of which, I'm very much looking forward to dessert."

"You *are* hungry," I teased.

"You have no idea." He took my coffee cup and set it on the floor with his own. "I'm a starving man, Alice. I haven't had a good meal in more than a week."

"You poor man." I climbed into his lap and held his face in my hands. "How about we just order subs for Team Two and skip straight to dessert?"

"You're going to need your energy for what I have in mind. As far as I know, all you've had all day is about a gallon of coffee and that one slice of pizza."

I gave him a look.

He turned serious. "Alice, I'm a shifter and an alpha. As long as we're together, there will never be a time when I'm not wanting to make sure you're safe and fed and happy."

I kissed him thoroughly and started to climb off his lap. "Then you'd best order the damn lasagna, because I am *starving*."

He laughed and reached for his phone.

Alice!

I heard Malcolm's panicked voice in my mind at the same moment I felt a yank on the blue-green magic trace that connected us. Someone was trying to pull my ghost away from me. Instinctively I yanked him back and it felt like someone drove a white-hot dagger through my skull—a blood magic attack that would have killed or incapacitated a weaker mage.

I made an involuntary sound that was half-gasp, half-cry and fell off the couch, my head bouncing on the wood floor.

"Alice!" Sean shouted. "What's happening?"

I couldn't talk because my jaw was clenched to hold in my screams. Through the agony, I realized a spell was trying to pull Malcolm away and someone with strong blood magic was attempting to sever the binding that connected us. Malcolm was resisting but he was losing his battle against the powerful spell.

I didn't recognize the magic but there was no time for me to think about who was on the other end of the attack. If whoever it was severed our binding, Malcolm would be lost to me forever—assuming I even survived. Stealing a bound ghost required the equivalent of a magical lobotomy and the pain was making it hard for me to think.

I heard Malcolm telling Sean someone was trying to take him from me and that if they succeeded I might die. Sean snarled at him to do something, but Malcolm wasn't a blood mage. He wasn't equipped for this fight, but I was.

From where I lay on the floor, I spooled my blood magic and yanked Malcolm to me. Startled, he tried to flit away, but I wrapped my magic around him like a cage. As he struggled to free himself, I thrust my hand into his body and ripped out the hidden spell that was trying to tear him away.

Malcolm yelped as the spell disintegrated. I released him and he flitted away from me, his eyes wide and horrified—whether at the attack or me or both, I couldn't tell.

The spell was gone, but I couldn't be sure there wouldn't be another attempt. Malcolm needed to be safe until I could figure out what the hell just happened.

"*Contain!*" I shouted.

With a tingle of magic, Malcolm went into a special crystal on my bracelet, one he couldn't jump out of or be taken from by anyone but me.

The stabbing pain in my head intensified as the blood mage stepped up his or her attack. Now that he or she had lost their ability to take Malcolm, they simply meant to kill me. Unfortunately for them, I was a better mage and a better killer.

I reached back through the magic trace and used my blood magic to kill my attacker. The dagger of blood magic in my head vanished with a sickening pop, leaving behind a vicious ache and a strange hollow feeling. Magic sizzled and then there was a familiar silence as somewhere the blood mage fell over dead.

And just like that, it was over.

Blood trickled from my nose. My arms and legs felt like they were full of lead. I tried to move but couldn't. My head hurt like it might split open.

"Alice," Sean said, his voice tight. "Alice, damn it, say something."

I opened my eyes. He was kneeling beside me, eyes bright with fury as he pulled me against his chest.

I forced myself to speak. "Nobody...takes...my ghost...from...me," I slurred, and then I passed out.

CHAPTER 8

WHEN I WOKE, I WAS IN BED AND VERY WARM UNDER WHAT FELT LIKE A PILE of blankets and quilts. Beyond my eyelids the room was dark, but I had no idea if it was day or night. My body ached down to the bones.

"*How* many dead?" The voice was more growl than human. It sounded like it was coming from the hallway outside my room.

A long pause.

"This has to be related to the Bell-Murphy war." Sean's anger prickled on my skin. "I don't know if it was a misfire of some magical weapon or these people were deliberately targeted. All she could tell me was someone tried to take away her ghost. Is it possible all of the victims—"

He broke off suddenly. I sensed movement before a warm hand brushed my forehead. "Alice? Are you awake?"

I made a small sound.

"I'll have to call you back." Sean put his phone on my nightstand. He pulled back the pile of blankets, scooped me up, and settled into the bed with me in his arms. I curled up against his chest and breathed in his scent, letting it ease the aches in my body.

He tucked my head under his chin. "Can you talk?" His voice was rough. "I need to know if you can understand me and how badly you're hurt."

I focused on putting syllables together. "Going...to be...all right."

He took a deep breath and squeezed me against his chest. "You're not lying to me, are you? We have an agreement: you don't tell me you're okay if you aren't."

"Feel like shit," I told him.

His laugh sounded strangled. I opened my eyes and moved my head so I could see him. He obviously hadn't slept and his eyes were bright, almost feverish, and shining gold, as if his wolf lurked just beneath his skin.

The curtains in my room were tightly closed but I saw daylight at the top and sides. "What time is it?" I asked.

"Almost noon." He kissed the top of my head. "It's been about fourteen hours since the attack."

I remembered what I'd heard him saying when I woke up. "What happened?"

"A lot of people died last night around the same time you were attacked and the hospitals are full of people in comas who aren't expected to survive. They don't even know how many victims there are yet; dozens, at least. People dropped unconscious or dead at home, in their cars, wherever they were, all over the city. There was a lot of panic at first, but things settled down when no one else seemed to be affected after the first wave hit."

"They tried to take Malcolm," I said. "There was some kind of spell inside him, hidden all this time. I broke it and killed the mage who tried to take him and kill me."

His chest rumbled with a low growl. "Good. So Malcolm is safe? I thought we'd lost him."

"I put him in my bracelet in case they tried again before I was recovered enough to defend us."

"Who do you think is responsible for this?"

"It has to be Bell. Malcolm died at the hands of one of his blood mages. I'm betting they spelled him before releasing him, so they could pull him back if and when they wanted to."

"But why release him at all? Isn't that unusual?"

"Very unusual; unheard-of, in fact. But if all of the dead and dying are people who had bound ghosts, then it's something Bell has been doing for a while." I laced my fingers with his. "Who was that on the phone?"

He squeezed my hand. "Adri Smith, calling to check on you when people started realizing that all the dead are mages. I don't think anyone has figured out the ghost connection, though."

"Bell has to be pulling in his ghosts because of Murphy's attacks," I said. "I don't know how or why, but he's either planning to use them as defense or offense."

"How would he do that?"

"Cabals use ghosts as energy sources, like Kendall used that ghost in the statue. They can amplify a mage's magic, be used as a focus for spellwork, and power wards, among other things. Maybe he's going to use them to strengthen the wards wherever he's holed up." I hesitated. "Or he's planning on using them to amplify a magical attack on Murphy or his people, either here or back in Baltimore."

"Why not just keep them stored at the cabal, in case something like this happens?"

My eyes widened. "Because they weaken if they're stored and go wraith over time. If they're free, they *gain* power, especially if they're bound to..." My voice trailed off.

"Bound to what?" he prompted.

"Strong mages," I whispered. "Son of a bitch, *that's* why he released Malcolm. We've been wondering all this time how Malcolm ended up with me when he died instead of at the cabal. Bell figured out a way to make his ghosts even stronger, by spelling them or arranging for them to be bound to mages and letting them build up power, then pulling them back when he's ready to use them, killing all those mages in the process. Not that he cared about that, obviously." My blood magic sizzled on my skin. "Murphy, Bell...they're all the same. Not an ounce of conscience among them."

Sean growled. "Is Bell likely to attack here, or back in Baltimore?"

"I'm betting Baltimore. Murphy took out Bell's compound and one of his most profitable businesses. If he can amass a cadre of mages like the one Murphy used to attack his compound, and he uses the ghosts to amplify their magic, and he doesn't care that it will kill most of them, he could obliterate Murphy's compound and everyone in it."

I turned my head away so he couldn't see my eyes, worried they would betray how I felt about that possibility. I'd fantasized about destroying the compound and killing Moses for most of my life, but it had seemed an impossible task. If Bell could do what I thought he could do, it might be the best chance anyone had of succeeding where so many others had failed. I tried not to get my hopes up, but my brain fixated on it and wouldn't let go.

"Murphy has to figure he'll be targeted," Sean said. "He might not know about the ghosts, but he's too smart to stay in his compound, knowing there's a target painted on it."

"He's arrogant. He thinks his wards will hold. No one has ever breached the perimeter walls, much less damaged the main building." Not from the outside, anyway, I thought, remembering the massive hole I'd blown in the compound on my way to freedom.

"So you think he'll stay home, despite the danger?"

"I guarantee he'll stay." I hesitated, then added, "Or at least that's my guess, based on what I've seen of him in the news."

"Well, you're probably right about that." He smoothed the hair back from my face. "Are you feeling any stronger?"

I nodded. "I'm a little foggy still, but I think it'll pass fairly soon. It's been a while since I had to fight a blood mage that way. Luckily, it's like riding a bicycle, I guess." I fell silent.

"You had no choice," he said firmly. "It was you or them, right?"

"Even after they couldn't get to Malcolm, they tried to kill me, I guess just on principle or in retaliation. They didn't have to, but they did and they paid for it."

"Will Bell's people be able to trace you through the dead mage?"

I shook my head. "No. What little trace of mine there was would have dissipated within moments. The only concern is whether Malcolm still has any of those spells hidden in him. I think it's best to leave him in the crystal for now, though, in case they're still trying to call him back. I need to be stronger before I let him out and try to look for more retrieval spells." I took a deep breath. "In the meantime, I'll get up and take a shower."

"Can you manage the shower by yourself?"

"I think so." Gingerly, I started to get up.

Sean resisted, holding me tight. "I thought I was going to lose you. I lay here all night, watching the news alerts about the dead and dying mages and wondering if you were going to wake up and what kind of shape you'd be in when you did."

"I'm not so easy to kill," I reminded him, then touched his face when his eyes darkened. "Thank you for taking care of me."

He squeezed my hand, then kissed it. "It's my privilege to do so." He sighed. "I'll call Karen and let her know we're probably not going to make it over there tonight."

"No, we're going."

"Alice, you just almost died. This isn't the time—"

"This is *exactly* the time," I countered. "I know an invitation like this is significant in shifter culture. It's a family dinner and I've been invited to sit and eat with you. That's an honor and an opportunity I'm not going to miss."

He kissed me then, carefully, as if afraid I might break. I grabbed him and kissed him hard.

When I leaned back, he was smiling. "Now I know you're feeling better. You need some coffee and some food. While you're in the shower, I'll order us some lasagna. By the time you're downstairs, it'll be here."

My stomach growled. He chuckled. "Get up," he said, rolling me gently off his lap. "Get clean, then come downstairs and get coffee and food."

I lay sprawled on the bed and smiled up at him. "You're my favorite werewolf."

"You're my favorite mage." He poked me in the side. "Get in the shower."

When I got out of the shower, I discovered Cait had sent me her preliminary report on Joseph Kendall earlier in the day. I took my laptop downstairs and Sean and I read through it while standing at the kitchen counter eating salad, lasagna, and breadsticks as Jack and Karen ate meatball subs outside in their SUV.

Unsurprisingly, the person Esther Aldridge and the others knew as Joseph Kendall didn't really exist—not on this plane of existence, anyway. The Joseph Kendall tied to the Social Security and SPERA registration numbers this man used belonged to a man who died in Indiana five years before. The mage claiming to be Kendall had stolen the dead man's identity.

Cait's attempt to identify the con man using facial recognition software had turned up several additional cases of identity theft that placed him in Dallas, Boston, and Denver in the past four years. In each of those cities, there were probably a half-dozen victims just like Esther Aldridge who had retained the services of someone like me to look into the thefts instead of notifying law enforcement. At this point, the con man had to have a small flock of private investigators and other less-legal hunters hot on his trail. He might have eluded justice up to now, but those chickens were going to come home to roost sooner or later.

So far, Cait hadn't connected the con man, who I'd creatively dubbed John Doe, to a real identity, but she was looking into it. In the meantime, she was also digging into his known associates in the city. I wondered if John Doe or one of his agents found new B&E-slash-safecracking crews in each city or if he had a team he worked with who came in to commit the burglaries, then left again.

"I'd like to pass this info on to Cyro," I told Sean. "I want to see about hiring him to get John Doe's phone records." Cait was a great researcher, but she stayed on the good side of the law. Black-hat hacker Cyro was firmly on the dark side.

He took a burner cell from his duffel bag. He sent off a text, then set the phone on the counter to finish his lasagna. A few minutes later, the phone rang.

He answered. "Maclin."

My ears weren't as sharp as his, but I could hear an electronically altered voice on the other end offering a terse greeting.

Briefly, Sean outlined what I was looking for and what we knew about John Doe. When he was done, the voice spoke again. Looking surprised, Sean held out the phone. "He'd like to speak to you."

Startled, I took the phone. "Alice Worth."

"Ms. Worth, this is Cyro," the voice said. "I understand you would like to employ my services."

I tried not to be creeped out by the strange computerized voice. "I would, assuming you're available. If the fee will be similar to what you charged the last time, I have the funds available in my business checking account for immediate transfer."

Cyro quoted me a price for John Doe's home, office, and mobile records. "I'll give you an account number. I'll begin the work when the funds are received."

My retainer from Esther would easily cover that amount. "Give me the number."

Cyro's mechanical voice relayed the number, which Sean wrote on a piece of paper.

"How soon can I expect a reply?" I asked. "Just so I have an idea of the time frame."

"I have a few jobs ahead of this today," Cyro said. "It depends on the difficulty of obtaining the information, obviously. Later this evening is probably the earliest I'll be able to send anything back. Tomorrow morning is more realistic."

"That's perfect. Thanks."

"Goodbye." The call ended.

I handed the phone back to Sean. "Wonder why he wanted to talk to me."

"It makes sense, if he's working for you directly this time."

"I guess," I said dubiously.

My phone rang and I answered. "Hey, Phil. Got some news for me?"

The fence's voice was gruff. "I sure do. You gonna come do me a favor?"

Sean's brows drew together. I mouthed *Wards* at him and his scowl faded.

"You know I will," I assured Phil. "My schedule's tight because I'm on a case, but I'll get it done ASAP. What do you know?"

"Got a line on a sparkly hand mirror."

My pulse sped up. "Who's selling it?" I took Sean's pen and pulled a notepad over.

"It's already been sold to a woman named Dora Quinn. She co-owns an antique shop just east of the Heights called Walsh & Quinn."

"Did she buy anything else?"

"My friend said no, just the mirror. He was glad to be rid of it, he said. Not sure what that means."

Considering the mirror's ability to show forgotten memories, I had an idea of why he'd been glad to get it off his hands.

"Rumor has it she paid three thousand for the mirror," he added.

"Good work, Phil. Keep your ears open and let me know if anything else interesting comes on the market. Also, if you hear anything about the whereabouts of a shady mage calling himself Joseph Kendall, I'd like to know."

"Will do."

We hung up. Sean looked up the antique store's website. The proprietors were two women who looked to be in their early forties. The store specialized in high-end "one-of-a-kind" collectibles, which was often a code for magical objects. Judging by the website and the photos of the store, their clientele were more *nouveau riche* than the kind of old money represented by Esther Aldridge.

"What's the plan?" Sean asked.

"I go in as a customer. If the mirror is on the premises, I'll probably be able to locate it unless it's behind wards. Once we know if it's there and I get a read on Dora Quinn, I'll decide which recovery method makes the most sense. Meanwhile, I guess I'm going to need my other good suit. Tell the mobile team we're rolling out in ten."

AN HOUR LATER, I strode into Walsh & Quinn, exuding the haughty confidence of Audrey Talbot, the persona I'd created for just this sort of reconnaissance mission. My skin buzzed with the obfuscation spell that disrupted the security camera's view of me. Sean was two steps behind me, radiating menace and wearing a Secret Service-style earpiece that connected him to Jack and Karen, who were in their SUV. He was taking his role as Audrey's hired muscle very seriously.

I didn't sense the mirror in the store, but that didn't mean it wasn't here, tucked away in the kind of warded safe that Esther Aldridge should have had.

One of the owners appeared from a back room and approached

us. She wore a black short-sleeved sweater and slim black slacks with heels, her shoulder-length blonde hair held back in a silver clip.

She took one look at Sean's glower and her blue eyes widened. "Good afternoon," she said, holding out her hand. "Welcome to Walsh & Quinn. I'm Dora Quinn."

"Audrey Talbot." I shook her hand briskly. "I'm looking for a special gift, and I understand you might have something unique."

"We specialize in unique gifts." Dora's smile was wide, but her eyes were calculating. "Can I ask how you heard about us?"

"A party, of course. I think it was the opera gala in March." I waved my hand as if the details were unimportant. "I heard your store is a place to find something special." I took a step closer and lowered my voice. "The gift is for my fiancé's mother. She has a small collection of one-of-a-kind items. We're...not close, but I hoped that if I could find something to add to her collection, it might smooth the waters. The wedding's only two months away, and I don't want her to cause trouble." I let my eyes water a bit, then bravely blinked away the unshed tears. "I love Dean *so much*."

"There, there," Dora said, patting my arm as she glanced at the large fake diamond engagement ring on my left hand. "I might have a few possibilities. What kinds of collectibles does your future mother-in-law like?"

"I haven't seen her collection," I sniffled, following Dora back toward the counter. "Dean's told me about it. That's what gave me the idea. I want something really special, something thoughtful."

"Wait here. I'll bring a few options out to show you." Dora disappeared into a back room.

Sean sidled up to me and lowered his head so that his mouth was near my ear. "Who's Dean?"

"Just some guy on a TV show," I murmured, my lips barely moving.

His fingertips slid over the small of my back, making me shiver. "Good," he said softly. He stepped back.

Dora returned carrying a small black velvet box. She set it on the counter in front of me. I sensed magic trace, but it wasn't from the mirror.

She opened the box and folded back a linen wrapping. I gasped. "Oh."

It was a statement necklace, made of swirling silver vines and diamonds. Fire magic danced along my senses. "Oh," I said again, my eyes wide. "What does it do?"

Her eyes sparkled with humor. "I haven't worn it myself, but I understand that its previous owner never left a party alone while wearing it."

A lust spell, then, held in the red crystal near the top of the necklace. "It's beautiful," I said, then shook my head regretfully. "My mother-in-law doesn't strike me as the sort who would wear it, though."

"She might like it simply as a collector's piece," Dora suggested. "Perhaps an item she could loan out for special occasions."

"Maybe," I mused. "She's very old-fashioned. Everything she has is antique. She even has one of those vintage dressing tables, like they had *ages* ago." I wrinkled my nose, showing my disdain for such a bizarre item, and hoping she'd take the bait and bring out the hand mirror.

Dora wrapped up the necklace. "Let me look and see what else I have." She closed the box and headed into the back room again.

We waited. This time, when she returned, she was carrying another flat box, and this one emanated familiar magic trace. She set it on the counter, lifted the lid, and unwrapped the mirror.

A sheet of tissue paper covered the mirror's reflective surface. "It's gorgeous," I breathed. "Why is it covered?"

Dora held out to her hand. "Don't get too close. It's—"

Without warning, the ground heaved beneath our feet as a wave of magical energy washed over us and an earthquake shook the shop.

Dora stumbled back with a startled shriek as items fell off the walls and tables. Everything on the counter slid off and fell. I grabbed for the mirror, afraid of what would happen if it shattered on the floor and released its magic.

The tissue paper fell away, revealing my reflection in the mirror. I tried to look away but it was too late. I felt a surge of magic and the shop and everything else faded into soft darkness.

I woke from a familiar nightmare, my heart pounding. I whimpered into the darkness of my room in my grandfather's compound. I expected my mother to come in to comfort me as she usually did, but she didn't appear.

I crawled out of bed, clutching Bernie, my stuffed rabbit, and crept down the hall. I could sneak into bed with my parents and they would hold me until I could fall asleep again.

As I approached their room, however, I heard voices. My parents weren't asleep and Mom sounded upset. I paused outside the door, trying to figure out if I should go in.

"She told me he made her do something that killed two people yesterday," my mother sobbed. "He's made her a killer, John. She's a baby."

I pressed my face against Bernie. Why did my mom call me a baby? I'm not a baby, I thought resentfully. Grandfather says I'm not a baby.

"We'll get her away from here as soon as we have a chance," my dad said. "I've been setting something up with some people from Paris. We'll get her out of the country, but we have to wait until the right time, until we know we can get there without leaving a trail. I know it's hard, Moira. You've got to hang on."

"I want to protect her from him, but I can't." My mother's voice was tight with pain. "Everything I've ever done, I did to keep her safe, but it wasn't enough. I can't even tell her who her father is, because if my father knew the truth he'd kill us all."

"You know you can't tell her, not yet," my dad said gently. "She's a

child. She'd never be able to keep that a secret. Someday, once we're away from here and she can understand, you can tell her about Daniel."

Mom took a deep breath. "I've never forgiven myself for not telling him, but he was getting out, leaving this nightmare behind. He bought a bookstore in California. He never would have left if he'd known I was pregnant."

"If he'd stayed, you'd all three probably be dead." The bedding rustled. "Maybe she can find him when she's older, if she wants to. In the meantime, I love her like she's my own. You know that. She's my daughter and I'm her dad. And I swear I will get us all away from here just as soon as I can."

"I know." My mother started to cry again.

My dad made soothing sounds. My mother's crying was muffled, as if she was weeping against his chest.

I tiptoed back down the hall to my room and slipped into bed, squeezing Bernie tightly. My parents' conversation didn't make sense, and I resented that my mother had called me a baby. Magic sparked on my fingertips as a breeze blew through my room.

I fell asleep, still frowning, the whispered conversation between my parents a fading fragment of a memory in the mind of a child who, at age six, had already killed on the orders of her own grandfather.

I FOUND myself huddled on the floor of Dora Quinn's wrecked antique shop, clutching the hand mirror so hard that my fingers were cramping. Someone had wrapped it in a cloth to cover the glass.

Sean was crouched next to me, his hand on my shoulder. "Audrey? Can you hear me?"

The memory was already fading, but I clung to pieces of it.

I can't even tell her who her father is, because if my father knew the truth he'd kill us all.

Someday, once we're away from here and she can understand, you can tell her about Daniel.

He never would have left if he'd known I was pregnant.

I love her like she's my own.

I let out a strangled sob.

Sean gently pried the mirror out of my grasp, put it in the box, and closed the lid. He slid it over so that it was next to him, then folded me in his arms. I trembled so hard that my teeth chattered.

Dora Quinn appeared, looking shell-shocked. I dimly recalled an earthquake and realized she was probably reeling from the damage to the shop's inventory.

"I have to call our insurance company and my business partner," she said shakily. "So many things are destroyed. I'll take this." She reached for the box.

Sean snarled. She jumped back with a frightened sound.

"That mirror is stolen property," I rasped. "You bought it from a fence. I'm returning it to its rightful owner. Be thankful the owner doesn't want to press charges. Receiving stolen property is a felony."

Dora's face turned beet red. "I have no idea what you are talking about. I have *never*—"

"Ms. Quinn, this is the best offer you could hope to receive under the circumstances," Sean said. "Now, why don't you go into the back and make those calls and Ms. Talbot and I will leave."

Dora took one look at Sean's golden eyes and made the right decision. "Fine," she snapped. She turned and stomped into the back office, slamming the door behind her.

Sean nuzzled my hair and held me. "Alice, whatever it was you saw, I'm sorry."

I shivered as a dozen emotions clashed inside me. How could I have forgotten something like that? I had other memories from when I was six; why didn't I remember that I'd heard my parents talking about my real father?

A thought occurred to me: was the supposed "lost memory" even real, or was it a cruel trick by the magic mirror? I'd been thinking about family lately. I'd encountered a lot of magical objects and many of them had had a mind of their own. Some were kind; others were malicious. The mirror might have plucked a real memory from my head, combined it with my longing for family, and generated a false recollection.

"We need to leave," Sean told me, interrupting my thoughts. He kissed my temple. "Can you walk?"

"I can walk." My voice was hoarse. "Get that box, and let's get the hell out of here."

CHAPTER 9

On the way home, we found out the earthquake was the result of another magical attack. This one destroyed two buildings only a mile away from the antique shop. Earth mages had taken out one of Darius Bell's smaller holdings. There was little structural damage to other buildings, but a lot of broken store windows and loss of shop inventory in the Heights.

When we returned to my house, I carried the box inside, holding it like it was full of angry bees. While Sean let Rogue in from the backyard, I took the box down to the basement, locked it in one of my cupboards, then went upstairs to my room to change.

When I came out of the bathroom in jeans and a T-shirt, Sean was waiting in my bedroom, standing at the foot of my bed. We stared at each other.

The tension in his shoulders and worry in his eyes told me he wanted to ask what I'd seen, but he didn't.

I wanted to tell him, but I couldn't. The secret was too big and too dangerous.

Was this what it was going to be like for as long as we were together? Secrets, half-truths, and lies? I tried to imagine how I would feel if our situation was reversed and it was Sean who refused to tell me anything about himself, who radiated guilt and anger, but wouldn't explain why. Would I be as patient as him? When would his patience run out?

Before he left for Seattle, Special Agent Trent Lake of SPEMA had figured out I wasn't who I claimed to be. He'd seen enough to know he didn't want to know any more than that. How long before Sean came to the same conclusion? He'd already inferred that I'd been a killer before I came to the city. It wasn't much of a leap from that to realizing my whole identity was a lie.

I looked at him and wondered—would there be a point when I'd trust him enough to tell him the truth? And if not, what was I doing having dinner with members of his pack and making him think there was a chance for something long-term between us?

"Penny for your thoughts," he said.

I took a deep, shaky breath. "I'm not sure they're worth even that much."

"If I can guess what you're thinking about, do I win a prize?"

I eyed him uneasily.

"You were thinking that you want to tell me what you saw, but you can't. Then you started wondering if you'll ever be able to tell me your secrets and you're not sure, so now you're asking yourself if there's any point to this." He gestured between us. "Am I right?"

"Something like that," I admitted.

He crossed the room and stood in front of me, pinning me with those beautiful golden-brown eyes. "Then let me be clear: I am not angry or resentful toward you because of your secrets. I am angry that there is someone out there who is a danger to you, forcing you to keep these secrets while they eat you up from the inside. At some point, I hope you will trust me enough to share those secrets with me, but I understand we are not there yet."

"Thank you," I said quietly.

"If it had been me who'd looked into that mirror, I can't say for sure if I would want to tell you what I saw, so let's put that aside for now and talk about what *does* frustrate me." His gaze hardened. "We've had this conversation before, but you don't seem to believe me when I say I am with you because I want to be here. Your secrets, whatever they are, have convinced you that you are not worthy of being cared for. Stop second-guessing how I feel about you. There's a lot of crazy shit going on the world, but if there is one thing you can count on, Alice Worth, it's me." His eyes blazed.

"It's probably hard to tell sometimes, but I hope you know I trust you more than I've trusted anyone in a very long time," I told him. "As for the rest...it's all just the bullshit in my head."

His expression softened and he laced his fingers through mine. "There's bullshit in my head too, but when I'm with you, it's better." Something dark lurked in his eyes.

"Tell me," I said. "Please." Maybe it wasn't fair of me to ask since I wasn't telling him my secrets, but if he had a burden and I could help carry it, I would.

He ran his nose along my hairline. I leaned my head against his chest and listened to the sound of his heart.

He took a deep breath. "A couple of years ago, I got wind of trouble in a smaller pack about two hundred miles from here. The rumor was the new alpha was abusing the women and girls in the pack and the local LEOs were the sort who weren't interested in helping any kind of shifters, even if they were minors. None of the other packs in the area wanted to get involved; we tend to stay out of each other's business, generally speaking. I wasn't in a hurry to get involved either until I got an e-mail from a woman named Jean, begging me for help because the alpha had raped her daughter and nearly killed her son when he tried to stop the assault."

I flinched.

"The next day, I went out there with Jack and a couple other members of my pack, but it was too late. The alpha had discovered Jean's e-mail and killed her." His voice was flat. "I killed the alpha. Jack killed the beta. Jean's children joined our pack. You've met them: Karen and Patrick."

I thought of Karen's kind eyes and magic sizzled on my skin.

Sean squeezed me tighter. "If I'd acted sooner, Jean might still be alive and Karen and Patrick might not have been hurt. I live with that, every day."

"A lot of packs wouldn't have done anything or even taken in the refugees, much less gone out there and challenged the alpha," I pointed out.

"I know that, Alice," he said patiently. "But that doesn't change the guilt I feel and it's precious little comfort when I go to Karen's house and see pictures of Jean. I know Karen and Patrick don't blame me for her death, but I blame myself and I always will."

We stood silently for a while. Sean slid his hand under my T-shirt and pulled me against his body, wrapping his arm tightly around my waist. The feeling of his skin against mine and his familiar scent comforted me.

"The memory I saw...I don't know if it's real," I said. "Magical objects aren't always what they seem. I only have Esther Aldridge's word that the mirror shows forgotten memories. It could just as easily have created something from bits and pieces in my head."

Sean stroked my hair. "Is there any way to know for sure?"

"Maybe."

I had a first name: Daniel. He'd been associated with Moses's cabal but left around the time I was born, heading—according to the memory—for California. A good researcher might be able to find him, if he existed. It wasn't that simple, though. If the memory *was* real, and I did have a biological father somewhere, he had no idea I existed. Who was I to go in and potentially turn his life upside down?

I had no idea who this Daniel might have been, but my mother seemed to think that if Moses knew he was my real father, he would have killed all three of us. If I tracked him down, would I be putting his life at risk still? Why would Moses kill Daniel for having a baby with my mother? And why would he kill me for simply existing? Who was this Daniel?

A father. I couldn't get the possibility out of my head. Would we resemble each other? I'd looked a lot like my mother, before the surgery that turned me into Alice Worth, but maybe I'd looked like Daniel too. My mind started conjuring images of how he might look, who he might be.

If I did find him, what would I even say to him? *Hi, you don't know me, but about thirty years ago you had a relationship with Moses Murphy's daughter Moira, and, well...ta-dah!* I let out an almost hysterical half-laugh. The entire situation was beyond surreal.

Sean held me tightly, kissing the top of my head. "If I can help, let me know."

"Thanks." I smiled up at him. "You were pretty menacing as Audrey's bodyguard, by the way. I've never seen that side of you. I gotta be honest...it was really sexy."

"I could tell you liked it."

I wound my arms around his neck. "Oh, yeah? How could you tell?"

He ran his lips along my jaw and nipped my earlobe. "Your scent," he murmured into my ear. "It was making me crazy. It *is* making me crazy."

I shivered. "It is?"

"It certainly is." He inhaled deeply and growled low in his throat. "Whatever you're thinking about, you need to either stop or take off your clothes."

"What time do we need to leave for Karen's?"

He grinned and glanced at the clock. "Seven."

It was almost four. "Plenty of time for you to nap, then."

His grin became a frown.

"You didn't sleep last night," I reminded him. "You can't be an effective bodyguard on no sleep. You look tired."

He didn't argue, which meant he really was worn out. "What are you going to do?"

"I think I'm recovered enough now to let Malcolm out of my bracelet, check him for any more hidden spells, and talk to him about what happened last night." I remembered the way the ghost had looked at me after I'd ripped the spell out of his body and wondered how he'd react to seeing me. It had been almost a full day since a blood mage had tried to steal him away, but for him it had only been seconds.

"You won't go outside." He looked uneasy.

"I promise I won't go outside. I'll be in the basement until I know Malcolm is safe from Bell." I kissed him deeply. "Get some rest."

He sighed and ran his hands through his hair. "I'd sleep better if you were next to me."

I hesitated. I could let Malcolm out when we got back from Karen's. I'd be more recovered by then, and it would be safer for both of us. Plus, the thought of napping wrapped in Sean's arms was just too good an offer to pass up. "Okay," I said reluctantly. I wagged my finger at him. "But we're going to *nap*. No funny business."

"No funny business," he promised.

I got my pajamas from the back of the bathroom door and brought them into the bedroom. Sean's reaction was very different from Arkady Woodall's. "I like the sheep." His eyes glinted. "Wolves like sheep. Very tasty."

I bared my teeth at him. He laughed and headed into the bathroom.

While he was in the bathroom, the mobile team radioed in to report a shift change. I hadn't realized that Jack's presence outside my house was causing me to feel tense until I thought about him leaving and my shoulders relaxed.

I changed into the pajamas and looked at myself in the mirror over my dresser. Part of me wanted to throw our "no funny business" agreement to the wind, but Sean needed his sleep.

I sighed. "Cold showers and baseball," I told my reflection.

"What was that?" he asked from the bathroom.

"Nothing. Just talking to myself."

By the time Sean came back out wearing lounge pants and a faded Quiet Riot T-shirt, I was already in bed. What little daylight there was sneaking past the curtains reflected gold in his eyes as he crossed the room and climbed in next to me.

I rolled onto my side and Sean curled around me, wrapping his arm around my waist and pulling me against his body. We fit together like pieces of a puzzle, I thought to myself. I wriggled in closer.

Sean buried his face in the back of my neck and kissed me. "I'm here and I'm not going anywhere," he murmured, his breath tickling my skin. "But you're going to have to stop wiggling or that promise I made about no funny business is going to get broken."

I stilled. His skin was hot and the warmth seeped into me.

I worried we wouldn't be able to relax, but it didn't turn out to be a problem. Within minutes, we were both asleep.

WE ARRIVED at Karen's house at seven thirty on the dot. Sean parked his SUV in the driveway of a two-story farmhouse not far outside the city limits and the mobile team parked off to the side of the drive-way, next to a sporty red car and a smaller SUV. He escorted me to the front door, carrying a bottle of Karen's favorite wine that we'd picked up on the way.

As we walked up the sidewalk, he bent down to murmur in my ear, "You look beautiful."

I wore a blue sundress and sandals with my monogram pendant, dangly earrings, and my charm bracelet. Despite the warm summer evening, I'd decided to wear my hair down. The look was somewhat spoiled by the bulletproof vest, but at least I'd get to take it off once we were inside.

The door opened as we approached and a smiling man who looked to be in his early thirties stepped aside to let us into the house. "Come on in, you two," he said warmly, shaking Sean's hand as he closed the door. "Everyone's in the living room." He turned to me and offered his hand. "Alice, it's great to meet you. I'm Cole, Karen's husband."

"Nice to meet you too," I said, shaking his hand. Sean had told me on the way to the house that Karen's husband was human. Several members of the pack had human spouses. It gave me hope that I might be more accepted at some point. Some packs didn't permit human mates, but the Tomb Mountain pack had always been more progressive, Sean said.

I took off the vest and Cole stuck it in the coat closet. I smoothed my dress, making a face at the wrinkles. As Cole turned to lead us to the living room, Sean squeezed my hand.

Four people were waiting for us. Karen was the first to greet me as we entered. "Alice!" She hurried to meet me and gave me a quick hug. I'd worried I would be underdressed, but she was wearing a light summer dress and sandals. She took the wine Sean had brought and set it on the table.

I recognized Felicia Lowell, though she looked very different than the last time I'd seen her, which was after several days of captivity and torture at the hands of the West-Addison harnad. She wore capri pants and a cute top, her long blonde hair in a neat braid.

"Alice, it's so good to get to meet you finally," she said, offering me her hand. "I never got a chance to thank you personally for rescuing me."

As we shook, I noticed faint scars on her wrists and ankles from the silver cuffs that had restrained her. Even werewolf healing abilities had their limits.

I shook hands with Felicia's brother David next. Then Karen introduced Nan, Felicia and David's mother.

The older woman threw her arms around me and hugged me tightly. "Thank you for saving my daughter," she told me as my ribs creaked.

"You're welcome," I wheezed.

Karen offered us something to drink. I requested a lemonade and Sean asked for a beer.

As Karen went to the kitchen, Sean glanced out the patio door to the deck, where a long table was set up for dinner. He counted the chairs and frowned. "Who else are we expecting?" he asked as Karen returned with our drinks.

She paused as she handed him a bottle. "Did Jack not tell you he was coming with Delia and they're bringing Caleb?"

At his expression, Karen took a step back and the others tensed. "I thought he told you," she said. "He said he was going to."

"It must have slipped his mind." Sean smiled at Karen. "Not your fault."

I wasn't sure how to react to the news of the unexpected guests. I didn't know enough about Sean's pack politics to think Jack had deliberately not told his alpha about his plans to crash the dinner party, but I suspected that might be the case. The tension in Sean's shoulders indicated that despite his reassurance, he wasn't very happy about this turn of events.

Felicia asked about my dress and we conversed for a few minutes, but the atmosphere in the room had turned noticeably edgy. I was angry at Jack for spoiling the mood but tried not to let it show. Sean would deal with the situation.

When all of the shifters turned toward the door at the same time, I guessed they'd heard someone pull up out front. Cole started for the foyer, but Sean held up his hand. "Let me," he said. It was phrased as a request, but Cole deferred to Sean immediately.

"Why don't we go out on the deck?" Karen suggested cheerfully as Sean headed for the front door.

We filed out the patio door and Cole closed it behind us. The back of the house faced east, so it was delightfully shady and cool.

"It's beautiful out here," I told my hosts, moving to stand at the railing and look out over their enormous backyard. "I love it. So peaceful."

"Where do you live?" Felicia asked, joining me at the railing.

"In town, on the east side. It's a quiet neighborhood, thankfully."

We chatted as the minutes ticked by. If the shifters could hear anything that was going on out front, they didn't let on. Finally, just when I was starting to wonder if one of us should go check on the rest of the dinner party, a group of people crossed the living room toward the patio doors with Sean in the lead.

When Sean slid the door open and stepped out onto the deck, I moved to join him. He was angry; I could see it in his eyes and in the tension in his shoulders, but when he kissed me, his mouth was gentle. I wasn't sure if he was staking a claim or if I was, but the kiss certainly made a statement.

The reaction among the shifters was palpable. I sensed pleasant surprise from Nan, Felicia, David, Karen, and Cole, and open hostility from the others. Jack's blue eyes were amber, a sign that his wolf was near his skin and angry.

The woman standing next to Jack, who I assumed was his wife, was much shorter than her husband, with shoulder-length curly brown hair and brown eyes. She wore slacks and a teal sleeveless top that showed off her toned arms. Behind them was a tall, surly young man with dark hair that hung in his eyes, wearing a black T-shirt and jeans.

Sean rested his hand on my lower back and turned to the others. "Alice, you've met Jack already. This is Delia, Jack's wife."

"Nice to meet you," I said, extending my hand.

After a beat, she took it. Her handshake was brief and she squeezed more forcefully than was necessary. "You too," she said shortly. Our eyes met and hers dropped before she looked back up, startled. Delia's wolf had recognized a more dominant female and indicated submissiveness.

Sean turned to the young man standing apart from the rest of the group. "Caleb Jennings, this is Alice Worth."

Grudgingly, he shuffled toward me, hand outstretched. As I shook his hand, he leaned close and sniffed.

Taken aback, I let go of his hand. "Hey."

"Caleb," Sean said sharply.

"Sorry," the young werewolf muttered. He stepped back and resumed staring at the ground.

"Well, we're all here, so let's eat!" Karen suggested.

We sat down as Karen and Cole brought out covered trays laden with pieces of chicken and steaks that looked like they had been placed on the grill just long enough to get them warm.

Before I could figure out how to politely request a salad, Cole set a plate down in front of me with a moderately sized steak cooked medium. "Wouldn't expect you to eat like a wolf," he joked, settling in across from me with his own steak. "It'll be nice to share a meal with someone else who doesn't like their steaks still mooing."

"Don't knock it till you've tried it." Sean looked over the table appreciatively. "Everything looks fantastic, guys. Thank you for inviting us."

"Our pleasure. Dig in!" Cole said.

The meal turned out to be pleasant, despite the unexpected guests. Whether by accident or design, Sean and I sat at one end of the table and Jack, Delia, and Caleb at the other end. I sat between Sean and Karen and across from Cole and Felicia. Our conversation was easy and cheerful. I answered questions about my work and chatted with the others as Sean ate and talked quietly with Nan. Several times during the meal, I sensed pointed stares from the other end of the table, but ignored them.

As I ate, I slid my foot out of my sandal and slowly ran my toes along Sean's calf. He calmly ate his food without so much as a glance in my direction, but I saw a gold sheen in his eyes. Nan's eyes twinkled as she watched us.

I started to get a sense of the pack hierarchy, at least among those at the table, based on nonverbal cues and the conversations around me. My brief exchange with Delia earlier had shown I had a relative position in the pack, despite being human and not a member, and the others had adjusted accordingly.

The mountain of food on the table disappeared at an alarming rate. The speed and single-minded efficiency with which they put food away was impressive and this was less than half the pack. Suddenly, my quip about needing five-gallon buckets of potato salad for the cookout seemed more like something I would have to actually look into.

Sean and I offered to help clear the table but Karen and Cole insisted on doing it themselves before bringing out dessert, which turned out to be homemade brownies with ice cream. I managed to eat almost half of mine before I couldn't take one more bite without risking busting a seam on my dress. It had been a little loose when we arrived but now felt a bit tight in the middle.

As we were drinking coffee and letting our food settle, Jack tossed his napkin on his empty plate, put down his coffee cup, and turned his piercing blue gaze on me. "So, I saw some interesting pictures online. You were quite the little hell-raiser back in Chicago, weren't you, Alice?"

Startled, I jerked and glared at him. We stared at each other. Amber rolled over Jack's eyes.

Sean's hand moved to my thigh and squeezed. "Lower your eyes, Alice," he said softly.

I resisted, not wanting to show submissiveness to Jack. A second ticked by. Two. Sean took my hand, lacing his fingers through mine.

The others watched Sean's beta warily as the large man leaned forward in his chair. No one breathed.

"Jack, stand down," Sean commanded.

"She's disrespectful," Jack growled.

"She's not pack," Sean said flatly. "She's shown you respect until now, but you were rude. You know as well as I do humans who don't spend much time around shifters don't react with the same instincts."

Jack's posture remained aggressive. "If she's with you, she needs to learn."

I bristled.

Sean's hand tightened on mine. "When she's around pack members, Alice will—"

"Don't talk about me like I'm not sitting here," I said.

The others looked startled that I'd interrupted their alpha. When Sean gestured for me to speak, I glanced at each of them. "When I'm around members of the pack I'll do the best I can to interact with you on your terms, but I'm sure we'll run into issues sometimes because I'm not a werewolf. You'll have to meet me partway."

"We don't have to meet you anywhere," Delia said curtly.

"You do," Sean said. If there had been a hint of his power in his tone before, now it was pure steel. "Because when you speak to Alice, you speak to me."

The werewolves around the table reacted as one, surprise rippling out in an almost visible wave.

"Is she your mate?" Jack demanded.

"Not yet," Sean said. He raised our entwined hands and put them deliberately on top of the table. "But I'm hoping." He stared at Jack as the others exchanged glances.

We'd have to talk about that later. For now, I looked around the table again, letting them see that I wasn't afraid. I even met Jack's eyes briefly. I wasn't trying to start a fight, but I wasn't going to be run over, by Jack or anyone else.

Finally, Sean defused the situation by rising from the table. The others followed suit, their eyes not meeting his. Even Cole, who wasn't a shifter, avoided Sean's hot golden gaze.

"Thank you for having us over," Sean told Karen with a smile. "Everything was excellent. Can we help you with the cleanup?"

"My kids and I are staying to help," Nan told him, winking at me. "We'll have it all done in a jiffy. You two run along."

"I don't think I'll be running anywhere anytime soon," I said, making a face. "I might need someone to roll me out to the SUV."

"I've got a wheelbarrow in the shed," Cole offered.

Everyone but Jack and Delia laughed at that. Even Caleb smiled fleetingly, though his face returned to its customary scowl quickly.

As evening turned to night, we filed inside carrying our dishes and made sure everything was in neat piles in the kitchen. I excused myself to use the restroom before we left.

When I came out, Sean waited by the front door with my vest. I groaned. "Oh, please don't make me put that on. I'm so full."

He looked sympathetic but stubborn. "It's adjustable. We'll leave it a little loose."

I grumbled as he slipped the vest over my head and fastened the straps. True to his word, he didn't tighten it as much as before, but I was instantly miserable and in no mood for any more trouble when Jack, Delia, and Caleb joined us in the foyer, which suddenly felt much too small.

Caleb stood next to me, bumping my arm with his. "Why does she have to wear a bulletproof vest?"

"It's a safety precaution," Sean said. "Alice is in a dangerous line of work."

His eyes it up. "Cool." For the first time all evening, the young werewolf looked interested instead of surly. He brushed against me, jostling me deliberately again.

I held my ground. "Back up, Caleb. You're in my space."

Caleb growled. His fists clenched and his eyes went golden. Fury and resentment rolled off him in waves as shifter magic surged. I tensed, spooling magic in case he shifted and attacked.

Instantly, Sean was between us. The force of his alpha magic made the others take a step back. "You will not shift in this house," he told Caleb. "If you can't control your temper and your shifting, you'll have to go out to the pack land until you can. You endanger all of us by acting like this and I will not have you threaten Alice. Is that clear?"

There was a long pause as Caleb fought to control his wolf. When he replied, his voice had an edge of growl in it. "Yes."

Sean turned to Jack. "Can he stay with you tonight?"

"Yes." Jack put a hand on Caleb's shoulder and the younger man seemed to relax. The surge of shifter magic dissipated.

"Good. Take him home and keep an eye on him."

Jack gave Sean a nod. However strained the relationship between Sean and his beta might be because of me, they seemed united in their concern about the pack's youngest wolf, and for good reason. I'd only spent a few hours around Caleb, but it was obvious he was far from stable. The phrase "ticking time bomb" came to mind, and those were not words you wanted to use when describing a werewolf.

We moved to the door, Sean staying between Caleb and me. He took the radio off his belt and told the mobile team we were heading out. Once we'd gotten the all-clear from Philip, Sean reached for the door.

"Alice!"

I turned at the sound of Karen's voice. She hurried over to me with a small gift bag. "This is for you."

I blinked in surprise and took the bag. "What's this?"

"Just a little gift from us." She hugged me and then stepped back.

"Are we set?" Sean asked, his hand on my waist.

"All set." I smiled at Karen. "Thanks again for having us."

"It was our pleasure. Come back and see us again soon."

"I will," I promised as Sean ushered me out the door.

Without being told, I stayed in Sean's shadow as we went to the SUV and let him load me into the passenger seat. I felt Jack's gaze on me as clearly as if he were touching me, drilling twin holes between my shoulder blades until the SUV door slammed closed.

As Sean went over to talk to the mobile team, I let out the breath I'd been holding and reached into the gift bag. I pulled out a small, heavy item wrapped in tissue paper. When I unwrapped it, I found a snow globe. Inside the glass dome was a tiny forest covered in white snow and a group of wolves, their muzzles raised toward the sky as if in mid-howl. In the center of the group was a black-and-gray wolf, a little larger than the others, with golden-brown eyes and big, magnificent teeth.

Inside the bag, I also found a card that read simply *Welcome to the pack*. It was signed by Karen, Cole, Nan, Felicia, and David.

I smiled and shook the globe, watching the snow dance.

CHAPTER 10

"You did good," Sean said as he turned the key in the ignition.

I gave him a flat look.

He heaved a sigh. "I didn't mean it like that. You don't need my approval. What I meant was that you showed them you aren't to be pushed around by anyone—not even me, and I'm glad you did."

I raised one shoulder in a half-shrug. "I didn't like the way Jack was treating me."

"I'm sorry." Sean squeezed my hand.

"Not your fault he's acting this way. Everyone else was wonderful. I just wonder how many other members of the pack are going to resent me as much as he and Delia do."

"They'll just have to get over it. Nothing matters but you and me." He grimaced and gestured in the direction of the mobile team's SUV. "Well, once this business with Kent Stevens is over."

I smiled and leaned over to kiss him, the mobile team, Jack, and Delia be damned. I grabbed a handful of his hair and teased his tongue with mine, turning up the heat. If they were looking over here, I wanted them to get their money's worth.

Finally, I pulled back, the skin around my mouth burning a bit from his beard stubble. Totally worth it.

Sean's eyes twinkled. "Trying to make a point?"

I settled back in my seat and belted in. "Maybe."

He chuckled and drove toward the main road. As we bumped down the gravel drive, he grew serious again. "If you ever feel threatened by anyone in the pack, no matter who it is, defend yourself. I hope it doesn't come to that, but if it does, do what you have to."

"That was my plan."

The corners of his mouth turned up. "I thought as much, but I figured it wouldn't hurt to say it out loud."

As we turned out onto the highway and accelerated, he said, "I noticed what happened when you met Delia. You don't seem surprised by her reaction. I didn't expect you to fall into the pack hierarchy so easily." He paused. "You know I want to ask."

I shrugged. "You already know I've spent time around shifters. It's not my first interaction with a group of werewolves and not the first time I've been recognized as a more dominant female. You could say I have a fairly well-developed sense of how pack hierarchy works, for a human."

"It's more than fairly well-developed. I'd say you have an instinct for it. Is it possible you have some shifter blood in your family?"

"Not that I'm aware of, but it would explain a few...oddities with my magic. It would have to be at least three generations back or more, though." I smiled. "It would be funny if I were part cat shifter."

Sean groaned. "Oh, please, *anything* but a cat shifter." He pondered that for a moment, then added, "It would explain a few things, however."

I poked him in the side, which had little effect through his vest. We drove in companionable silence for a while.

When we were about ten minutes from my house, my phone rang. I glanced at the screen and answered. "Hello, Charles."

"Alice, my dear, how was your meal with the wolves?" he purred.

"Was dinner served on the hoof or were they actually quite civilized?"

There was no chance he didn't hear Sean's growl. I made an exasperated sound. "The meal was wonderful. Do you have any news? Is Stevens in custody?"

"Not yet." Charles's voice lost its mocking tone. "Our people are searching the city, but have found no trace of him."

I sighed and pulled unhappily at the side strap of my vest. "Then why are you calling?"

"I may have located one of your missing items."

I perked up, the vest and my discomfort forgotten. "Which one? Where is it?"

"I believe I know where your magic cup will be tonight."

"Where?"

"An auction."

I blinked. "An auction? What kind of auction?"

"A very exclusive auction." Charles's voice held a note of amusement.

"*How* exclusive?" I asked impatiently.

"Invitation only. Impenetrable security. Location known only to a handful of carefully selected individuals whose discretion is beyond reproach."

My eyes narrowed. "So you know where it is."

"I do."

I was in no mood for Charles's games. "Can you get me in or not?"

"Get *us* in," Sean interjected.

Charles overheard Sean's comment. "You, yes," he said. "The werewolf, on the other hand—"

"Vampire, where she goes, *I* go," Sean stated flatly.

"Well, you heard him," I told Charles. "So, what's your plan for sneaking Sean and me into this super-secret, ultra-exclusive auction?"

"I will not be sneaking you in," Charles said.

Sean growled.

The vampire chuckled. One of these days, he was going to find out why it was a bad idea to bait a werewolf. "You will be walking in through the front door."

I walked in through the front door.

Charles handed our invitations to the enormous tuxedo-clad security guard and rested his hand on mine where it was curled around his arm.

As the doorman looked over the invitations, I took the opportunity to glance around. The auction was taking place at a private mansion not far from Northbourne Manor, headquarters of the Vampire Court of the Northwestern United States. The interior of the house looked more like a museum than a residence.

The man-mountain at the door slipped our invitations into the basket at his elbow and gave Charles a small bow. "Welcome, Mr. Vaughan, Ms. Worth. You may wait in the main hall. The event starts promptly at twelve. Please be in your seats in the salon before it begins."

Charles inclined his head and we moved into the foyer. Behind us, Sean and Bryan, our escorts, stepped inside and the doorman greeted the next couple.

The entryway led to a wide hall. Paintings covered the walls and antiques and relics took up every available surface. Some held magic. I gave those a wide berth. About a dozen well-dressed vampires and a few humans sipped wine and champagne, browsed the art on display, and conversed quietly. Wait staff circulated among the guests, offering drinks and hors d'oeuvres.

Charles and I each took a glass of champagne. His was pink. Not rosé champagne, though, I decided immediately, as my magic tingled—champagne with a few drops of blood added for color and taste.

Bryan and Sean stood behind us, silent and watchful. Charles, like the other guests, had been limited to one security escort per person. Bryan appeared to have healed from his wounds, though his eyes were shadowed and he'd been uncharacteristically quiet since Charles's limo had picked Sean and me up at my house.

The forty-minute drive from my house to the mansion had been tense. When Sean had asked Charles where the vampire was residing since the ambush at his gate, Charles had evaded the question and repeated his invitation for me to stay with him. Sean had not taken that well. We'd avoided bloodshed, but only just.

Charles raised my hand to his cool lips. "You look divine, my dear."

I wore a floor-length, shimmery midnight-blue dress that clung like a second skin. Though it covered my back and arms, hiding my scars and tattoos, the front showcased my cleavage. The slit in the front went to mid-thigh. The dress and the four-inch stiletto heels had been supplied by Charles and both were a perfect fit. They'd arrived at my house less than fifteen minutes after we'd returned from Karen's house, accompanied by a professional makeup and hair stylist who trapped me in my bathroom for over an hour. I looked sultry and bronzed and not at all like myself.

I sipped my champagne. "I'm here to work, Charles. Stop flirting."

"One does not necessarily preclude the other," he said easily, exchanging a nod with a passing male vampire I didn't recognize. "We have little opportunity to see one another in a social setting. I have certainly never seen you wearing anything so alluring."

"It's a costume, nothing more," I said, my voice pitched so only Charles's ears could hear me. "I'm arm candy, as far as everyone here is concerned."

Charles leaned close, his lips a millimeter from my ear. "It is expected I should flirt outrageously with my 'arm candy,'" he murmured. "They will presume we are lovers, and suspect nothing of you." He slid his arm around my waist, brushing my butt with his fingertips as he did so.

"If you do that again, you may lose a hand," I muttered.

He arched an imperious eyebrow. "Your werewolf would be foolish to attack over so little a provocation."

I smiled with my teeth and tapped his glass with mine. "I wasn't talking about Sean."

He chuckled. "Oh, Alice, I do believe you mean it."

"I assure you I do."

Charles finished his champagne and a server appeared as if by magic to exchange his empty glass for a full one. I continued to sip my own drink slowly. I needed to keep my head clear and my senses sharp.

An unfamiliar vampire approached us, glass in hand. I didn't recognize him, but Charles apparently did.

"Vincent," my companion said, his voice suddenly glacial. "I was led to believe this was an *exclusive* affair, but your presence leads me to conclude that standards have slipped somewhat."

The tall, dark-skinned vampire chuckled. "Vaughan, how nice to see you again. And who is this lovely woman?" He turned to me and extended his hand. "Vincent Barclay, at your service."

I offered my hand. He caught it in his cool grasp, bowed, and brushed his lips across my skin.

"May I present my guest this evening, Ms. Alice Worth," Charles said formally. "Alice, Mr. Barclay is visiting from Seattle."

"Pleased to meet you," I murmured.

The other vampire released my hand almost reluctantly, sliding his fingers through mine in a deliberate provocation. Charles drew me possessively against his side.

"Have you ever visited Seattle, Alice?" Barclay asked. He lingered over my name, as if savoring it, and I didn't like the sound of my name in his mouth.

"I didn't care for it," I said shortly. "Far too much rain."

He chuckled. "Perhaps you have not adequately explored the pleasures of being wet."

Charles's anger became white-hot fury. Behind us, both Sean and Bryan took a step closer.

"I do hope your stay is brief," Charles told the visiting vamp before I could respond. "I am sure you are needed back home. Safe travels." It was a clear dismissal.

Barclay's eyes glowed silver in anger. He and Charles eyed each other for several long moments. Finally, the other vampire bowed to me, turned, and departed.

"Well, that was interesting," I said.

Stay away from him, Charles said in my head. *He is known to take women by force for both blood and sex.*

Why does that not surprise me? I responded.

Barclay rejoined a small group of vampires standing near a grotesque painting of a group of young women being led to an altar that dripped blood. He caught my eye and raised his glass in my direction.

I deliberately turned away and leaned my head toward my companion. *Ten bucks he calls his home his lair*, I said to Charles.

He chuckled aloud, but his eyes remained fixed on the Seattle vamp. I had rarely seen Charles lose his trademark cool, but clearly Barclay was odious enough to rate overt loathing.

Why hasn't the Court dealt with him, if they know this about him? I asked. *Drinking blood from non-consenting donors is a violation of both vampire and human law.* And a capital crime in many states, though not in California or Washington state.

Charles finally returned his attention to me. *He is not without allies in both the human and vampire world. The situation is complex.*

I scowled and sipped my drink. I still had Trent Lake's phone number; he'd insisted I keep it after he moved to Seattle to become the assistant director of the SPEMA field office there. Barclay was from Seattle. I was willing to bet Trent would go after Barclay, regardless of whatever allies the vampire had. I didn't think about it too much now, not in such close proximity to Charles, who might overhear a stray thought, but it might be worth giving Trent a call to see if anything could be done about Barclay.

I longed to turn around and look at Sean, but I kept my attention on Charles and the scene in front of me. Around the room, the guests chatted quietly among themselves, but no one paid the least attention to their security. Doing so might jeopardize my cover as Charles's arm candy.

More importantly, Sean was wearing a tailored tuxedo and I was trying very hard not to think about how good he looked and how much I wanted to get him home and take that tuxedo off with my teeth.

I sipped my champagne and focused on the other guests before my hormones got the best of me and Charles mistook my body's reaction to Sean in a tux as a response to his flirting. I recognized a few faces in the crowd, but most of them were vampires and not ones I knew personally.

So, besides the cup, what are the other items up for bid tonight? I asked Charles. I disliked talking to Charles telepathically since the ability to do so was a result of him biting me without my consent, but with so many sharp ears around us, this conversation was better had in our heads.

I understand there are six lots, all collector's pieces. I am interested in a few for my own collection. Neither of the other items you are seeking is among them.

I've already obtained the hand mirror, so after this, the only thing I'm missing is the cuff. For the record, I'm authorized to bid on the cup, up to ten thousand dollars.

He tilted his head. *If I may, perhaps it would be more seemly if I were to bid on your behalf.*

When I started to object, Charles added, *You are here as my guest, as my 'arm candy,' as you so colorfully put it. If you were to bid, you would attract quite a lot of attention, which I am sure you would prefer to avoid.*

He wasn't wrong about that, but I frowned. *If you win the bidding, you'll have possession of the cup. What guarantee do I have you'll turn it over to me or my client?*

Charles smiled and flashed his fangs. *Perhaps you will have to take my word?*

Only Herculean effort kept me from scowling. *That is not very reassuring.*

He grew serious. *You wound me. Have I not kept my word in all our dealings, from the moment you first began working for the Court?*

He had me there, though I might have pointed out that drinking my blood while I was in a coma might not have been a violation of his word, but it had been a terrible violation nonetheless. We'd come to a kind of fragile understanding about that, however, and there was little point in revisiting that discussion since each of us possessed the means of the other's destruction. He knew I wasn't the mid-level earth and air mage I claimed to be, and I could use our connection to control his body or even kill him. Neither of us was anxious for anyone else to know about either of those facts.

I could tell by Charles's expression that he knew what I was thinking, and he sensed I'd chosen not to bring it up. He gave me an almost imperceptible nod and turned his attention back to watching the room.

At ten minutes to midnight, two doors opened at the end of the hall and a man appeared. "If you would all please follow me," he said.

Charles offered his arm. I set my glass down on a table and we joined the rest of the guests.

As we approached the doors to the salon, there was something of a bottleneck and our movement halted. A familiar warm body moved up directly behind me. I knew without turning who it was.

It was a risk, but I reached back with my free hand. Strong fingers caressed mine and hot golden shifter magic ran over my skin as Sean squeezed my hand. The scent of forest filled my nose and a little of the tension drained out of my shoulders. Then we were moving again and he let go. I missed his touch immediately.

I wasn't sure if Charles had seen or sensed our brief contact, but he covered my hand with his and drew me closer.

Stop provoking Sean, I snapped. *You're being childish, and I'm not a prize for you to be fighting over.*

I have no idea what you are referring to, Charles replied, his voice in my head pure innocence. *I am merely concerned that you may lose your footing on the marble floor. It appears to be treacherous.*

My response was brief and quite profane. Charles shook with silent laughter.

Game face, I told myself as we reached the doors of the salon.

At an ordinary auction, the goal was to win the bidding on the item you wanted.

At this midnight gathering, the goal was to bid, win, and get out alive.

***

IT BECAME QUICKLY apparent the kind of auctions Charles regularly attended were very different from any I'd seen before.

There were sixteen bidders in attendance, plus that many security escorts lined up along the walls in the salon. A solemn vampire named Marcus introduced each item, opened the bidding, and acknowledged bidders with a somber "Sir" or "Madame" rather than by name. There was certainly no crass, loud, fast-paced auctioneering; this was a high-class affair where all the bidders were deadly serious about their bids.

The hosts of the event were equally serious about security. As we entered the salon, we crossed strong wards and a magic suppression spell settled over us like an invisible, prickly blanket. It didn't smother my magic entirely, but neither I nor anyone else would be able to unleash any strong magic or spells without first breaking the wards, which I assumed were full of landmines designed to incapacitate or kill anyone who tried. Considering the kind of clientele who came to these events and the powerful nature of the items for sale, it made sense the hosts would do everything in their power to ensure both the safety of the participants and the security of the valuables.

Lot 1201, the first item up for bid, was a dagger resonant with blood magic. Marcus informed us the weapon would drain the magical energy of its victim into the person who wielded it. A low murmur ran through the assembled guests, and then the bidding began at the reserve price of five thousand dollars.

Charles didn't bid on the dagger and I tuned out as the bids went back and forth, climbing in increments of five hundred dollars.

Despite my resolve to not think about it, my brain returned to the alleged "lost" memory conjured up by the hand mirror and the possibility that my biological father might still be alive. I made sure my shields were strong so Charles didn't accidentally overhear any unguarded thoughts and tried to put it out of my mind. There was nothing I could do about it right now; there would be time to think about it all later, when I wasn't sitting in a room full of vampires.

The sudden sound of wood striking wood startled me out of my reverie. Instead of a traditional gavel, Marcus had a fist-sized wooden ball that he tapped on his podium to close the bidding. The dagger had been sold for ten thousand dollars, to a beautiful female vampire I didn't recognize. Assistants took the dagger backstage and Marcus informed the winning bidder she would be able to take possession of the dagger at her time of departure, once payment was made in full.

Lot 1202 was a vampire relic: a wine bottle spelled to preserve the life energy in human blood kept inside. Lot 1203 was far more intriguing to me. It was an object of power, a flat golden ring about eighteen inches wide designed to focus a mage's power. They went for twelve and eighteen thousand dollars respectively. A male vampire I didn't recognize bought the bottle. The ring went to a human man in a dark suit who looked to be either a broker or some-one's proxy. Charles bid on each, but only at the beginning and never seriously. Court mages were capable of creating bottles like Lot 1202 and presumably the profit margin on objects like the ring were too small to make it worth his while.

Most of the audience appeared to be here as spectators rather than active bidders. Perhaps none of the items offered so far were of interest to them, or events like this were a place to be seen as much or more than a way to acquire magical items of, as my client had put it, "questionable legal status."

Lot 1204 was Esther's cup.

It was presented in a velvet-lined wooden box by a silent assistant. As the assistant walked the cup past the assembled bidders, Marcus spoke. "This cup is a unique item dating from, we believe, the early sixteenth century. While it is rather plain in appearance, the cup is quite remarkable. Drinking from it permits a vampire to remain awake for one hour past dawn and to walk without harm in direct sunlight."

A murmur ran through the guests. I almost sighed aloud. I'd hoped the cup's power would remain a mystery, but someone had recognized its magic. If I got outbid, I'd have to either attempt to recover the cup some other way or report to Esther that it had gone for more than I'd been authorized to spend. Though she had seemed far more interested in recovering the cuff, I wanted a one hundred percent success rate for this job.

That's the cup, I told Charles.

Understood.

The bidding began at the reserve price of five thousand dollars. The female vampire who had won Lot 1201 opened the bidding. Charles inclined his head and Marcus accepted his bid for five thou-sand five hundred dollars. The female vamp bid again, and again Charles put in a bid. Back and forth it went, until the price reached ten thousand dollars and the female vamp declined to offer another bid.

I was about to breathe a sigh of relief when I glimpsed movement out of the corner of my eye and Marcus said, "A new bidder. Ten thousand five hundred. Thank you, sir."

Vincent Barclay. Son of a bitch.

Marcus looked at Charles questioningly. Without hesitation, Charles nodded.

"The bid is eleven thousand," Marcus said.

Charles, what are you doing? I asked. *Ten-thousand-dollar limit, remember?*

No response.

To our left, a deeper nod from Barclay. "Twelve thousand," Marcus said, reading the other vampire's body language.

Charles inclined his head again. "Thirteen thousand."

Charles.

Barclay raised his index finger. "Fifteen thousand."

Charles raised two fingers. "Twenty thousand."

Barclay made the same gesture. "Twenty-five thousand."

Charles again. "Thirty thousand."

I started to sweat. *Charles?*

Barclay raised his eyebrows. "Forty thousand," Marcus said.

Charles followed suit. "Fifty thousand."

Barclay hesitated for a fraction of a second, then nodded. Something flashed in his eyes: frustration, maybe, or irritation. Either way, he looked to be reaching his limit.

Charles made a kind of seated half-bow. "Sixty-five thousand," Marcus intoned. He looked at Barclay.

No response. The Seattle vamp was expressionless and still.

A few beats passed. Marcus tapped his ball. "Bidding is complete."

Mindful of the many vampires in the room, I'd kept my breathing slow and steady, but as the assistant vanished behind the red velvet curtain with the cup, it was everything I could do to stay calm. *Charles, what the hell? I was only authorized to spend ten thousand dollars.*

Then the cup is mine, he replied, his voice in my head as emotionless as I'd ever heard him be. *You were outbid by a factor of six. Your client will hardly be able to complain.*

I seethed. *Your little pissing contest with Mr. Vincent Barclay just cost me a big bonus.*

No response. I chanted swear words in my head and hoped he was hearing them.

Lot 1205 was already on exhibit: a wide gold cuff covered in a delicate vine pattern, with a network of tiny red crystals forming four stylized flowers. As the assistant passed me, I sensed ancient blood magic.

Marcus addressed the audience. "This cuff is believed to have belonged to the Borgia family, but its age is estimated to be more than two thousand years old. Its purpose is to rein in a newly risen vampire's bloodlust, ensuring a smoother transition. Bidding will begin at the reserve price of five thousand dollars."

Charles won the cuff, agreeing to shell out nineteen grand for it. I wondered if he intended to use it himself when he created new vamps or resell it. If I ever decided to speak to him again, I'd ask.

The auction paused for a brief interlude before the final lot was presented. Wait staff circulated with trays of champagne and hors d'oeuvres. I took a glass when it became clear I would be the only one who didn't, and a cracker topped with fancy cheese and a thin slice of smoked salmon.

When everyone was settled and the wait staff had departed, Marcus reappeared behind his podium. "Honored guests, I am pleased to present the evening's featured item, Lot 1206."

The crown jewel of the auction turned out to be a painted stone that had once belonged to Vlad Tepes when he resided at Poenari, his fortress in Romania. Where Vlad currently resided was one of the vampire world's most closely guarded secrets. Charles had told me once that humans should hope they never found out.

Marcus cleared his throat and the low murmur of conversation faded to silence. "Ladies and gentlemen, the bidding shall commence at the reserve price of twenty thousand dollars."

The bidding was intense and Charles was in the thick of it. By the time the sale price surpassed eighty thousand dollars, most of the bidders had dropped out and it was down to Charles, the female vampire who had won Lot 1201, and—of course—Vincent Barclay.

Barclay hadn't wanted to spend more than sixty grand on the cup, perhaps because he was here for the stone. Judging by the bidding frenzy, there had to be more to that stone than its value as having once belonged to Vlad Tepes, but I sensed no magic from it. The stone was about four inches long and roughly oval-shaped. It had originally been brightly painted, but now the paint was mostly gone, making it impossible to discern what the image had once been.

At seventy-five thousand, the female vamp dropped out and once again the bidding was between Charles and Barclay.

Back and forth they went. One hundred thousand. One-ten. One-twenty. I discovered I was holding my breath. Vampires didn't breathe, of course, but even the fangy undead appeared to be watching the bidding war with bated breath.

I was watching Barclay when Charles bid one-fifty and saw the almost imperceptible tightening of his eyes that signaled the Seattle vamp was reaching his limit. This was looking to be an expensive night for Charles if he won.

Barclay bid one-sixty, but a heartbeat too slow if he wanted Charles to think he wasn't backing down. Charles went in for the kill and bid one-eighty.

After a pause, Barclay demurred. Marcus tapped his strangely shaped gavel and bidding ended.

My curiosity got the better of me. *What is that doohickey, anyway? I asked Charles as everyone rose. I don't sense any magic.*

Not all objects of power use the same kinds of magic, he replied.

At Charles's summons, Bryan and Sean approached. "Stay with her," Charles instructed Sean. "I must render payment and arrange to take possession of my purchases. We will return in a few minutes."

Sean gave him a nod. Charles and Bryan disappeared behind the red curtain, along with the other winning bidders and their escorts. I feigned the bored expression of a piece of brainless arm candy left with the hired help.

Sean leaned close, his lips almost brushing my ear. "I thought you had a spending limit of ten grand for that cup."

"That was all Charles," I murmured, my eyes scanning the room as the other guests filed out. "Believe me, we're going to talk about it once we're in the car."

I was about to apologize for the way Charles had been needling him when my eyes met those of Vincent Barclay.

The Seattle vamp was standing by the doors with an enormous bodyguard who looked, impossible as it might seem, larger than Bryan. I had the thought, and not for the first time, that bodyguard physiques were a kind of power-play thing for vamps. When it came to hand-to-hand combat, size wasn't the deciding factor for enforcers whose reflexes, strength, and stamina were enhanced by regularly drinking vampire blood. I'd seen Adri beat the stuffing out of men twice her size, so having the biggest bodyguard was less a matter of security than good, old-fashioned dick-measuring.

It wasn't the size of the enforcer that made me pause, however; it was Barclay's eyes. They were pure black and filled with hate. After years of torture and abuse at the hands of my grandfather, few things frightened me anymore, but I would be lying if I said I didn't feel a chill as the Seattle vamp glowered at me.

Beside me, Sean went still. Shifter magic rose and he stared at Barclay, his eyes going bright gold. Two vampire security guards appeared from behind the red curtain and watched the stare-down, ready to intervene if a fight broke out.

Finally, Barclay turned away from us and left the salon with his enforcer. The security guards followed, apparently wanting to ensure that Barclay left the property without causing trouble.

"Does Vaughan have a history with this guy?" Sean asked, his voice growly.

"I think so," I murmured. "Not sure what it is, but I'm pretty sure the hate is mutual."

With the drama over, a passing waiter offered me champagne. I took a glass to have something to do with my hands, but found myself drinking it as the minutes ticked by. The female vamp left with a long wooden box tucked under her arm. The other winning bidders left a few minutes after that with their purchases, and still there was no sign of Charles and Bryan.

Nearly fifteen minutes after they'd disappeared behind the curtain, Charles and Bryan reappeared. Charles carried the wooden box that contained Esther's cup and another I assumed held the vampire cuff, but there was no sign of the stone.

The vampire gestured at the doors. "Shall we?"

When we'd entered, Charles and I had gone first with our escorts behind us. On the way out, Sean walked in front of us and Bryan followed.

When we reached the front doors, our limo waited with Adri at the wheel. It looked like we were the last to leave; no other vehicles remained in front of the mansion. A doorman opened the rear door and Charles offered me his hand as our escorts guarded us. As I settled myself into the seat, the vampire got in, followed by Sean and finally Bryan. Sean sat next to me and Bryan sat next to Charles.

As soon as the door closed, Adri pulled away, gliding around the circular drive and accelerating smoothly down the long driveway toward the main road. Charles put the wooden boxes next to him on the seat. The cup's magic teased my senses, reminding me that I'd failed my client, through no fault of my own.

Before I could bring it up, Sean spoke, addressing Charles. "You want to tell us about this vamp from Seattle?"

"Vincent Barclay is contemptible," Charles replied, his voice cold. "He trafficks people throughout the region for sex, blood, and other purposes. It is known that his companions are not always willing. He is not welcome in this city, which he knows very well. He risks much to defy the Court in this way."

That settled things, as far as I was concerned. When I got home, I'd put in a call to Trent Lake about Vincent Barclay. "He came for the

Tepes stone, that much was obvious. Speaking of which, where is the stone? Did you not bring it with you?"

"I have it with me." He looked out the window as the limo slowed, turned onto the main road, and accelerated.

"Where are we headed?" Sean asked.

"You asked where I am staying," Charles said, his eyes on the scenery. "We are going to visit my temporary place of residence."

I started to object. Sean was tired after being up all night and only getting a few hours of sleep this afternoon. Plus, going to wherever Charles was staying seemed like a recipe for more of the same hostility that had made our ride out to the auction so tense. There was something in Charles's tone that made me stay quiet, however. I couldn't quite put a name to it, but he sounded almost...wistful?

Sean covered my hand with his. Charles's eyes flicked to our hands, then back to the window. I suppressed a smile. After spending most of the night needling Sean, he could hardly object to—

The limo swerved sharply, throwing us violently against one another. Sean dove on top of me, knocking me flat as the others hit the floor next to us.

A second vehicle plowed into ours, its engine roaring. Metal crunched, glass exploded, and the limo went sideways, the entire side caved in where Charles had been sitting a fraction of a second earlier. Sean curled around me, trying to shield me with his body as glass and broken pieces of the limo's interior pelted us.

The other vehicle's momentum pushed our limo sideways, tires squealing, as Adri fought in vain to keep us from going off the road. At the edge of the pavement the car turned on its side and we fell in a pile against the undamaged side of the limo. The limo teetered for a heartbeat before the other vehicle pushed us over and we began to roll down the steep embankment.

Seats, roof, floor, glass, grass, sky, and bodies whirled around me for what felt like an eternity as the limo rolled. Sean lost his grip on me when Bryan collided with us in midair. The four of us smashed into each other, our elbows, knees, and skulls battering each other's bodies relentlessly.

Through the broken window, I glimpsed the tree line approaching fast. If we'd been sliding down the hill I could have used my air or earth magic to slow or halt our movement, but since we were rolling there was little I could do but try to hang on to something.

The second impact was only slightly less terrible than the first and our roll down the hill came to an abrupt halt when we hit the trees. Someone grabbed my arm, but not fast enough. My face smashed into something hard and then there was only darkness.

CHAPTER 11

When I woke, at first all I could see, taste, and smell was blood. Judging by the traces of shifter and vamp I could sense, not all of it was mine, but I suspected most of it was. It bubbled from my lips, trickled from my nose, ran down my face.

Disoriented and confused, I wiped the blood from my eyes. I recognized the effects of shock and possibly a mild concussion. My body ached like I'd been beaten up, which wasn't far from the truth. The worst pain radiated from the middle of my back, where Bryan's knee had hit me during the rollover, and I wasn't sure if I'd be able to stand up or walk if I tried. My left arm ached. Someone had grabbed me just before we hit the trees and my shoulder felt like it had almost been wrenched from its socket.

I managed to focus and discovered I was alone inside what remained of the limo, which was upside-down and smashed to hell.

Charles? I asked. Even my mental voice sounded woozy.

A pause, then a terse reply: *Stay where you are.* He cut our connection so abruptly that I winced.

I couldn't see what was going on outside, but I heard the distinctive sound of fighting. That meant Charles, Sean, and the enforcers were facing whoever—or whatever—had run us off the road, and they were having to fight hand-to-hand.

I forced myself to move, crawling toward the opening where a door had either been torn off or kicked out. Broken glass cut into my hands and knees, but I ignored the pain and focused on finding out what the hell was going on and where Sean was.

Finally, I emerged from the wrecked limo and tried to figure out what I was seeing.

To my left, Charles appeared to be fighting two other vampires. No wonder he'd blocked me out so he could concentrate; they moved so fast that all I saw was a blur. I couldn't tell who he was fighting or if I recognized them, but he appeared to be holding his own.

Meanwhile, Bryan and Adri, both bloody from the crash, battled two black-clad men who, based on their size and speed, appeared to be enforcers. They moved almost as fast as the vampires. One of them was bigger than Bryan, and I suspected I knew who had attacked us.

As I watched, Adri knocked her opponent down. He flipped back to his feet, a blade in his hand. In a blur of movement, she kicked the blade away and met his charge with a boot to the face. He went back down, dazed.

I heard a growl and turned to my right.

Sean, in wolf form, his fur standing up, ears back, and teeth bared, stood between me and a third vampire. I pushed bloody hair out of my eyes and looked up.

"Alice, my dear," Vincent Barclay said, his eyes silver. He looked me over and made a *tsk* sound. "Look at all that wasted blood. Such a shame."

I pulled myself to my feet, unwilling to face him on my hands and knees, no matter how much it hurt to stand up.

Barclay smiled, revealing his fangs. "Yes, do stand, love. No need to crawl to me. Not yet, anyway."

Sean snarled and snapped his teeth. On my left, one of the vampires went down and didn't get back up. Yay, Charles.

Barclay didn't bother to check on his fallen buddy. "What a lovely woman you are. I can't decide if I want to keep you for myself or see how much you might be worth on the open market. How much *are* you worth, Alice Worth?" He chuckled.

"Not funny," I muttered.

He tilted his head. "What did you say?"

I raised my head, my hands tingling with spooled magic, and met his glowing eyes with my own. "I said, that's not funny."

He came for me, vamp-fast. Sean met him in midair with a vicious snarl, his teeth sinking into the vampire's throat, and the fight was on. Sean was a blur of teeth and claws. While Barclay got in a few hits, the wolf was tearing him apart. Blood sprayed across the grass and it wasn't Sean's.

A strange pulse of magic from my left made me glance over just in time to see Charles pinning the second vamp to the ground, his palm against the other vamp's chest. A tendril of dark magic was coiled around Charles's arm. As I watched, the vamp on the ground convulsed, his back arching as a wave of energy ran up Charles's arm and disappeared. The vamp went still and Charles smiled, his eyes shining silver.

Before I could figure out what that was about, Barclay tore free of Sean's teeth and came after me.

The vamp's momentum drove me back into the side of the limo so hard that it knocked the wind out of me. Barclay's mouth was open, fangs extended, as he went for my throat.

I wrapped my hands around his torn neck and sliced through it with my spooled blood magic just as Sean hit him from the side. Barclay's head went one way and his body went another. Cool vampire blood fountained across my face and down the front of my dress.

Barclay's head rolled and came to a stop next to my bare foot, his face frozen in an expression of shock.

Sean stood over him and snarled as the Seattle vamp's body and head turned to ash. A frisson of cold gray vamp magic tingled on my skin and faded as Barclay died.

"Alice."

I wiped blood out of my eyes and looked up at the sound of Charles's voice. He, Bryan, and Adri were bloody but in better shape than I was. Barclay's enforcers were either unconscious or dead. The other two vamps were still down and not moving.

The wind sent some of the ash swirling into the air and it stuck to my bloody dress. "Am I going to be in trouble for this?" I asked Charles, gesturing at what was left of Barclay.

"He stated his intention to kill us and take you and the Tepes stone," he said. "There will be a hearing before the Court, but I have no doubt your actions will be deemed justified."

"That's good to hear." I leaned back against the limo. The shock was beginning to wear off and I was acutely aware that I was hurting all over, except the parts that were numb.

Three black SUVs screeched to a stop up on the road next to the mangled stretch Hummer that had smashed our limo. Black-clad Vamp Court enforcers spilled out and rushed down the embankment.

Charles's people cleaned up Barclay's remains and loaded the unconscious vamps and enforcers into the SUVs. I crouched to burn my blood and ended up sitting against the side of the wrecked limo, unable to rise because my back had become a giant knot of pain. I pulled a few shards of glass from my knees and palms that looked like what was left of the highball glasses from the limo's minibar.

Charles tried to approach me. Sean moved between us and gave him a warning growl. "I mean her no harm, wolf," the vampire said.

Another growl, this time with more teeth.

"I'm all right," I said. "He's on edge because of Kent Stevens. You'd best give him some space and go see if you can find the stuff you bought at the auction somewhere in this wreck."

You are injured and require healing, Charles said in my head, annoyed. *This is no time for such behavior.*

He's just protecting me. Get Barclay's cronies out of here and he'll shift back. I hoped so, anyway.

Sure enough, as soon as two of the SUVs left with the prisoners, Sean shifted back to human. I knew I was in bad shape when the sight of him naked failed to elicit the usual response from me.

He crouched and touched my face. "How badly are you hurt?"

I thought about that. "Pretty badly." I lowered my voice. "I can't stand up."

He scooped me up and headed for the road, where two more SUVs had arrived with reinforcements. I spotted one of my missing shoes halfway up the hill, where it had apparently fallen out of the limo during our roll down the embankment.

"Why didn't you stay in the limo?" he asked as he carried me.

I rested my head against his chest. "Would you have stayed put if it was me facing some unknown attacker?"

"No," he said automatically.

"Well, there's your answer."

He kissed me then, vampire blood and ash and all.

THE BATHROOM DOOR opened and closed. Familiar footsteps crossed the tile floor. "Aren't you clean yet?"

I didn't open my eyes as Sean came to sit on the side of the gigantic tub where I'd been soaking for a very long time. "Don't rush me," I murmured, sliding a little farther down under the bubbles. "This tub is amazing." Not to mention the hot water and massage jets did wonders for my battered body.

He brushed hair back from my face, careful to avoid tender bruised areas. "How do you feel?"

"Sore." Which was the understatement of the year.

It turned out Charles was staying with Niara of the Vampire

Court. As soon as we arrived at her home, a human physician examined me and determined I had no broken bones and had not been concussed. I did, however, have dozens of cuts and bruises, and my back hurt like I'd been kicked by a mule. The doctor removed shards of glass from my arms, legs, and hands and cleaned the wounds with what I could only assume was battery acid.

I'd refused both Charles's and Niara's offers of blood in favor of a mid-range air magic healing spell, which had helped but not healed me completely. My decision had angered Charles and left Sean conflicted. He didn't like seeing me hurting, but he didn't want me drinking from Charles again any more than I did.

Sean stayed at my side until I'd showered and climbed into the tub for an extended soak. He finally agreed to go shower and put on clothes when Bryan promised to guard the door.

He leaned down and kissed me. "If Malcolm were here, he would be able to heal your injuries."

"When I get home, I'll use a stronger healing spell and then I'll be fine." I opened my eyes and stared. "*That's* what they gave you to wear?"

He grinned down at me. "I always thought the enforcer look was unimaginative." He inhaled deeply and his eyes turned golden. "But if me wearing all black gets you this turned on, I might make this my standard attire when I'm not at work."

"There's no way you can smell anything from me over this bubble bath," I retorted, raising my hand and blowing some frothy bubbles in his direction. "Niara's housekeeper poured half a bottle of the stuff into the tub. It smells like a florist shop in here."

"It does," he agreed. "But I'd know your scent anywhere."

I pulled him down again for another kiss. When we broke apart, he reached for a towel, draped it over his knees, and gently lifted me out of the tub. I sat on his lap as he dried me carefully. Then he kissed me thoroughly enough to make me wish we were at home instead of a bathroom in Niara's house with Bryan standing outside the door. I was sitting on ample evidence that Sean agreed.

Finally, he nudged me off his lap. "Get dressed and let's find out why Vaughan brought us here."

"And what the hell that stone is." I caught a glimpse of myself in the mirror and winced. I was covered in bruises and half-healed cuts that stood out as angry red lines all over my skin. A knot on my forehead marked where I'd been knocked out, and my right knee had gotten twisted in the rollover and was now painful and stiff.

Sean made a growly sound and gently put his hand on my bruised back. "You'll finish healing yourself when we get home."

"I will," I promised. "Believe me, I have no desire to go around any longer than I have to feeling like a three-hundred-pound enforcer kicked me in the back. I'm almost afraid to ask, but what clothes did Charles give you for me?"

He gestured at a stack of folded clothes on the counter. "These are from Niara, actually."

The clothes turned out to be a pretty, sleeveless purple top that left my midriff bare and a colorful, multi-layered ankle-length wrap skirt.

Sean raised his eyebrows at the sheer black bra and matching skimpy undies, both of which fit too well to be coincidence. "Anything I should know about this?" he asked, gesturing at my sexy lingerie.

I hesitated.

His eyebrows went higher. "Really. And here I thought Vaughan was the only member of the Court I had to keep an eye on."

"No need to worry. I made it clear I wasn't interested," I told him as I tied the skirt around my hips. I pulled the top on over my head and stepped into a pair of sandals.

"And vampires are always *so* respectful of boundaries when it comes to these things," he said dryly. "As evidenced by that very lovely lingerie, which she must have had on hand and which I look forward to taking off later."

I started combing through my wet hair. "Speaking of which, I'm sorry your clothes were ruined in the wreck and then finished off when you shifted. I wanted to take that tux off of you myself."

"I know." He kissed me. "You'll have to settle for taking off this enforcer uniform, I guess."

I looked him over and decided I could make do with that.

WHEN WE EMERGED from the bathroom, Bryan was waiting on us. We followed the enforcer through a maze of hallways and out onto the back patio, where Charles and Niara waited.

Niara's residence was as beautiful and colorful as Charles's was elegant and understated. She'd decorated her veranda in bright fabrics and rattan furniture. Beyond stretched an enormous garden. The scent of flowers filled the air.

Dark shadows moved along the walls of the garden: heavily armed Vampire Court security watching for trouble. I'd almost forgotten Kent Stevens in all the excitement of the auction and Barclay's attack, but the sight of the guards brought all the tension and uneasiness back in a rush.

Charles had changed into a light gray summer suit. He rose as we approached, looking me over appreciatively, but his eyes were dark with anger. *You are limping*, he said in my head. *Why do you refuse my offer of healing?*

It's only cuts and bruises, Charles, not a bullet wound. Nothing a strong healing spell can't fix.

Out loud, I said, "It's beautiful out here, Niara."

Tonight, her hair was in long, tiny braids and held back from her face with a colorful scarf. She wore a long purple shift dress and her feet were bare except for a gold anklet and toe rings.

I no longer had Niara's blood in me, but the warm copper glow in her eyes made me remember the feeling of her hands on me in the stairwell at Hawthorne's the night it was bombed. I'd be lying if I said there wasn't a spark of attraction there, but even if it weren't for Sean, vampires of either sex were a no-fly zone for a list of reasons longer than my arm—not that either she or Charles seemed put off in the least by my repeated refusals. I got the impression that one or both of them were simply in no rush to force the issue. And why should they? Vampires had all the time in the world to plot and wait until they thought the time was right.

Niara smiled. "My refuge from the world," she said, her voice low-pitched and musical. "No matter the ugliness beyond those walls, I am surrounded by beauty here. Your presence makes it all the more lovely. Please, sit." She gestured at the two empty chairs.

Sean and I sat as Charles reseated himself next to Niara. The table held a bottle of champagne in a bucket of ice, four glasses, and the box containing Esther's cup.

As Charles reached for the champagne, I asked, "What are we celebrating?"

"Many things," he said, removing the foil and *muselet* with practiced ease. "My success at the auction, our survival, and Vincent Barclay's long-overdue true death."

The cork slid free of the bottle with a muffled *pop*. He divided the champagne among the four glasses.

We raised our glasses in a toast. As we enjoyed the champagne, I spoke up. "Speaking of Barclay's attack, what exactly *is* that stone, and what did it do to that vamp?"

"As you heard at the auction, the stone was one of many that once belonged to Vlad Tepes," Charles said. "The magic is ancient. Few know its origin. I know only that it predates our earliest records. Tepes's collection of vampire objects of power was the largest ever known. Pieces from the collection become available on occasion. Their powers vary, but the object I purchased tonight possesses the ability to transfer life energy to the one who wields it."

I stared at him. "That's what I saw you do to that vamp on the side of the road. You took his life energy. Did it kill him?"

"No. A vampire's immortality cannot be taken in that way. He is merely very weakened and mortal for a time."

"But if you used that weapon on a human or a shifter?" Sean asked.

"They would most likely die." Charles sipped his champagne.

"Do you plan on reselling the object or keeping it?" I asked.

"I have not decided. I must study the market, determine if it could be sold for a sufficient profit at this time. If not, I will keep it in my collection until such time as I can make an adequate profit, or I choose to keep it."

"And the cup?" I gestured at the box on the table. "What's your plan for that, now that you've got it?"

"I plan to use it," he said matter-of-factly.

I almost dropped my glass.

Niara's expression was grim. "You risk much." Her tone indicated they'd already argued about this before Sean and I came outside. "You have not seen it used. You have only the word of the expert brought in by the broker as to what its power is. If they are wrong—if Alice's client is wrong—you may die under the sun."

"I have not stood in the sun for more than two hundred years," Charles said. "Perhaps I am willing to risk much to feel that warmth once again."

Her gaze became distant as she toyed with her champagne glass. "I have felt the sun," she said, her voice softening. "Not so long ago, I was tempted, as you are now, by magic and the promise of walking in the daylight. It had been so very long since I had felt the caress of the sun that once blessed me as I walked the plains of home. My people called themselves children of the sun. I thought I was parted from it forever, and then I received a great gift: a magical talisman that allowed me to see the sun again, as if I had not become a vampire and a child of the night. It was not long before I knew it was a great folly."

"You regret that you walked beneath the sun?" Charles asked in disbelief.

Niara seemed to be considering what to say. Finally, she said, "Perhaps I cannot explain in a way you would believe. But if you do this, you risk more than you know." She glanced at the eastern horizon. "Dawn comes within the hour. You have time to consider this decision, but I will leave you to it." She rose.

We stood as well. It took some effort on my part since my back and knee had stiffened again. Niara brushed her lips across Charles's mouth, then disappeared into the house.

"Well, that was sobering," I said as we reseated ourselves. "Are you reconsidering?"

"No," Charles said firmly.

"Niara's right that we don't know for certain what the cup's power is. I have only my client's word, and any expert the seller called in can only give their best guess at what the spell will do. What if they're half right and the spell only lasts thirty minutes?"

"I will put on sunscreen."

I stared at him, nonplussed. "You don't seem to be taking Niara's warning very seriously."

He finished the last of his champagne and set the glass on the table. "I take her warning very seriously. Still, I choose to accept the risk for the chance to walk in these gardens in the sunlight."

"Sir."

We all looked up at the unexpected sound of Bryan's voice. The enforcer stood in his customary spot to Charles's right. "I will accompany you with a large umbrella or a covering," he said. "If the spell fails, I'll do my best to see that you are returned to the safety of the house and healed, should it be necessary."

Charles inclined his head. "Thank you, Mr. Smith. Your offer is greatly appreciated but unnecessary. Alice alone will accompany me."

Bryan stiffened, Sean made a low growly noise, and I jerked in surprise. "Me?" My voice had a hint of squeak in it.

"She wouldn't be able to protect you from the sun or return you to the house," Bryan objected.

"This is true," Charles acknowledged. "But I wish to take a walk in a garden in the sunlight accompanied by a beautiful woman."

Bryan looked at me, clearly unhappy. "Then ask Adri," I suggested. "She's gorgeous, and she'd be able to bring you back to the house if—"

"It is your company I desire," Charles interrupted. "If you wish, you may consider it a last request."

My stomach lurched. "Damn it, Charles," I ground out. I reached for the box, flipped open the lid, and grabbed the cup.

It wasn't really a good idea to pick up a magical object, but I was angry and more than a little uneasy at the thought I might witness Charles cindered by the morning sun. We might have had a difficult relationship and I didn't doubt that he wouldn't hesitate to sell me out if he ever figured out who I was, but that didn't mean I wanted to watch him burn to death in front of me.

The magic in the cup seared my senses. My head jerked back and my vision faded as I lowered my shields and plunged headlong into the cup's magic.

I knew the spellwork that would allow a vampire to walk in daylight by heart; my grandfather had me learn it not long after my blood magic manifested when I was twelve, because vampires would pay astronomical sums for the chance to experience daylight after decades or centuries—or millennia—of moonlight. I found the spell easily, woven through the blood magic and the peaceful green of the earth magic, and traced its lines and runes, feeling their familiar curves and edges. Finally, I raised my shields slowly, disengaged from the cup's magic, and returned to awareness.

I opened my eyes and found myself staring into Sean's fiery golden gaze. He was crouched in front of my chair, gripping the armrests. "I have been trying to get you to respond for almost five minutes," he snapped. "What the hell did you think you were doing?"

"Trying to find out if this cup is the real deal," I said, my voice uneven. I looked past Sean at Charles, who sat on the edge of his chair watching me. "As far as I can tell, the cup is exactly as advertised: a spell that keeps you awake past sunrise and permits you to be exposed to the sun without burning."

"As far as you can tell?" Bryan asked skeptically.

"I'm familiar with this kind of spell," I said. "That's what it is."

"For one hour?" Charles asked.

"I'm reasonably certain the spell will last for one hour, but it's not as if there's a timer in the spellwork. 'Reasonably certain' is as good as it's going to get on the timing. I can't guarantee anything, Charles."

"There are no guarantees, in this life or any other," he told me. "Your 'reasonably certain' is enough for me. I accept the risk."

"I'm not sure I do. If I'm wrong—"

"Then I was sufficiently warned and chose to proceed against the advice of my companions." He regarded me. "I cannot force you to join me, but I would be...grateful if you would."

Sean and Bryan were plainly displeased, although for very different reasons. I didn't need to be able to read his mind to know Sean was thinking about who might be blamed if the spell didn't work the way it was supposed to and Charles ended up severely burned or turned to ash.

Bryan was no doubt thinking that his entire job—his life, in fact —was dedicated to keeping Charles safe from harm, and I'd caused all this by bringing Charles into my search for the missing magical objects. If something did go wrong, I'd have to answer to Bryan before I even got a chance to answer to the Court.

But I saw something in Charles's eyes that I'd not seen in the five years I'd known him: a glimmer of life. Even in moments of levity, which were few and far between, Charles's eyes had never belied any hint of humanity. And yet, when he looked at the cup, I saw an echo of the man he must have once been, before he'd been turned.

Maybe it was stupid and sentimental of me—in fact, it almost certainly was incredibly stupid, given the possible consequences I might face if the spell failed—but I was having a difficult time talking myself into refusing his request.

I put the cup on the table. "I accept. There's only one important question left to answer."

Charles ignored the low growl from Sean and Bryan's frown. He tilted his head. "And that would be...?"

"What do you want to drink?"

⁂

AFTER BROWSING Niara's well-stocked cellar, Charles chose a 1914 merlot and brought the bottle up to the sitting room that overlooked the veranda.

Ten minutes before the sun was expected to rise, he pulled the cork from the bottle and poured wine into the cup and a wineglass. He handed me the glass and we walked to the doors that looked out over Niara's garden.

Charles touched the rim of the cup gently to my glass. "To you," he said. We drank.

Magic coiled down Charles's arm as he swallowed the wine. It faded and his aura changed from its usual cool gray to peaceful earth-magic green.

I lowered my shields and touched him. "How do you feel?"

"Warm," he said.

We turned to face the eastern horizon. When he took my hand, I didn't pull away.

It began as gradual lightening of the sky over the hills and then dawn broke in a spectacular array of oranges, reds, and yellows. Charles flinched as the first rays of sunlight touched us, but the spell held and he was unharmed. We stood motionless as the sun peeked over the top of the hill and the day began.

Slowly, as if in a dream, Charles reached out and opened the door. I followed him out onto the veranda, my hand in his. We left our glasses on the table and descended to the garden. The grass and flowers sparkled with morning dew.

I wondered what Charles was thinking about as we strolled down the path, heading away from the house. His face was impassive and I couldn't read his eyes. Sean and Bryan stood at the edge of the veranda, watching us.

When we reached a point about three-quarters of the way across the garden, Charles stopped and turned to me. His mask of impassivity vanished and he raised his face to the sky, his eyes full of wonder. "So bright."

"It's a beautiful sunrise," I said.

"It is perhaps the most beautiful I have ever seen." He fell silent.

We started walking again, wandering between rows of flowers and neatly trimmed hedges. He seemed lost in thought and I stayed quiet, not wanting to intrude on this miraculous daytime excursion.

He surprised me when he spoke. "Have I ever told you of my life before I was turned?"

"A little. When we first met, five years ago or so, you told me you fought in the Revolutionary War as a teenager. That's all I know." Well, and that he'd been eviscerated before his death, but I didn't want to bring that up. He might regret revealing that to me. I knew very well the emotional weight of scars.

"Many years ago, before I was turned, I was married."

My steps faltered. He smiled slightly and pulled on my hand, urging me to resume walking. "Her name was Emma. We married when I was seventeen and she was fifteen. Such things were common in those days. Our families had little money, but we were very much in love."

We turned away from the house, wandering nearer to the far end of the garden. "We had a small home near her parents' residence where we lived for fourteen years. She bore me six children, three of whom lived past infancy: two daughters and a son. Our lives were difficult. We were not always happy, but we were always in love. I considered myself quite fortunate to be wealthy in love, if not in worldly goods."

Charles paused to run his fingertips over the warm brick of the garden wall. "In the year 1792, I was returning to my home from visiting a friend when I was arrested on suspicion of committing a murder. The victim was the pregnant wife of the local magistrate. A witness described a man seen fleeing from the scene. I had the great misfortune of wearing similar clothing and resembling the man who was described. The magistrate believed me guilty. I was tortured in order to obtain a confession. You have seen the scar."

I nodded.

"I survived the wound, but once I had confessed, though it was under duress, my guilt was decided. I asked to see my wife and was told her parents had taken her and my children away to another town so they would be spared the infamy of having a murderer for a husband and father. My own parents wanted nothing to do with me. I was branded a rapist and a killer. Even the minister of our church refused to visit my bedside. I was forsaken by everyone. My execution was to be held as soon as I was able to climb the steps to the gallows. Had the situation gone on much longer, I am sure the magistrate would have simply dragged me up the steps and put the noose around my neck himself."

We walked on in silence. I snuck glimpses at the watch I'd borrowed, watching as the minutes ticked by.

"One night as I lay in my bed in the jail, delirious with fever, as the wound had become infected, the bars were torn from the window. The smell of my blood had drawn a newly risen vampire. I could see little through my delirium, but I felt the pain when he bit my throat. I could not fight back, but neither did I desire to do so. It would be, I decided, a death preferable to hanging in front of my neighbors and those I had once called friends."

My stomach twisted. I squeezed his hand, but he did not return the gesture, as if too caught up in his memories to notice it.

Charles continued, "My attacker drained me to the point of

death. Just as I felt myself slipping away, the door burst open and two more vampires rushed in. They pulled him away from me and I lost consciousness. The next night, I rose as a vampire."

"One of the other vamps turned you?"

"Yes. They could not leave me behind, for my wound would have been proof vampires lived nearby. The elder of the two took me to his home. They decided because I had so stubbornly clung to life despite my grievous wound, I would be likely to rise as a vampire. And since I was a condemned man with no friends or family to claim me, I would not be missed by anyone."

Though we had made a final turn back toward the house, Charles continued to walk slowly. There was only twenty minutes until the hour was up, but he was in no hurry.

"What about your wife? Did you ever see her again?"

"Some months later, when I had control of my bloodlust, I followed her to a village where she had gone to live with her new husband. I observed her caring for our children and keeping the house. She was with child, the child of her new husband. I watched as he returned home from working in the fields and she greeted him with a smile and a kiss. I left then and did not return."

We walked in silence back toward the house. When I looked at Charles's face, I was startled. "Charles, you have a sunburn!"

He smiled, but it didn't reach his eyes. "Do I?"

I remembered something he'd said before the bombing, when he'd visited my house and found me drunk on my back porch. "The night you showed me your scar, you said part of the reason you kept it was to remind you of a lesson you'd learned. What was the lesson?"

"That those you love and trust can and will turn against you," he said quietly. "And people will commit great evil and call it justice."

We climbed the steps to the veranda. Sean and Bryan watched us pass as we walked to the table, where the cup and my wineglass waited. Charles picked up the cup and regarded it.

I stole another glance at my watch. Nine minutes before the spell would break. My stomach churned as the seconds ticked by and the vampire made no move to return to the house.

Finally, Charles held the cup out. *Return this to your client,* he said in my head. *Take it far from me and never tell me who possesses it.*

Why? I asked, stunned.

Because I think I have come to understand what Niara was attempting to tell me when I was too stubborn to hear her words. I have walked in the sun and remembered what it was like to be human. I will never be human. If I were to use this cup again, I believe I might not return to the safety of my home before the hour ended.

My stomach contracted. *You wouldn't commit suicide by sunlight, Charles. I know you.*

He smiled without humor. *You do not know me, Alice. Never presume to know what is in my heart. Take the cup away.*

I can't repay the sixty-five grand, I reminded him.

This hour with you has been repayment enough. He kissed my cheek, startling me with the warmth of his usually cool lips. *I feel the pull of sleep. My stolen hour is almost gone.*

I took the cup. This use had depleted its magic, but it would regenerate. My fingers brushed his and he paused, savoring the moment.

Finally, Charles released my hand and went inside. I followed, but he'd already vanished into the recesses of Niara's mansion. Somewhere in the house, a heavy door closed and locked.

Sean came inside and picked up the wooden box. I nestled the cup in its velvet-lined interior and closed the lid. I looked up at him.

He used his thumb to wipe the single tear off my cheek. "Let's go home."

CHAPTER 12

ADRI DROVE US HOME. SEAN CONTACTED MOBILE TEAM ONE, JACK AND Karen, and gave them our ETA. He'd put his shoulder rig back on and we both wore our bulletproof vests again. I was too tired and emotionally drained to waste energy thinking about how uncomfortable I was. Our drive was silent.

When we pulled into my driveway, Jack and Karen were already parked in front of my house. Sean gave the mobile team a wave and escorted me inside. He locked the door behind us as Adri backed down the driveway and I tossed my vest in the coat closet.

While he let the dog in and checked the doors and windows, I took the cup down to the basement and put it in the cabinet with the hand mirror.

Back upstairs, I stifled a grimace as I sat on the couch and called Aaron Riddell. My back and knee ached mercilessly.

"I have good news," I told the attorney when he came on the line. "I've got two out of three. The cup and the hand mirror are in my hands."

"Two days and two down. I knew you were the best in the business," Aaron said. I could hear the smile in his voice. "You sound kind of rough. Did you have to get them the hard way?"

"You don't really want any details, do you?"

"No, I do not, but if you end up needing legal representation—"

"—I'll have to call someone else. There's no way I'd be able to afford your rates."

He chuckled. "I'm sure I could offer you a discount. And what about item number three?"

Sean came downstairs and headed for the kitchen, still wearing his all-black enforcer clothes. My eyes followed him. Yum.

"Alice?" Aaron prodded.

"Yes?" I shook myself as Sean disappeared into the kitchen. "Yes, sorry, I was distracted." I heard him pouring dog food into Rogue's bowl.

"You'll let me know as soon as you have any news on the cuff?"

"Yep. You'll be the first to know as soon as I've got it."

"Great. I'll let my client know about your success. I'm sure she'll be very happy to hear it."

We said our goodbyes.

Sean stuck his head out of the kitchen. "Do you want coffee?"

I shook my head. "I'm recovered enough to release Malcolm from my bracelet and check him for hidden spells. Once that's done, I'm going to finish healing myself and take a nap for a few hours."

He came into the living room and sat on the couch next to me. "Are you all right?"

I hesitated. "How much did you hear of what Charles was telling me?"

"Very little. I did hear the last bit about learning a couple of lessons."

I stared in the direction of the fireplace. "He told me how, when, and why he was turned."

"Oh." He put his hand on my thigh and squeezed. "It wasn't a happy story, I take it. Those stories seldom are." Something about the tone of his voice made me look up. His eyes were haunted.

Though I'd never asked Sean if he'd been born a werewolf or been bitten, I'd assumed the latter, and the way he spoke more or less confirmed it.

Sean figured out what I was thinking. "I will tell you, Alice," he said quietly. "You only have to ask."

I read his expression and knew it wasn't the right time. "I want to hear the story, but it can wait until another day," I told him, leaning over to give him a quick kiss.

When I sat back, I shook my head. "One thing I have to remember is that no matter what stories he tells me, he's still Charles Vaughan of the Vampire Court. I can't forget either where his loyalties lie or that he's dangerous. He never does anything without a reason. If he told me that story—assuming any of it is true—he did it because he thinks it was to his advantage to do so."

"That's my Alice," Sean teased, lifting my hand and pressing a kiss to my knuckles. "You never allow sentiment to cloud your vision. It's one of the things I love most about you."

"I don't know if that's true," I countered, while my stomach did a somersault and then tied itself into a pretzel. "I feel like I've let Charles pull the wool over my eyes a couple of times. Maybe I've finally learned from those mistakes, though." I started to push myself to my feet.

Sean rose and pulled me up carefully to minimize the strain on my sore back. I rested my forehead against his chest.

He hadn't said he loved me; he said there were things about me he loved. It wasn't much of a difference, but I wondered if he was trying out the word to see how I would react.

There was love in the way he cared for me when I was hurt, the way he both protected and supported me in front of his pack, the way my well-being and happiness were essential for his own. There was love in everything he did.

He hadn't come out and said it, but I was pretty sure he loved me. Did I love him? Did I even know what love felt like? I remembered loving my parents, but that was a long time ago, and not the same kind of love. Was I even capable of loving someone? I hoped I was, but I was very much afraid that I couldn't.

He kissed the top of my head. "You're awfully quiet all of a sudden."

"I got lost in thought." I gave him a quick squeeze and headed for the basement door. "I'm going downstairs to check on Malcolm. It might take a little while."

"Alice."

I paused with my hand on the doorknob. "What's up?"

"I understand why you need those wards on your basement and why you haven't granted me passage through them." His eyes glowed. "I'm not asking you to change that, but I want you to know if you get hurt down there or I think you're in danger, I'm coming through those wards."

He wouldn't get through them, but he wouldn't let that keep him from trying. He'd fight them until he was either unconscious or dead.

I'd been thinking of my basement as some kind of retreat or escape and not from Sean's perspective. To him, it was a source of worry and that worst of emotions for an alpha: helplessness. It must have been gnawing on him constantly since we'd gotten back together, and the close call with the blood mage had made it impossible for him to stay quiet anymore. He was probably imagining what might happen if someone else tried to take Malcolm and I ended up unconscious or worse and he couldn't get to me.

I couldn't do that to him. As much as I needed my own space and a place to retreat, it didn't have be locked to him. In fact, it *shouldn't* be.

"Come give me your hand," I said softly.

"Alice—"

"Sean, give me your hand."

He joined me at the door. I traced four runes on the doorframe and the wards hummed. As I had done once before, I took his hand

and drew two more runes with our index fingers. The wards chimed as magic ran through us.

"They feel powerful," he said. "I wish I could see them."

"I can show them to you." I placed my palm on the doorframe and suspended the obfuscation spells, revealing the wards.

Sean caught his breath.

Hundreds of layers of wards appeared, colorful and neon-bright: white air magic, green earth magic, and purple, red, and black blood magic, interwoven in seemingly endless chains of runes and spells that ran along the walls, floor, and ceiling of the basement.

As we watched, a golden thread—Sean's shifter trace—snaked its way along the existing wards, weaving itself through the spellwork until it was visible throughout, permitting him to enter the basement unharmed.

"I've never seen anything like this," he said, looking over the wards in awe. "This is a masterpiece. You are the most incredible woman I've ever known."

I took my hand off the doorway and the wards vanished, once again hidden by their powerful obfuscation spells. "You are welcome in the basement, but don't come down unannounced in case I'm doing spellwork or if I'm down there because I need alone time. You remember what to touch down there and what not to?"

"I remember." He took me in his arms and held me. "Thank you. This means a lot to me."

"It means a lot to me too." I kissed him, then reached for the doorknob. "I'm going to let Malcolm out and check him for spells. I'll be back upstairs when that's done."

"Let me know if you need me." He let go of my hand and headed for the kitchen. "In the meantime, I'm going to make an omelet for breakfast. I'll make yours when you're done."

"Thanks." I hesitated. "I love the way you make omelets."

He paused at the doorway to the kitchen and turned around. His grin made my heart skip a beat.

Smiling, I opened the basement door, pushed through the wards, and headed downstairs.

SINCE I DIDN'T KNOW whether Malcolm still had any of those retrieval spells hidden in him, I spent a good twenty minutes drawing runes and turning the three inlaid concentric circles into a fortress that even a team of blood mages wouldn't be able to get through.

When I charged the circles, the power level made my hair stick out. I took a deep breath, exhaled, and touched the blue crystal on my bracelet. "*Release.*"

Malcolm popped into existence, his eyes wide and full of panic. He saw me, flitted back, and hit the inner circle, which zapped him and sent a bolt of magic back into me. He bounced away from the circle and flitted around me in a whirlwind.

"Malcolm, it's okay," I said, trying to keep track of him as he moved. "It's okay. We're in my basement. No one's going to take you."

He stopped as suddenly as he'd appeared, flickering with anger. "What the *hell,* Alice?" he yelled.

I blinked at him. "What did I do?"

"What did you do?" Malcolm moved as far from me as he could within the small circle. He'd gone from panicked to furious in record time. "You caged me in blood magic and ripped a spell out of me!"

"You were trying to get away—"

"From the blood magic! Which is how I *died,* if you'll recall, so I'm a little edgy about it!"

"—and if I hadn't gotten that spell out of you, they would have taken you and I would have probably died, and you'd be in a crystal at Bell's cabal like all the other ghosts!"

"Like all the other…? What other ghosts?" Malcolm floated back and forth in confusion. "Wait, whose clothes are those? Why is your face all bruised? How long have I been in your bracelet?"

I hesitated. "Don't get mad."

Malcolm's irritation buzzed on my skin. "Alice, when you say that, I feel like I will probably have a good reason to be mad."

I sighed. "It's been about thirty-six hours since the attack."

"*Thirty-six hours?*"

"A really crazy thirty-six hours."

He closed his eyes, appeared to count to ten, then reopened them. "Okay, let's hear it."

I told him about the attacks on mages, my theory that Bell had pulled back all his bound ghosts, our outing to find the mirror, my dinner with the pack, the auction, Vincent Barclay's attack, our visit to Niara's mansion, and Charles's walk in the sun. Malcolm listened with varying levels of anger, disbelief, sympathy, shock, and surprise.

When I finished, he was quiet. "Is that all?" he asked finally, his tone dry.

I rubbed my forehead. "I intended to take you out of the bracelet last night after dinner with the pack, but then Charles called about the auction."

"It's okay." Malcolm's anger had faded. "You did what you had to do under the circumstances. Thank you for not letting me end up back at the cabal, stuck in a crystal for all eternity. Also, I'm glad you're not dead."

"Hey, me too. Speaking of which, I need to make sure you don't have any more of those spells hidden in you."

He floated back and forth nervously. "How are you going to do that?"

"There's only one way. I need to search by hand."

He flitted back to the far side of the circle. "Alice…please."

"There's no other way. Neither you or I sensed the one that almost got you the other night. The only way to be sure there aren't more of those spells hidden in you is for me to look really, really closely. You know I'm right."

"I know," he said miserably. "It's not that I feel pain, exactly, but it's like I'm being cut open over and over again."

I hated that I had no choice but to do this to him. "I'll wait until you're ready," I promised.

He floated over to me. "Can you talk and search at the same time?"

"Yes. What do you want me to say?"

"Tell me more about your dinner with Sean's pack."

"Okay." I rolled my shoulders. "Let me know when you're ready."

"Just do it."

I started at his feet, passing my hands slowly through his non-corporeal form, my shields down and senses wide open, searching for any trace of another hidden spell.

I talked as I worked, describing my visit to Cole and Karen's house, the surprise visit by Jack, Delia, and Caleb, Jack's hostility, Sean's statement that he hoped I might be his mate, and the snow globe I'd been given. Malcolm shuddered as I passed my hands through his body, but didn't make a sound.

I found two more hidden spells, one of which was another retrieval spell. Since I had the luxury of time, I unwove it instead of tearing it out. When I finished, the spell dissipated in a puff of blood magic.

The second spell gave me pause.

It wasn't a retrieval spell; it was the spell that bound Malcolm to me. I'd theorized to Sean that Bell had found a way to have his ghosts bound to high-level mages in the area, but Malcolm had been bound to me specifically. When he'd first manifested in my office, he'd told me he'd been assigned to haunt me because of my past. The spell that bound us wasn't made of blood magic. The magic was silver—afterlife magic—and nothing on this plane of existence had made it. I could not unweave or break it, since that kind of magic was beyond even my abilities.

Strangely, the spellwork contained an element I couldn't identify. I sifted through the magic until I figured it out. The spell wasn't permanent; there was a condition that, once it was met, would free Malcolm and me from each other. What that condition was, I couldn't tell. I wondered if Malcolm knew, but this didn't seem like the time to ask.

"Alice?" he asked, his voice hollow. "Are you finished?"

"I'm finished." I raised my shields and withdrew my hands. They were bluish with cold and almost numb. "I found another retrieval spell and the spell that binds you to me. Other than that, I'm pretty sure you're free of hidden spells."

"Okay. Can you break the circles, please?"

I'd never seen him so subdued. There was no snark, no sarcastic quip, not even a smirk. I hesitated to use the word, but he looked... haunted.

I dropped the circles and he floated toward the steps. "I need to go out for a while and clear my head," he told me. "Is that okay?"

"Take as much time as you need. If something comes up, I'll summon you." I paused. "I'd break our binding and free you if I could."

He shook his head. "I don't want you to. If I have to be a bound ghost, I want to be bound to you. I need some space right now, that's all."

I didn't know what to say to make him feel better, so I just said, "Okay."

He vanished. My house wards tingled as he crossed them.

With a heavy heart, I cleaned up the runes I'd drawn in the circles, then slowly climbed the stairs, enduring stabbing pains in my back and knee with each step.

When I opened the basement door, I found Sean sitting on the couch. He took one look at my face and put his phone down. "What's wrong?"

"I found another of those spells in Malcolm." I pulled the door closed and headed for the stairs. "I got rid of it and he's clean of spells now, as far as I can tell. He needed some alone time after we finished, so he went out for a while."

Sean met me at the foot of the steps. "Let me make you breakfast. I've got everything ready. It'll only take a few minutes."

The thought of food made my stomach churn. "I'm really not hungry. I need to use a healing spell and then rest if I'm going to be able to do anything later today about tracking down that cuff."

I expected him to argue, but he didn't. He touched my hand and recoiled. "Why are you so cold?"

"Occupational hazard when working with ghosts." I headed up the stairs.

Sean followed me to my room and stood quietly while I changed into pajamas and a tank top. I washed my face, got my first aid box from the drawer in the bathroom, and returned to the bedroom.

Sean was sitting on the bed. "I have to use a blood magic healing spell," I told him, tracing runes on the lid of the box and opening it. "It's going to be painful."

"I know." His voice was gruff.

I selected a strong spell in a blue crystal, closed the box, and put it on my nightstand. "I'd rather you didn't watch."

"I'd rather you not go through it alone." He rose and moved to my side, taking the hand that didn't hold the spell crystal. "That's what this is about, you know: not having to face anything by yourself. I can ease your pain; I've done it before."

He'd used his alpha shifter magic to take away my pain on several occasions and had even been able to relieve my cravings for Black Fire after I'd been exposed to the drug.

"Don't make me stand by helplessly while you're hurting." He squeezed my hand. "It was damn near impossible when we first met after you'd been burned. Now I won't be able to bear it." The growl in his voice told me his wolf was close to his skin and very unhappy.

"All right." I climbed onto the bed as he moved to the other side and lay down facing me. "Don't touch me until I tell you the spell is done," I reminded him as we settled in.

"I remember the rules." He leaned over and kissed me. When he withdrew, his eyes were bright. "Do you trust me?"

"Yes."

A rush of golden shifter magic rolled through me, taking away the pain in my back, arms, and legs.

I lifted my tank top, pressed the crystal to my stomach, and invoked the spell. "*Helios.*"

Healing magic pulsed through my body. Instead of the agony I was used to, the pain was distant, muted by Sean's magic. I locked my eyes on his and lost myself in their glow. Sean's jaw tightened as the strong healing spell rolled through me in waves.

I lost track of time in the haze of magic. When the last of the pulses faded and the spell crystal was empty, I dropped it on the bed. I was dazed and shaking, but not nauseous or hurting except for a dull, distant ache.

Sean's shifter magic dissipated. He touched my face. "Alice?"

"Why didn't you tell me my pain became yours?" I asked, my voice tight.

He set his jaw. "I'm an alpha. It's part of my role. I take pain from a new wolf who's learning to shift, from a mother giving birth to a child, from a pack member who's grieving or injured."

My stomach knotted. "Every time you've done this for me, you've suffered? When you took away my cravings for Black Fire, they didn't just go away? You felt them instead?" The need had been so terrible, and he'd taken it. The thought of him suffering on my behalf made me feel sicker than any healing spell had ever done.

His eyes darkened. "Alice—"

I started to get up. I don't know why or where I intended to go, but he caught my arm and held on. "Stop, please. Don't run. Hear me out."

I pulled away but sat on the bed, my arms wrapped around my knees. "I'm listening."

He leaned against the headboard. "I don't feel the pain or the addiction as badly as you would, but that's not the point. Even if it was ten times worse, I would still do it. I do it for my pack because I am their alpha. For you, I do it because I can't bear to see you hurting." His eyes searched my face. "If that's not enough to convince you, I can tell you it would hurt me more to see your pain than to take it for myself. You are worth that much to me."

"You should have told me," I protested. It was surely the height of hypocrisy for me to fuss at him for holding things back from me, but I couldn't help it.

He didn't point out my double standard. "If I had, would you have let me do it?"

"Maybe," I hedged.

He shook his head. "I know you better than that. You'd have refused on principle and suffered. Or you would have given in to the cravings and found a Black Fire dealer." His face was grave. "I could tell you were close to the breaking point several times. You had no choice about being exposed to the drug and you would have had little choice about whether to use it again. I could save you from that, and whatever discomfort I felt was well worth it to know that I'd never have to see you trapped in addiction. What was a brief sick feeling for me might have been devastating to you. I didn't even have to think about it."

I rubbed my face with my hands. "I know I said thank you for helping me through that, but now I realize how woefully inadequate that was. I can't ever make it up to you."

"Stop." He took my hands. "You owe me *nothing*. Our relationship does not have a ledger of debts and credits. It never has and it never will."

When I said nothing, he let go of my hands and sat back. "You've been keeping track, haven't you? All this time, you've been counting up all the things I've done for you and you think you're in my debt."

I didn't have to admit it; he saw it in my face.

He looked like he'd been slapped. "Damn it, Alice, I don't care what kind of life you had before you came here, where no one gave you anything unless you earned it or offered you anything without getting something in return. That is not what love is. Love is taking care of each other and not keeping score. If you need me, I'm here. If I need you, you're here. That is what this is. *There are no ledgers.*"

"It's all I've ever known," I confessed.

"I know." He pulled me into his arms and pressed a kiss into my hair, then rested his cheek on my head. "There may come a time when I'll need you to be my strength. I know you'll be there when I need you because somehow, despite everything you've been through, or maybe because of it, you are a good and unselfish person. You put everyone else ahead of your own safety. I worry that you'll give too much of yourself again, like when you sacrificed yourself to destroy the *Kasten* or used the Black Fire overdose to take out Spencer Addison and his wards."

We sat quietly. Finally, he asked, "Can you bring up your cold fire in your hand?"

Puzzled at his request, I raised my right hand and spooled earth magic. Green flames appeared on my fingertips, then spread to engulf my whole hand. We watched the fire dance.

"Take our ledger and put it in the fire," he told me. "Burn it. No more keeping score."

I closed my eyes and envisioned the list of things Sean had done for me since the night we met at Hawthorne's. It was a long list. I hesitated.

"Burn it, Alice," he murmured, his lips against my ear. "Please."

In my head, I dropped the list into the fire and watched it turn to ash. I snuffed out the fire on my hand.

"No more ledgers, no more keeping score," he said. "No more owing. Take what you need when you need it and know that I am happy to give."

I looked up at him. "Take what I need?"

"Whenever you need it."

"And if I need something now?"

"Whenever you need it," he repeated.

I kissed him with all my pent-up desire and he made that growly sound I liked, the one that made me crazy. I pulled his tight black shirt out of his pants and he slid it off over his head, tossing it to the floor. My tank top followed a second later.

I straddled his lap and cupped his face with my hands. "How much do you like these pants?" he asked me, his voice half-growl.

I shrugged. "They're not my favorite."

He tore them off, leaving me naked. He toed off his shoes and unfastened his belt.

"How much do you like these pants?" I asked him.

"I thought you liked the way they looked," he said, his eyes twinkling.

"I did, very much, but right now they're in the way."

Fabric ripped and the pants were gone. As I'd suspected, he hadn't been wearing anything under them. I rose up on my knees and lowered myself slowly, teasing him until I couldn't stand it anymore and slid down. I cried out and he groaned, pulling me down until I was full of him.

He held me still and looked in my eyes. "I love the way you feel."

I kissed him deeply and rested my forehead on his. "I love how you know what I need, even before I do."

He released my waist and guided me with his hands on my hips. Though it had been nearly two weeks since we'd made love—an eternity for us—we moved slowly, enjoying every moment, every touch, every little bit of sensation.

When I started moving faster, he slipped a hand between us and stroked me softly. I gasped, my head falling back as his gentle movements became more earnest and deliberate. My legs began to shake and he pulled me close to carefully bite my shoulder.

When the wave of bliss broke over me, he held me against his chest as I shuddered. A tiny sound that was almost a sob escaped and he kissed me, his hand cupping the back of my head. He moved his lips along my jaw to my ear. "My beautiful Alice," he murmured.

He rolled us over so that he was above me and took control of our pace, his movements catching the last of my aftershocks and drawing them out until I trembled and gasped for air. He was tender and patient, exactly what I needed at this moment to feel whole again.

The healing spell had mended my cuts and bruises, but it was Sean who repaired my heart. I didn't know how to say that, so I tried to show him with my eyes how much that meant to me.

He leaned down and ran his nose along my hairline, drinking in my scent. "I'm yours, Alice. Never doubt it."

When we finally went over the edge together, I released my magic and it swirled around us in a gentle storm of green, white, black, red, and purple, with traces of golden shifter magic.

The release of energy helped me regenerate the magic I'd expended dealing with Vincent Barclay and helping Malcolm. Its return made Sean stronger and increased his alpha magic, which gave him more power to strengthen and lead his pack. It also brought a second wave of pleasure that we shared.

Beyond the practical benefits, Sean had confessed that he enjoyed seeing our magic blended together, and I'd realized I did as well. We watched the magic swirl around the bed, then held each other as it rolled back through us.

Afterward, I lay in his arms and listened to his heart. "I love the way you smell after sex," he told me, nuzzling my hair.

I smiled lazily and poked him in the side. "Because I smell like you?"

He nipped my earlobe lightly with his teeth. "Because you smell like *us*."

"What do I smell like normally?"

"Honey and vanilla and that body wash you use. And magic."

"What does magic smell like?"

He thought about that. "It's hard to describe. Sometimes it's like how the air smells when it rains. When you're angry, your blood magic smells like a high-voltage wire."

I nestled deeper into his arms. "You smell like a forest to me."

"I smell like a forest?" He sounded surprised.

"Like green leaves and shade and earth." I rolled over and he curled around me, pulling me close with his arm around my middle. "It's the most wonderful smell."

He kissed my shoulder. "A forest. I didn't know that."

"A forest in spring," I murmured, and fell asleep.

CHAPTER 13

THE MAN CALLING HIMSELF JOSEPH KENDALL HAD BEEN LIVING IN A 2,400-square-foot condo just north of downtown, in the trendy Castle View neighborhood. Apparently, being a con man and criminal mastermind paid fairly well.

At the moment, however, we were far from the condo and its posh uptown address. Instead, Sean and I were in his SUV, parked across the street from a seedy motel near the airport, watching the door to room 220. Light peeked through a gap in the curtains and the television was on, but we'd seen no hint of movement in the room since we arrived several hours earlier.

Phil texted me mid-afternoon to pass along a tip that Kendall/John Doe was staying here. A motel like this was a perfect place to lay low, but it seemed like such a step down from his Castle digs that I was skeptical. Still, we'd come to check it out.

Sean went into the motel office, showed John Doe's picture to the clerk, and traded cash for a room number and some information. According to the desk clerk, who spoke to Sean from behind bullet-proof glass, our shady mage had checked in as Tom Nelson last night and paid for three days in cash with the stipulation that housekeeping not enter his room. The clerk hadn't seen him since. Sean returned to the SUV, where I'd waited under the watchful eyes of Mobile Team Two.

As the hours passed and we saw no sign of anyone moving in the room, it became increasingly likely the room was empty. We'd debated whether Sean should walk past to see if he could get a glimpse through the gap in the curtain, but decided to wait until after dark.

In the meantime, I looked through the phone records Cyro had sent over earlier in the day. In addition to the raw records from the cell and landline phone companies, Cyro had provided a report identifying the numbers that had called and been called from John Doe's home, cell, and business lines. Sean loaned me a tablet so I could see the reports better than on my phone screen and highlight names and numbers of interest.

The report was a list of people who were probably clients and potential victims of John Doe's crime spree. I wasn't sure what good those names would do me, but I noted them anyway.

Since John Doe had been staying ahead of the law and anyone else who had been chasing him for so long, I had to assume he was meticulous and probably paranoid about leaving any kind of trail someone like me could follow. That meant burner phones, VPNs, and probably no paper trail, but a good investigator always did due diligence because even the best criminals made mistakes. I wasn't seeing any so far, though.

As I picked up my coffee and drank the last of it, I glanced at Mobile Team Two's SUV. "I hope Philip and Tom brought magazines or something. This might be a long, dull night if we decide to stick around for a while."

"I hope they *didn't*," Sean said. "They need to be vigilant. You're looking for signs of John Ice. They're watching for Stevens."

I propped my elbow on the door and rubbed my forehead. "This is driving me crazy."

"Do you feel self-conscious or guilty because all of these people are focused on protecting you?"

"Yes," I said reluctantly.

"You have to get over that. They're doing their job. It's what they love to do. Ask any of my people if they'd rather be doing anything else and they'll tell you no. Protecting an asset is way more interesting than most of the other work they do. I know you think they're over there bored out of their minds, but I can promise you they aren't. They're on alert, watching everyone and everything around us. This is a challenge for them. Most of them are adrenaline junkies. When I asked for volunteers for the mobile teams and told them what we were up against, I had three times more people wanting the gig than I had spots available. So relax; nobody's here because I forced them to be."

I stared at him. I hadn't really thought of it that way. I'd felt like I was imposing on Sean and his people from the moment he showed up on my doorstep. How had he known that?

He put his hand on my thigh. "I think there's some part of you that questions whether you're worth all this." At my look of surprise, he smiled. "I know a little bit about how you think."

"Thanks," I said softly. "That helps. But I'm never going to be comfortable being the center of attention." Not when my life depended on staying below the radar.

"I know." Sean rubbed my leg. His touch felt good. "I wish I could make this go away, but I can't. The best I can do is keep you safe while the vamps and the feds look for Stevens."

"I wonder where he is. I wish he'd go after Charles again. It might even be worth it for Charles to leave Niara's house and visit a couple of his businesses to try to draw him out."

"I suggested that to Bryan Smith," he said, surprising me. "He's pretty certain Stevens won't be able to evade the Hunters for much longer. If Stevens is smart, he won't fall for an obvious trap. Hell, if he's smart, he headed to another country after he missed Vaughan the other night."

"He won't run. He's still here. He wants Charles dead. He wants Julie Day dead. Maybe..." My voice trailed off.

Sean's hand froze on my thigh. "Don't even think about it."

"I could do it," I argued. "I could go back to the hotel where Julie was staying. With your people around, and the vamps and the Hunters—"

"No. You are not going to offer yourself as bait."

"You just suggested Charles do it."

"Vaughan is a vampire. He can heal virtually any injury. Stevens can't kill him unless he puts a stake in his heart or cuts off his head or drags him out into the sunlight. You...you, he can kill a hundred ways." His eyes shone gold. "You are *not* bait, Alice. They'll get him some other way."

"If I'm not bait, I'm going to be a sitting duck. I don't know how Stevens might figure out who I am, but if he does, wouldn't it be better to have him find me when we control the situation, instead of waiting to be surprised? I could go back to the hotel or Mike Robinson's house. We could arrange to have gaps in the security. He'll never be able to resist coming after me and the Hunters will get him."

Sean's eyes glowed gold. "No," he growled.

"You're not thinking like a professional right now," I accused him. "You're letting your feelings for me cloud your judgment. If I were a different client—"

"I don't care *who* you are. No client of mine is going to set themselves up as bait for a highly trained Marine."

"You're treating me like I'm a fragile flower who needs protecting," I protested. "I'm a high-level mage and a private investigator. My whole life I've been in danger in one way or another and I survived. Stevens is no more of a threat than John West or Spencer Addison or a dozen other people I've faced. Why is this any different from a month ago, when I posed as a prostitute to get myself kidnapped and taken to the harnad warehouse?"

Sean took a deep breath, exhaled, and gripped the steering wheel until his knuckles turned white. "Alice, you know I don't think you're any kind of fragile flower. I didn't try to talk you out of going into that warehouse or out of any other dangerous situation. I do try to protect you when I can, because it's important to me that you're as safe as you can be given your line of work and the kinds of threats you face. What's different about Stevens versus someone like John West is that Stevens's weapons aren't magic—they're grenades and high-powered rifles. I believed you could beat John West and you did. But when it comes to the kinds of weapons Stevens has, what can you do against someone who could shoot you from a hundred yards away?"

"He won't shoot me from a hundred yards away. If I'm any judge of character, Stevens will want to be up close and personal when he tries to take me out. He'll want me to see him coming. He could have taken out Charles and Bryan that night from a distance if he'd wanted, but he came right at them. It's personal for him. And if he's anywhere near me, I can take him out before he gets me. I have more weapons at my disposal than my fire whip."

"You may be right about him wanting to face you." He rubbed his chin and stared ahead through the windshield. "You asked what's different now. It's not just that Stevens is coming after you with rifles. My wolf thinks of you as his mate and he knows you're in danger. He wants to kill the person who is a threat to you, but that isn't an option right now and it's hard for him to understand that. I want Stevens dead too, or at least taken off the board. We're both angry and unhappy with the situation."

"And to top it off, you're at odds with Jack and Delia because of me."

He took my hand, a sign that he needed my touch to calm himself and his wolf. "You aren't the cause of the trouble; the disagreement over my 'ideal' mate predates you by a couple of years. Jack and some of the others have different ideas about what's best for me and the pack and that's what's causing the conflict. What he can't understand is that I believe—I *know*—you would be good for all of us."

My stomach knotted. I didn't agree that I would necessarily be good for Sean or the pack as Sean's mate. I'd always been a loner and as nice as Karen, Cole, Nan, and the others were, I couldn't imagine ever being comfortable as part of a pack. Besides, I had a murderous crime lord grandfather. I was a danger to them, not a benefit.

While I was thinking about that, Sean continued. "The other thing Jack doesn't understand is human dating and human relationships. Both he and Delia were born shifters. They've never been human. Their courtship took all of a couple of weeks. The concept of dating for months or years before committing to a bond is as alien to them as the idea of the mating bond is to you. But I was human before I was a werewolf, and even if my wolf thinks of you as his mate, I'm not wired to think that way. I still think like a human most of the time, and my human self knows we've only been dating a couple of months—not nearly long enough for either of us to be sure about anything long-term."

He lifted my hand and kissed my knuckles. "Do I think you and I might have that bond someday? Yeah, I do. But I'm in no hurry to get there."

"Thank you." I squeezed his hand. "I am sorry about your pack troubles, though."

"They'll have to get used to you," he said firmly. "They'll come around, or they'll learn to live with it."

We sat in comfortable silence for a few minutes. Finally, I made a decision. "Let's go take a look at that motel room. He's either not there or he's in there dead. Either way, I'm ready to find out."

"I agree." He picked up his radio. "Mobile Unit."

Tom's response was immediate. "Go for Mobile Unit."

"We're getting a look at the room. Going to earpiece for contact. Keep your eyes open."

"Ten-four."

Sean stuck his earpiece in his left ear, turned down the volume of the walkie-talkie, and clipped it to his belt in the back under his jacket. I put my phone in my back pocket and waited while he exited the SUV and came around to my side.

We crossed the street and the motel parking lot to the stairs. I heard music playing and the sounds of televisions as we climbed up to the second floor and made our way down the walkway toward room 220.

When we passed the window, I caught a glimpse of the small room. The bed was unmade, a towel tossed on top of the rumpled covers. Two suitcases and a duffel bag were piled in the corner. The room appeared to be empty.

Sean touched his earpiece. "Raven and I are checking out the room. Keep an eye on traffic." I assumed that meant listen in on the police scanner in case someone saw us and called the cops. That didn't seem likely in this part of town, but I didn't want to have to explain to anyone in uniform why we were breaking into the room, especially if there was a body in there.

He slipped a small black case from his inside jacket pocket. I took it and crouched to look at the lock. "I'll get the door. You keep watch."

As I went to work with his lock picking tools, Sean murmured, "I do love a woman of many talents."

"Which of my many talents do you like the most?"

He pondered that. "It's a tough call. It might be a tie between your precision with your fire whip and that thing you do with my—"

The lock clicked. "Hold that thought," I said. I handed him back the lock pick set and we slipped inside room 220.

Sean closed the curtains as I took a quick look around. "No bodies," I announced after I checked the tiny bathroom. "But I wish I'd thought to bring some gloves. I'm going to take a bath in hand sanitizer after we get done searching this place."

He reached into an inside jacket pocket and took out two pairs of black latex gloves. He held them aloft and raised his eyebrows.

I sidled over and pulled him down for a kiss. "You know what I find sexy?" I asked softly, my lips against his.

He rested his hand on my butt. "What do you find sexy?"

"A man who knows not to leave fingerprints." I took a pair of gloves from him and pulled them on.

As the latex snapped against my hand, Sean grinned. "I don't know how, but you make those gloves look hot."

I winked at him. "I think we need to explore your latex kink later when we're somewhere a little more sanitary. You want to search the bags while I do the room?"

"Let's do it."

We worked in silence for a while. I started with the bed, checking between the sheets, inside the pillowcases, and even under the stained mattress. *My kingdom for a hazmat suit*, I thought as I dropped the mattress back onto the sagging box spring. I looked under the bed using my flashlight, then moved on to check the small dresser.

Meanwhile, Sean was looking through John Doe's suitcases and duffel bag. He was extremely thorough, checking each garment and even the lining of the suitcases and bag. Ordinarily, I would have felt compelled to double-check. It was nice to work with someone whose skills I could trust.

When my search of the dresser came up empty, I searched Doe's toiletries, which were expensive. "How many moisturizers do you have?" I asked as I rummaged through the bottles on the counter.

"Uh, one, I think. Why? How many does he have?"

"Three, and one of them has gold flakes in it." I waved the bottle. "Maybe you should try it. It might make you sparkly."

"Werewolves do not *sparkle* under any circumstances," he informed me. "You finding anything?"

"Not a damn thing," I said grumpily. "You?"

"Nope. Well-made but generic clothes only. No paperwork of any kind and nothing that might give us a hint to his identity. No identification. No pictures, nothing of any sentimental value."

"I'm not giving up. There's something here; there has to be." I searched under the sink, behind the toilet, and even inside the toilet tank, finding nothing.

When I came back into the bedroom, Sean was standing by the door. "Ready to head out?"

"In a second. There's one more place I haven't checked." I went to the window A/C unit. "Got something I can use to pry the cover off?"

He produced a pocketknife. I carefully slid the blade into the casing of the A/C. The plastic cover popped off easily. I handed Sean the knife and took the cover off. There was a key taped to the inside of the A/C cover.

"I'll be damned," Sean said, impressed. "What made you think to look in here?"

"It's the sort of place I'd hide something in a room like this." I pulled the key free and studied it. "Looks like the key to a heavy-duty disc padlock. He could have a storage unit somewhere, if this is his key."

He leaned in to get a closer look at the A/C cover. "There's no dust or dirt on top of the tape. I'd say there's a good chance this is John Doe's key."

"Yeah, but where's the lock it goes to?" I scrutinized the inside of the A/C but couldn't see anything else inside it. "I think that's all there is. We should probably skedaddle."

I pocketed the key and put the cover back on the A/C as Sean alerted the mobile team that we were heading out. Once we got the all-clear from Tom, we left the room and locked the door on the way out. We took off our gloves and I stuck mine in my pocket in case I needed them again. I was hoping for at least one more B&E opportunity in the near future.

By the time we got back to the SUV, I had a plan for that. I knew from Cait's report that John Doe had been leasing an Infiniti while in the city. The car was still parked in front of the condo, but it might still be of use.

"I have a job for Cyro," I told Sean as he got in and shut his door.

"It's a long shot, but I'm sure John Doe's fancy car has a built-in navigation system."

He smiled. "And you're wondering if it could tell us if he's been visiting a self-storage facility?"

"Bingo."

"Let's find out." He took a burner phone from the center console and sent a text. "In the meantime, do we stay and watch the room or go home?"

I thought about it. "We should stay," I decided. "The towel on the bed was still damp, so he's been in the room recently."

"The only thing in that room worth going back for is the key," Sean pointed out. "The rest of it he could leave, but if that key goes to a storage unit, either he's going to need it or someone else is. Either way, it's your best lead unless something else turns up."

"Exactly. I hate to say it, but I think we have to stay."

Sean informed the mobile team that we were going to stay to watch the room. Tom had just radioed his acknowledgment when Sean's burner phone rang. He answered. "This is Sean."

I heard Cyro's familiar electronic voice on the other end. Sean explained what we needed, then held the phone out to me. "He'd like to speak to you."

I took the phone. "This is Alice."

"Hello, Alice," the electronic voice said. Keyboard keys clicked rapidly in the background. "I like this challenge. You bring me the most interesting projects."

"I do try."

"I'm intrigued by this man who calls himself Kendall. He's very good at covering his tracks and hiding his real identity—better than most people I run into. I might have to make identifying and finding him a personal project."

"He certainly has a lot to answer for."

"Oh, not because he's a thief," Cyro said. "I couldn't care less that he travels from city to city swindling rich people out of their junk. It's more about the challenge. I get bored."

"I can see that." I hesitated. "I don't know if it matters, but when I went to my client's home yesterday I discovered Kendall had been using a ghost trapped in a crystal as a power source. She'd been in there for years. It was his magic binding her to the crystal, so he's the one who put her in there."

A long pause. "Where is she now?" I could hear his anger even through the electronically modulated voice.

"She passed on and he won't be able to get her back."

"Thank you for that," Cyro said. "I'll bump this to top priority. You'll have the info from the car's navigation system as soon as I can get it. You're looking for a self-storage facility?"

"Thank you. Yes, we believe so. We have a key we think goes to a heavy-duty padlock. If you don't find a storage facility, I'll take the raw records. Maybe we can retrace his movements and figure out what the key goes to if it isn't storage."

"I'll see what I can do. Take care." The call ended.

I handed the phone back to Sean, who frowned. "What are you thinking about?" I asked.

He drummed his fingers on the steering wheel. "I've been talking to Cyro for almost five years. He's always been all business. He's never made small talk, revealed anything personal, or told me to 'take care.' And he's certainly never wanted to speak to anyone else when I ask about a project, even if it would be easier to get the information he needs directly from the client instead of relaying it through me. These conversations between you are completely different from any I've ever had and I'd like to know why."

"I'd like to know why too." I kept my tone light, but Sean's words were troubling.

I didn't need a hacker like Cyro sniffing around me. As secure as I felt that my identity was safely hidden, if anyone could uncover the truth—that I was not the real Alice Worth, or that I was Moses Murphy's granddaughter—it would be someone like Cyro. I was beginning to regret coming to his attention in any way. I did not want a talented hacker to find me interesting. I didn't want *anyone* to find me interesting.

Sean took my hand. "After this, we don't need to contact Cyro for anything anymore. We both have other resources we can call on. They might not be as good or as fast or as willing to break federal law as him, but they're a safer option. No case or client is worth endangering you."

For a moment, I didn't know what to say to that. Sean knew I had secrets. He'd figured out that I was probably hiding from someone and my life before I arrived in the city had been dangerous and violent. If I acknowledged that I needed to distance myself from Cyro, I was more or less confirming that I didn't want a hacker getting interested enough about me to dig into my past. I was so paranoid about revealing anything about my previous life that I didn't even want to confirm that I'd had one.

I should run.

The thought popped into my head out of nowhere. Just a few months ago, I'd felt reasonably secure in my new life. It had been lonely, but was as safe as I could be given the circumstances. Things changed quickly around the time I'd met Sean. Malcolm showed up, bound to me as a result of things I'd done while part of the cabal. Then Charles bit me and discovered I wasn't a mid-level mage. Federal agent Trent Lake figured out I wasn't really Alice Worth, and I worried Sean might be getting perilously close to coming to the same conclusion.

Now I'd come to the attention of a hacker who liked challenges and finding out people's real identities. If he figured out who I was, the best I could hope for was probably that I'd be blackmailed. At worst, he'd sell me out to Moses. And it wasn't even just my own life that might be in jeopardy—now it was Malcolm, Sean, and Sean's pack too. All those lives depended on Moses not finding me.

I didn't want to run. This mess with Kent Stevens aside, I liked my life as Alice Worth. I liked being a mage private investigator. I liked my home and the small group of people I called friends. I liked

Sean. I liked the idea of having a family in the form of a pack, even if it scared me too.

If I had to run, I had options. Alice Worth wasn't the only identity I had. There were others, sitting on digital shelves across the country and even in Europe. I could leave Alice behind and become one of a dozen women anywhere from Dallas to Dublin.

I thought of John Doe, who ran from city to city with nothing but a couple of suitcases. Would that be my fate? Was it delusional of me to think I could have anything more than that? To think that I *deserved* to have anything more? Wasn't it entirely selfish of me to put everyone around me in danger by staying?

"Alice, please stop." Sean's firm voice broke into my thoughts. "I can feel how dark it just got in your head. I think I know what you're thinking about." He squeezed my hand. "I'm going to say this, even if it pisses you off. If someone comes looking for you, they will have to go through me. I don't care if it's an ex-Marine with a grudge or an army. Don't run because you think it's the best option you have. You have a better one: staying here. Out there, you're alone and vulnerable. Here, you are not alone."

"I'd only run if I had to."

His eyes went golden. "I'm telling you that you don't have to."

"Aren't I the best judge of that?"

"Aren't I the best judge of whether I want to fight for you or not?" he countered. "I thought we settled this when we faced the demon Ravan together. You told me it was my decision to make. You trusted me to make that choice then. Unless something's changed, you should still trust me now."

"I do trust you to make that decision. That doesn't mean it's ever going to be easy for me to see you put yourself in danger."

"It's never going to be easy for me to let you go into harm's way either. I guess the only thing we can do about it is face threats together."

I wanted to punch the dashboard in frustration. "Why is this so stressful?"

He grinned. "Us caring about each other is causing you stress?"

"Yes!"

He laughed. Despite the lead ball of worry in my stomach, I had to smile.

I took off my jacket, wadded it up, and put it on the center console between us. I laid down across the jacket, resting my head on Sean's thigh, and shifted with a pained grunt as the stupid vest and cup holders dug into various parts of my anatomy.

"That can't be comfortable," he said, gently brushing my hair back from my face. "Why don't you climb in the back seat for a bit and lie down if you're tired?"

"I'm not tired," I lied. "It's not even midnight." I wiggled a bit until I found a position that was merely uncomfortable instead of painful. "Tell me a story."

He rested his hand on my hip. "I'd like to tell you the story of how I became the alpha of our pack."

"I'd like that."

A pause. "In order to explain how I became the alpha, I have to tell you how I became a werewolf."

I put my hand on top of his. "If you're ready to tell me, I'm ready to hear it."

He took a deep breath. "I was twenty-two. My friends Danny and Matt and I decided to go camping. We packed up and drove out to the middle of nowhere, then hiked for a half a day to find the right spot to camp. Nobody had cell phones back then, not that you'd be able to get a signal out there. We had compasses and balls and we figured that was all we needed. We wanted to prove how tough we were, I guess."

When he went quiet, I glanced up at him. Sean was staring into space, as if looking back through time. "The first couple of days were great," he said. "We sat around and bullshitted each other the way twenty-two-year-olds do, with all our big plans for the future. We fished for food and swam in ice-cold water and shared the couple of bottles of vodka that we brought."

Another pause. I waited.

"It happened on the third night. We were asleep when they found us. It was two werewolves—a mated pair who didn't belong to any pack. They were lurking on the edge of the Tomb Mountain Pack's territory, hunting. It was a full moon."

I grimaced. At any other time, werewolves could shift back and forth between their human and wolf forms at will. But on the full moon, they were forced to shift at the moon's rise and stay in wolf form until dawn. They were at their most feral and violent.

"I didn't even know what happened for a long time," he said finally. "I was asleep when we were attacked. All I remembered was teeth and claws and blood and hearing Danny and Matt screaming. They tore us apart. The next morning, I woke up. The others didn't."

I squeezed his hand.

"When I came to, the first thing I saw was Henry, the Tomb Mountain Pack alpha, standing over me. The sunlight was blinding. I could hear every rustle, every little sound. I didn't understand what was going on. Then I saw his eyes. They were gold. He told me to sleep, and I did."

"The next couple of days were basically a blur. I shifted to my wolf and back a half-dozen times without having much control over it. Henry or his beta, Seth, were always with me. Without them, I don't know what I would have done. When I was finally able to stay in human form and think clearly, Henry told me Danny and Matt were dead. Apparently only one of the werewolves who attacked us was capable of transmitting the virus. Whichever one it was bit me. The other one killed Danny and Matt. That's why I lived and they didn't."

His voice was heavy with sorrow. I entwined our fingers and waited for him to continue.

"The werewolves who attacked us got away. They must have realized what they did and left the region. A park ranger found Danny and Matt's bodies two days later and called in the feds. They looked for me for a week. In the meantime, I stayed with Henry until

I had enough control to go back. I went to the feds and told them what happened. They ran tests, determined I was newly turned and not responsible for my friends' deaths, and sent me on my way."

His hand tightened on mine until it hurt, but I stayed quiet. "I was so afraid to go home, afraid I wouldn't be able to control my shifting. I told my parents I was upset about Danny and Matt and I was going to take a road trip. I went back to the pack and stayed with them for six weeks. When I felt like I could control myself, I went back home."

"When did you finally tell your family?" I asked.

"Four months after the attack, when I hadn't shifted involuntarily in more than two months. They took the news pretty well, all things considered, except they were angry that I'd kept it from them for so long. I'm lucky. They accept me and they love me. A lot of werewolves get disowned by their families, or worse."

We sat quietly for a while, holding hands and lost in our own thoughts. I imagined Sean, young and afraid, a new werewolf who couldn't control his shifting, having to rely on complete strangers to help him adjust. "At least you had Henry and the pack," I said softly.

"Henry could tell my wolf was very dominant," he said. "He was old, and he knew someday soon he wouldn't be able to run the pack anymore. I'm not saying he helped me entirely for selfish reasons, but he knew what he was doing when he brought me into the pack. He told me later that he saw the potential for me to be the alpha someday, even in those first few days. If something happened to him, he needed to make sure Seth didn't become the alpha." His tone changed when he said Seth's name.

"What happened?"

"About ten years ago, Henry turned eighty. He was still strong and sharp and a good alpha, but Seth and a couple of the other younger males thought he was too old and weak. Seth ambushed Henry during a full moon and killed him. Technically it was his right to do so under shifter law, but most modern werewolf packs don't fight to the death to establish a new alpha. Simply defeating him would have been enough, but Seth wanted to make a point. He killed Henry, then dragged his body into the open so we could all see it. That was the sort of alpha Seth wanted to be. He liked to kill. He wanted to rule by fear, and he thought all the females in the pack should belong to him first, even before their spouses."

"And that's why Henry made sure you survived and joined his pack, so someday you could protect the others from Seth."

"And that's what I did. The same night Seth killed Henry, I fought Seth and I killed him." His fingers stroked mine. "Does that bother you?"

"Of course not." I squeezed his hand again. "It wouldn't have been enough just to beat him. Someone like that...they would never have accepted you as their alpha. He wouldn't have stopped trying to kill you." I looked up at him. "What made you want to tell me all this now?"

"I've been thinking about telling you for a while. After the conversations we've had tonight and given everything else that's going on, it seemed like the right time to put my cards on the table."

"I'm glad you told me." I wiggled until my head and neck were nestled comfortably against his leg. "Tell me about some of the people you've worked for. I bet you have all kinds of funny work stories."

Sean ran his fingers through my hair and told me about an investment banker who had three girlfriends who found out about each other when they showed up at his apartment at the same time. The catfight that ensued involved a lot of screaming and broken glassware.

I closed my eyes and laughed softly as he described how his employees tried to separate the women from the banker and each other.

"Three girlfriends at the same time? What an idiot," I murmured sleepily when he finished.

"I agree," Sean said. "You find the right woman, you only want the one."

"Mmmm. Tell me another story."

He described some of the misadventures his employees had while attempting to upgrade the surveillance cameras at Nyx, a vampire burlesque and sex club near downtown.

I dozed a bit as he talked, not wanting to sleep, but feeling secure with him watching over me. Eventually, not long after Team Three arrived at midnight, sleep stole me away.

CHAPTER 14

I napped until three thirty, then stayed awake to watch for John Doe.

We remained parked in front of the motel until just after dawn, but there was no sign of anyone trying to get into the room. At seven, with Team One getting ready to come on duty, I decided to call it off and we headed back to my house. Sean met briefly with his people, then joined me in bed for a few hours of sleep.

I was in the shower when Sean knocked on the bathroom door and stuck his head in. "Cyro just sent over the navigation records for John Doe's Infiniti."

I shut off the water and reached for a towel to wrap around my hair. "Tell me there's good news."

"What's that? I can't hear you through the shower curtain."

"Uh-huh. So much for werewolf hearing." I grabbed another towel off the rack and pulled the curtain back. He was leaning against the counter and grinning. I rolled my eyes and stepped out of the shower. "Can you hear me now?"

"Loud and clear." He kissed my forehead. "How are you feeling?"

"Better than you, I'm sure." Unlike me, Sean hadn't slept during the stakeout and we'd only napped a few hours at home. I sniffed the air. "Do I smell coffee?"

"There's a whole pot in the kitchen with your name on it."

"Awesome," I said fervently as I dried myself off. "What were you saying about the records from the car?"

"Cyro came through with the navigation data. It looks like John Doe regularly cleared his history in the car, but that data never really goes away. It's stored on a server somewhere."

I draped the towel over the rack and started dressing. "Well, don't keep me in suspense...where are we going?"

"A self-storage company on the west side. John Doe was last there two days ago. Cyro went ahead and got into the company's records and found out he's renting the unit under the name of Ted Nickerson."

"Tom Nelson, Ted Nickerson," I mused as I pulled my shirt on over my head. "Same initials. Might be a clue to his identity. Let me dry my hair and finish getting ready. We'll be able to roll out of here in about fifteen minutes if you'll pour that coffee into a travel mug for me."

Sean went back downstairs, humming "Eye of the Tiger" under his breath. I chuckled and reached for my hair dryer. It looked like I wasn't the only one excited about finding out what was in John Doe's storage unit.

Twenty minutes later, with Jack and Karen following us, Sean and I were on our way to the west side. I'd spent the extra five minutes consuming a breakfast burrito that he'd whipped up in the time it took me to dry my hair, put on makeup, and get downstairs.

"You're trying to fatten me up," I accused him as we drove. "I tasted butter in those eggs."

He gave me an innocent look. "How else are you supposed to make them?"

I sighed and guzzled coffee. "I don't have a werewolf's metabolism. If you keep feeding me like one of your pack, I won't be able to run after anyone if I have to."

"That was hardly a werewolf-sized meal. A werewolf would have eaten four of those burritos. Besides, you were hungry, and you ate every last bite."

"I was just being polite," I huffed.

He laughed. I put my hand on his leg and sipped my coffee.

Our destination turned out to be a medium-sized self-storage business that looked like it had been built in the late eighties.

"Interesting," I said as we pulled into the drive. "I was expecting something a lot more high-tech and secure for someone who runs a burglary ring."

"The high-end places have a lot more security and a lot more traffic," Sean pointed out. He pulled up to the gate, rolled down his window, and punched a four-digit code into the small keypad. The gate rolled open.

"You get that code from Cyro?"

He nodded. "Yes. When we're done here, I'll let him know and he'll erase the security cam footage of our visit."

"Great." I was still uneasy about Cyro, but I couldn't argue that having a master hacker on call was advantageous.

Sean drove through the gate and rolled slowly down the passageway between the long storage buildings. "We're looking for unit 303."

I looked around. "These look like buildings one and two. Building three is probably on the other side."

Behind us, Jack and Karen entered through the gate and followed us around the back. Building three was on the left. Unit 303 was third from the back.

Sean parked in front of the unit. Jack backed their vehicle against the fence so he and Karen had a clear line of sight down both passageways.

We got out of the SUV and went to the rolling door of the unit. Sean pulled the key from his pocket and reached for the padlock.

"Wait. There are wards." I placed my hand on the door and felt the wards pulsing against my skin. They were much more powerful and intricately made than the wards on Esther's house. "I need Malcolm's help."

"Has he been back since you took the other retrieval spell out of him yesterday?"

I shook my head. "No. I can still sense him, so he's okay. I guess he just needed some time alone. I'll see if he's ready to talk." I found the familiar blue-green trace in my mind that connected us and gave it two gentle tugs.

A few seconds later, I felt the telltale buzzing in the crystal on my bracelet as Malcolm jumped to me. I touched the crystal. "*Release.*"

Malcolm appeared beside me. He looked better than yesterday, and some of the sparkle was back in his eyes. "Hey, Alice. Heya, Sean." He glanced around. "What are we doing here?"

I explained how we'd ended up at the storage unit and why I'd paged him.

He floated over to the wards and studied them. "It's air magic, obviously. More complex than the other ones, but not anywhere near expert level." He frowned. "These other wards are, though."

"What other wards?"

"There are black wards inside the door. They're masked to you, but I can see them."

I pinched the bridge of my nose. "Black wards. Fantastic."

"They aren't that bad. I'm thinking he hired someone; they seem...generic."

I tapped my lip with my index finger. "Do the wards go around the perimeter of the unit?"

"No, only along the door. How big of a circle can you cast without drawing a line?"

"Why?"

"If you can control the flare, I'm pretty sure I can break the wards rather than spending hours unweaving them."

"I can tap a ley line to hold a circle big enough, but what if there are landmines?" I worried aloud, thinking about the hidden curses that had almost taken me out the last time I'd tried unweaving someone else's wards.

He shrugged. "Landmines don't seem to affect me much. They'd have to be specifically made to target ghosts, and I doubt these were. I can't imagine he'd be too concerned about a ghost getting into the storage unit."

"As soon as we break the wards, he'll know we're here, assuming he's still alive, that is."

"How dangerous is what you're about to do?" Sean asked.

"About a three for her," Malcolm told him. "Unless I'm wrong about those landmines, about a one for me. Relax, dude. This is a walk in the park for a couple of bad-ass mages like us."

I was glad to see Malcolm getting back to his old self after the scare with the retrieval spell and yesterday's unpleasant search for additional spells. I didn't like seeing him upset, especially if I was the cause of it, either directly or indirectly.

I gestured. "Sean, you need to stand over by the SUV." He moved to where I pointed. "Let me know when you're ready," I said to Malcolm.

He gave me a grin. If I didn't know any better, I'd have said he was having fun. "Ready."

The city was located at the intersection of two ley lines, which was one of the reasons I'd chosen to move here after leaving my grandfather's compound. As an earth mage, I could make better use of the lines than air, fire, or water mages. I rarely did, however, because it hurt like hell and because I hadn't really had the need to siphon that much power. It also had the potential to attract attention, but I wasn't planning on tapping the line for very long.

I closed my eyes and reached out to find the closest ley line. It felt like a high-voltage wire on the edge of my awareness. I breathed deeply, exhaled, and grabbed the line.

The sensation was pure power, like one of those cartoons where someone gets electrocuted and they light up like an incandescent bulb. My hair stuck straight out with the force of it. Every cell in my body seemed to vibrate. It didn't hurt yet, but it would.

I envisioned the bubble I wanted to create around the door of the storage unit and focused my magic and the ley line energy. With a heavy *pop* sound that only I could hear, the bubble formed. Pain sizzled along my skin, a familiar sensation.

Malcolm didn't need me to tell him when the circle was in place. Only seconds after I'd formed the bubble, he broke the air magic wards. The energy hit the barrier of my bubble. I gritted my teeth as it crackled and faded. *That wasn't so bad*, I thought.

Then Malcolm broke through the layers of blood wards. It was like the difference between a little Fourth of July popper and three bundles of dynamite going off one after the other: blam, *blam, BLAM*. On the third wave, the discharge of energy made me stagger and fall to my hands and knees. I set my jaw and didn't yell, but that *hurt*. I barely registered the gravel that bit into my palms through the pain of the wards bursting against my containment bubble.

Despite their power, the broken wards dissipated quickly. As soon as the energy faded, I released the ley line and dropped the circle.

I couldn't get up right away, not because of the pain, but because conducting that much power and focusing it left me disoriented. When I'd lived at my grandfather's compound I'd worked with ley lines regularly, but since I'd been in the city, this was only the second time I'd tapped into one. Using ley lines regularly or for very long got you noticed by local mages and harnads, and I had no desire to come to their attention.

I heard Sean telling Jack over the radio that I was fine. They'd apparently seen me go down and wondered what had happened.

Malcolm's cold hand touched my shoulder. *How long has it been since you used a ley line?*

I took a deep breath. *Too long. I need to practice more often.*

Yeah, you do. You don't want to be in a situation where you need to tap a line and you can't do it. He took his hand off my shoulder.

"I'm all right," I said out loud as Sean came to stand next to me. My voice sounded a little wispy, but my head was clear.

"So that was a three?" he asked mildly, offering me a hand.

"Actually, yes." I pulled myself to my feet and gave him a quick smile to show I was okay. "The wards packed a little more of a punch than I expected, but the circle held without any trouble and now we can get into the unit."

"Without getting fried," Malcolm added.

"Thank you for helping us with the wards," Sean said. "You good?"

"Yeah, I'm good. Sorry I needed some space."

"Don't apologize," I told the ghost. "You can take some 'me' time whenever you need to. You mind sticking around? I'm not sure what we're going to find in there."

"Yeah, no problem. I got no place to be." Malcolm grinned at me and I smiled back.

Sean and I pulled on another pair of black latex gloves. He used the key we'd found to unlock the padlock. "Let's get in here and see what's what." He took the radio from his belt. "Going to check out the unit. Keep an eye out for visitors."

"Ten-four," Jack said briskly.

Sean raised the door halfway and we slipped inside. He found the light switch by the door and flipped it before rolling the door back down to hide us from anyone passing by.

The unit was about ten feet by ten feet and nearly full. Boxes of various sizes, all marked with runes, filled three tall metal shelves. A half-dozen large paintings wrapped in paper were stacked against the wall.

"This is the tidiest storage unit I've ever seen," Sean said, surveying the room. "Malcolm, do you sense any more wards?"

"Not from here, but you guys stay where you are and I'll do a more thorough search."

We waited by the door while Malcolm floated around, checking every inch of the storage unit. Finally, he came back to us. "No more wards I can sense," he reported. "Most of the boxes are spelled, but they should be pretty easy to unweave. Some of the boxes have containment spells, though, which means whatever is in them could go kaboom if we're not careful."

I pursed my lips. "Well, I don't want to open any of those boxes. There's no telling what's in them and I have no desire to blow up the building."

"So what's the plan?" Sean asked.

"See if we can find the cuff, I guess," I said. "Then we have a choice of whether to just leave things where they are and let the situation sort itself out, or tip off SPEMA about a cache of magical objects and let them look for John Doe."

"You could sell them to Charles," Malcolm said, half-jokingly.

I shook my head. "I'm not getting into the stolen magical objects trade. There are others hunting for these items and not all of them play nice. All I'm taking out of here is the cuff if we can find it."

"It's probably not in one of the containment boxes, so I'll start unweaving the spells on the other ones," Malcolm said. "Some of them have blood ward locks, so I'll start with those since it's safer for me to unweave them than you."

We went to work as Sean watched. While Malcolm focused on unweaving blood ward locks, I looked through the boxes that just had simple masking spells designed to hide the magic trace of their contents.

In the third box I opened, I found a bracelet that matched the lust-spell necklace Dora Quinn had shown me at Walsh & Quinn.

"That wench is selling all kinds of stolen goods," I fumed, showing Sean the bracelet. "I'm starting to think half the stuff in that shop was obtained in the same way she got Esther's hand mirror."

"Maybe we should drop a dime to SPEMA about the shop," Sean said.

"Maybe we should." I closed the box and put it back on the shelf before opening the next one.

Not all of the boxes housed magical objects; some contained

antiques and jewelry. I checked to see if any of it belonged to Esther. If I managed to recover any of her missing jewelry, maybe she'd bump up that bonus. To my disappointment, none of it matched the photos of Esther's stolen pieces.

The pieces in the boxes with the blood ward locks were more expensive magical items. The boxes with containment spells had me worried; some of them might pack a wallop and I had no way of knowing what was in them. By the time I finished looking in all the boxes on the first and second shelving units, I'd decided we had to tip SPEMA off about this stash before those items fell into the wrong hands.

I was beginning to think we were going to come up empty in our search for Esther's cuff when I opened a medium-sized box and whooped. "Got it!"

"Excellent." Sean joined me and examined the cuff. It was about four inches wide and made of what looked like hammered brass. The edges were lined with runes, the fire magic spellwork that gave its wearer the extra zip that Esther and her husband had apparently enjoyed.

Sean's thoughts must have mirrored my own. "Maybe we should take this for a test drive before you give it back to your client," he said with a wink.

"You don't need any help in the virility department," I told him, patting his butt affectionately. "If you had any more sex drive, it might literally kill me. I can barely keep up with you as it is."

"Oh my God, you two. Get a room," Malcolm complained. He'd stopped unweaving blood ward locks when I found the cuff and was now floating by the door.

"I plan to." Sean grinned. "Alice and I are going to have a lot to celebrate once she gets this stuff back to her client. I can't believe Aldridge was willing to pay five or six grand for this thing. It sure doesn't look like much, does it?" He reached for the cuff.

It happened faster than any of us could react. As soon as Sean's fingers got near the cuff, it flipped and closed around his right forearm with a flare of magic.

He snarled and tried to pull the cuff off with his other hand, but it had closed completely around his wrist without even leaving a visible seam.

Magic pulsed from the cuff and each wave was stronger than the last. Sean staggered and grabbed the shelving unit for support as he went down. The shelf fell over, sending boxes crashing to the floor.

Whatever the cuff was doing to Sean, it sure as hell had nothing to do with his libido. He was on his hands and knees, his muscles straining as if he was fighting something. When I heard joints popping, I realized he was trying not to shift. It had to be agonizing.

"Alice, get this thing off me," he growled.

"Hold still," I told him. My earth magic spiraled out of my hand and formed a short, thin whip. I lashed the cuff with the power and precision of someone who'd been practicing that skill her entire life.

The cuff should have split instantly. Instead, a backlash of magic traveled up my whip and punched me in the chest so hard that my heart stuttered. The blast knocked the wind out of me and sent me crashing to my knees.

As I went down, Malcolm zipped to Sean and tried to unweave the spells on the cuff. The moment he made contact with the spells, a powerful flare of magic disrupted his form.

"No," I gasped as he fractured before my eyes. I'd never seen magic affect a ghost that way. "Malcolm!"

He vanished. Fear gripped me until I recognized the tingle of magic as the spell he used to jump back to one of the crystals in my basement. He would be protected there and hopefully regenerate and heal whatever damage the cuff had done to him.

"Get...Jack," Sean ground out, his eyes bright gold. His voice was more than half growl.

As I reached for the radio on his belt, the rolling door was yanked up so quickly that I heard metal bending.

Jack appeared in the doorway, framed by sunlight. He must have sensed trouble through the pack bonds. He slammed the door back down and crouched at Sean's side. "What happened?"

"The cuff—" I began.

"I wasn't asking you," Jack snarled.

He grabbed the cuff with both hands, attempting to tear it apart, but was knocked back by a burst of magic. The damn thing was warded against magic *and* physical force. What the hell *was* that thing?

Sean was growling now, his eyes golden as he fought to stay human. "Lead...the...pack," he ordered Jack. "Protect...Alice. Even... from me."

"I will," Jack said. "Shift now before resisting it kills you."

Sean looked at me, his eyes almost full wolf. There was no fear in them, only anger and pain. I wanted to take the pain from him, but I couldn't and it was breaking my heart.

"I will get the cuff off you," I promised him.

He held his human form for one more second, and then he shifted with the sound of bones popping and a pulse of golden magic.

Sean's wolf was enormous, black and silver with golden eyes. I'd hoped that when he shifted the cuff would fall off, but instead it appeared to have changed sizes so that now it fit snugly on the wolf's front leg.

My thoughts raced. Clearly, the cuff was much more than a libido-enhancing accessory. Perhaps that was its effect when worn by a human, but its effect on a shifter was dramatic.

"Sean?" I asked tentatively.

The wolf lowered his head and growled softly, his eyes on me. Sean had told me that though the wolf was in the driver's seat when he was in wolf form, he was aware of everything that was going on and could speak to the wolf.

Jack turned on me, his eyes bright. "What the fuck is that thing on his leg?"

The wolf snarled at him and snapped his teeth. He moved

between Jack and me and growled warningly at his beta. The message was clear: back off.

Jack's demeanor instantly changed. His posture became less aggressive and the glow in his eyes diminished. "I'm not going to attack her," he said calmly. "I'm just trying to figure out what happened."

The wolf seemed to not understand what Jack was saying. He bared his teeth, his ears back as if preparing to attack.

"Sean, everything is okay," I said, trying to make my voice soothing. "Can you hear me? We're going to help you."

The wolf stood his ground, watching Jack closely and growling. I started to move around to his side, thinking if he could see my eyes and body language I might be able to communicate better.

The wolf turned his head and snapped his teeth at me. I froze.

In the blink of an eye, Jack pulled out a gun and shot the wolf.

The dart hit the wolf in the neck. He whipped his head around and snarled at Jack, who held his ground as the wolf tried to leap. Instead, his legs went out from under him and he fell.

Stunned, I asked, "Why did you have that gun?"

Jack stuck the gun back in the holster at the small of his back. "It was for Caleb," he said shortly.

I went to the wolf on my hands and knees. His eyes were half-closed but he managed to look at me. I saw pain, worry, and anger.

I ran my fingers through the wolf's fur and lowered my forehead to his. "I will get that cuff off you," I told him again. "Just hang on."

The wolf let out a tiny, almost imperceptible whine. Then his eyes closed and he went limp.

I laid my head against his side and listened to the steady, slow beating of his heart. He was so warm. I wanted to cry. I wanted to tear something or someone apart. But mostly I wanted to find out what the hell this cuff was and how to get it off him.

Jack pulled his radio from his belt. "Mobile Unit, back our vehicle up to the door and open the back."

"Ten-four," Karen replied, her voice strained. I wondered if everyone in the pack could sense what had happened to Sean.

I raised my head. "What are you doing?"

"Taking my alpha somewhere safe, somewhere far away from you."

I was on my feet before I realized I'd moved. My magic surged and the ground trembled beneath us. "The hell you are."

His fury was so intense that it scoured my skin like a sandstorm. "That tranquilizer won't last more than an hour or two, and you have no way of caging a werewolf."

"I have to get that cuff off of him," I argued.

"We'll get the cuff off. If you're too stupid and weak to do it, we'll find a mage who can."

My rage went ice-cold. "I am neither stupid nor weak. I just need time. That cuff is heavily warded, but every spell has counter-spells. Every ward can be broken, eventually."

Tires crunched outside as Karen backed their SUV up to the rolling door. A door slammed and footsteps approached.

"We'll find someone who can remove the cuff. It's no longer of any concern to you." Jack crouched and picked up the wolf's unconscious body. "Open the door," he called to Karen.

As she rolled the door up, I said, "That's not your decision to make, Jack. Sean and I are a couple whether you like it or not, and his well-being is of great concern to me, as mine is to him."

"Which is why you're still in one piece," Jack snapped. "Now move out of the way."

"What happened?" Karen asked, her eyes wide and horrified as she watched Jack carry Sean to the open back of the SUV.

"I'll explain later," Jack told her, placing the wolf carefully into the cargo area. "You drive the other vehicle and follow me."

Karen froze. "And leave Alice here alone?"

"I'll send personnel from Maclin Security to come get her. She can wait here." Jack shut the back of the SUV.

Karen hesitated, looking at me helplessly.

"Get his phone and radio. We need to go *now*," Jack ordered.

"It's okay," I told Karen. "Go. I'll be all right."

As she bent to pick up Sean's things, Jack snarled at me. "Don't give her permission to obey an order. She's pack."

"I wasn't giving her permission; I was reassuring her. There's a difference." I approached the open door where Jack was waiting for Karen. "When I figure out how to remove that cuff, I will come for him. Don't get in my way."

Karen seemed to shrink as Jack loomed over me. "Are you threatening me?"

The last time Jack and I had squared off, at Karen's house, Sean had advised me to avoid looking his beta in the eye. It had felt wrong then and it felt wrong now. My gut told me facing him was the only way to show Jack he had no authority over me and never would.

I met his gaze and didn't back down. "I'm making it clear where we stand. Take it however you want."

We stared at each other. His hands curled into fists and he made a low growl. Shifter magic rose.

I pushed my blood magic through my fingertips, forming razor-like claws. I kept my hand at my side, but he saw the blades.

Someday, Jack and I might have to settle our differences, but today was not that day. Sean was more important. As much as it rankled me to do so, I took a step back to show that I didn't want to fight. "Take him somewhere safe."

Jack turned on his heel and left with Karen behind him. She sent me an apologetic look just before Jack reached up and pulled the door down. He slammed it closed, leaving me alone in the semi-darkness.

Moments later, an engine started and the SUVs drove away.

CHAPTER 15

THERE WAS SO MUCH I NEEDED TO DO. I HAD TO GET HOME TO CHECK ON Malcolm. I needed to figure out what the hell the cuff was and how to get it off Sean. Then I'd have to deal with Jack, assuming Sean didn't kill him outright for leaving me high and dry.

First, in the privacy of John Doe's storage unit, I sat down on a cardboard box, put my head in my hands, and gave myself exactly sixty seconds to break down.

In the space of just a few minutes, the ground had been yanked out from under my feet. Malcolm was hurt. Sean was possibly stuck in wolf form as the cuff did God-knew-what to him.

The wolf's final whine echoed in my ears. I doubted I'd ever forget that sound. I'd only heard it once before: when the demon Ravan broke his ribs while they were fighting in my backyard. Hearing Sean in pain did something to me that I'd never felt before. It made me furious beyond what I would have thought possible. I supposed that was a taste of what Sean felt when he saw me hurt or in danger. I rubbed my face with my hands.

My phone buzzed. I dug it out of my pocket. The caller ID read *C Rose Calling*. I didn't recognize the name or number.

Frowning, I answered. "Alice Worth."

"This is Cyro." The electronic voice was tense. "What is your status?"

Sean had told me a while back that Cyro's full pseudonym was Cyanide Rose. That explained the caller ID, though not why he was calling me now.

When I didn't respond immediately, he spoke again, more urgently. "Ms. Worth? Are you all right?"

"I'm fine," I said. "Why are you calling me?"

"I saw what looked like trouble and the Maclin Security SUVs left without you. What's going on?"

I blinked. "Were you watching the security cameras?"

"Yes, obviously." Cyro sounded irritated. "Why is Maclin in wolf form and unconscious, and why did his beta leave you there alone and unprotected?"

"There was a medical emergency and they had to leave." I didn't want Cyro involved any more than he already was. "I have someone coming to pick me up."

"Ms. Worth—"

"I need to make some calls, Cyro," I told him. "Once I'm gone, please erase the security footage of us being here. I'm going to tip the feds off about what we found in the storage unit and I don't want anyone to know we were here."

"Consider it done," he said briskly. "Do you want me to send an anonymous tip to SPEMA instead so it can't be traced back to you? No charge."

I couldn't think of a downside to accepting. "Okay. I appreciate it."

"I'll keep an eye on the cameras until you're safely away."

"Thank you."

"Goodbye." Cyro disconnected.

I scrolled through my contacts and made a call. The phone rang once. "Miss Alice," Bryan rumbled.

I took a deep breath. "I need your help."

ABOUT THIRTY MINUTES LATER, tires crunched in the gravel outside the storage unit. My phone buzzed with a text message. *Bryan: Your ride has arrived.*

I texted back an acknowledgment and opened the rolling door. A black Vampire Court SUV was backed up to the storage unit, its engine running. I rolled the door closed, locked the padlock, and went around to the passenger door. I opened it and blinked in surprise.

"Hop in," Arkady Woodall said. She was wearing a black jacket over a black shirt, black jeans, and tall black boots. Her blonde hair was back in a ponytail. The butt of a gun peeked out from under her left arm and I saw another in a holster on her right ankle.

"Sorry. I was expecting Adri." I climbed into the passenger seat, put the box that had held the cuff on the floor at my feet, and dropped my messenger bag next to it. My door shut with a heavy sound. The Court had sent me an armored vehicle with bulletproof glass. Fancy.

She headed for the main gate. "I asked to come instead. Seatbelt."

I buckled in. "Bryan told you why I needed a ride?"

"Yes. He let Maclin Security know the Court is taking over your personal safety until further notice."

She slowed as she approached the gate. A second Court SUV waited on the street. Like ours, its windows were darkly tinted. I could only make out two hulking shadows in the front seats. The gate rolled aside slowly.

I glanced up at the security camera mounted above us. Somewhere, Cyro was watching and hopefully ready to erase the footage of our visit as soon as we were out of sight.

As we drove through the gate, she asked, "Where to?"

"My house, please." My worry about Malcolm gnawed at me. Our link felt thin in a way it never had before and I feared for him. I needed to know how he was doing before I could do anything else.

Arkady turned left out of the drive and accelerated. The backup SUV fell in behind us as we headed east across the city.

"Catch me up on your case," she said. "How did we end up here?"

I gave her an abbreviated version of what had happened since I was hired to recover the three magic objects. I left out the identity of my client and didn't mention Malcolm.

As she listened, her eyes swept our surroundings as Sean's did when he drove. I felt hollow without him next to me.

"What happens if you figure out how to get that cuff off and Jack Hastings tries to block access to Sean?" Arkady asked.

"I would hope he wouldn't, for the simple fact that his alpha's well-being should be more important to him than his objection to me. But if he does interfere, I'll have to go through him."

She glanced at me. "I'm your security against Kent Stevens, but I won't be able to help you with Hastings if it comes down to that. As an employee of the Court, I can't interfere in a pack disagreement."

I'd figured as much. Interfering with pack business was a quick way for the Vampire Court to get sideways with the Were Ruling Council. "I don't need your help against Jack Hastings."

She smiled. "You don't really think you need my help with Stevens either, but you need a ride home because you're not sure if you can trust Maclin Security or anyone else from the pack without Sean in charge. I get it. If I were in your shoes, I'd be pissed about the whole thing too. That's part of the reason I asked for this gig."

"What's the other reason?"

"Curiosity." She slowed to make a turn. "Mr. Vaughan mentioned that he offered you a chance to be a Court investigator but you turned it down."

I was somewhat surprised Charles had revealed that fact to her. "Did he say why I turned it down?"

"He said you preferred to run your own company and remain an independent associate of the Court. I assume there's more to the story than that, since I've never known vampires to care very much about what a human prefers."

In fact, he'd attempted to blackmail me into accepting, forcing me to turn the tables and do some blackmail of my own. Naturally, I didn't reveal that to Arkady.

When I didn't comment, she added, "I also found it rather interesting that after Stevens almost took him out, Mr. Vaughan's first priority after saving Bryan Smith's life was to come to your home to check on your welfare, in direct violation of Valas's orders."

"He disobeyed Valas to come to my house?" Hoo boy. I could only imagine how tongues wagged about that back at Vamp Court headquarters. This was not good news. I didn't need anyone associated with the Court wondering too much about the exact nature of my relationship with Charles, or asking questions about why he'd allowed me to turn down his job offer.

"Valas ordered him to either come to Northbourne or go to Niara's home. Instead, he jumped into the vehicle with Matthias and me and headed straight for you without even waiting for additional backup. And you answered the door in sheep pajamas." Her eyes twinkled.

I crossed my arms. "I apologize for nothing. I love those pajamas."

"I have a pair with cats sleeping on clouds. If you tell anybody that, I will shoot you."

We exchanged a smile.

"So you were curious enough about me to take babysitting duty." I dug in my bag until I found my bottle of water. "I'm not that interesting, honestly."

"I'm also hoping Stevens shows up so I can shoot him in his kneecaps," she said conversationally. "I liked Fortune."

I took a deep breath and exhaled. I'd buried my grief over Fortune's death by keeping busy, but her words brought it back full force. "He was a good guy."

"We were sleeping together." Her voice was flat, unemotional. I recognized that tone; I'd used it often enough myself when I didn't want others to know I was hurting.

I stuck the water bottle back in my bag. "I didn't know that. I'm sorry, Arkady."

She gripped the steering wheel and stared straight ahead. "I'm okay. I'll be better when Stevens is dead."

I remembered the night Fortune died and Bryan was shot, when Charles had brought Arkady to my house. She had been entirely professional, hiding her pain from all of us while we dealt with the aftermath of Kent Stevens's attack and the logistics of arranging protection for Charles and me.

I was no longer ambivalent about wanting Stevens to find me. Between Arkady's guns and my magic, I liked our chances versus the former Marine. Sean hadn't wanted me to use myself as bait, but something told me my new bodyguard might not object quite as strenuously to the idea.

First things first, though: check on Malcolm and try to figure out how to get the cuff off Sean. Then we'd see about arranging some payback.

WHEN WE GOT to my house, Arkady escorted me to my front door. I dropped the house wards briefly to grant her passage. Once we were safe inside, I gave her clearance through the wards, figuring my bodyguard needed to be able to get in and out freely without getting fried.

Once we were inside, Sean's absence was like a punch in my gut. Everywhere I looked, I saw signs of his presence in my life, from the coffee mugs on the kitchen counter to the dishes in the sink and his clothes in the laundry room.

"Make yourself at home," I told Arkady as I headed for the basement door. "I have to do some work downstairs. If you need me, call or text. Don't try to come through the wards."

"Got it. I'm going to make some coffee, if that's all right."

My chest hurt. I forced myself not to think about how Sean usually made coffee for us. "Help yourself. There's some whole beans in the cabinet above the coffeemaker. The grinder is on the counter. Mugs are to the right of the sink."

I left Arkady upstairs, closing the basement door behind me.

When he needed to jump to the safety of my basement, Malcolm ended up in a medium-sized blue crystal I kept on the work table. Unlike the crystal I'd kept him in after the blood mage's failed attempt to recall him, he could release himself from the crystal in the basement. My worry grew when I realized he hadn't this time.

When I picked it up, the crystal buzzed against my skin. Malcolm was still inside it. The buzzing felt thready, though. Something was terribly wrong.

I closed my fist around the crystal, shut my eyes, and carefully funneled energy into it. I sensed a tug on the flow of power, as if Malcolm was trying to draw more energy from me. He'd always said that being in the crystal was like being asleep, but he still had some level of awareness. He might be drawing on my energy out of instinct rather than consciously. Either way, if he needed more, he could have it.

I funneled energy into the crystal until I wasn't sure how much more it could contain. My connection to Malcolm was stronger, but something was still off.

For better or worse, I had to know what kind of shape he was in. I took a deep breath, exhaled, and spoke. "*Release*."

Malcolm appeared beside me. He was jumbled, like a puzzle still in pieces in its box. Slowly, as if it took a lot of effort, he reformed in human shape, but maybe half as opaque as normal and with hollow eyes.

"Are you all right?" I asked, my heart in my throat.

"I feel thin, like I'm not all here," he said, his voice faint. "Where's Sean?"

"I couldn't get the cuff off him. It forced him to shift and he became aggressive. Jack darted him and took him somewhere."

"Alice, I'm so sorry." He floated back and forth slowly, as if trying to figure out how to move. "What should we do?"

"I'm going to figure out what that cuff is and how to get it off of him. What happened to you?"

"I tried to unweave the spells on the cuff and hit wards I've never felt before. The cuff was warded against ghosts or anyone who tried to interfere with the spellwork. I felt myself disintegrating." He went quiet. "I thought I was a goner. When I jumped here, I didn't know if I'd make it to the crystal or if I'd go poof and wake up somewhere else. Then, when I got here, I didn't start regenerating like I normally do, and even with all the energy you gave me, I'm still not whole."

His vulnerability and powerlessness made my heart ache. "We'll figure out how to get you back to one hundred percent. What can you tell me about the magic on the cuff?"

"I didn't recognize it."

I frowned. "You mean you didn't recognize the spellwork?"

He shook his head. "No, I mean I didn't recognize the *magic*. The fire magic spellwork was easy to see and feel. What zapped me, and what made the cuff latch itself onto Sean, is some kind of magic I've never encountered before. It felt ancient. It wasn't fire magic, or air, or earth, or water, or even blood magic."

I recalled something Charles had said to me after the auction: *Not all objects of power use the same kind of magic.* I hadn't sensed the magic in the Tepes stone, but it had power; I'd seen it with my own eyes when Charles used it to drain the vamp on the side of the road. I hadn't sensed anything but fire magic on the cuff, but it clearly had much more than that in it. My studies in magic were extensive, but I'd encountered two new forms of magic in as many days and I needed to know more about both.

At this point, I'd take any clues I could get. "What color was the magic?"

He thought about it. "Brown? No, not brown. More like copper."

Copper-colored magic? I'd never heard of such a thing. I didn't know of any magic that was any shade of brown, but if Malcolm said it was copper-colored, that's what it was.

Maybe the clue wasn't the brown, but its variant shade. "So, it was a kind of dark golden brown?"

He nodded slowly. "You could say that. What are you thinking?"

"Shifter magic is golden. You said the magic felt ancient. What if it's some kind of ancient shifter magic?"

Despite his depleted condition, Malcolm's eyes lit up. "Maybe it was some kind of old shifter magical object and someone added the fire magic spellwork later?"

"That's what I'm leaning toward at this point. It makes sense. The cuff didn't react to me, so the spells must only activate when in the presence of a shifter." I rubbed my forehead.

"Do you think Esther Aldridge knew the cuff was a shifter relic?"

I thought about it, then shook my head. "I don't think she did. I didn't sense any trace of shifter magic in her safe, which means that aspect of the cuff hadn't been used while it was in her possession. She probably thought of it only in terms of what it did for her husband and never suspected it was anything more than that. Yet another good reason for non-mages to leave magic objects the hell alone."

"The thing I don't understand is what the damn thing is supposed to do. What's the benefit of forcing a shifter to go furry and making him more aggressive?"

"Not all magical objects are designed to be beneficial." I headed for my bookcases. "It could be punishment, or it could have been designed to harm the wearer outright. Or it might just have a mind of its own and do whatever it wants. If we're right and it's ancient magic, there's no telling what it's designed to do, or what it might be doing to him."

"Do you want me to try to check on Sean?" he asked. "I have enough juice to get to him. I could keep an eye on him and let you know if there are any...developments."

My heart hurt. I wanted to know that Sean was all right. My only other option was to call someone in the pack for updates, like Karen or Nan, but that might put them crossways with Jack. Despite what I'd declared to Jack about Sean and I being a couple, I had no formal claim on him, no authority to ask a member of the pack to go against the acting alpha.

"Please check on him for me," I said finally. "Be careful and don't let them sense you."

He floated over to me. "You'll figure this out, Alice. You'll get that cuff off him and then you'll deal with Jack. You and Sean are the real thing. You can't let some stupid bracelet and a jerk beta mess up the second-best thing you've got going for you."

"What's the first-best thing I have going for me?" I asked, not quite sniffling.

He grinned. "Me, of course."

I couldn't help but smile at that. With a wink, he disappeared.

When he was gone, I went to work pulling books from the shelves and stacking them on the table. I grabbed anything on shifter magic or forms of ancient magic. I didn't have much. When I finished looking through my library, I had only ten books in the pile, and I wasn't sure any of them would have information that would be helpful to me. At times like this I sorely missed my library back at my grandfather's cabal, which had been enormous. No doubt I could have found what I needed there. I sat down at the table and started skimming.

An hour later, I set the tenth book aside and sighed. As I'd feared, nothing in my library had anything helpful in the way of information about ancient shifter magic. I was also curious about the magic of the Tepes stone, but that had to go to the back burner for now.

I pushed my chair back, stretched, and headed for the steps. I'd almost forgotten I had a houseguest.

When I emerged from the basement, I found Arkady sitting on the couch. The TV was on, tuned to a news channel and muted.

She put down her phone as I closed the door. "Any luck?"

I didn't tell her about Malcolm; the fewer people who knew about my ghost sidekick, the better. I shook my head. "I have a theory about what the cuff might be, but I'm having a hard time finding any information that might be helpful."

"You could call Kim Dade, the Vampire Court researcher, and see if she has any ideas," she suggested. "I'm not sure what she's working on right now, but I know you two are good friends."

On the surface that sounded like a good idea, but I was reluctant to reveal too many details about the situation to the Court. Information was a valuable commodity, as Charles liked to remind me. There were other packs in the area, and any one of them might be interested in knowing the alpha of the Tomb Mountain Pack was temporarily out of commission. If that news got out, one of the other packs might try to make a move, and though Jack was no pushover, a beta—even a strong one—was not an alpha.

On the other hand, I could ask Kim about ancient shifter magical objects in general and see what resources she could point me toward.

"Not a bad idea," I said finally. I sent her a text asking her to call me when she had a moment.

My phone rang as I was in the kitchen pouring myself a cup of coffee. "Hey, Alice," Kim greeted me. "How are you holding up with all this mess with Kent Stevens?"

I added milk and sugar to my coffee and stirred it. "I'm hanging in there. I've got plenty of security keeping an eye on me. Arkady Woodall is over here now."

"Stevens better hope the Hunters catch him before she does," she said ominously. "What can I do for you?"

"This might be outside your area of expertise, but I'm needing to find some information about shifter magical objects, possibly of ancient origin. What are my best resources for that?"

"The Court has a pretty extensive library, of course. Do you know what you're looking for? I could run a search."

"I'm not exactly sure yet," I hedged. "I don't suppose I could access the library and do some searching?"

"Unfortunately, not without clearance," Kim said, sounding regretful. "Is it Court business? You could ask Juliet LaRoche or Ezekiel Monroe for authorization if so." LaRoche and Monroe were the daytime representatives of Niara and Valas, respectively.

"It's actually personal. If I can't get into the Court library, what's the next-best thing?"

"Have you tried the MOP website?"

I frowned. "Really? The last time I used that, it was a mess. There was more false information on it than real."

"It used to be a dumpster fire, but about a year ago a group of mages took it over and became full-time administrators. They cleaned it up, took down the fake stuff, and started moderating posts. It's actually a pretty good resource now. You have to register to use it, but it's worth it for you, in my opinion."

"That's an idea. I'll check it out."

"Let me know if you find what you're looking for and I might be able to dig something up in our library. In the meantime, stay safe."

"You too. Thanks, Kim."

We said our goodbyes and disconnected. I topped off my coffee and took it into the living room.

As I settled onto the other end of the couch with my laptop, Arkady asked, "Was she able to help?"

"She suggested I look in the MOP database." I opened the laptop and searched for the website.

"I'm assuming that has nothing to do with actual mops."

I smiled. "It stands for Magic and Objects of Power. It's basically an online database resource for mages and researchers to find information. It used to be about as helpful and trustworthy as the walls of a public bathroom, but Kim says they've cleaned it up and it's reliable now, so I'm going to give it a try."

When I found the website, it looked nothing like what I remembered. Instead of disorganized pages full of links to error-filled articles written by anyone with access to the internet, I found a very authoritative site with public pages offering helpful information to non-mages and a registration system for mages wanting access to the database.

I opted for a premium membership, which allowed me full access to the site. I was still skeptical, but I figured I could cancel my membership if the site didn't live up to expectations.

Once I was logged in, I was amazed at the amount of information and how well it was organized. The site was hosted by a foundation with a board of directors who were all credentialed mages. Many articles were written by authors affiliated with the site, while others were written by members of the public and then fact-checked by employees of the foundation. The forums were moderated, and I saw quite a few discussion threads where the questions and comments seemed insightful and accurate.

As a test, I searched for a cup like the one that had granted Charles an hour in daylight and found an entry that described a cup very like the one I'd recovered for Esther. The photo was of a different cup, but the description of the spellwork was consistent with what I knew.

To my surprise, a recent update to the article noted that one such cup had just sold at auction for more than sixty thousand dollars, though that was considered anomalous and nearly five times the expected price. The database's sources were clearly up-to-date on recent transactions in the world of magical objects, since that sale had taken place less than forty-eight hours before. I was impressed.

A second search led me to a section of the site devoted to mirrors. Mirrors had countless uses in magic, from divination to spirit communication. Some could be used as portals between realms, offering passage at a price to the demon realm, fae realm, or the in-between places. Wall and floor-length mirrors were most often used in magic, but hand mirrors were no less powerful because of their size.

After some reading, I found an entry on hand mirrors spelled to reveal hidden memories. I'd set the possible memory the mirror had shown me aside to think about later, half-convinced the mirror had invented it from bits and pieces in my head. According to the database, the spellwork was real and a double-edged sword capable of uncovering repressed and traumatic memories. The article's author included a heartfelt warning about using such mirrors. Reading between the lines, I wondered if she had found out the hard way that some memories were better off left buried. If my own recovered memory was true, I would have a lot to think about once this mess with the cuff was resolved.

Having verified that the database was in fact a much-improved and useful resource, I began my search for information about ancient shifter magic and magical objects. Shifter magic was as complex and varied as my own, and some objects dated back hundreds or even thousands of years. These objects varied in strength, purpose, and application, and ranged from stone teeth to obelisks and everything in between.

I had a better understanding of shifter magic than the average mage, but only as much as I'd needed to do spellwork, such as wards within my grandfather's cabal compound that blocked shifters from gaining access to certain areas. I understood how magic allowed shifters to change from human form to furry form and back again, and how the pack bonds allowed shifters to sense each other and draw strength from their alpha. Having spent time around Sean, I had a better understanding of how an alpha's magic differed from members of the pack, and how he could draw power from the pack if needed. Shifter physiology included abilities like faster healing and enhanced senses, but the magic of the shift itself was powerful enough to heal injuries, even potentially fatal ones.

When it came to shifter magic objects, however, I knew next to nothing. No human magic could create them and they could not be used by anyone who was not a shifter. Human magic could hide them or contain their power, but that was the extent to which a non-shifter could interact with them. As such, I had never studied them and found myself engrossed in reading basic shifter magic theory in order to understand the source of their power and the mechanics of their spellwork. I hadn't done this sort of research in a very long time, but it didn't take long to remember how much I enjoyed it. Learning about magic was more than a hobby or a job; it was part of who I was.

I took a break after a while to refill my coffee cup and to let Rogue into the backyard so he could potty and run off some of his seemingly boundless energy.

As I closed the back door, Arkady looked up from her phone. "So, do you mind if I ask what's up with your garden back there? I went out on the back porch earlier when I let the dog in and if I didn't know better, I'd say the plants leaned in my direction like they were sizing me up."

I stretched, putting my coffee cup on the floor so I could bend over and touch my toes. My back popped. "It's kind of a long story, but the short version is that the plants are magical and probably hungry, so you should keep a safe distance."

Her eyebrows went up, but she seemed to take that bit of news in stride. "What do you feed hungry plants? I'm guessing not normal plant food."

"They seem to be carnivorous, so I'm thinking I might have to run by a butcher shop and pick something up."

"There are a couple of shops in town that deliver. You can order on their website and they'll bring you what you need."

I hadn't thought of that. "Good point." I didn't have a good sense yet of how much I might need or how often I'd need to feed the garden, but I could start with a small whole hog, the kind you'd buy if you were going to have a barbecue, and go from there.

I found the website of a local carnicería and put in an order, then returned to reading about shifter magic.

My search for cuffs with shifter magic turned up a surprisingly high number of hits. It appeared that cuffs were a common type of magical object for shifters, which made sense. The cuff that had latched onto Sean's arm had changed size when he shifted.

The question was: what type of spellwork was on the cuff? If the magic had been natural human magic, I could have explored it as I had the spellwork on the cup and probably determined its purpose. But between those heavy-duty wards and my unfamiliarity with shifter magic, I was at something of a loss.

My best option at the moment seemed to be reading through the entries on magical cuffs on the MOP website. If that didn't pan out, I'd be forced to decide whether to ask Charles for authorization to search the Court library. No doubt he would find out what had happened at the storage unit as soon as he woke at sunset.

Most of the entries in the database had pictures or drawings of the cuffs. That was enormously helpful, but I didn't go by the images alone. The appearance of the cuff might have been altered along the way, so I read through each article, looking for hints as to what this particular cuff might be. It felt like I was looking for a needle in a pile of needles.

By late afternoon, my eyes were bleary and I hadn't found any answers. I was just getting up to refill my coffee cup when I sensed Malcolm cross the wards as he jumped to his crystal downstairs.

I put my cup on the counter and headed for the basement door. "I need to go downstairs for a few minutes."

"Okay." Arkady was watching the news and snacking on some chips she'd found in the pantry.

When I got downstairs, I found Malcolm floating by the work table. He was still distressingly weak, so much so that I felt guilty for asking him to go check on Sean. Normally when I was near the ghost, his aura buzzed on my skin and the blue-green thread that connected us hummed with energy. Since the run-in with the wards on the cuff, our connection had felt almost completely diminished, and even standing two feet away, I couldn't sense his energy at all.

Judging by his expression, the news was grim. "How is he?" I asked.

Malcolm didn't even try to sugar-coat his response. "Not good. They've got him at Jack and Delia's house, in a cage they apparently keep on hand for when they've got a wolf who's gone mad. As soon as the tranquilizer wore off, he went berserk and Jack had to dose him again. Not to knock him out, but enough to make him too tired to hurt himself trying to get out of the cage."

"Why is he being so violent? Is it the cuff?"

"Everyone thinks so. The wolf almost took a chunk out of Jack's arm when he got too close to the cage. I think he knows Jack was responsible for carting him off and leaving you unprotected. If—*when* Sean shifts back to human, he's gonna have Jack's ass for that."

"I was hoping that since you were gone so long, no news was good news." I sat on the work table, my legs dangling.

Malcolm shook his head. "Jack called a pack meeting. That's why I was gone all afternoon; I wanted to stay until the end and see what was decided. It got pretty ugly."

I could only imagine. "Let's hear it."

"Everyone's upset and angry about Sean's condition and Jack blamed you for everything. He basically said that either you knew what the cuff would do and let Sean get trapped on purpose, or that you were incompetent. Either way, he's got some of them believing you're the worst thing that's ever happened to Sean. He brought up how Sean ended up in Vamp Court custody after he got in a fight with Charles and blamed you for that too. Some of the pack seem to agree."

"What about Karen, Nan, and Felicia?"

"They don't believe you did it on purpose, and Nan told Jack he was wrong to have separated Sean from you. Ben said so too."

"Ben said that?" I was surprised. I'd only met Ben once, at Esther's house, and I certainly hadn't expected to hear him speak up on my behalf.

"Yep, he came to your defense pretty strongly. He seems to be third in the pack hierarchy, just below Jack, so his voice carries weight. He reminded Jack and the rest of the pack that Sean had stated his feelings about you quite clearly and it wasn't their place to interfere with the alpha's courtship of a potential mate. He also reminded Jack that Sean told him to protect you and that he left you stranded in the storage unit without so much as a sharp stick. The others didn't take kindly to that. Criticizing you is one thing, but Jack basically disobeyed a direct order from Sean. Jack tried to say he had no choice, but the others didn't buy it. Even the ones who don't seem to think you'd be a good mate didn't think Jack should have gone against Sean's directive. It reflects poorly not just on the pack, but on Maclin Security as well."

That was something, at least. "So where did it end up?"

"Jack's determined to find out what the cuff is and how to get it off. He's made some calls to experts and the Were Ruling Council. In the meantime, he's decreed that you're not allowed any contact with Sean. The others argued that letting you visit him might calm him down, but Jack's word is law until Sean is better and he wasn't budging an inch on that."

"They can't keep Sean drugged the whole time," I protested.

"Ben pointed that out. Jack said they'll have the cuff off before it becomes an issue." He floated over to me. "Here's what's really got me worried, Alice. Once the pack meeting broke up, Jack and Delia were talking about what's going to happen once Sean shifts back. Delia asked what Jack will do if Sean still wants you as his mate. Jack said, and I quote, 'Then we'll have to deal with her some other way.'"

I took a deep breath and exhaled. "In a weird way, I'm kind of relieved to hear that. Before, I wasn't sure exactly where we stood. Now I know. It's always better to know for sure who your enemies are. If Jack comes for me, I'll be waiting."

"You want me to go back there and keep an eye on things?"

"I'm worried about you. I don't know what those wards did to you, but you're down in power by at least half and you aren't regenerating like you should. You're vulnerable right now until we figure out how to undo the damage. As glad as I am to know how Sean is doing and how the pack meeting went, it was selfish and dangerous of me to ask you to leave the safety of the house and go out there."

"Well, the good news is that I can pretty much jump between Sean and here now, so that limits my exposure. None of the shifters seemed to sense my presence, so my masking and obfuscation spells seem to be holding up well. I *am* running on about half power. Other than siphoning power from you, the fastest way I know to regenerate is in a crystal."

I held out my arm. "Take what you need."

He shook his head. "Without Sean here, you can't regenerate magical energy like you normally could."

I gave him a look.

He sighed. "Alice, sex regenerates magical energy; everyone knows that. I'm not trying to embarrass you by bringing it up, but I'm not going to siphon energy from you and risk leaving you vulnerable right now with everything that's going on."

"Fine. If you want to regenerate in the crystal, I can at least speed up the process." I gestured at the circles inlaid in the floor.

He nodded slowly. "A power circle? That would work. Good thinking, Alice."

"I have my moments." I picked up Malcolm's crystal and held it out. "Hop in. When you feel like you're back to full strength, you can jump out and break the circle."

"Thanks." Malcolm hesitated. "Everything is going to be all right. Just don't go up against Jack without me, okay?"

"I'll try not to," I promised.

Malcolm vanished. The crystal buzzed faintly in my palm.

I put the crystal in the center of the smallest circle on the floor, grabbed a piece of chalk, and went to work drawing runes. When the spellwork was complete, it formed a web with the crystal at the nexus. I placed my palm on the circle and fed energy into the web until every line and rune pulsed with power. The energy formed a loop, feeding power into Malcolm's crystal and hopefully speeding up his regeneration.

I got to my feet and took a moment to just breathe. The news about Sean and the pack was bad, but not as bad as I'd feared. Jack could be as angry as he wanted, but I wasn't going to be intimidated. It had never been my nature to back down and I wasn't going to start now. Sean was worth fighting for.

Jack might think he knew what he was up against by picking a fight with me, but he had no idea what I was capable of, or what I would be willing to do to hold onto one of the few chances at happiness I had ever had.

CHAPTER 16

WHEN I GOT BACK UPSTAIRS, I FOUND ARKADY IN THE KITCHEN. "So, I couldn't help but notice that you seemed to be talking to someone downstairs," she said as I got a glass and filled it from the sink.

I'd wanted to keep Malcolm under wraps, but unless I wanted to claim I was having a conversation with voices in my head, I didn't have much choice but to acknowledge that there had been someone else in the basement.

"I was getting a report from a ghost," I said.

"As one does," she said dryly. "Is he keeping an eye on Sean for you?"

She put two and two together faster than about anybody I'd ever known. "Yes."

"How are things going?"

I drained the water and set the glass in the sink. "Not well. Speaking of which, I should get back to my research."

She glanced out the window. The sun was beginning to set. "You'll probably be getting a call soon."

Somewhere in or below Niara's home, Charles would be waking soon, if he hadn't already. "I figured as much. When's your shift change, by the way? I just want to get a sense of how this is going to work."

She smiled. "There is no shift change, Alice. I'm with you twenty-four seven until this situation is resolved. The team out in the SUV will switch off every six to eight hours, depending, but you and I are best buddies until Kent Stevens is on ice."

"I had a thought about that," I said.

We headed back to the living room and settled on the couch. She muted the television and looked at me expectantly. "What's on your mind?"

"What are your thoughts on trying to draw Stevens out?"

She tilted her head. "My orders are to keep you out of harm's way and leave the search to others." After a pause, she added, "However, with the hunt for Stevens dragging into its fourth day, there might be some flexibility there. If nothing else, your case might take us near some of the locations Stevens could be watching, like Mr. Vaughan's new wine and cocktail bar, where his temporary offices are located while Hawthorne's is being rebuilt."

"That wasn't a spontaneous suggestion, was it?"

"Not entirely, no. I wasn't going to bring it up, but I thought you might suggest something along those lines. I'm kind of surprised you didn't before now."

"I did bring it up, actually, but my previous bodyguard vetoed the idea."

She nodded slowly. "I can see that. An alpha werewolf wouldn't like the idea of his girlfriend using herself as bait. In that case, maybe we should hold off and let the Hunters find him."

"Sean's not here," I pointed out. "And I'm the one who makes decisions about what I do and don't do. I guess I *am* wondering why Charles isn't willing to do it."

"Oh, he *is* willing, very much so," Arkady assured me. "But Valas has forbidden him to go near any of his properties. He hasn't left Niara's house since Fortune was killed, except to attend the auction with you the other night. Valas wasn't very happy about that either, especially given what happened afterward."

"Charles was hardly to blame for that," I protested. "That creepy Seattle vamp attacked *us* trying to steal the item Charles bought at the auction."

"And you as well, from what I understand. Well done dealing with him, by the way. It's another reason I like the idea of stopping by the wine bar and seeing if Stevens is hanging around. I get the impression you're a force to be reckoned with. If you can take out a vampire, you can deal with Stevens, especially if I'm there too. The Hunters can have him when we're done."

The more I thought about it, the more I liked her plan. As much as it had bothered me to be under guard these last few days, what had frustrated me more was that we had been doing nothing to take Stevens out. The Court had dispatched Hunters and other resources to find him, but sitting on my hands while someone else acted had never been my style. I did feel some guilt about doing this against Sean's wishes, but if we could eliminate Stevens that would be one less problem for Sean to deal with. It looked like Sean was going to have his hands full with Jack as it was without also worrying about whether Stevens was still out there gunning for me.

"How about this," I said. "Let me keep researching for about another hour or so. That will give you time to think about our strategy and contact whoever you need to coordinate with about baiting a trap tonight at the bar. When the pieces are in place, we'll head out."

She grinned. "I like how you don't even hesitate once you've made up your mind. I'll start making some calls. One thing: the bar has a dress code. I'm assuming you've got something appropriate to wear?"

"I have a couple of options. What about you?"

"I'll have someone bring me what I need." She cracked her knuckles and reached for her phone. "Let's do it."

While Arkady went to the kitchen to make phone calls, I got back to the database and its entries on magical cuffs. I noticed that a number of the articles were by the same person, an Ella Potter from Portland. She seemed to have quite a bit of knowledge about shifter magic, particularly spelled arm cuffs. If I couldn't find what I needed in the database, I might be able to contact her for information. Her webpage invited inquiries by e-mail.

My phone rang about a half-hour into my reading. I took a deep breath and answered it. "Hello, Charles."

"I should never have left your safety in the hands of the wolves." His voice was as cold as I had ever heard him be. He wasn't just angry; he was livid.

I found myself trying to defuse the situation. "It was my decision to hire Maclin Security, and it was the right one. Sean and his employees provided excellent security up until this afternoon. It was also my decision to ask Bryan to send someone from the Court to take over this afternoon instead of waiting for a replacement team from Maclin Security. I'm grateful to the Court for responding so quickly. I'm not going to defend what Jack did because he went against Sean's orders and he'll have to answer for that to both the pack and his employers."

"Mr. Hastings's actions constitute a breach of contract." His tone was icy. "I have instructed one of my attorneys to proceed with legal action on the matter."

I sighed. "Charles—"

"Alice, *this is not acceptable!*" he thundered.

I stared at the phone in shock. I'd only heard Charles raise his voice one other time in the entire five years I had known him, and that incident occurred on the first night we met, when he thought I'd killed a Court mage without warning or provocation.

He lowered his voice, but his fury was still evident. "The Court placed an enormously valuable asset in the hands of a contractor and you were left unarmed, without so much as a vehicle with which to transport yourself to a safe location. Other companies who work for the Court must understand that such a violation of trust will not be tolerated."

"I'm never unarmed, Charles," I reminded him. "I have magic. The storage facility was a pretty secure location, all things considered. I was less vulnerable there than almost anywhere else. I'm not telling you not to be angry, because I'm angry too, but don't assume I was defenseless and left out in the open, because I wasn't."

Silence.

"Arkady is here with me now," I said when he didn't reply. "There's an SUV full of Bryan-sized enforcers parked outside. I'm safe."

"A condition which you must find irksome, as I understand you wish to use yourself as bait for Kent Stevens." He was still angry, but his tone was dry.

"I'm tired of hiding, Charles. I'm a mage, Arkady's got two really big guns, and we have the full force of the Court as backup. I want this over with. I want him to come at me and I want Arkady to have the chance to put bullets in both of his kneecaps."

His tone hardened. "As much as I endorse Ms. Woodall's desire to do so, I would have refused her request for the operation, which is why she asked Valas instead."

I smiled to myself. Crafty Arkady. "The sooner we nail this bastard, the sooner we can all get back to our normal lives, including you."

"If you are harmed in any way, I will hold Ms. Woodall responsible."

That got my hackles up. "Don't be ridiculous. It was my idea. The only person responsible for my safety is me."

"Ms. Woodall cleared this plan with Valas last night," Charles informed me.

That changed nothing, as far as I was concerned. All it proved was that Arkady had been planning a way to get to Stevens, probably since the moment she found out Fortune was dead. I would have done the same.

"She didn't bring it up; I did this afternoon. I've been wanting to do something to draw him out but Sean wouldn't go for it."

"How very annoying to find myself agreeing with the wolf."

I paused. "You haven't asked about Sean's condition, so you must know what happened."

"I understand the cuff attached itself to his arm and forced him to shift. He was taken to a place of safety, where his condition has deteriorated to the point that he must be sedated to prevent him from harming himself or others."

I wasn't surprised he knew the details; the Court had eyes and ears all over the place. I did, however, take exception to the cold way he said it, as if it hadn't turned my life upside down. "Then there's nothing more you and I need to talk about."

"Alice." Charles's voice stopped me before I could end the call. "There is no love between the wolf and I, as you well know. But I would not have you suffer, and I know his condition weighs heavily upon you. What assistance can I offer?"

"What would you want in return for your assistance?"

His response was exactly what I expected. "The answer would depend on what was required."

I sighed. "What would it cost to give me access to the Vamp Court library so I can try to find out what this cuff is and how to remove it?"

"That is not a simple request. A great deal of the information we possess is considered confidential and our resources are designated for Court business only. However, the welfare of an alpha like Maclin is of interest to the Court because the stability of local packs benefits us as well. As such, I believe that as a gesture of goodwill it would be possible to assign one of our researchers to the task."

I closed my eyes. A Court researcher was more than I could have hoped for. I might have an answer in minutes or hours instead of days.

Charles's next words, however, brought me crashing back down to earth. "If we do this research on behalf of the shifters, we will have to share our findings with Maclin's pack as well. It cannot be given to you alone."

My heart sank. "So if you find out what the cuff is, you'll have to call Jack?"

A pause. "We would pass the information to the Were Ruling Council, who would no doubt pass it on to Mr. Hastings, as he is currently acting as the head of the Tomb Mountain Pack."

I read between the lines and recognized an opportunity for negotiation. "How much of a head start can you give me with the info before you contact the Council?"

I heard the smile in Charles's voice when he replied. "Perhaps a few hours. Communication between the Court and the Council is a delicate matter that must be handled carefully. It will take some time to compose the document and have it reviewed by the necessary personnel."

"Do it," I said. "Please."

"I will see if Ms. Dade is available, since you have worked with her before. Would you prefer to be alerted as soon as she has discovered something?"

"Yes, anytime day or night." I took a deep breath. A little of the weight lifted off my chest. "Thank you, Charles."

"I would prefer to be with you during this operation tonight," he said quietly. "You are not merely an asset of the Court to me, nor is your safety purely a matter of protecting a resource. Others may look at you as such, but I do not. Some may consider it a higher priority to apprehend Stevens than to ensure your safety. I do not believe Ms. Woodall is one of the latter, or I would send Adri Smith in her place. Even so, be cautious."

I'd been thinking about that in the back of my mind since I'd first proposed using myself as bait to Arkady. The Court wanted Stevens. They wanted to protect me too because I was useful to them, but if it came down to it there were undoubtedly some who would throw me under the bus if it meant getting Stevens. Like Charles, I didn't think

Arkady would be among them, despite the fact Stevens had killed Fortune.

I might have even wondered about Adri and Bryan if it came down to it. Arkady worked for the Court; Adri and Bryan *belonged* to the Court. I hadn't known Arkady long, but I was usually pretty good about reading people. You got good at that sort of thing when you were a prisoner of an organized crime syndicate and surrounded by enemies. My instincts told me Arkady wanted Stevens's hide, but not at the expense of mine.

"Thanks for the warning," I said finally. "Wish me luck."

"I do not believe in luck, only in planning and strength. I wish you success and a safe return."

"Good night."

We disconnected. Arkady appeared in the kitchen doorway. "What was the warning about?" she asked.

I put my laptop aside and stood. "There's a chance some of our backup tonight might want Stevens in custody more than they want me to come out unscathed."

She snorted. "As I'm sure you'd already guessed. Good thing I've got your back."

"And I've got yours. If he does show up, he'll never know what hit him."

My perimeter wards tingled, signaling a visitor's arrival. "Are we expecting someone?" I asked.

She didn't ask how I knew. "That's my change of clothes. We're due at the bar by nine-thirty, so we'd better get moving."

I frowned. "It's not even seven yet. How long will it take you to get ready?"

Arkady headed for the front door just as footsteps crossed the porch and someone knocked loudly. "Oh, honey, you have no idea."

UP UNTIL TWO NIGHTS AGO, I had wondered how Charles's newest wine and cocktail bar had gotten its name. Thanks to our walk in the sun and the story he'd told me, now I knew: it was the year he'd become a vampire.

Our SUV pulled up in front of 1792 at precisely nine thirty. Our driver was a Court enforcer named Kirwin. I'd met him not long after I moved to the city and saw him occasionally at Northbourne. Our other escort was Matthias, who'd accompanied Charles and Arkady to my house the night Fortune was killed—and who, unless I was very much mistaken, had a bit of a crush on Arkady. I hadn't noticed it that night, but I caught him making googly eyes at her at least twice during our drive from my house to the bar.

Matthias opened the rear door and gallantly offered his hand to help Arkady out of the back. She was wearing an emerald green pantsuit with heels, her hair back in a loose twist. The matching jacket covered her shoulder holster and the long pants hid her ankle holster. She had the skills of a professional makeup artist and put them to good use on both of us. She looked absolutely gorgeous, like a Norse goddess.

I'd resigned myself to wearing something that would hide my vest, but Arkady had surprised me with a form-fitting and very feminine vest shaped like a corset. She assured me it would stop rifle rounds. It was no more comfortable than the one Sean had given me, but at least I didn't look like I was wearing a vest. I quickly made up my mind to try to keep it when this was over.

Though his eyes were on Arkady, Matthias helped me out of the SUV. I wore a short purple dress with over-the-knee boots. Like Arkady, I'd styled my hair up. I wore diamond earrings and a charm bracelet with Malcolm's crystal on it, but the ghost was still in his crystal in my basement, regenerating slowly. The crystal would allow him to jump to me, or for me to stash him in it, should trouble arise.

Matthias stayed with us as Kirwin drove away to park nearby. Well-dressed couples came and went through the front door of the club. We waited outside for a few seconds to make sure Stevens saw me, if he was watching.

I felt exposed on the sidewalk with tall buildings on all sides, offering Stevens an almost infinite selection of sniper nests. But as I'd told Sean, I doubted Stevens would try to take me out from a distance. He'd want me to see his face. I felt no itchiness between my shoulder blades, however. That wasn't a surefire way of knowing whether we were being watched, but I was willing to bet Stevens wasn't here, not right now. I couldn't help but be disappointed, but the night was only just getting started.

At Arkady's nod, Matthias opened the door to the club and ushered us inside. 1792 reminded me immediately of Hawthorne's: dark wood, subdued lighting, and private booths along the walls with tables in the middle of the floor.

The bar had the well-deserved reputation of serving the finest martinis in the city and its wine list was second to none. A pianist provided quiet music from a nook near the front windows. The men wore jackets, the women evening wear. The bar certainly catered to a much different clientele than Hawthorne's, where I had been comfortable wearing jeans and a T-shirt and hanging out for an hour or two nursing a Scotch or beers. I doubted I'd be returning here anytime soon unless it was for business.

We approached the host with Matthias behind us. Arkady unleashed a smile that could only be described as her third-most-lethal weapon, possibly her second. The host looked positively gobs-macked and couldn't take his eyes off her.

"We have a table reserved under the name of Vaughan," she told him. "Party of two."

It took him several seconds to process her words and realize who we were. His eyes widened. "Yes, of course. This way, please."

He led us to one of the best tables in the club, a corner booth with an excellent view of the entire room. It had no clear line of sight to the front window, eliminating the threat of a sniper shot through the glass. Once we sat, I realized the lighting ensured we could see the room while we remained in shadow. The booth also had dark red velvet curtains that could be drawn for additional privacy. Very nice. Being guests of the owner certainly had its perks.

The host had only taken two steps away from our booth when a tuxedo-clad young man appeared and presented us with menus. "Ms. Woodall, Ms. Worth, welcome to 1792. My name is Anthony. What may we serve you tonight?"

I scanned my menu. There were several pages of martinis that were specialties of the house, and then the wine list. I'd never been much of a wine drinker, and I wouldn't know a good martini if it walked up and introduced itself.

I glanced at Arkady over the top of my menu. Her expression mirrored mine.

Our dismay must have been obvious. Before either of us could speak, our server gestured at another young man standing off to the side holding a tray with two glasses on it.

"With the compliments of the owner." He placed one of the glasses in front of me with a flourish. "A fifty-year Glenfiddich single malt Scotch whisky, neat." The second glass went to Arkady. "And a sixty-month tequila for Ms. Woodall."

I raised my eyebrows. "I didn't see any whisky or tequila on the menu."

Anthony smiled. "Mr. Vaughan anticipated your desires and sent some from his private stock. Would you like me to draw the curtains?"

"Not at the moment," I said. "I think I'll people-watch for a bit."

"Thank you, Anthony," Arkady added.

He gave us a small bow and retreated. I didn't see Matthias, but I assumed he was somewhere nearby, keeping an eye on us and listening in on the conversation among the various members of the Court security team positioned in and around the building.

Arkady raised her glass. "To revenge."

I tapped her glass with mine. "May we serve it cold tonight."

My Scotch was almost unbelievably smooth, with a seemingly endless finish. I hadn't been drinking much lately, so the whisky was a rare treat on multiple levels. I didn't even realize I'd closed my eyes until Arkady chuckled. "I take it yours was good too?"

I opened my eyes and set my glass back on the table. "Very, very good. I think I need a cigarette."

She surprised me by saying, "Me too." She leaned forward conspiratorially. "What do you think they'd do if we both lit one?"

"I think we'd see how quickly and politely Anthony could ask us to put them out."

She sighed. "Maybe later we can smoke in celebration back at your house."

"Any sign of Stevens?" I asked.

She shook her head. Like Matthias, she wore an earpiece so she could listen to the security teams outside. "No sign of him. Trust me, I'd tell you if there was."

"Maybe this was too obvious of a setup," I ventured. "He'd have to know we wouldn't be dumb enough to show up at Charles's place practically wearing targets around our necks unless it was part of a plan to draw him out."

"Of course he'll know it's a setup." Arkady leaned back in the booth, crossed her legs, and sipped her tequila. "Part of what I've been doing the last couple of days is reading everything the Court has dug up on Stevens, from his military record to his involvement with fringe 'Human rights' groups since his brother died. This is about the psychology of a man who's not just bent on revenge, but to whom a trap is a challenge—especially a trap laid by women. He has a history of domestic violence. He never went to jail for it because the women always dropped the charges, but his misogyny is another factor I'm counting on. The only thing better than what we've laid out tonight would be if it was Adri Smith instead of Matthias with us. If he lets us leave here unscathed, it's a blow to every part of his ego. He won't be able to walk away, even if he knows it's a trap. And that's why we'll get him."

"I hope I'm right about Stevens wanting to look me in the eye," I confessed. "If he does decide to snipe me instead from the building across the street, my last thought in this life is probably going to be 'Oops.'"

She smiled without humor. "I think you're right, for what it's worth. He didn't open fire on Mr. Vaughan's vehicle the other night until he was in sight of its passengers. He could have taken them out before they'd known what hit them, but then what would be the point?"

We sipped our drinks and waited for word from the security teams outside. I wondered if Arkady was thinking about Fortune. My own thoughts kept drifting back to Sean. Part of me felt guilty for being here while he was lying drugged in a cage, but there was a Court researcher working on finding out about the cuff and I had no doubt Kim Dade would get the answers many times faster than I could. Since I could do little to help Sean until I got some answers from Kim, I might as well stay busy and do whatever was in my power to eliminate a different kind of threat.

As for setting myself up as bait against his wishes, I reminded myself that it was better to have the situation resolved so he wouldn't have to deal with Stevens once we got the cuff off. He'd have enough on his plate dealing with Jack. I was surrounded by Court security and I had my magic.

To distract myself, I sipped my Scotch and scanned the people sitting at the tables and in the row of booths behind Arkady. I saw no empty chairs anywhere. I made a mental note to compliment Charles on the bar's success. It might not be my scene, but I recognized a well-run and high-quality establishment when I saw one. In this city, it was no small feat to reach this kind of success and maintain it.

As my eyes passed over the couples and small groups in the

booths, I caught sight of a red-haired woman in a green cocktail dress sitting with her back to me a couple of booths away. She was slim, wearing diamond drop earrings that had to be several carats each. She gestured dramatically as she spoke to her companions and a diamond tennis bracelet sparkled on her wrist. But that wasn't what made me pause with my drink halfway to my mouth.

It was her ring.

She waved her right hand and the ring glittered. From here, it appeared to be made of white gold with black diamonds forming an *M*.

I put my drink on the table before I dropped it.

No, it can't be her.

Just as that desperate thought crossed my mind, she turned and signaled to a passing server, allowing me to see her face in profile.

Time seemed to slow and then stop. I went cold all over faster than if someone had dumped a bucket of ice water over my head. My heart pounded in my ears loudly enough to drown out everything else.

I suddenly knew who my grandfather had sent to the city to lead the war against Darius Bell: his oldest daughter, Catherine Murphy Atwood. My mother's sister.

My aunt.

CHAPTER 17

As much as my mother had abhorred my grandfather's cabal and everything he did, Catherine had always embraced her role as one of his lieutenants. Though I was her only niece, I had never been anything more than a tool or a weapon to her, something to be used in whatever way was needed to make money and gain more power for the syndicate. I was not allowed to refer to her as "Aunt Catherine," only Catherine.

In the days and weeks after Moses murdered my parents, I'd tried, out of desperation, to turn to Catherine for love and comfort, but there was none to be had. I'd realized later that she blamed me for my mother's death, since my parents had been attempting to flee with me when Moses was tipped off to their plan and burned them alive. Her sister's horrible death had been my fault, as far as she was concerned, and if she'd treated me with indifference before my mother died, her coldness had become outright hatred afterward.

Like Moses, she was a high-level fire mage. Unlike Moses, she'd never tortured me herself; she left that to others. But she didn't mind watching, and she hadn't offered any care after. She also didn't have blood magic, which was why she thought Moses was reluctant to name her as his successor. The real reason was that she didn't command the same level of fear that he did, and since the big cabals ran on fear and loyalty, that was a serious strike against her case for becoming the new Davo. She was a perfectly competent lieutenant, however, and followed Moses's orders to the letter.

It hadn't occurred to me that Moses would send Catherine here, but it should have. The more I thought about it, the more it made sense. Catherine was less well-known than some of Moses's other senior lieutenants, despite being his daughter. She stayed under the radar. People underestimated her and her ruthlessness. She would be able to go unnoticed for longer than the others. If Darius Bell was looking for Moses's people in the city, he wouldn't be looking for a woman in her mid-fifties who could pass as anything from a teacher to a lawyer without attracting attention. She could smile convincingly at bank managers, hotel concierges, even restaurant servers, and no one would suspect who she was or what she was capable of doing.

Catherine ordered another round of drinks for her group. The server scurried away to the bar to put the order in. I wondered who she was sitting with. I didn't recognize the man across from her, but I couldn't see who else was in the booth.

I had to regroup before Arkady or anyone else who was watching us wondered why I was staring at that booth and its occupants. There would time enough later to think about Catherine and the danger she represented. For now, I needed to be thinking about our current mission to catch Kent Stevens.

I picked up my glass and took a much-needed drink. "How long do you think we should stay here?"

Arkady raised her shoulder in a half-shrug. "An hour at least. If he's not here, he may be watching this location via some kind of surveillance camera. If he saw us go in, he'll be headed this way. He's probably already staked out several ways of approaching the bar. We need to give him time to get here."

"That makes sense." I picked up the menu and glanced at the

first page. My stomach growled, reminding me that I'd had nothing to eat since the breakfast burrito Sean made this morning. That meal felt like an eternity ago. "Some of these appetizers look interesting. Are you hungry at all? I could snack."

"I am actually starving to death." She picked up her own menu and read through the options. "Seared tuna, mini-croquettes, artisanal cheeses...what I wouldn't give for a pepperoni pizza," she muttered.

It was hard to ignore Catherine and I didn't want anyone from her group noticing me looking at her. I scooted over so she was no longer in my line of sight. "Well, the croquettes sound good, and I'm thinking the meat and cheese board is the closest we're going to get to a pizza. Unless you think the thing I can't pronounce with the marinated olives sounds good."

"No, I do not." Arkady raised her hand.

Anthony materialized almost out of thin air. "What may I bring out for you?"

"We're hungry," Arkady told him. "How about two orders of the croquettes and a meat and cheese board? What else do you recommend?"

He didn't even blink at the amount of food we were ordering. "I can highly recommend either the empanadas or the seared tuna."

"Empanadas. Thank you."

He left in the direction of the kitchen.

I reached for my water. "Well, you read my dossier, but I know next to nothing about you. How did you end up working for the Court?"

"It's kind of a long story, but the short version is that I got kicked out of the Army for punching my CO when he tried to pressure me into sex. After that, I went into private security while I got my PI license."

"Did you like private security?"

She nodded. "I did, actually, though I liked the investigative work a lot more. I worked with a friend of Fortune's, and when the Court let it be known that they were looking for investigators, I sent in my résumé and Fortune put in a good word. I interviewed with Mr. Vaughan and Bryan Smith, and then with Niara and her head of security, Nadya."

"Have you met Valas?"

She shook her head. "I've spoken with Juliet LaRoche, Valas's daytime representative. I haven't been invited to actually meet Valas yet, though I understand that she ultimately made the decision to hire me. I hear she's quite impressive."

"That she is." And also more than a bit terrifying.

We chatted about the members of the Court until our food arrived. Mindful that there was a chance our booth was bugged and our conversation was not private, we kept the conversation light. Once the food arrived, however, if anyone was listening all they would have heard was the sound of two hungry women eating everything in sight.

Anthony reappeared as we were finishing the last of the meat and cheese tray. He looked suitably impressed by the way we'd cleaned our plates. "May I bring you anything else? Perhaps a dessert?"

Arkady covered her mouth to hide a burp. "I think I'll pass. Alice?"

"No, thank you. Could you point me toward the ladies' room?"

He smiled and gestured grandly toward the back of the club. "Allow me to escort you."

"Me too," Arkady added quickly. Apparently I wasn't allowed to use the bathroom by myself.

We slid from our booth, purses in hand, and followed Anthony along the booths to the end, where two hallways branched in opposite directions. Anthony indicated the hallway on the left. "Second door on the right, ladies."

The bathroom was worthy of a two-page spread in a design magazine, but I couldn't really appreciate it fully until I'd relieved my bladder. While we were in the stalls, someone else entered the bathroom and took the stall farthest from the door.

Business concluded, I flushed the toilet, double-checked to make sure my undergarments were in place and my dress wasn't tucked into my underwear, and emerged from the stall to find Arkady already washing her hands at the sink.

I joined her. "This place is really nice," I said as I washed my hands. The soap smelled like lilacs.

Arkady took a folded paper towel from a basket and dried her hands. "That was the best tequila I've ever had. I was about to ask Anthony how Mr. Vaughan knew what my favorite drink was, but then I realized there's probably nothing about me that Mr. Vaughan doesn't know, down to my bra size and what kind of ice cream I have in the freezer."

"More than likely." I took some lipstick from my bag and applied it as the toilet flushed in the last stall. "You don't seem upset about that."

She took out her own lipstick. "Bra size and favorite ice cream flavor, no. But every girl has secrets she wants and needs to keep buried, and there are some invasions of privacy I won't accept. This is a good job, but it's a job. I won't hesitate to walk away if certain lines get crossed. I made that pretty clear."

I wondered what kinds of secrets Arkady might have buried and how she intended to keep the vamps from digging them up. I knew all too well what a minefield secrets were. I hoped she would have more luck protecting hers than I'd had.

The stall door opened and Catherine emerged. Our eyes met in the mirror.

Hers were the same gray as my mother's had been, the same as Moses's were. Mine were dark brown, a gift from my dad, my mother had always said. She'd loved my brown eyes. I'd never understood why, really, until I figured out that the things she loved most about me were the things that weren't part of the Murphy family legacy. I'd always thought my eyes were a darker version of my dad's, but now I had to question that given what the mirror had revealed to me. Perhaps they reminded her of my biological father, Daniel.

I dropped my lipstick back into my purse and stepped aside to allow Catherine to reach the sink.

"Excuse me," she said, reaching for the soap dispenser and turning her attention to washing her hands.

The sound of her voice made the hair stand up on the back of my neck. I hadn't heard her voice in more than five years, but it sounded exactly as I remembered it.

I wanted nothing more than to run from that bathroom and then away from the bar as fast as I could, but I forced myself to smile at Arkady and walk leisurely out into the hall, as if I couldn't sense my life crumbling around me.

"Is it about time to leave?" I asked as we returned to our booth and slid into the seats.

She checked the time. "It's been a little over an hour. Let's give it another fifteen minutes, shall we? I'll let them know we're almost ready to leave."

As Arkady texted the security team, Catherine walked past me on her way back to her table. Her hand passed within inches of my arm. I held still as she went by.

I looked nothing like her niece anymore, thanks to surgery. My magic was unrecognizable under so many layers of spells. There was absolutely no cause for her to suspect I was even alive, as far as I knew, much less reason to think I might be here now in the same bar, mere feet away. It was sheer paranoia to think that she had passed by me so closely on purpose to try to sense my magic or that she'd gone to the restroom at the same time I had to engineer an encounter.

It was equally paranoid for me to think the reason her attractive male companion had glanced at me twice since we'd come back to our seats was because she had mentioned me. At any other time, I would have thought his glances were simply admiring a woman in a bar, but I couldn't help but wonder.

He caught my eye and smiled. I gave him a slight shake of my head to indicate that I wasn't interested and turned my attention to Arkady, hoping for an all-clear signal to move out. The sooner we were out of here, the better.

Arkady raised her eyebrows. "Is someone checking you out?"

"Yeah, but he's not my type. Plus I've got a werewolf boyfriend, you know?" I realized I'd just referred to Sean as my "werewolf boyfriend." Suddenly I was a character in a teen shifter romance. Ugh. I picked up my Scotch and tossed back the remainder.

Arkady tilted her head, listening to the voices on her earpiece. "Well, we have people in place all around. The net is set. I'll have Kirwin bring the car to the front."

"Let's walk to the car."

She studied me. "That was not the plan."

"New plan. Let's make the bait super-shiny."

She sent a text, received one, and then sent another. "They don't like it, but they're ready. The SUV is parked in a lot two blocks to the north."

My heart raced in anticipation. "Then let's go."

I'd once told Charles that I was addicted to danger, and it was true. I needed the adrenaline, the risk, and yes, even the pain of fights. Thanks to my grandfather, I'd known little else since I was a child. The need for danger had become a part of me. I couldn't get rid of it any more than I could my magic.

Until Sean, I felt most alive when my life was on the line. Now I felt that way when we were together, too, but I still felt compelled to run toward danger rather than away from it. Sean would need to accept that about me, as difficult as it would be for him to do so. He could stand beside me if he wanted, but I wouldn't be left behind or kept safely put away. It just wasn't in me.

As much as I'd enjoyed our conversation and my drink, Arkady and I were here on a mission. Catherine's sudden appearance had unnerved me, but that was a problem I would have to think about and deal with later. Right now, we had business outside.

We got up from our booth and headed out to meet it.

"Why the hell didn't it work?" I demanded.

Arkady tapped her foot, clearly irritated, as Matthias drove us back to my house. Kirwin had received a request for him to return to Northbourne, so we'd left him at 1792. Most of our drive had been ominously silent.

"Heck if I know," she said finally. "I thought we had him figured out. There's no way he could have resisted that bait if he saw you, and I would have bet real money he'd be there. It's the obvious best spot for him to find Vaughan or you. We'll just have to try again tomorrow, I guess."

I didn't punch the seat in frustration, but I wanted to. I worried that I might bust the leather upholstery wide open if I did. I'd spooled magic during the walk, preparing to face Stevens, and now all of that power sizzled on my skin, refusing to be put back in the bottle.

Like me, Arkady was restless and short-tempered. I was starting to think she might love a good fight as much or more than I did, and we were both all wound up with no one to pound. Maybe we could take turns punching my heavy bag when we got home.

I also hadn't gotten a call yet from Kim Dade about the cuff, which gnawed on my already-frayed nerves. My fingers itched to call her, but she'd said she'd let me know as soon as she found something. A phone call would do nothing but interrupt her research.

The SUV turned onto my street. "I'm going to stay and watch the house until dawn," Matthias told Arkady, catching her eye in the rearview mirror. "If Ms. Worth needs to leave for any reason, we'll be her escorts."

"Good." Arkady's attention was out the window as the SUV

pulled into my driveway and parked, so she missed the look Matthias gave her. Poor guy had it bad. I wondered if she'd noticed it yet.

Matthias left the engine running but opened his door. "I'll escort you into the house."

"Wait for us to come around to your side," Arkady reminded me, opening her door.

"I remember," I said, hoping I didn't sound as sullen as I felt.

They got out. Matthias opened my door and offered me his hand as Arkady kept watch on our surroundings. He flinched when my spooled magic gave him a little zap, but he didn't let go until both of my feet were on the ground.

Arkady and I headed toward my front door with Matthias at our six. I opened my handbag and reached for my keys.

Behind me, I heard four quick, heavy *thumps*. Matthias grunted, staggered, and fell.

In the time that it took me to realize he'd been shot, Arkady spun around, her gun raised as she searched for a target. "Take cover!" she ordered me.

Thump thump. She went down with a pained sound, two neat holes punched in the front of her jumpsuit right above her heart. The bullets hit her vest, but their impact knocked the wind out of her. She lay crumpled on the lawn, struggling to breathe.

Matthias, bleeding from at least a couple of wounds, crawled to her and shielded her with his body. "Get inside," he rasped.

If I went into the house I'd be safe behind my wards, but the shooter might pick me off before I could get the door open. Besides, I wasn't about to leave Arkady and Matthias wounded and undefended.

I dropped to a crouch just as bullets hit the sidewalk next to me, pelting me with pieces of cement. The shots seemed to have come from the direction of the carport, but I couldn't see anyone. More bullets peppered the sidewalk in front of me. Were there two shooters? Did Stevens have a partner, or a whole team?

I was a sitting duck in the middle of my walkway, so I scuttled behind the SUV just as three or four rounds hit the bullet-resistant glass above my head. I realized now that my escorts were down, all of the shots were directed at me. Clearly I was the primary target. I needed to draw their fire farther away from Arkady and Matthias.

I got up and ran for the backyard gate as bullets thumped into the grass behind me. I expected to feel shots in my back at any moment as I got the gate unlatched, swung it open, and dashed into the darkness of my backyard. I left the gate ajar, hoping Stevens would follow me and leave Arkady and Matthias alone.

Sean had told me that the vamps had people watching my house, so where the hell were they? Why hadn't they found the shooters and taken them out? What were they waiting for?

There wasn't much cover in my backyard except for some bushes, a couple of skinny trees, and my new garden. The plants rustled in excitement as I ran around to the side of the garden and put the mass of swaying greenery between me and the backyard gate. I peered through the plants, watching the side of the house and waiting for Stevens to show his face or for the Vamp Court's team to find Stevens and whoever was helping him.

I sensed an obfuscation spell break behind me. I spun and raised my left hand, forming an air magic shield, as my cold-fire whip spiraled out of my right palm.

Kent Stevens appeared seemingly out of thin air, gun in hand, and fired five shots straight at me. All five hit the shield and were deflected away.

I lashed out with my fire whip, striking Stevens across the chest and throwing him back into the bushes. To my surprise, he held onto his gun and fired several more shots before I could get my shield back in place. Angry hornets tore past my upper left arm and hip. I ignored the flashes of heat and pain and raised my shield, sending the rest of the bullets into the fence on my left.

Stevens rolled to his feet—

—and vanished.

Shit.

Obfuscation spells powerful enough to make someone invisible were rare and very, very expensive for non-mages. Now I knew how he'd slipped past the Vamp Court team watching the house and made it seem like there were multiple shooters instead of just one.

These spells were air magic, though, so as an air mage I had a slight advantage. I'd also been practicing engaging an invisible target with Malcolm, and I had a second to be thankful for our recent sparring sessions before I sensed magic to my left. I raised my shield just in time to block three shots. I lashed out with my whip, but missed him.

Footsteps rustled in the grass to my right; I lashed again and this time my cold fire whip made contact, sending him flying backward. Blood splattered on the fence and something hit the ground and became visible: his gun, a Glock with a suppressor and extended magazine. I lashed it with my whip and the barrel bent, rendering the firearm useless.

Silence.

Breathing hard, I backed up against the fence and tried to sense where he was, but it was hard to focus with the pain in my arm and side and the sensation of blood dripping down my leg.

The sharp point of a knife punctured my right side, just below the edge of my vest. A spell broke and I found myself staring into Stevens's eyes from inches away. I hadn't seen him since that day at Robinson's house, but he looked almost like a different person. His face was a cold mask, his eyes dark and murderous. I was right; he wanted to look me in the eye, up close and personal, when he took me out. That decision doomed him.

I didn't wait for him to speak or drive his knife farther into my flesh. I pushed my blood magic out through my fingertips and plunged the wide red-and-black blade deep into his gut, twisting it as hard as I could.

He grunted and dropped his Ka-Bar knife. Hot blood poured over my fingers. I pulled my magic blade out and hit him on the chest with both hands. Air magic sent him flying back to land on the grass next to the garden. He lay stunned, his hands on the bloody, gaping wound in his stomach. I backed toward my house, watching him.

Two figures ran through my backyard gate, moving too quickly to be human. A pair of Hunters—one male, one female. They must not have been able to find him when he was using the obfuscation spells, but the smell of blood had drawn them like a magnet.

They headed straight for Stevens, fangs bared and eyes black. If they got hold of him, they would tear him to shreds.

I raised my hand. Red, purple, and black blood magic flared on my fingers. I sensed the dark magic of the Hunters and grabbed it with my mind, bending their will to mine. "*Stop,*" I commanded.

They stopped, frozen, staring at me in a combination of fury and confusion.

Arkady appeared, walking unsteadily, her gun still in her hand and her breathing labored. She gave the Hunters a wide berth and joined me in the middle of the yard.

"The Hunters," she rasped. "How...*why* are you stopping them?"

How was not an answer I was willing to share with her, but the *why* was important. "Because he's yours to take down," I told her. "Two in the kneecaps, remember? For Fortune."

She swallowed hard. I saw a flash of something in her eyes— grief, maybe, or pain—and then it was gone. Despite the soreness in her chest, she straightened. "Thank you."

Stevens must have moved, because when I'd left him lying on the ground, he hadn't been within reach of the garden. Somehow, despite his guts spilling out, he was able to move. Maybe he was going for another weapon; maybe he was trying to get back on his feet.

Either way, he didn't get very far.

The plants moved fast. One moment, Stevens was on the ground next to the flowerbed; the next, a thick vine wrapped around his legs and yanked him into the garden. His short scream ended abruptly in a wet gurgle.

Arkady and I ran for the garden, but it was too late. The plants thrashed wildly and I heard a sound that was somewhere between chewing and slurping. The thrashing subsided, but the sound continued. I had a feeling I'd be hearing it in my nightmares for a while.

Finally, Arkady stuck her gun back in her shoulder holster and studied the plants as they enjoyed their dinner. "I really wanted to shoot him, but I think I like this even more. Do you think the plants will eat everything, or—?"

The garden rustled and a gloppy wet boot plopped on the grass at my feet, followed by its mate. A thick leather belt landed next to them a moment later, still buckled. It had been chewed in half.

Arkady turned a little green. "I think I'm going to be sick."

I pressed a hand to my bloody side and glared at her. "Don't you dare."

We turned and headed for the front of the house. Behind us, the garden slurped and sighed.

It was a well-planned ambush, and it had almost worked.

Matthias swore we hadn't been followed from the bar, so at first it was a mystery how Stevens found me. Not long after we returned to 1792 for medical attention and a debriefing, however, the vamps found Stevens's vehicle, a stolen truck, two streets away from my house. In it was a prepaid mobile phone with one incoming message from a blocked number that read simply *Identity Confirmed: Alice Evelyn Worth* and gave my address. They speculated that someone working for Stevens had surveillance in place at 1792 and used facial recognition software to identify me. There wasn't much chance of figuring out who had sent the text that directed Stevens to my home, but the vamps were on it. They were also looking into where he might have bought the obfuscation spells.

Charles and Bryan arrived at 1792 at the same time we did. Matthias had taken four shots in the back. Two hit his vest, but one hit him in the neck and the other his upper left arm. He lost a lot of blood, but he lived, thanks to a little luck and Charles's blood.

Arkady had a spectacular and very painful bruise on her chest from the bullets that hit her vest. She declined all offers of healing and said she'd be fine with some aspirin and an ice pack. We made plans to meet for drinks soon and she went home to recuperate. Matthias watched her go with a hangdog look, then left as well, headed for Northbourne.

My own wounds were fairly minor. One bullet had grazed my upper left arm and the second left a slightly deeper trench across my hip. I had an inch-deep puncture in my right side from Stevens's knife. Like Arkady, I declined Charles's blood, preferring standard first-aid remedies. I'd heal the injuries myself at home with spells later.

Bryan, a former Army medic, dressed my wounds, gave me ibuprofen and a bottle of fancy water, and hovered next to me like a very large, very stern mother hen as I reclined on one of the enormous overstuffed sofas in Charles's office above 1792.

It was my first visit to the office Charles was using as his primary workspace while his former digs were being rebuilt. This room was more spacious than his office above Hawthorne's had been, with a large sitting area, a full bar, and an enormous L-shaped desk. The walls were lined with bookcases and display cases full of antiques and artifacts.

"I like the sofas," I said, wincing as I adjusted the pillows I was leaning against. "Super-comfy. I could almost fall asleep right here."

"You are welcome to do so, or you may stay in one of the furnished apartments upstairs," Charles said. He'd been in a good mood since he'd heard what had happened to Stevens. He was less happy about my refusal to let him heal my wounds and frowned when I grimaced.

The ibuprofen took the edge off the pain, but my arm, side, and hip throbbed mercilessly. Bryan had offered me stronger pain meds, but I declined. If Kim called about the cuff, I wanted a clear head.

I finished the last of the fancy water and handed the bottle to Bryan. "Thanks for the offer, but I'd rather sleep at home in my own bed. I'll get up and go here in a minute." Maybe five or ten minutes. The couch was ridiculously plush and I strongly suspected I was going to need help getting up.

"There is no hurry. May I offer you a drink?" Charles asked.

I shook my head. "I better not. Thanks, though, and thank you very much for the fantastic Scotch you served me down in the bar earlier. That was quite a special treat."

"I suspected neither you nor Ms. Woodall would find much on the drink menu downstairs that was to your liking." Charles poured himself three fingers of whiskey and joined me in the sitting area, settling into the armchair across from me so we could converse easily. "What is your assessment of Ms. Woodall?"

"You knew I'd like her. Crack shot, highly trained, cool as a cucumber under pressure, fearless, driven, total adrenaline junkie."

He smiled. "Those words describe someone else I know."

I scoffed. "That last thing maybe."

He waved his hand. "This is unnecessary modesty. We are well aware of your skills, Alice—though not all of them, it would seem. I speculated that you might be able to control Hunters, but it is quite something else when it happens."

Before Charles had bitten me, I'd kept the fact I was a blood mage hidden from him, as well as some of the more unique skills I had developed. He now knew I was a high-level blood mage, however, and some powerful blood mages shared an affinity for the dark magic that bound Hunters to their master. My ability to command Hunters was rare but not unique. I hadn't planned on revealing it, but I had weighed the value of keeping that ability a secret from

Charles versus permitting Arkady the opportunity to take her revenge and decided her need was greater.

Charles contemplated his Scotch. "As I am sure you recall, the first night we met, five years ago, I engineered an encounter between you and two Hunters. I suspected then that you had blood magic, though you had so carefully hidden it. The Hunters' reactions to you —and your reaction to them—was further evidence of this. Amira, their Master, thought so as well." He studied me. "I cannot help but wonder what else you are capable of."

"Well, I've been known to make a mean grilled cheese." I shifted position again and stifled a groan.

At least 1792 had an elevator so I didn't have to either climb stairs or suffer the indignities of being carried as a result of my injured hip. I hoped Charles had added one to the new Hawthorne's. He disliked elevators as a rule, but had acknowledged that not all of his visitors appreciated having to climb several flights of stairs to visit his office, especially if they were a bit worse for wear.

As I was debating whether to force myself to get up or lie on the couch for a few more minutes, my cell phone rang. I dug around in the couch until I found it. The screen read *Kim Dade Calling*.

My discomfort forgotten, I sat up and answered. "Hi, Kim."

"Hi, Alice."

I knew her well enough to recognize that tone. My heart sank. "You have bad news."

She sighed. "Well, the good news is that I did find out what that cuff is. The fire magic spellwork you sensed must have been added sometime in the past twenty years or so. The original shifter magic dates back at least a thousand years."

So our guess about its age and origin were correct. That was something, at least. "What's its purpose?"

"It's designed to be worn by the alpha of a pack. The original spellwork is supposed to strengthen the alpha and bolster the pack bonds, thus fortifying the pack and assuring strong leadership and dominance."

"The hell it is," I said hotly. "That cuff forced Sean to shift and made him violent and irrational."

"That's because you've only got one cuff." She took a deep breath. "That's the bad news. It's one of a pair, Alice. There's a second cuff that's supposed to be worn by the alpha's mate. Together, the cuffs reinforce their bond and provide strength and stability to the pack. That cuff Sean is wearing is not supposed to be used individually. The magic is incomplete, and you know how dangerous broken spellwork can be."

Shock left me speechless for a moment. "What will happen to Sean if someone doesn't put on the other cuff?"

Her voice was full of sorrow. "Without a mate to wear the matching cuff, Sean is going to die."

CHAPTER 18

My world shrank to the feeling of the phone in my hand and the pain in my chest. "How long?" I asked hoarsely.

"Days at most. Maybe less. He's probably weak already and going downhill rapidly. I'm sorry, Alice."

And Jack had dosed him with a sedative. I felt a surge of rage and fought to focus on figuring out what to do. "How do we get the cuff off of him?"

"As far as I know, you can't. The magic is bound to him. It only comes off if he dies, so it can be passed to the next alpha."

That settled that. "Then we have to find the other cuff. Do you know where it is?"

"I've been looking, but there's no trace of where it might be. It's not in a museum as far as I can tell, so it's probably in a private collection. It could be here, or it might be on the other side of the world. I'll keep trying, though. If it's out there, I'll try like hell to find it."

"Thank you, Kim. Please call me the second you know something."

We disconnected.

I put my phone in my lap and looked up to find Charles and Bryan standing in front of me. "I have to get to Sean," I said, struggling to rise.

"Miss Alice, let me help you." Bryan took me by my right arm and lifted me to my feet. "You're in no condition to confront a pack of werewolves."

"He's dying alone in a cage," I said, pushing Bryan away. I was well aware that he moved only because he chose to do so. "I can't leave him like that. He needs me."

"He needs someone to find the other cuff and put it on," Charles said. "Are you willing to do that, Alice?"

I hesitated.

It made me sick to my stomach, but I hesitated. Sean loved me. I didn't want him to die. I would give almost anything, *do* almost anything, to save him. But at the thought of putting on the other cuff and binding myself to him for the rest of our lives, even if it was to save his life, I hesitated.

I hated myself so much in that moment that I was sure Charles sensed it.

I tried to remember how Sean and I had talked about a mate bond only yesterday. He'd said he thought we might have such a bond someday, but not yet. Though his wolf wanted me as a mate, Sean knew we'd only been dating a few months and neither of us were ready for that level of commitment.

And then there was my grandfather, who had quickly gone from distant danger to imminent threat. It was one thing if I told Sean the truth about Moses and he chose to accept that risk, but putting the cuff on meant Sean had no say in whether he would become a target.

Even knowing that, we were talking about life and death. If I found the other cuff—and that was a mighty big *if*—I'd have to choose whether to put it on and save Sean's life, or refuse and watch him die. I knew couldn't watch him die, but I didn't think I could put the cuff on.

The debate was academic unless we found the second cuff. Sean's current condition was much more critical.

I swallowed hard and turned to Charles. "Please call Jack and tell him what we know. When you're done, I would like to speak to him."

"I do not believe he will allow you to see the wolf," he told me gently. "I cannot ask him to grant you access. It is a pack matter and the Court has no authority."

"I have to get in to see Sean." I paced, limping from one side of the sitting area to the other. "I have to tell him that I'm trying to find the other cuff. I have to tell him…something important. And if I can get into the cage, touch the cuff, and sense the magic, I might be able to use the trace to locate the second cuff."

"That magic could have killed you the first time," he reminded me. "It may kill you outright if you touch it now that the spellwork has degraded further. You cannot risk it."

"I have to. I have no choice." I took a shaky breath. "Please call Jack, Charles. Before it's too late."

LEFT HOOK, right hook. Left hook, right hook. Jab, cross, jab. Left hook, right hook. Left hook again. *Bam bam bam.* My gloved fists pounded the bag. I reset my feet and started again. Left hook, right hook. Jab, cross, jab.

Malcolm hovered in the hallway outside the spare bedroom, his worry a faint buzz on the edges of my senses. "Alice, you've got to stop this. You just got shot twice, for Pete's sake. Why aren't you resting?"

"You think I can rest right now?" I delivered three quick punches to the bag and wiped sweat off my face. My arms and shoulders were screaming. "Do you really believe I could go lie down and sleep while

Sean is locked in a cage dying and Jack Hastings won't let me see him?"

"Okay, maybe you can't sleep, but you sure as hell don't have to be in here running yourself into the ground. I thought you were past doing this sort of bullshit."

Left hook, right hook. Jab, cross, jab. "What bullshit am I doing, Malcolm?"

"Damn it, you know exactly what I mean. You're punishing yourself because you think this is your fault. It's four o'clock in the morning and you've been punching that bag since you got home and healed your arm and side. What would Sean say if he were here?"

I turned on him, my gloves raised. "He's *not* here, Malcolm. That's the point!" I turned and punched the bag three more times, my eyes stinging.

Malcolm floated over next to me. "Alice, stop," he pleaded.

One second, I was pulling my arm back to deliver another set of punches, and the next I was sitting on the floor, dazed.

Malcolm floated above me, looking furious. "I said *stop!*" he yelled.

I blinked up at him. My butt hurt from landing on the floor but I had no memory of going down. My chest felt kind of tingly. "Did you just zap me?" I asked in confusion.

He crossed his arms, still angry. "Did you just spend the last forty-five minutes doing the closest thing to beating the crap out of yourself and ignoring me when I told you to stop?"

"What do you want me to do?" I rested my gloved hands in my lap as sweat trickled down my face. "You said I couldn't go out to Jack's house and cut my way through the pack to get to Sean."

"I'm pretty sure Charles told you that too," he pointed out. "I'm equally sure you know you can't do that, not if you want any kind of future with Sean. I know your usual solution to a situation like this is to go in with magic blazing, but that's not going to work this time. You have to go a different route."

"I wish I knew what route to take. Jack won't even talk to me, much less let me see Sean, even when Charles said I might be able to trace the second cuff if I could touch the one Sean's wearing. He just said they'll find the other cuff and it's no longer any business of the Court's, or mine."

"What good will it do them if they find the other cuff?" Malcolm asked. "You're Sean's mate. They'll have to let you put it on if they find it, right?"

When I frowned at him, he looked surprised, then thoughtful. "Oh."

"What do you mean, 'oh'?" I demanded.

"You're not sure if you want to put it on." When I started to protest, he shook his head. "No, I get it. You're not Sean's mate, not yet. You've only been dating a couple of months. But you have to put the cuff on, or Sean dies." He grimaced. "Crap, Alice, that's tough."

"This is all speculative anyway, probably. I don't see any way we could find the other cuff, especially if Jack won't let me use the trace."

"That magic would probably kill you if you touched it anyway. It's undoubtedly warded against doing exactly what you want to do: use the trace to find the other cuff. Everything about it is designed not to let anyone mess with the spellwork or the cuffs themselves. We're both lucky we're not dead from it already." He made a face. "Well, in my case, deader."

I suddenly felt every ounce of the exhaustion I'd been trying to ignore. I pulled off my gloves and started unwrapping my hands. Malcolm watched me, floating back and forth.

When my hands were free, I left the gloves and the hand-wraps on the floor and got to my feet. I started toward the door, then paused and turned back. "I'm a bad person, aren't I?"

He stared at me, nonplussed. "Of course you aren't. Why would you think that?"

My eyes burned. "Because Sean will die if I don't find that cuff and put it on, and I'm not sure I can put it on, not even to save his life."

He floated over to me. "Alice, you are absolutely, positively *not* a bad person. I may not know anything about what happened to you before you moved here, but I am one hundred percent certain that you are a good person and that you will save Sean's life, whether that means putting on the cuff or figuring out some other way."

"There is no other way, apparently," I said wearily. "Find and put on the other cuff, or Sean dies. The cuff only comes off if Sean dies."

"Well, so says Kim Dade," Malcolm pointed out. "Maybe you need to get a second opinion. Is there anyone else you can ask?"

"Maybe." I told him about Ella Potter, the shifter magic expert from Portland who seemed to know a bit about magic cuffs.

"Send her an e-mail right now, then go to bed," Malcolm told me. "You can try to catch a little bit of rest until you hear from her. Take something to help you sleep if you have to. You got almost no sleep last night and if you don't get at least a couple of hours tonight, you'll be useless if you've got to swing into action later."

I couldn't argue with that, though I found it highly unlikely I'd be able to fall asleep anytime soon.

I went downstairs and fetched my laptop, then took a shower because I was sweaty and gross. I put on my sheep pajamas—the ones Sean liked, because wolves thought sheep were tasty—and sat on the bed with the computer in my lap. Malcolm had gone downstairs to give me some space.

I found Ella Potter's e-mail address on the MOP website and wrote a detailed message explaining the situation. I attached a photo of the cuff, explained what another researcher had uncovered, and asked if she knew anything more that might help us. Though I knew it was a very long shot, I also asked if she had any idea where the second cuff might be or how else it might be traced if I didn't have access to the magic on the one Sean was wearing.

I read back over my message to make sure it was clear that my inquiry was urgent but didn't sound like I was begging for help. I decided it was reasonably professional and hit Send.

With that done, I closed the laptop and turned off my lamp. I slid down under the covers and curled into a ball. I couldn't remember my room ever feeling so empty and silent.

After a few minutes, I rolled over to the other side of the bed, the side closer to the bathroom where Sean usually slept. The forest scent was much stronger on that side of the bed. I buried my nose in the pillow and inhaled.

This morning, in the minutes before we fell asleep together, I'd laid in his arms thinking about the story he'd revealed to me while we were staking out John Doe's motel room. It was the most painful and personal story a werewolf could tell: how he'd become a shifter. It was proof of his trust in me. He was waiting for me to tell him my story, but in the meantime, he offered me his. He'd put his cards on the table, hoping I might do the same.

For the first time I thought I might be able to tell him my story someday soon. When, I wasn't sure, but soon, assuming I figured out a way to save him.

With my nose filled with the scent of a forest in spring, I could almost feel his arm around my middle and his nose against the back of my neck. I wrapped my arms around myself and slept.

I DREAMED OF THE WOLF.

He lay on his side in a glass cage in the middle of an empty, dark room, his golden eyes full of pain and hurt. Need mate, *he said in my head.*

I pounded my fists against the glass walls. I'm trying to get to you, *I told him.*

He summoned up enough strength to bite at the cuff on his front leg, but it held fast. He lay his head back down and showed his teeth. Bad magic.

I know. There's another cuff that matches that one. If I can find it, I can save you. You've got to hang on. Please don't give up.

A clawed hand grabbed me by the shoulder, spun me around, and slammed me up against the glass wall of the cage. Jack's face was half-wolf, half-human, with an oversize jaw and huge teeth. His eyes were bright gold with fury. "I told you to stay away," he snarled in my face. His breath was hot.

The wolf growled and snapped his teeth. Protect mate, not hurt, *he commanded.*

Jack ignored the wolf and grabbed me by the throat. I pushed my blood magic out through my fingertips and slashed his face, opening four long, bloody gashes.

With a snarl, he flung me down and towered over me, his face twisted with rage. Blood dripped down the front of his shirt. "You are not welcome in our pack," he growled.

My pack, the wolf snarled. *He struggled to his feet and moved stiffly to the glass wall.* My mate, my pack.

Jack turned on him with a growl. I slashed at his legs with my blood magic and he came at me, teeth bared. The last thing I felt was the pain as he sank his canines deep into the soft flesh of my throat.

☙ ❧ ☙ ❧ ☙ ❧ ☙ ❧ ☙ ❧ ☙ ❧

I woke with a short scream, my hands on my throat as I shook uncontrollably. The dream had seemed so real that it took several seconds to process that I was in my own bedroom and not the eerie, empty room with Jack and Sean's wolf.

Strangely, my shoulder hurt where Jack had grabbed it in the dream, and my neck was sore. I must have been sleeping in an uncomfortable position, I reasoned. There was obviously no way I had actually been interacting with either the wolf or Jack in a dream.

With my blackout curtains closed I couldn't tell what time it was, but I sensed that it was late morning and my bedside clock confirmed it. The message light was blinking on my phone, indicating I had two voicemails from my office line.

The first message was from Aaron Riddell, inquiring on the status of my search for the cuff. He asked me to give him a call at his office. With everything that had happened, I hadn't even given any thought to what I would tell him or Esther about the cuff. If I was able to somehow get it off Sean, I had no idea if I would be able to return it to my client, or if the pack would want to keep it in case the second cuff turned up. I wasn't even going to consider the possibility that it would fall off on its own. I wasn't going to let that happen to Sean.

When I played the second message, I got a surprise. "Alice, this is Karen Williams from Sean's pack." Her voice was tense and angry. "I didn't have your cell, so I'm trying your office number. Jack ordered us not to contact you, but you deserve to know what's happening."

My stomach knotted.

"Sean is...in really bad shape," she continued, her voice breaking. "He can barely eat or drink and he isn't moving around very much. I know you're trying to find the second cuff. Please hurry. I don't know how much longer he can hang on. We've tried to talk Jack into letting you come see him, but he won't even consider it."

She took a deep breath. "You need to know what Jack's trying to do. A year or so ago, he and Delia set Sean up on a date with Lily Anderson, a female shifter from another pack. They dated for a while but Sean wasn't all that taken with her. She fell in love with him, though, and their alpha has kept in touch with Jack, hoping they might get back together even though Sean has said he's not interested. Well, Jack is looking for that other cuff too, and if he finds it he's going to have Lily put it on and make her Sean's mate."

For a moment, I couldn't get a breath. A bubble of rage filled my chest and threatened to burst through my skin. How dare Jack even think about binding Sean to someone for life without his consent, whether or not it would save his life to do so? The thought made me sick to my stomach.

Karen went on. "Jack says that if they're bound together, whether it was Sean's choice or not, he'll have to accept Lily or risk war with her pack. He's probably right. Sean won't have any choice. I'm so sorry about this, Alice. I know you care about Sean very much and he cares about you. That's why I'm calling to warn you. Please, *please* find that cuff before Jack does. It will break our hearts if he does this to Sean and to you. I know this probably isn't how you envisioned your relationship would go, but I believe that you'll find the cuff and save Sean. Just *hurry*, Alice. Please hurry." *Beep.*

I put the phone on the bed and sat with my legs dangling over the side, too stunned to move at first. I'd never even considered that Jack might give the cuff to another woman if he found it. He had to know how angry Sean would be if he was bound to this other woman. I couldn't imagine Sean not killing him over it.

I remembered Jack's size and felt a sudden rush of fear. Sean was weakened tremendously by the cuff. What if Sean challenged Jack and lost? In fact, what if Jack was counting on Sean to fight him in a weakened condition so he could kill Sean and become the new alpha?

I rubbed my face. Was Jack that ruthless and disloyal? He just might be. I'd been wondering how he thought he was going to get away with everything he'd done since the cuff got onto Sean's arm. Maybe he was well aware of how angry Sean would be and he was planning to use that anger to his advantage.

My search for the cuff had just taken on additional urgency. I grabbed my laptop, hoping to find an e-mail reply from Ella Potter, the shifter magic expert.

I opened my e-mail and found three messages in my inbox. One of them was from Ella, sent about twenty minutes ago. My heart in my throat, I opened the message.

Hi, Alice. Thanks so much for contacting me! I'm so sorry to hear about what the cuff is doing to your friend.

First, the bad news: I don't have any information about where the other cuff might be. I've seen cuffs like this before, but not this particular set. I can confirm what your researcher has told you about their purpose and that the cuff's magic will keep it affixed to the alpha's arm until either he or his mate dies, in which case both cuffs fall off so they can go to the new alpha pair. The spellwork is potentially deadly to anyone who attempts to remove the cuff, either physically or by interfering with the magic. It sounds like you know that already from personal experience.

I do have some potentially good news for you, however. Since you can't touch the magic on the cuff you have, I do know of a spell that might work to help you find the cuff you need. I've attached a copy of the spell and the instructions for using it. I'm hoping you have enough of your friend's shifter magic that it will work. I don't know if you are a mid or high-level mage, but obviously the more powerful you are, the more likely you'll be able to get it to work.

Just so you know, I was contacted via e-mail this morning by a shifter named Jack Hastings, who told me essentially the same story you did, except his version wasn't very complimentary toward you. I told him that as far as I knew his information about the cuff was correct and that I didn't know where the other cuff might be. I didn't tell him that you had also contacted me, or about the spell. I didn't much like the way he spoke about you.

I sincerely hope you can find the other cuff. I will ask around and see if anyone I know has any information that might be helpful, either about the cuff or ways of locating the other one. In the meantime, good luck with the spell and let me know if I can do anything else to help. Peace and best wishes, Ella.

I opened the attached image and studied the spellwork. Most of the runes were new to me, but the basic structure was familiar and based on air magic, as most tracking spells were. The accompanying instructions stated that the probability of the spell working increased based on the power of the mage using it, the amount of shifter magic they could draw upon, and how much—if any—of the trace from the known cuff was available.

I was a high-level air mage, so that would help. Sean and I blended our magic on a regular basis, as Malcolm had recently—and so awkwardly—pointed out, so I had that going for me. I did have the box the cuff had been stored in, and if anything would have some of the cuff's trace, it would be that box.

I also had Malcolm, whose magic skills were better in some areas than my own. If there was a way to increase the chances of the spell working, he would know how.

There was no time to waste with Sean's condition deteriorating rapidly and Jack hunting for the other cuff too. There was a good chance he would find out about the tracking spell some other way and there were other high-level mages around who might be able to use it. Time was ticking.

I printed off the spellwork and the instructions Ella had sent, e-mailed back a quick and heartfelt thanks for her help, got dressed, and hurried down to the main floor. "Malcolm!" I called.

He came up through the floor from the basement. "I'm glad you got at least a little bit of sleep," he said. "What have you got?"

I told him what I'd received from Ella and showed him the spell-work. We studied the diagram together in the kitchen while coffee brewed and I made a couple of pieces of toast with jelly for breakfast. Magic took energy, so I needed food even if it tasted like sawdust.

"Holy crap, this might work," Malcolm said finally as I licked jelly off my fingers. "I take back all the complaining I did about you guys going at it like bunnies, because all that shifter magic in your aura is going to really help us out here."

"I swear, if I hear you say one more thing about bunnies, you will be sorry." I poured my coffee into a large tumbler, snapped on the lid, and headed for the basement. "Let's get a move on. We've got to hurry."

On the way downstairs, I told him about Karen's warning and Jack's plan to find the cuff and put it on Lily Anderson.

As I'd expected, Malcolm went nuclear at the news. By the time he got done swearing, I was on my hands and knees in the smallest circle on the basement floor, using chalk to draw the spellwork.

Malcolm hovered nearby, watching me work. "I'm thinking we

can increase the chances of this working with two sets of amplification spells in the second and third circles. I can close and power them while you focus on the tracking spell and channeling the shifter trace. You'll have to be in the center circle anyway."

That was a hell of a lot of spellwork and it would take hours to draw it all, but Malcolm was right: it was our best chance of getting the spell to work. Magic like this would take a lot out of me, so everything would have to be right the first time because I might not have enough juice to try again.

It took well over an hour just to draw out the spellwork for the tracking spell. It was intricate and a lot of the runes were new to me because it was based on shifter magic. Malcolm watched, learning the new spellwork along with me.

I had to take a short break before I started the first set of amplification spells. I used the time to sit on the couch for a few minutes and call Aaron.

He greeted me warmly. "Alice, thank you for returning my call. I hadn't heard from you in a day or two, so I just wanted to touch base and see how things were going."

"I'm still hunting for the cuff," I told him. I disliked lying to Aaron, but the situation left me little choice at the moment. "If you want me to hand the cup and the mirror over while I'm looking for the cuff, you could send a courier to my house with a check from Ms. Aldridge and I'll box them up."

"Let me ask my client what she prefers and I'll get back to you. Are you doing all right? You sound tired."

"I've been putting in some long hours on this," I said truthfully. "I had a couple of leads that didn't pan out, but I'm not giving up."

"Don't forget about that bonus for wrapping the case up within a week," he reminded me. "I know you're working as fast as you can, but that extra cash could pay for a nice vacation for you and Sean."

I thought of the trip to the Bahamas that Sean had been trying to talk me into taking. If we got out of this mess—*when* we got out of it

—I thought I just might take him up on the offer. Goodness knows we'd deserve some real rest and relaxation after this.

"That's a good way to look at it," I said, hoping he didn't notice the way my voice trembled. "I'll keep looking for the cuff. Just let me know if you're sending someone to pick up the other two items."

"I will. Take care of yourself, Alice. I know you forget to do that sometimes."

"I'll try. Bye, Aaron." We ended the call.

Aaron was a good man. Our affair had been short but passionate. I'd broken things off when I sensed he was starting to want more than just a physical relationship. Back then, two years ago or so, I would never have considered allowing someone to get as close to me as Sean was. Every once in a while, I felt guilty about kicking Aaron to the curb just because he'd started having feelings for me. We'd both moved on, however, and luckily we were still friends.

Arkady texted to ask how I was feeling. I told her I was fine. She sent a photo of what the bruise on her chest looked like today. I winced, then texted back that if she needed company while she recuperated, Matthias might be willing to help nurse her back to health. She replied with a "Wow" emoji.

Me: How did you NOT notice that??

Arkady: I was busy trying not to get killed!

Huh. Maybe Arkady wasn't quite as observant as I'd thought.

Having gotten my second wind, I went back downstairs with a tumbler full of ice water and a turkey sandwich. I needed to be at my best for this to work, which meant more real food and drinking something other than just coffee.

I worked on the first set of amplification spells, which would fill the second circle on the basement floor. That went much faster than the tracking spell even though it was larger, since I'd been doing these spells since I was six. I took a quick break, and then drew the amplification spells in the enormous third circle. That took longer just because the area was so large, but I worked quickly.

When I finally finished, it was late afternoon and I had three circles full of intricately drawn spellwork ready to be used. My fingers were cramping from holding the chalk and my knees hurt from crawling around on the floor, so I sat on the work table for a few minutes to rest and drink more water before doing the final steps for the spell.

Something had been bothering Malcolm for a while, but he hadn't brought it up while I was working. I figured he'd speak up when I took a break and I was right.

"Alice, I'm really sorry for knocking you down last night," he said, looking ashamed. "It was wrong of me to do that. I've been feeling horrible about it ever since. It doesn't matter how frustrated I was; violence is never the answer. I deserve for you to rip me a new one, so have at it. I'm ready." He braced himself.

I smiled. "I accept your apology. I'm not going to rip you a new one. Neither of us were our best selves at that moment. Let's just both learn our lessons and move on. Sound fair?"

Relieved, he returned my smile. "Sounds more than fair."

My phone rang. The screen read *C Rose Calling*. I debated sending it to voicemail, then decided Cyro wouldn't be calling if it wasn't important. I answered and put the call on speaker so Malcolm could hear. "Alice Worth," I said cautiously.

"Congratulations on taking down Kent Stevens last night," the electronic voice said. "You and Ms. Woodall make a good team."

I blinked. "You saw us? How?"

"The Vampire Court had video surveillance in place at your home. I hacked into the feed after you left 1792. I was concerned when it looked like he got the drop on you, but you handled the situation."

"How did you know we were springing a trap on Stevens?" I asked suspiciously.

"I didn't," Cyro said. "I've been keeping an eye on the area around 1792, using facial recognition software in case Stevens showed up, and got a ding when you arrived at the bar. The only reasonable explanation for you being there was to set a trap for him, and it worked. Well done."

"Thanks."

"The main reason I'm calling is the cops found a body in a dumpster behind a motel near the airport early this morning. It's in pretty bad shape, but there's a good chance it's your guy who called himself Kendall. Somebody worked him over with a baseball bat or a pipe with particular attention to his face. The M.E. thinks the body's been in the dumpster since yesterday. They're running fingerprints but no hits so far. I just thought you should know."

I exhaled. "I'm not surprised at all. If you go around stealing from people long enough, it's going to catch up with you sooner or later. The cops have any leads?"

"There's a rumor it might have something to do with the Murphy cabal."

In shock, I blurted out, "*What?*" I calmed myself and added, "Why would they think so?"

"A security camera caught the license plate of a vehicle that might have dumped the body and it traces back to someone who is a known associate of the cabal, Darren Walker. He's been seen hanging around with Catherine Atwood, who is Moses Murphy's only surviving daughter. She's been in town for a couple of weeks, coordinating the attacks on Darius Bell's cabal. Now she's hunting for Bell himself, but he's gone into hiding since his HQ was destroyed."

It was surreal to hear Cyro talking about Catherine, but it did confirm why my aunt was in the city.

"But what's the connection to John Doe?" I asked.

"You know the magical objects you found yesterday in the storage unit? I tipped off SPEMA, as we discussed, and they confiscated the whole stash. There are some items in the collection that are listed in the SPEMA reports as 'highly volatile magic weapons.' If I had to guess, I'd say maybe John Doe was procuring those weapons for Murphy's cabal and when the feds got them instead, Atwood or someone else working for Murphy was pissed and put him out of business permanently."

That made as much sense as anything. Now I was doubly glad we'd given the magical objects to the feds instead of letting my aunt get her hands on them. A powerful magic weapon in the hands of a high-level fire mage was a disaster waiting to happen.

There was a good chance Catherine would find another supplier, obtain weapons, and go after Bell with them. I'd been thinking it had been too quiet in the city these last few days; now perhaps I knew why.

I had my own problems to deal with at the moment, however. Catherine had to stay on the back burner for now. "Thank you for letting me know about John Doe, Cyro. I appreciate the call."

"You're welcome. Take care." The call ended.

I put the phone down on the table, stood up, and stretched. "Well, RIP John Doe, I guess."

"I guess so," Malcolm said. "Idiot got mixed up with Murphy's cabal. How did he think that was going to end? Murphy kills everybody, sooner or later. Everyone knows that."

"Some people think they can make a lot of money getting involved with cabals and find out too late that they've gotten in too deeply to get out." I took off my shirt and put it on the table. I was wearing a sports bra underneath. "Okay, enough delays. We need to get this show on the road."

Malcolm hovered next to me as I used a tube of henna to draw the rest of the tracking spell on my arms and chest. That done, I went to one of the cupboards along the wall, took out the box that had contained the cuff, and set it on top of the spellwork in the center circle.

Barefoot, I sat in the center circle in front of the box. In my head, I ran through the steps I would need to follow for the spell to work. I had used tracking spells many times before, but the inclusion of the shifter magic was new.

Finally, I rolled my shoulders and gave Malcolm a nod. "Ready."

"All right. Let's do this."

I shut my eyes. It wasn't necessary to do so, but I always saw magic and spellwork a little better with my other senses. I closed the inner circle and fed energy into it until my skin buzzed.

I sensed Malcolm close the second circle and then charge the amplification spellwork within it. A second wave of energy followed as he closed the third circle and charged the second set of amplification spells. The power buzzed, waiting for me to use it.

Most tracking spells acted like homing beacons, allowing the user to follow the trace to the object. Instead, this one was designed to show me the cuff's location, which made sense since it could be—though hopefully wasn't—thousands of miles away. I was far more familiar with the former type of tracking spell than the latter, but I had plenty of experience with both.

I held the tracking spell in my mind and drew on the shifter magic in my aura. Suddenly the white lines of air magic spellwork ignited bright gold. I'd never used shifter magic before, but it was beautiful. I sensed the tracking spell forming, waiting for its target, waiting to be unleashed.

Carefully, I opened the box that had held the cuff and put my hand inside.

Before, I'd only sensed the trace of fire magic, but now I had shifter magic coursing through me and the residual golden magic in the box blazed in response.

I had all of the components. Now to put them together and light the fuse.

I grabbed the power from the amplification spellwork and fed it into the tracking spell underneath me. The surge of energy was incredible. Once I had control of the power, I fed the shifter magic into the tracking spell, then drew the power through me to the spellwork drawn on my chest and arms. The sensation was of enormous pressure, like a wave about to break, or a gun about to go off.

I took a deep breath, exhaled, and connected the trace from the box to the tracking spell. "*Adinvenire.*"

With the power of the amplification spells behind it, invoking the spell felt like being fired from a cannon. Images flew past my inner eye like a movie being fast-forwarded. Buildings, streets, grass, pavement, cars, and trees flashed by as the spell searched for the missing cuff at metaphysical speeds with my consciousness along for the ride.

To my surprise, the search seemed to take only a few seconds of real time. That meant the cuff was relatively close by. I barely had time to register relief about that before the spell slammed me face-first—metaphysically speaking—into a wall made of wards.

I fell back with a startled sound, banging the back of my head on the concrete floor. The tracking spell fractured, threatening to release all of its energy in a giant flare. Instinctively, I broke the spell and the inner circle, dropped the amplification spells, and lay dazed, staring up at the basement ceiling.

Malcolm broke the second and third circles and appeared above me, worried. "What happened?"

I tried to process what I'd seen in the last milliseconds before the spell hit the wards and broke. There was a house, and a hallway, and a door, and a room, and then a wall safe. The wards were on the safe, so the cuff must be inside.

I ran the movie backward, trying to recall the room it was in and the outside of the house. I remembered lots of dark wood inside the house and large rooms. It was very elegant...and somehow familiar.

I sucked in a breath and sat up.

"Alice, you okay? Did you see where the cuff is?"

"Yeah, I saw it." I staggered to my feet. The back of my head hurt and my body ached like I'd gone ten rounds with a professional boxer, but at the moment, I didn't care.

Blood magic ignited on my hands. "It's in a safe at Charles's house. That fangy son of a bitch has the cuff."

CHAPTER 19

Not long after sunset, I pulled up to the gate of Charles's estate.

The gates swung open as I reached for the button to roll my window down. I drove up the long driveway and parked in front of the mansion's front steps next to two black SUVs. I got out of the car and headed for the front door.

The door opened, revealing Bryan. "Miss Alice."

"Bryan. I assume he's here?"

He stepped aside to let me walk past and closed the door behind me. "He is. Would you care to wait in the office? He'll be with you in a few minutes."

"All right." I followed Bryan through the foyer and down a hall to a pair of doors. He opened them and ushered me into the office.

Charles's home office was large enough to accommodate a game of field hockey, with room left over. Two stories tall, it boasted floor-to-ceiling bookcases on two walls. The third wall was a two-level art gallery. Narrow wrought-iron staircases led up to a walkway that ran around the three interior walls. Tall west-facing windows offered a panoramic view of the estate's backyard.

Like his office above 1792, the room was divided into three main areas: the desk area, a sitting area with several couches and chairs, and the bar, with its enormous granite counter and tall chairs.

Everything about this meeting was part of a chess match, from the timing of my arrival to the room Charles had chosen for our meeting and my choice of where I sat. With that in mind, I settled into one of the chairs in front of the desk.

Bryan headed for the bar. "What can I get you to drink?"

"Just water, please."

He selected a bottle from the fridge, removed the cap, and brought it to me wrapped in a cloth napkin. He placed a coaster on the table at my right and set the bottle down. "You look like you've recovered from last night. How are your arm and side?"

"All healed. Neither were all that serious." I picked up the bottle and took a drink. "I'm sure you're all relieved to have the Kent Stevens situation resolved and be back home."

"Very much so." Bryan moved around in front of me, leaning against Charles's desk. "It was very courageous of you to risk your life to draw Stevens out. Mr. Vaughan and I would have preferred to have done that ourselves."

"So I gathered." I crossed my legs and studied him. "I meant to ask before, but will there be a funeral for Fortune? I'd like to attend."

"His family requested a private service, from what I understand. Mr. Vaughan is covering the costs of the funeral and burial, naturally, but the Court is respecting their wishes."

"Oh." I set the bottle down on the table. "The construction project looks like it's going well. Any idea when Hawthorne's will reopen?"

The answer came from behind me. "We hope to reopen in two months."

Charles strode into the office. He wore a gray summer suit, with a purple tie and matching silk handkerchief perfectly folded in the breast pocket. It was the color combination he knew I liked most on him and another deliberate choice in our chess match.

He walked around the desk and settled into the oversize leather chair as Bryan returned to the bar to pour his employer two fingers of Scotch from a crystal decanter. He brought the glass to Charles and set it on the leather desk pad.

"Thank you," Charles said. "If you will excuse us?"

"Of course." Bryan inclined his head and turned to me. His expression was carefully neutral, but I read concern in his eyes. If I'd had any question of whether he knew the reason for my visit, that look dispelled it. Everyone in the room knew why I was here and what was at stake. He departed, closing the doors behind him.

Charles and I studied one another, reading each other's body language. To the untrained eye he might have seemed as expressive as a rock, but I knew him well enough to see he had anticipated this meeting. Arkady loved a physical fight. Charles enjoyed a battle of wits.

I had come prepared for both.

In the hours between my realization that Charles had the cuff and my arrival at his house, I had allowed myself to be angry. I embraced the fury, and then I let it go. I could not afford to allow anger to be a part of this chess match. Anger made you stupid. It sucked away your ability to think five steps ahead and strategize. I wasn't here to lash out or retaliate or even demand explanations. Charles would be coldly strategic, so I couldn't afford to be any less calculating. My years as a prisoner in my grandfather's cabal had taught me many things, but perhaps the most valuable lesson of all was to never let the bastards see that they got to you. Show your enemies no anger, no grief, no hurt, and no happiness, because they will use your feelings as a weapon against you.

I spoke first. "How long have you had the cuff?"

He picked up the glass and took a sip. "Since early this morning."

"How long have you known there was a second cuff?"

"For certain, since the night of the auction."

"When did you suspect there were two?"

"From the moment you sent me the images of the items you had been hired to locate."

"And when did you find out the second cuff was the cause of Sean's condition?"

He put the glass back on the desk. "Last evening, while you and Ms. Woodall were at 1792."

His responses felt like truth. "So Kim found out about the second cuff and told you, and you held back that information until after the operation to catch Stevens was over. You had her call me with the news once the dust had settled."

He gave me a nod.

"So I wasn't distracted during the operation, or so I went ahead with it instead of backing out to focus on looking for the second cuff?"

"Both."

In other words, it was more important to Charles that Stevens be caught than for me to know about and begin my search for the second cuff. I was not in the least surprised by that, nor by any of his other responses. I had expected as much.

I took a drink of water. "What made you suspect there was a second cuff to begin with?"

"When I saw the picture of the cuff you sent, I recalled selling a similar object a few years ago to a client from another city. There was, of course, a chance it had since changed hands, or that your client was in fact the person I had sold it to, but the cuff I had seen did not have the additional spellwork. It required some time to ascertain that they were, indeed, two different cuffs."

"And when did you begin the process of obtaining the other cuff?"

"The moment I suspected they were likely a pair: the night of the auction."

I hadn't thought it would be possible for me to be any angrier than I was, but I went even colder at the realization that the chess match had started days ago, even before Sean and I went to John Doe's storage unit.

"You couldn't have known the cuff would end up attaching itself to Sean, so why not just tell me about the second cuff to begin with? Why keep it a secret and go to all the trouble to obtain the second one?" I studied him and thought about it. "Were you hoping to find my client's missing cuff before I did and then sell the set to the highest bidder?"

He inclined his head. "Unfortunately, my agents were not able to locate it before you did. The man calling himself Joseph Kendall left little trail for them to follow. Once the cuff had affixed itself to Maclin, I accelerated my plan to obtain the second cuff and adjusted my strategy accordingly."

I had one last question. "Does Jack Hastings know you have the cuff?"

"I have not yet revealed that fact to him, nor has he contacted me to request a meeting."

Charles's deliberate word choice was not lost on me. He had not *yet* told Jack about the cuff, but that was on the table.

Our relative positions in this match were complex. We both knew I wanted the cuff, and that my need for it was great. We also knew Jack wanted the cuff. I assumed Charles already knew what he planned to do with it and what the possible fallout from that might be.

On the surface, those facts seemed to put me at a disadvantage. Charles had something I wanted and there was another interested party. But because of my magic coursing through his veins and his knowledge about my power, and because I had something *he* wanted just as much, nothing was as simple as it might appear.

One point to Charles for keeping the cuff at his house so that I would come here to get it. One point to me for being calm instead of furious at the games he'd played. He'd chosen to meet me in the office, as opposed to another room or on the back patio, knowing I'd decide to sit across from each other at the desk rather than at the bar or in the sitting area. He'd chosen our battlefield and I'd accepted his terms in that regard.

The office setting told me he was approaching our discussion as a business negotiation. The cuff was for sale if we could decide on terms.

I didn't inquire about his asking price; he would have declined to name a figure. I'd heard someone once say that in a dark room, the ceiling was always higher. Besides, we both knew quite well what he wanted in return for the cuff. Like chess strategy, we had to follow a series of expected moves...at least, up until a certain point.

I rested my hands on the arms of the chair. "According to my sources, the fair market value for the cuff, given its age and purpose, is twelve thousand dollars." That number came from Ella, with whom I had exchanged several e-mails before I arrived at Charles's house. "I am willing to offer fourteen thousand four hundred dollars, or twenty percent above market value."

He remained impassive. "And if Mr. Hastings were to offer more?"

"Then I will exceed his best offer by the same percentage."

I was not at all surprised when he replied, "Perhaps cash is less interesting to me than the services I might receive from a potential buyer. No doubt the pack could provide many benefits whose value far exceeds that of the cuff's potential sale price. What might your counteroffer be?"

I paused a moment as if contemplating my answer, when in fact I'd had it prepared knowing he wouldn't accept a cash offer.

"Your new building will be completed soon and no doubt you'll require a great deal of wards and spellwork to protect it. You know very well both the cost of creating wards on that scale and the value of it. In exchange for the cuff, I will provide the wards for your new building, to your specifications, as expediently as my physical ability will allow."

That got a reaction. It was only a slight narrowing of his eyes, but I'd surprised and impressed him with my second offer. He'd set the stage for me to offer my magic skills by mentioning what the pack might be able to do, but he hadn't expected me to make such a large bid. It was big enough to throw him slightly off his game. He'd been prepared to pretend to consider and then reject my proposal, but it was a hell of an offer and he hesitated just a little too long if he'd wanted me to think he wasn't tempted by it. Point to me.

The question was, was it big enough to derail his plans for how this negotiation was going to go?

The answer, it turned out, was no, but it had made the train wobble a bit.

Charles steepled his fingers. "That is quite a tempting offer, but I would prefer to pay you a fair price for that work rather than set the rather dangerous precedent of you bartering your services to a member of the Court. Others on the Court might see it as an opportunity to exploit you in the future, and I am loath to be the cause of it."

It was a nice parry; I had to give him credit. There was just enough truth in his reasoning that it wasn't an outright lie.

So here we were, arriving at exactly the place Charles had wanted this negotiation to go. That might have seemed like a failure on my part, but I'd known from the beginning this was where we'd end up, and I'd come prepared for it.

Part of Charles's game plan was for me to be the one who made the offer. He wanted me to say the words. I had no doubt it would give him pleasure to hear them. As such, I was willing to do what he wanted, because it would be to my advantage in the end...if I acted the part and made just the right moves.

I took a deep breath, as if steeling myself, and thought about Sean so I felt a stab of pain, fear, and anger that Charles could sense. It was pure method acting. "In return for the cuff, I will let you drink from me."

Charles raised an eyebrow, feigning surprise. "That is a very generous offer."

"You know I want the cuff," I told him, leaning forward. "And we both know you'd like to drink from me again, especially if I'm awake and able to share the experience, unlike last time."

Judging by the flash of surprise in Charles's eyes, I scored a palpable hit with that comment. Charles had indeed already bitten me, but I was in a coma at the time and unaware of it. Part of his reason for biting me was to discover what secrets my blood held—that I was a high-level mage, not the mid-level mage I'd claimed to be—and to establish a kind of dominance over me.

A not-insignificant purpose for a vampire's bite is the intimacy of it; not just the physical and sexual intimacy, but the emotional one. Charles wanted to bite me with my consent not just because he enjoyed the taste of my blood and would benefit from the power of my magic, but because he believed it would bind us together, much like that walk in the sun and his seemingly spontaneous story were designed to do. He hadn't known I was onto his game until this moment. As I'd told Sean, I'd suspected Charles's decision to share his story of how he became a vampire had an ulterior motive, but it wasn't until I knew he had the other cuff that I put it all together.

Charles wanted me; he'd been clear about that since our first meeting when I'd smirked in his face and then threatened to burn down Vampire Court headquarters. He'd bided his time for the last five years, playing a long, carefully calculated game as I settled into my new life and the walls I'd built around myself started to come down. He'd even let me leave Hawthorne's with Sean the night we'd first met, when he could have covertly interfered. He'd wagered my relationship with Sean wouldn't last. He was still betting on that, even to the point that he was willing to hand over the cuff, because he was sure I wouldn't put it on. My reaction to him asking me if I would do so last night had no doubt confirmed that belief.

He was banking on that walk in the sun, his story, and his bite to strengthen the bond between us just as my conflict with Jack and the problems caused by the cuff made my future with Sean even less certain.

I had no doubt that he'd considered selling the cuff to Jack. It had to have been an attractive prospect, at least at first. If Jack put the cuff on Lily Anderson and bound her and Sean together for life, Sean was no longer a rival for my affections. Hard on the heels of that thought must have been the realization that if word got out that Jack had obtained the cuff from Charles, it would torpedo once and for all any chance of me ever being interested in him.

At the same time, he couldn't just keep the cuff hidden until Sean died. If the other members of the Court or the Were Ruling Council discovered Charles caused Sean's death, either directly or indirectly, there would be hell to pay and the Court wouldn't protect him. They'd throw him to the wolves, quite literally.

So he'd arrived at the only logical conclusion: a business transaction. A drink of my blood for the cuff. I get what I want, Charles gets what he wants, Sean lives, and because I wouldn't be putting the cuff on—or so he believed—Charles's plans to add me to his collection were coming along nicely.

He might suspect I had figured some of this out, but his surprise at my reference to his earlier bite told me he hadn't credited me with deciphering his motives. My advantage was my past as a prisoner of my grandfather's cabal, where there were plots within plots within plots and no one's motivations were simple. Charles was very, very good at 12-D chess, but so was I, as he was about to find out. Magic and sarcasm weren't my only weapons.

"I confess you are correct," he said, choosing to acknowledge that I'd accurately assumed he wanted to share the intimacy of his bite with me. "While I found your blood sweeter than any wine I have ever tasted, and the power of your magic strengthened me more than I could have imagined, I found the experience unsatisfying. In some circumstances, a vampire's bite is not merely for sustenance. You are as far from a food source as could be, Alice. For me, you are a joy."

Time to negotiate. "Then let's come to an agreement. You will hand over the cuff to me, with no strings attached. In return, you may bite me and drink from me once, at a time of my choosing but within the month."

"Very well, but I will choose the time," Charles said. "I choose tonight, before I present you with the cuff."

I had expected that counteroffer, but I pretended to be insulted. "Do you think I'll go back on my word?"

"Not at all, but I strongly suspect that the wolf will object most strenuously to our agreement and I think you will agree that it would be much easier for all concerned if our transaction is completed prior to his recovery."

I couldn't disagree with that. "All right; agreed. You can bite my wrist."

He smiled. "My terms are for your throat only. On this I will not negotiate."

Again, not a surprise, but I didn't accept right away. It was time to play a very big card. "In return for biting my throat, you will not bring any pleasure with your bite."

His poker face disappeared. I saw surprise, anger, concern, and dismay before he managed to get his mask back in place.

He'd counted on the intense pleasure of the bite to make it intimate, and he certainly hadn't thought I would figure that out and refuse it. I knew very well, though not from my own experience, that a vampire could bring their food source to climax with a bite, and it would not have surprised me in the least if Charles had planned to do that to me.

I was willing to trade a bite and pint for the cuff and let it be a business transaction, but I wouldn't allow Charles to give me an orgasm. The bite was intimate enough. At the moment, there was only one person who was allowed to see and share my pleasure, and that was Sean.

"If there is no pleasure, there will be only pain," Charles said finally. "I do not wish to hurt you."

He'd hurt me plenty by keeping his knowledge of the cuff a

secret, but it would do no good to point that out. That was in the past and dwelling on it would not help me negotiate with him now.

"Those are my terms, Charles. One bite, right now, on my throat, with no pleasure. You will not attempt to turn me. I will stay fully dressed. Then you will hand over the cuff and allow me to leave without any delay. You will do me no harm, physical or otherwise, other than the bite. And though it goes without saying, any attempt to deviate from our terms will end very badly for you."

His face darkened. "I have never reneged on an agreement, Alice, and I do not intend to start now."

"Good. Then we have a deal?"

"We do."

"Shall we drink on it?"

"Indeed." Charles rose and moved to the bar. He selected a glass and poured two fingers of Scotch.

While his back was turned, I entertained a brief fantasy of reaching into my boot, pulling out the stake I'd hidden inside, and planting it right in his lying, scheming heart. My fingers itched. I tapped them on the arm of my chair and put the fantasy aside... for now.

He brought me my glass and picked up his own. "To you. A masterful negotiation."

I rose and tapped the rim of my glass to his. "And to you, for a masterful scheme."

We drank.

FOR ALL OF my careful negotiations, I had overlooked one detail: where Charles would administer his bite. That would teach me to think I could ever completely outmaneuver a vampire. I'd thought he'd given in on the no-pleasure debate too quickly; perhaps now I knew why.

I'd planned to sit on one of the sofas in the office while he bit me. Unfortunately, since I hadn't made that part of our agreed-upon terms, we had to hash it out after the fact, which meant I had little bargaining power when push came to shove on the topic of location.

As a result, we ended up in bed.

Actually, *on* a bed, and not Charles's own, not that he hadn't tried his damnedest to talk me into doing precisely that.

He escorted me to one of the mansion's many guest rooms. Before I surrendered to the inevitable, as it were, I took a moment to "compose myself" in the adjoining bathroom while Charles presumably set the mood.

I ran water in the sink while I let Malcolm out of my earring and gave him instructions on what to do if Charles deviated from the terms we'd agreed upon—up to and including the separation of his head from his body if he tried to turn me. I was ninety-nine percent certain he wouldn't attempt it, but if he did, I wanted to make sure it didn't happen.

Malcolm, needless to say, was extremely unhappy about the entire situation. He'd already voiced his objections back at home, so he had nothing to add now except to glare in the direction of the bedroom. Even my assurance that I was fine with the way our negotiations had turned out wasn't enough to lessen his anger at Charles. I figured I'd be hearing about all this later too.

I washed my hands, turned the light off, and opened the bathroom door.

I'd half-expected Charles to have changed into a silk robe and turned the room into a candlelit, rose-petal-strewn love nest while I'd been in the bathroom. Indeed, he'd turned off the overhead light in favor of a bedside Tiffany lamp that cast a rosy glow, but there were no candles and no actual roses. Nor was he undressed, other than he'd removed his suit jacket and tie and draped them neatly over the back of a chair. His shoes waited next to the bed.

He stood in his socks, collar unbuttoned and hands behind his back, as I emerged from the bathroom. At my surprise, the corners of his mouth turned up. "You were expecting something quite different?"

"I wasn't expecting you to be wearing checkered socks."

He glanced at his feet. "I do allow myself a bit of whimsy on occasion."

"You're on a slippery slope with this, Charles. Today, it's checkered socks. Tomorrow, who knows, a polka-dot bow tie?"

"I said whimsy, Alice, not lunacy." He gestured grandly at the bed. "Please, be comfortable."

I intended to stay fully dressed, but I couldn't bring myself to put my dirty boots on the very expensive-looking comforter. I unzipped them and steadied myself against one of the bedposts as I toed them off. I wasn't exactly stalling, but I didn't rush the process either.

With my boots lying beside Charles's shoes on the floor, I sat on the side of the bed. "Okay, I'm ready."

"You should lie down," Charles advised gently. "If you remain sitting up, you may faint."

That was a fair point. Feeling self-conscious, I swung my feet up onto the bed and lay back, my head resting on a pillow as light and airy as a cloud. The comforter was silk and velvet and somehow almost as weightless as the pillow. I lay with my arms at my sides and spine as straight as a board, my gaze fixed on the ceiling.

His eyes glowing softly, Charles walked around to the other side of the bed. He moved like silk himself, somehow making the climb onto and across the bed look elegant instead of awkward. Despite everything, my heart raced as he lay down at my side.

I cursed my failure to think about where he would want to be while he bit me and returned my gaze to the ceiling. Trying to slow my heart rate, I pictured myself standing in an ice-cold shower while someone read me baseball scores.

He chuckled. "A cold shower, Alice?"

Too late, I realized I might have been focusing a little *too* hard on that image. "Damn it, Charles, stay out of my head," I snapped.

"You broadcast your thoughts," he countered. "I made no attempt to eavesdrop, as you call it."

"Whatever. Let's just do this." I turned my face away.

Carefully, he used his fingertips to turn my head back. "I am open to renegotiating our terms," he said quietly. "Specifically, your edict that I cannot mitigate the pain of the bite. I have not bitten anyone in such a way in a very long time. I told you that I do not wish to hurt you, and I spoke the truth."

He might truly not want to hurt me, but he was willing to do so to get what he wanted. I would not have expected any different. "You've seen the scars on my back. You know I'm no stranger to pain."

His eyes darkened. "If I ever encounter the person or persons who inflicted those wounds on you, I will show them their own entrails before they die. I have no desire to be remembered in the same category as your past tormentors."

I kept my mind carefully blank so Charles didn't catch any stray memories or thoughts of Moses. "I offered you my throat, Charles. It's not the same category at all." I turned my head again. "Please just bite me and let's get this over with. I have a life to save."

He brushed hair back from my neck and leaned close, his lips cool against my skin. My pulse raced and I knew he could sense my blood rushing millimeters away from his fangs. I shivered.

"Sweet Alice," he murmured, and bit me.

The pain of his fangs piercing my skin made my vision go white. I managed not to cry out but I couldn't do anything about my flinch. He held me still so I didn't jerk away and tear my own flesh.

The agony did not lessen; if anything, it increased. My chest heaved and my breathing became ragged, almost like sobs. I felt a strange pulling sensation in the midst of the pain and realized Charles was drinking.

The pain was so great that I almost told him I'd changed my

mind about the pleasure, but I pictured Sean and that killed the impulse. If I could withstand hours of torture by a blood mage, I could hold up under a few minutes of pain from a vampire bite, or had I grown weak? The fear that I'd become cowardly was enough to banish all thoughts of asking him to ease the pain.

Charles made a sound low in his throat. I'd heard it once or twice before, a kind of sensual growl. I realized my body was responding in a very unexpected way to the pain of his bite. Whether my arousal was a result of his or vice-versa, no amount of imagining a cold shower had any effect on the growing heat between my legs.

At first, I thought he'd broken his word and given me pleasure, but there was nothing but pain. I'd always liked a little pain with my pleasure—sometimes more than a little—but this was the first time I'd become so aroused by pain alone. I'd experienced agony before and never had this reaction.

Unless it was Charles I was reacting to.

I banished the thought as quickly as it popped into my head. We were lying in bed and he was drinking my blood. It was by definition an intimate act and it had triggered an automatic response. There was nothing more to it than that.

Then why was my hand on his, where it rested on my hip?

I wanted to let go of him, but I couldn't. My hand wouldn't obey; instead, my fingers tightened around his and he made that low sound again. Dimly, I realized the pain had indeed diminished as endorphins kicked in and my arousal grew. I couldn't stifle a moan. His hand squeezed my hip, though I had long since stopped struggling to get away.

I lost track of time as he drank, drifting in and out of awareness and caught between pain and pleasure. It was something of a surprise when his fangs slid out of my flesh. His cool tongue laved my neck, cleaning up the blood that trickled from the bite and healing the punctures. I realized then that I'd forgotten a second item while negotiating. Vampires often branded their cattle by leaving visible bite marks. Charles had healed the wound of his own accord.

I sensed my magic coursing through his body, blending with his own. He would be stronger for a time because of it. More importantly, my influence over him increased as well, and that would not fade away. It shifted the balance of power between us ever so slightly in my favor—another reason I'd been willing to make this trade.

Finally, he raised his head. His eyes were deep black. He looked fully sated, his skin slightly pink. He was also quite aroused, but so was I, so I couldn't fault him for it. To his credit, he kept a little space between us and ignored the visible evidence of his excitement.

I wanted to get up and leave, but I couldn't, not just yet. Not until I thought I could stand up without falling.

He took my warm hand in his cool one. "Your blood tasted slightly of whisky."

"I wondered why you gave me a glass of that fifty-year single malt to seal our agreement. Now I understand." My voice was stronger than I would have expected, all things considered.

We stared at each other. I wondered if he would mention my reaction to his bite.

Instead, he raised my hand to his lips and kissed it. "I would give you the world, if you would take it from me."

"I don't want the world," I said, pulling my hand out of his grip. "I've been offered that before and turned it down. It would never be worth the price I'd have to pay."

"Perhaps the price is negotiable. You drive a hard bargain, as they say. I have no doubt you would come out the winner."

"I highly doubt I would." I pushed myself up until I was sitting. I had a moment of lightheadedness and then it passed.

Charles watched as I swung my legs over the side of the bed, picked up my boots, and put them on. When I started to stand, he rose and moved vamp-fast around to my side. "Slowly," he cautioned me.

"It ain't my first rodeo with blood loss," I told him. I lowered my feet to the floor and carefully stood.

He cupped my face with his hand. "You should eat a meal and drink water. May I call for some food?"

"No, thank you. I have to be going." I pushed his hand away. "Can I have the cuff, please?"

"It is on its way. I can have a light meal here in moments."

"I really don't have time. Sean's dying, remember? I'm in a bit of a rush."

"What will you do with the cuff once you have it?"

"Whatever I have to do to save Sean."

He studied me. "Perhaps it would best not to disclose how you came into possession of the cuff. I am sure you can concoct a reasonable explanation for obtaining it that does not mention my name."

"I'm sure I can."

Someone knocked at the door. I suspected it was Bryan, and when the door opened, I found I was right.

He didn't look surprised or relieved, so I assumed Charles had already told him that I was fine. He carried a wooden box with runes inscribed on all six sides.

Charles took the box and handed it to me. "The spellwork hides the contents from tracking spells until the box is opened. As such, you should not open the box until you reach your destination."

At my raised eyebrow, he sighed. "I give you my word the cuff is in the box."

"Good." I picked up my messenger bag and put the box inside it. I touched my right earring, as if checking to make sure it was still there. At that prearranged signal, Malcolm jumped into the earring.

With my ghost safely stashed, I turned to Charles. "I'll be in touch."

"I have no doubt we will speak again soon." He glanced at Bryan. "Please escort Alice to her car."

"Yes, sir." Bryan headed for the door. "Miss Alice, please follow me."

I headed for the door. At the threshold, I paused and turned back. Charles was watching me, standing in his checkered socks next to the rumpled bed.

I didn't thank him, nor did I tell him what a bastard he was for keeping the information about the cuff from me. He knew how I felt and that I wouldn't forget or forgive what he'd done anytime soon. He didn't tell me he didn't think I'd put the cuff on, or that he wouldn't forget my reaction to his bite. Everything we didn't say hung in the air between us.

"Good night, Charles," I said finally.

"Good night, Alice."

I followed Bryan into the hall and closed the door behind me.

CHAPTER 20

About ninety minutes later, scrubbed clean and wearing different clothes, I pulled up in front of another enormous gate and rolled down my window.

A black-clad Court enforcer approached my vehicle. "Ms. Worth, what brings you to Northbourne tonight?"

I recognized him. "Hello, Carlos. I'd like to see Valas."

"Do you have an appointment?"

He knew very well I didn't, or I'd have been expected. "No, I don't, but I have with me the only way to save Sean Maclin's life and if I don't see her, he'll die."

He got a faraway look that told me he was speaking to someone telepathically. I waited.

The metal barricades in front of the gate retracted into the ground and the gate began to swing open. "Proceed directly to the main entrance," he instructed me. "Someone will meet you there."

I thanked him and passed through the gate. Northbourne's driveway was nearly a quarter of a mile long. As I drove, my earring buzzed reassuringly, reminding me that I was not going into Northbourne alone.

I'd let Malcolm out when we got home. To his credit, he'd said nothing about what he'd seen and heard while Charles was drinking from me. Instead, he asked me if I was sure I was going through with my "crazy" plan to ask Valas for help. When I said yes, he told me in no uncertain terms that he was coming along. I surprised him by readily agreeing. If any part of my plan did go sideways, I might need his help just to survive.

While I showered, I'd sent Malcolm to do a quick check on Sean's condition. He reported that Sean was weak but aware enough that when Malcolm got near him he raised his head slightly and appeared to hear the ghost when he spoke. Malcolm told the wolf that I was coming and that he needed to hang on. The wolf seemed to understand.

He'd also overheard Jack shouting at someone on the phone, a mage he'd hired to locate the other cuff. The hired mage wasn't having any luck. According to Malcolm, Jack and Delia were discussing whether I had the cuff and had found some way of hiding it from anyone else. That was uncomfortably accurate. They were debating whether to come to my house looking for it when Malcolm jumped home to warn me that we'd better get moving.

Ahead loomed Northbourne, the headquarters of the Vampire Court of the Northwestern United States. The estate had once belonged to a shipping magnate. The Court had renovated it into a fortress that was part residence, part courthouse, part magic workshop, and part prison. Though Valas was the only member of the Court who resided there full time, the others had apartments where they stayed when they needed additional security or when their Court duties required them to be close at hand.

From what I understood, Valas had not left Northbourne in years. How many was a matter of conjecture, but the consensus was that she did not pass its gate except on the rarest of occasions.

I was hoping that tonight would be one of those occasions.

When I parked in front of the estate's wide front steps, a Court enforcer I didn't recognize opened my door. "Ms. Worth, this way, please."

We entered Northbourne's enormous main lobby, with its marble floor, soaring rotunda, and sweeping grand staircase. The enforcer led me to the right of the stairs and down a long hall lined with artwork. I'd never been down this corridor before.

"What's your name?" I asked, scurrying to keep up with his long strides.

He looked straight ahead. "Hanson, like the band."

"There's a band called Hanson?"

A pause. "Never mind."

"Okay. Where are we headed, Hanson?"

"You asked to see Valas. We are going to her audience chamber."

Of course Valas had an audience chamber.

At the end of the hallway we encountered a pair of doors. Hanson paused outside, presumably asking permission to enter. After a moment, he turned the handles and swung them open.

The room was less ostentatious than I had imagined, but it still made Charles's home office look like a broom closet by comparison. High above us, the chandelier glowed dimly, leaving the room in near darkness. Two large chairs sat in front of an enormous stone fireplace. Despite the warm night, a fire burned in the fireplace. A long and very heavy-looking conference table ringed with ornately carved chairs took up a good part of the other side of the room. The large open area in between must be for gatherings or ceremonies. The deep carpet seemed to swallow my boots.

I expected to be led to the conference table. Instead, Hanson directed me to sit in one of the chairs by the fire. I wondered at this choice of seating. The conference table signaled a business meeting; the chairs, a cozy fireside chat. I doubted my conversation with Valas would be anything close to cozy.

I perched on the edge of the chair. "Shouldn't I stand and wait for Valas?"

Before Hanson could reply, a familiar voice answered from the shadows. "I do not think you care much for such proprieties."

Hanson bowed in the direction of the voice. "Madame Valas, Ms. Worth."

I rose as the tall, slim vampire seemed to appear out of the shadows themselves. Her long, straight black hair framed her hawk-like face. Tonight, she wore a floor-length midnight-blue dress. Her slippered feet made no noise as she crossed the floor.

The one and only time I had met her before now was when I gave a progress report to the entire Court during my investigation into the West-Addison harnad. At that time, I'd been some twenty feet away, far enough that I hadn't sensed her dark magic until she wished for me to do so—and then she almost crushed me with it, or tried to.

Tonight, as she sat in the chair across from me, her power felt like I was standing too near an open furnace. As she was perfectly capable of containing her magic behind her shields, I assumed she was reminding me, and none too subtly, of her power.

"Please sit," Valas said graciously, indicating my chair.

It was a far cry from the last time, when she'd used her power to drop me into a chair like a marionette with its strings cut. She'd been trying to make a point then. Tonight, she'd agreed to see me without an appointment. I must have piqued her interest when we'd met before, or perhaps my reference to saving Sean's life had been intriguing. Either way, I had my audience. Now I had to make it count.

Unlike Charles and Niara and every other vamp I'd ever encountered, the head of the Court had not one scent but many. She was ancient. Before I'd met her, I'd heard she was at least a thousand years old, but her power felt much older than that. Her accent sounded vaguely Middle Eastern or eastern European. I had not been able to identify her accent, probably because the language she had spoken when alive no longer existed.

"You have come to me for help," she said without preamble.

When I started to object, she raised her hand. "Ms. Worth, your situation is a desperate one. You have obtained the cuff that is the mate to the one currently draining the life from your lover, but his beta, Jack Hastings, has declared you *persona non grata*. You cannot reach him without risking great harm to yourself or members of his pack. All this is known to me. What I do not know is why you have come to me, or what you believe I can or will do to assist you. The Court, as you know, cannot interfere in a pack matter."

It would appear there was little I could tell Valas that she didn't already know. "If no one knew or suspected anyone from the Court was involved, you'd have nothing to worry about in that regard."

She raised an imperious eyebrow. "Perhaps that is true, but again I ask: why would I risk war with the Were Ruling Council to help you?"

"Because Sean is a good alpha and the stability of his pack benefits the Court. Jack may have designs on taking Sean's position. You and I both know he'd make a very bad alpha. Their troubles will become your troubles sooner or later—probably sooner."

She regarded me. "He schemes to unite his pack with another through a mate bond with the daughter of another alpha."

"True, but there's no way that goes the way he wants it to. Sean loves me. He'll never accept Lily Anderson without making Jack pay dearly for what he's done."

Valas nodded slowly. "You fear for Maclin's life if he challenges Hastings."

"He's weakened because of the cuff, but he wouldn't let that stop him from challenging Jack for stranding me, barring me from seeing him, and trying to get the cuff before I could. Again, it's in the Court's best interest to do what it can to keep that from happening, even it means covertly helping me."

"Let us stipulate that I do not disagree with your assessment of the situation. I am still unclear as to what you want of me." She leaned forward, her eyes so dark that they seemed eternal. Her ancient scent enveloped me and the air became thick with power. "And I wonder, Alice, what you offer me in return."

Earlier, I sat across the table from Charles and painstakingly negotiated for possession of the cuff. Those stakes had been high, but I had prevailed.

For the second time in a single night, I opened negotiations with a vampire, with Sean's life—and mine—hanging in the balance.

THE SPEEDING CAR hit a pothole and the bone-jarring impact rattled my teeth.

"Perhaps your speed is excessive," my companion suggested, her hands folded neatly in her lap. "The road conditions do not appear ideal for your vehicle. Had I known, I would have insisted on taking a different mode of transportation."

"We're in stealth mode," I reminded her, narrowly avoiding another pothole as my car flew down the country road. "The Court SUVs and limos might have better suspensions, but they aren't stealthy. I promise we'll get there in one piece."

"Do humans find that comment reassuring?" Valas asked. "'In one piece' could mean many things."

I slowed as a couple of deer ran across the road. "Generally it's meant to be somewhat tongue-in-cheek."

"Ah, a form of sarcasm. I see." She nodded and continued looking out the window, studying the houses and empty fields as we passed.

My navigation app informed me that we were a little over a mile away from our destination. "We're getting close. I'll park a little ways up the road and we can go in on foot."

"You will park directly in front of the residence," she told me. "Additional 'stealth' will not be required."

"Are you sure?"

The scent of lost empires filled my car, indicating her displeasure. "You will trust and obey."

I wasn't very good at doing either of those things, but I didn't have a hell of a lot of choice in the matter. "Okay," I said, hoping I sounded more certain than I felt.

Ahead in the darkness, I saw a two-story house set back from road. Despite it being the middle of the night, all the lights were on. Almost a dozen trucks, SUVs, and cars were parked out front. It looked like the whole damn pack was at Jack and Delia's. That was a lot of werewolves to wade through.

Hoping Valas was right about not needing to sneak up on the house, I turned into the driveway. There were so many other vehicles already here that the only empty space was directly in front of the garage, blocking in a large truck I assumed was Jack's. I parked and turned off the car, leaving the key in the ignition in case I had to leave quickly. I got out, put my messenger bag on my shoulder, and listened.

The house was eerily quiet. I expected pack meetings to be loud events, but I heard nothing but nighttime insects and the wind.

"We must go inside," Valas said, closing her door. She'd opted to wear the same long blue dress to come with me to Jack's house. My suggestion that she change into something less formal had been met with an imperious stare.

I headed for the front door with Valas behind me. Perhaps it would have made more sense to send the immortal and immensely powerful vampire in first, given we might be walking into a den of very angry werewolves, but hiding behind someone else had never been my style. It was bad enough that I'd had to ask for her help; I wasn't going to cower behind her too.

I opened the door, stopped, and stared.

The front room was a large formal living space. Beyond it, through a wide arched doorway, I saw a family room. I counted well over a dozen men and women—most or all of the adults in Sean's pack—in the two rooms.

And they were all unconscious.

"What did you do?" I breathed.

"What you requested that I do." Valas moved past me into the house and closed the door behind us. "You wished to get to your lover without confronting members of his pack and to execute your plan without their interference. This was the easiest and most efficient way to accomplish both."

Jack, Delia, Ben, and Nan were in the front room, along with an older man and woman I didn't recognize. In the family room I found Karen, Felicia, Felicia's brother David, and several others. Some were sprawled on the floor, others slumped over in chairs or sofas. Jack, Delia, and Ben seemed to be in a tight group in the middle of the living room, as if they had been standing close to each other, perhaps arguing, when Valas's magic had hit and dropped them where they stood.

One pack member who was conspicuously absent was Caleb. I wondered if Jack had decided it was best to keep the volatile young werewolf far away from such a stressful and emotional situation. I hated to agree with Jack on anything, but it was probably the right call.

I became aware of a strange keening sound drifting up from below. By the time my brain processed what it was, I was already in motion, headed for a door just off the enormous kitchen. I flung the door open and ran down the stairs.

Patrick, Karen's brother, lay unconscious on the floor near the foot of the stairs. I stopped short when I realized Jack and Delia's basement was large and unfinished—an enormous, nearly empty concrete space that was straight out of my dream.

The wolf, however, was not in a glass cage. It was made of steel and looked like the sort used to hold lions or tigers. I shook myself and went to the cage.

The wolf stopped keening when I appeared. He'd apparently sensed the rest of the pack being spelled and dragged himself to the side of the cage to throw himself weakly against the bars. He'd been too feeble to injure himself very badly, for which I was grateful. He lay on his side, his golden eyes full of fury and pain.

"Sean, I'm here," I told him, my voice sounding choked. "I'm here, I'm here."

If the wolf understood what I was saying, he didn't react except for a heartbreaking whine. I went to open the door of the cage, but it was padlocked.

The wolf raised his head and growled. I turned to find Valas right behind me. I hadn't heard her come down the stairs.

She held out a key. "From the pocket of the beta. He did not entrust it to this one." She nodded at Patrick. "He is a poor beta if he mistrusts his pack. As an alpha, he would spell disaster. You were correct in coming to me with this matter."

"You got all that from a key?"

"Much can be learned from apparent trifles. Go to your wolf."

I took the key and unlocked the padlock. The wolf raised his head as I opened the door and entered the cage.

"Don't try to get up. Save your strength," I told him.

He settled back but kept a wary eye on Valas as I knelt beside him. She stayed outside the cage, watching us.

I buried my face in the wolf's fur and drank in his scent. There was a part of me that had worried I would never smell him again, never hold him in my arms in either form. I realized my face was wet with tears. It was a hell of a thing to care about someone so much that it gave you pain to see them hurt.

"I'm here. I'm here." I repeated the words like a mantra. It still didn't feel real to be reunited with Sean. The situation had seemed so hopeless only hours ago, until I'd discovered Charles had the cuff.

"Ms. Worth, I cannot hold the spell indefinitely, and there is other magic to be done that will require a great deal of power. We must not delay."

I let myself hold the wolf for a little longer before I sat up. I opened my messenger bag and took out the box that held the second cuff.

"If you wish to change our plans, you must do so now," Valas told me. "There will be no going back. Only death will remove the cuff."

"I never go back." I wiped my tears away and set the box in my lap. "The only way is forward."

I opened the box. The spellwork that hid the box's contents from tracking spells broke when I lifted the lid. Inside the wooden box was a second box identical to the one that had held the cuff now affixed to the wolf's front leg. I opened that box and found the second cuff inside. Charles had indeed kept his word.

I picked up the cuff. Golden magic pulsed.

The wolf raised his head and gave a short yip. I couldn't tell if it was concern, a question, or a warning.

I lowered my face to his. "You have to trust me. It's the only way to save you. We'll be okay. I know what I'm doing."

Charles had bet I wouldn't put the cuff on. He'd been so certain of it that he'd handed it over without an ounce of hesitation. I guess he didn't know me quite as well as he thought.

I slid the cuff onto my right forearm. The cold metal made me shiver. I sensed shifter magic, but it was dormant. I wasn't a shifter, so the cuff didn't react.

The wolf whined.

"The only way is forward," I whispered, and touched my cuff to his. "*Este comparia.*"

The cuff closed tightly around my wrist. My world turned gold. Shifter magic seared my skin, traveling through my bones. I threw my head back and screamed. Beside me, the wolf raised his head and howled.

The magic was pure golden power. It pulsed between the wolf and me and filled me up, igniting every cell and synapse. The wolf staggered to his feet. I wondered if the magic was having the same effect on him. I hoped so. He would need every bit of strength he could get.

Then I felt the pack.

The pack bonds were like doors opening in my head. I sensed

Jack, Delia, Ben, Nan, Felicia...one by one I became aware of them all. They were all still unconscious, except for two who weren't at the house: Caleb and one other. In those lying upstairs, I sensed an echo of fear, as if they'd had just enough time to realize what was happening before they lost consciousness.

I also sensed that they'd become aware, in a distant way, that something big had just happened. There was a kind of restlessness in their sleep and I wondered if Valas's spell was about to break.

A voice cut through the chaos in my head. *Alice, what have you done?* It was Charles. He sounded furious...and fearful. I had never heard fear from Charles before, not once in five years. Did he fear that he had lost me, or did he fear for my life?

I owed him no explanation and I had no time to waste; the wolves were beginning to stir. I shut the link between us and opened my eyes.

Valas knelt outside the cage. She'd closed the door but not locked it, shutting me inside with the wolf. He paced and growled, but not in anger. Through our new bond, I sensed confusion and wonder and fierce protectiveness.

Mate, the wolf said in my head, his voice a growl. *Mine.*

"Our time grows short," Valas said. "The spell is finished?"

"Yes." My eyes felt warm and I wondered if they were golden like Sean's. "The cuff's magic is complete. The bond is set."

"Remember our arrangement." Her eyes turned dark and the shadows gathered around her. "The terms we agreed upon must be fulfilled."

"I know what I agreed to. Now hold up your end of the bargain."

She smiled slightly. "You have no fear. I should like to know how you came to be so fearless."

Above us, in the house, I heard movement and voices. The werewolves were waking up.

"That's a story for another day." I met her ancient, fathomless eyes with my own. "Make it quick."

"As you wish." She reached through the bars and touched my chest.

Behind me, the wolf snarled and leaped at her, but it was too late.

Dark magic rose. My vision went black. My breathing ceased. My heart stopped. My thoughts became dust.

And I died.

CHAPTER 21

I was no stranger to death. I'd died a number of times under torture at my grandfather's cabal, only to be revived either by magic or medical intervention each time. The only thing that hurt worse than dying was coming back.

When I'd died after fighting Amelia Wharton and the *Kasten*, I had felt no pain, only serenity. My return to life was equally peaceful, like waking from a long sleep. Then I'd wandered alone in darkness for what felt like an eternity while my body lay in a coma in Charles's care.

My demise at Valas's hands was so fast that I scarcely had time to realize what was happening before it was over—which was, I supposed, the point of asking for a quick death. I had no idea what magic she used, but it was sharper and faster than the finest blade.

I woke much the same way, like a switch had been flipped from off to on.

As my senses came back online, I realized my ears were filled with the sound of howling. A dozen voices were raised in what could only be described as a chorus of grief. It was strangely beautiful. The sound was definitely wolf in nature, but something about the intonation made me think the howls came from human throats. That didn't seem possible, but I'd given up on the concepts of possible and impossible long ago.

"*Quiet!*" Sean thundered.

The howling cut off instantly.

Someone picked up my arm and pressed two fingers into my wrist, searching for a pulse. I felt a weight on my chest, as if they were listening for a heartbeat or for the sound of me breathing.

The weight lifted off my chest. "Alice, can you hear me?" The hope in Sean's voice made my heart hurt.

Speech seemed beyond my ability at the moment, but sensation was creeping back into my limbs and I could remember how to move.

I opened my eyes.

I heard several gasps and a voice I thought was Nan's whisper, "Thank God." Clearly we were not alone, but the only thing I cared about was the familiar face above mine and the red-rimmed golden eyes that stared back at me in disbelief.

And then Sean kissed me so hard, and for so long, that I almost passed out from lack of air.

When he finally raised his head, he smoothed my hair back and held my face in his hands. Neither of us spoke for a very long time. For me, it was enough to see him back in human form, and—I glanced at his bare arm to confirm it—without that damn cuff.

I became aware that we were still in the cage in Jack and Delia's basement and the entire pack was gathered around outside it, watching us in stunned silence. It felt like a punch in the stomach when I realized they'd all been howling over my death.

I didn't know I was crying until Sean used his thumbs to wipe away my tears. He kissed the tip of my nose. "My Alice," he murmured.

For the first time, I didn't feel weird when he said it, not even in front of an audience.

"I missed you." My voice sounded wispy, not surprising since I'd been stone-cold dead only moments ago.

He smiled. I loved the way his eyes crinkled when he smiled. "I missed you, too."

"Where are they?" I asked.

He figured out what I meant and hooked his thumb over his shoulder. "Over there, in their boxes, where they'll stay."

"What are you going to do with them?"

"I haven't decided. Maybe melt them down. Maybe put them in a safe, fill the safe with concrete, and then drop the safe over the side of a boat a hundred miles out into the Pacific."

That made me smile back at him. "It sounds like you've given this some thought."

"Trust me, I had a lot of time to think about how to dispose of those damn things." He pressed his forehead to mine the way I'd touched my face to the wolf's. His skin felt blazingly hot against mine. "I thought I'd lost you for good this time," he said roughly.

Before I had a chance to reply, someone spoke. "I believe the decision of what to do with those cuffs is something the pack should discuss." The speaker was behind me, but I recognized Jack's voice.

Sean's eyes blazed. He raised his head and shot Jack the deadliest stare I'd ever seen from him. His fury seared my skin and alpha power rose until the air crackled around us. "This topic is not open for debate." The words were clipped and full of warning.

It was a warning that went unheeded. "The cuffs are a source of enormous power," Jack said.

"The cuffs are a prison." Sean looked down at me. "Can you stand?"

It didn't matter if I could or couldn't; I was going to. Sean and I would face Jack together. "Yes."

He offered me his hand. I took it and he lifted me to my feet. Everything got a bit hazy and he steadied me by my upper arms until my ears stopped ringing and I could see clearly again. He was naked, but nudity mattered little to werewolves, especially in front of the pack.

When I was standing on my own, he opened the door of the cage and ushered me out. I made it one slow step at a time, letting him half-support me with one arm around my waist. I was happy that Sean seemed to have recovered from his ordeal. If he felt any weakness or shakiness, I couldn't see it. The power we'd shared after I put on the cuff must have helped him regain his strength.

Valas was long gone. Her part in this was over. Whatever the magic was that killed me and then resurrected me once the cuff fell off, she hadn't needed to be physically present for it to finish its work. All that remained was for me to fulfill my obligations to her. I put aside thoughts of our bargain until this mess was cleaned up.

Nan pushed her way through the group and met us just outside the cage door. I thought she was there to greet Sean, but instead she put her arms around me and squeezed gently. "Alice."

I returned her hug a bit awkwardly. "Hey, Nan."

She released me and smiled tearfully up at Sean. He smiled back briefly. His expression hardened as Jack moved to the front of the group. For the first time since I woke up, I got a good look at the beta's face.

Four faint scars cut across the left side of his face, slashing diagonally like someone had clawed him exactly how and where I had in my dream. With their ability to heal it was rare to see a shifter with scars, but wounds left by magic were the hardest to heal completely, as the scars on my back could attest. It didn't seem possible that I had inflicted physical harm on him in a dream, but what other explanation could there be?

While I was processing that, Sean stepped forward to meet Jack toe-to-toe. Jack had a couple of inches and maybe twenty pounds on Sean, but Sean still seemed larger somehow.

"Where did those scars come from?" Sean asked.

Jack jerked his head at me. "Ask *her*."

Sean glanced my way. "Alice?"

Maybe they would be able to explain how it happened. "Last night I had a dream that I was here speaking to your wolf. Jack attacked me in the dream. I slashed his face in self-defense. I had no idea it was anything but just a dream until now."

"You found a way to use the pack bonds against us," Jack snarled at me. "I was defending our pack."

"I wasn't attacking you or anyone else in the pack. I didn't even do it on purpose. I was asleep."

"It shouldn't be possible for you to contact Sean through the pack bonds," Ben said, moving to stand next to Sean and Jack. "You're human and you're not his mate—not yet, anyway."

I raised my hand and concentrated. Golden magic ran along my fingertips. "I'm no ordinary human." I'd only just learned how to use shifter magic, but they didn't need to know that.

My simple demonstration had a seismic effect on the pack. On the faces of those I knew, I saw astonishment, wonder, and happiness. Several others seemed equally pleased. The older couple whose names I didn't know exchanged a glance. Jack, of course, only grew angrier.

Delia stepped out of the group to stand next to her husband. The look she gave me was pure venom. "So she knows a few magic tricks. That doesn't make her worthy of you *or* the pack, and it sure as hell doesn't give her the right to wear the cuff."

"Watch yourself," Sean warned. "A month ago, Alice risked her life to save Felicia from the West-Addison harnad. She just died for me and the pack. Everyone here is in her debt, twice over."

"She doesn't look dead to me," Delia retorted. "It was just some cheap stunt, Sean. She's trying to trick you and all of us."

"You felt her die, Delia," Ben said. "We all did. That was no stunt. I don't know how she did it; maybe she'll tell us someday. But the fact of the matter is, she was dead for close to seven minutes in order to free Sean from that cuff."

Holy shit, seven minutes? Not only had I been dead, I'd started going cold before the damn cuffs fell off and Valas brought me back.

That wasn't mostly dead; that was *all the way* dead. Hearing news like that was enough to make me need a stiff drink or three.

I wondered if the cuffs had been spelled to wait a certain amount of time before falling off to prevent someone from doing what I'd just done. I felt a bit smug that I'd tricked that blasted shifter magic.

"Our pack would benefit from those cuffs," Jack told Sean. "If the right people wore them, we'd be stronger. Faster. More stable. Our dominance over the other packs would be beyond questioning. You felt the power, all of you." He turned his bright amber stare on the others. "Tell me you don't all want that power for our pack."

No one spoke at first. Several of them exchanged glances, even Felicia, Karen, and David. I remembered the power too, how it filled me and made me feel like I could face anything or anyone, as if my magic was endless.

Power like that was a drug; I'd learned that the hard way. Once you got a taste of it, you could never have enough. You'd kill for it, betray anyone and everyone, inflict unimaginable suffering to get more. My grandfather was a prime example. So were Adelbert and the *Kasten* and the harnad blood mages John West and Spencer Addison. Even I had felt a taste of that desire for power when I'd been injected with the drug Black Fire and experienced what it was like to have so much magic that my body couldn't even contain it all.

Sean wanted his pack to be safe and strong. Jack wanted power and to bring other packs to heel. That and his lack of compassion would make him a disastrous alpha.

Karen spoke. "Not if it means locking those cuffs on Sean and his mate." Her voice was quiet but firm.

Jack glared at her, but then Nan said, "Not if Sean says it's the wrong choice for us."

Ben joined in. "Not if the purpose of that power is to subjugate anyone else."

Karen's brother Patrick spoke up. "Power like that will only end up destroying us."

One by one the rest of the pack shook their heads, leaving Jack and Delia alone in their desire to use the cuffs.

"You got your discussion," Sean told Jack. He addressed the rest of the pack. "While I'm glad to hear that almost everyone is in agreement, the decision about what to do about the cuffs is mine to make, with Alice's input because there is magic involved and because she has earned the right to have a say."

Jack's anger was still palpable, but he said nothing. His silence worried me. Delia tried to stare me down, but she couldn't hold my gaze for more than a few seconds before she looked away.

"Everyone, please go upstairs so I can speak to Alice privately," Sean said. "Those who need to leave may do so. Ben, I'd like you to stay, and Karen too."

"I'll tell Cole I'll be a bit longer," she said. "It's no problem."

"I'll stay," Ben added. "I'll let Casey know not to wait up."

The pack headed for the stairs. Karen squeezed my hand as she passed.

When the door closed behind Ben, leaving us alone in the basement, Sean rubbed his face and turned to me. "Where do things stand with Kent Stevens?"

I might have known that would be his first question. "He's dead."

He stilled. "Alice, tell me you didn't use yourself as bait."

"It was a Court-run operation. I was safe—"

"Don't lie to me, Alice. Not about this."

I was starting to feel a little wobbly. Being dead could take a lot out of you. I glanced at the couch. "Can we sit, please?"

We moved to the couch and sat. "Tell me what happened," he said.

I told him the whole story, from when Arkady picked me up at the storage unit through Stevens getting munched by the garden. He inspected my arm and hip and saw for himself that the wounds were healed.

He got up and paced, his anger prickling on my arms. "You knew

I didn't want you to do that. It was the Court's responsibility to catch him. It should have been Vaughan out there, not you."

"Stevens escaped me too, that first day at Mike Robinson's house," I reminded him. "And as long as it was my life on the line, that made it my responsibility to help catch him. Do I think Charles should have been the bait? Yes, but that wasn't my call. It was Valas who decided he needed to stay sequestered. I don't know why, and they're not likely to tell me."

When he didn't reply, I added, "I needed him caught or dead, Sean. I knew that cuff was hurting you and I couldn't save you and watch out for him too. I couldn't do what I needed to do to help you with bodyguards dogging my every step. I was tired of waiting."

"Do you think it was easy for me to wait it out on the sidelines?" he demanded. "Don't you know how badly I wanted to find Stevens and tear him apart for hurting you?"

"Of course I did; that's why I took care of it. You have enough trouble with Jack and the cuffs without having to worry about Stevens and me too."

He spun around to face me, his eyes bright and furious. "Alice, damn it, do you think I couldn't handle Stevens *and* my own pack? You're always reminding me that you're a high-level mage and I should treat you as one, but you don't treat me as an alpha. You keep thinking that you have to protect me. It's not just an insult; it diminishes me in front of my pack and in the eyes of others, from the vampires to the Were Ruling Council."

Shocked, I said, "I never meant it as an insult or to make you look weak."

"Of course you didn't. You're too busy thinking that you have to save everyone and protect everyone. I love that about you, but sometimes there are other considerations beyond your compulsive need to throw yourself on every grenade."

Still angry, he returned to the couch and touched my face. I leaned into the warmth of his hand. Finally, he exhaled. "You put on the matching cuff and then died for seven minutes so we'd both be free of them. I want to be angry with you for doing that, but I can't. Just tell me it was the only way."

I covered his hand with mine. "It was the only way."

"Whatever magic you used to kill and then resurrect yourself, you could have used it on me."

I realized then that he had no idea that Valas had been here. Had she wiped his memory somehow, or had he not been aware of her presence?

"The hell I could," I snapped. "As if I would ever have done that to you."

"Yet you have no problem doing it to yourself." He shook his head. "All right. Now explain how you found the second cuff."

This was the part I had been dreading. "After Kim Dade, the Court researcher, found out there was a matching cuff, I did some research online and found an expert in shifter magic who had a tracking spell. I found out that it was here, in the city."

He read my expression. "Tell me what you're not telling me, Alice."

"Charles had the cuff."

His face was like a glacier. "Did he know all along?"

"He suspected there was a second cuff and tried to find it before I did so he could sell the set to whichever pack would pay him the most. He only found out last night, just before we set the trap for Kent Stevens, that without it you would die. As soon as that was over, he had Kim call me with the news."

"And how long did he have the second cuff?"

"Since this morning, he said. The second the sun set tonight, I went to get it from him."

Sean leaned forward and inhaled.

Shocked and furious, I jumped up and nearly fell when a wave of dizziness made me grab for the arm of the couch. "What did you think, that I had sex with Charles to get the cuff?"

He shook his head. "I didn't think that, but there is no way in hell Vaughan gave you that cuff without getting something big in return." He read my eyes and his expression went flat. "He bit you."

"Sean—"

He stood, his hands balled into fists and fury rolling off him in waves. "The first time he bit you, it was an unforgivable violation—you said so yourself. And now you let him bite you again?"

He turned and punched the door of what turned out to be a storage closet. He pulled his fist out and punched it again, demolishing it completely.

"Sean, hear me out. I knew that was what he wanted and I was ready to negotiate. He drank from me, but it was just a bite, nothing else. We were fully dressed. I didn't allow him to give me any pleasure with the bite. It was nothing but...nothing but pain for me. When it was done, he handed over the cuff and I left. It was a business transaction."

No answer.

His silence infuriated me. "Damn it, you were *dying*. I had no choice."

He spun around, his eyes flashing fire, but I kept talking. "It was nothing but a bite and a pint of blood. You would have done the same for me, if our roles were reversed. Look me in the eye and tell me you wouldn't."

"That would be different."

I put my hands on my hips. "How would it be different? Because you're a man, or because you're an alpha?"

He ran his hands through his hair. I'd just caught him in a double standard and he knew it. "You are a high-level mage and an associate of the pack. You are not just some vampire's meal."

"No, I'm not a meal. I've never allowed any vampire to bite me, not ever. I've been offered sums of money that you wouldn't believe. Gifts fit for kings. I turned them all down. But I did this *for you*, because..." I stopped.

"Because why, Alice?" he asked. "Tell me why."

"Because the thought of losing you was more than I could bear.

Because Charles thought he had me right where he wanted me and I showed him he was wrong. Because you are the one chance at happiness I've ever had, and I'd be damned if I was going to let you down when you needed me." When he didn't respond, I added, "And because if he got hold of the cuff first, Jack was going to put it on Lily Anderson."

Sean's face went blank. Alpha magic rose and I stumbled, almost falling to one knee.

Finally, he spoke. "Jack was going to put the second cuff on Lily?" His voice was deadly.

"Yes. Jack wouldn't let me come see you, but Karen called and warned me that—"

Ben's voice interrupted me, calling to us through the basement door. "Sean? A Vamp Court SUV just parked in the driveway and there's a vampire—"

CRASH. It sounded like someone had come through the front door without bothering to open it.

"Where is Alice?" It was Charles, upstairs. His voice was almost a roar. "*Where is her body?*"

Sean started for the stairs, still cold with fury.

"Wait," I said.

He turned around. "What?"

"He doesn't know I'm alive," I said softly. "That means he's lost his connection to me, the one he got by biting me while I was in a coma. He felt me die and he still thinks I'm dead." I smiled. "He's not in my head anymore, Sean. I'm free of him."

"Good." He came back and scooped me up. "You're in no shape to climb stairs."

I would have protested except he was right, so I let him carry me up the steps. When we got to the top, he pressed his lips to my ear. "Our conversation is not finished," he murmured. "But I have a beta I have to deal with, and a vampire who needs to understand once and for all that three's a crowd."

He kicked the basement door open and stepped into the kitchen.

CHAPTER 22

CHARLES HAD INDEED BROKEN THROUGH JACK AND DELIA'S SOLID OAK FRONT door, reducing it to a pile of splintered wood and broken glass. He stood in the front room with Bryan at his side, facing off with Jack, Delia, Ben, and Karen.

Gone was his trademark icy calm. He was shrouded in shadow, his face a mask of pure rage and eyes pitch black. Dark magic made the air heavy.

The werewolves' eyes were golden but they held their ground and their human forms—at least for now. I had to grudgingly give Jack credit for not attacking Charles, despite the vampire's intrusion into his home.

When Sean stepped into view, Charles looked past the others and spotted us. It took several seconds for him to process the sight of me alive. His anger gave way to relief and then confusion.

Bryan, for his part, looked as close to nonplussed as I'd ever seen him. He stared at me like he thought I was a ghost.

Sean spoke first. "Get out of this house, Vaughan. You'll be hearing from my attorney about the damages to the Hastingses' property."

If Charles heard what Sean said, he didn't acknowledge it. "Alice," he said, his voice rough with only a hint of its usual suave tones. "I do not understand."

Sean lowered me down carefully and steadied me with one hand on my back. He knew me well enough to know I wanted to face Charles on my own two feet. His touch made my skin warm and tingly. Maybe a fragment of our bond from the cuffs remained, or maybe the magic of the cuffs had awakened some trace of shifter blood in my veins. If so, that was something I would have to figure out later once Charles and Jack were dealt with.

"What don't you understand, Charles?" I asked. "I told you I would do whatever I had to do to save Sean's life."

"A statement that turned out to be far from mere hyperbole." He took a few steps toward the kitchen. At Sean's nod, the others reluctantly moved aside so Charles could approach us.

He entered the kitchen and stopped on the other side of the center island. "I felt your death, but not your return to life. Our link has been terminated as if it never existed. No human magic I have ever known would be capable of this. How is this possible?"

I'd been wondering that myself. Valas must have severed the connection, but I hadn't thought to ask her to do so; I hadn't even known it was possible. Why she'd done it was a question I wanted an answer to. She must have thought it would benefit her in some way. That would be something else I'd have to fret about later.

"You have no idea what I'm capable of," I told Charles truthfully. We might no longer share a telepathic link, but he could still sense emotions and deception. Good thing I excelled at partial truths and evasive answers.

"I certainly never thought you capable of giving your life for his." Charles glowered at Sean, who returned his gaze impassively. "There was no guarantee that your life could be restored. You might have truly died. He is not worthy of such a sacrifice. You are worth ten of him."

I opened my mouth to object, but Sean spoke first. "On that we agree," he said. "Regardless of how you or I feel about it, the choice was Alice's to make. Her choice seems clear, doesn't it, Vaughan?" In other words: *Alice chose me.*

Something dark flashed in Charles's eyes. His anger began to give way to the cool calculation I was used to seeing. I suspected he was about to go on the attack, and I was right.

"Did Alice tell you how she came to be in possession of the second cuff?" he purred.

I almost smiled. Charles had advised me not to tell Sean that I'd obtained the cuff from him. Even then I'd thought that he intended to use it against me at his first opportunity. I'd never considered holding that information back. As angry as Sean had been at the news that I'd traded a bite for the cuff, it would have been far worse if he'd learned of our arrangement from Charles instead.

"Of course she told me," Sean snapped. "First you bite her while she's in a coma and defenseless, and now you coerce her and try to pass it off as just another business transaction. Even for you, this was a new low."

The corners of Charles's mouth turned up and his eyes glowed silver. "But did she tell you how much she enjoyed my bite? The scent of her arousal still lingers on my bed."

In the front room, Jack and Delia looked at me with contempt. Neither Ben nor Karen reacted visibly; either they assumed Charles was lying or they were taking their cue from Sean, who just shook his head. "It means nothing," he said. "It was an involuntary physiological response. Don't delude yourself into thinking it was anything more than that."

"Perhaps it is you who is deluded." Charles studied Sean. "She saved your life because she owes you her own. She chose to risk death rather than wear the cuff and bind herself to you."

"You know nothing of Alice if you think that was her motivation," Sean said coldly.

I'd had enough of them talking about me as if I wasn't standing right there, and I wanted Charles gone before I lost my tight control over my anger and found myself tempted to fry him where he stood. "Now you know I'm not dead, and you're trespassing on private property. You need to leave before this becomes an incident and the Court gets involved in a dispute with the Were Ruling Council."

"As you wish." Charles gave us a slight bow and backed toward the front doorway. "I can see that you all have much to discuss. I will compensate you for the damages to your home, Mr. Hastings, and please accept my apology for my intrusion. Good night."

Bryan watched the werewolves as Charles departed, one hand near his gun. He glanced at me, his face unreadable, then followed his employer down the front steps and out of my line of sight.

Jack went to the door as Charles and Bryan got into their SUV. Tires crunched on gravel as they backed down the driveway.

When the sound of the engine faded, Jack turned around to find Sean advancing on him, radiating alpha power and fury. The force of it scoured my flesh. Wincing, I rubbed my arms and leaned against the kitchen island.

Before Jack had a chance to react, Sean had him by the throat. "Before I shifted, I gave you an order to protect Alice." He slammed the larger man against the wall hard enough to shake the house as Delia looked on in shock. "You stranded her at the storage unit without any weapons or even a vehicle. As your boss and your alpha, I gave you a clear directive and you deliberately refused to obey it. The Court will sue Maclin Security for breach of contract because we were hired to provide security and we left an asset vulnerable to assassination. But more to the point, I trusted you to carry out my orders and you betrayed me."

"You ordered me to lead the pack and that's what I did," Jack growled.

"And your plan to find the second cuff and give it to Lily Anderson?" Sean demanded. "Was that your way of leading the pack? To bind me for life to a woman you know I don't love and never will, without any regard whatsoever for what I wanted?"

"Better that than let you be bound to *her*." Jack jerked his head in my direction. "She's not pack and she never will be. She's a human and a vampire's whore."

The last word hadn't even left his mouth before Sean picked Jack up and threw him out the front door.

I felt a strange pull and the others staggered slightly. By the time I realized he'd drawn power from the pack to shift faster, Sean—already in wolf form—was out the front door with Ben, Delia, and Karen right behind him.

I was still shaky and Sean had used some of my energy to shift, so I lurched through the kitchen and front room using walls, furniture, and then finally the doorframe to steady myself.

By the time I made it to the front porch, the fight was already underway in the yard. Jack's wolf was larger than Sean's and tawny brown with darker coloring on his ears, face, and tail. The fight was vicious; both wolves were already bloodied before I got to the door.

I worried that his ordeal in the cage had weakened Sean more than he'd let on, and the fast shift couldn't have helped even if he'd drawn on the pack bonds. As we watched from the porch, Jack ripped at Sean's leg with his teeth. Sean snarled and came up limping, his leg bloody and torn.

Delia turned on me as the wolves growled and circled each other. "You're the cause of all this, Alice. We were fine before you got your hooks in Sean. Get out."

"What exactly is your problem with me, Delia?" I asked. "Is it that I'm human, or that you can't push me around like you do the others?"

Delia's eyes went bright yellow. Karen took a step back, but Ben stared Delia down. "You know damn well Sean and Jack had their problems long before Alice even met Sean. And it doesn't matter one bit what Jack thinks about Alice; his orders were to protect her and he didn't."

"Sean told Jack to lead the pack," Delia argued, echoing her husband's earlier argument. "The pack comes first."

"Sean told Jack to protect Alice and Jack said he would," Karen said, her voice gaining some strength despite the more dominant woman's glower. "If we can't trust Jack to keep his word, he's not the beta this pack needs. In fact, maybe he's not a wolf this pack needs."

Furious, Delia started to go after Karen, but Ben caught Delia's wrist. "Stop," he warned her. "If you have a problem with a member of the pack, you talk to Sean."

Delia pulled away and crossed her arms. "Fine."

We turned back to the fight in time to see Sean's wolf leap at Jack and take him down. Jack might be bigger, but Sean was the alpha and despite the injured leg and smaller size, he was stronger and his fury gave him the advantage.

Delia made a fearful sound when Sean's teeth closed on Jack's throat, but Sean didn't intend to kill Jack. The brown wolf let out a short whine, signaling surrender. Sean shook him none too gently, then let go and backed away. Jack rolled onto his side to show Sean his belly, and then crouched with his tail tucked in a submissive posture. Beside me, Delia took a few steps back and bowed her head, echoing her husband's pose.

The wolves shifted back to human, their wounds healing in a pulse of golden shifter magic. Sean watched as Jack got to his feet. Both men were breathing heavily and sweating, but Jack seemed the worse for wear.

When Jack was standing, Sean approached him. "You are never to speak to or about Alice that way again," he said coldly. "When I give you an order, I expect to be obeyed. You've never disobeyed me before and I need to know you never will again if I'm even going to consider giving you a second chance."

"You have my word," Jack said.

Jack had his back to me, so I couldn't see his face or read his body language except the deliberate hunch of his shoulders and the way he seemed to shrink in size in the face of Sean's anger. He certainly appeared and sounded submissive and contrite, but appearances could be deceiving.

Sean studied his beta. Finally, he said, "You're suspended

without pay from Maclin Security for two weeks. What happens after that may depend on the legal action the Court takes. As far as your role with the pack goes, this is my last warning. If we have to have this discussion again, there will be a different and more permanent solution. Am I clear?"

"Perfectly clear."

"Good." Sean glanced up. "Everyone, please go inside. I'll join you in a few minutes." He looked at me. "Alice, a word?"

"Sure." I leaned against the wall as the others filed past. Ben and Karen gave me small smiles. Delia and Jack ignored me altogether.

When they were inside the house, Sean opened the back of the Maclin Security SUV parked off to the side of the driveway. He found his duffel bag and pulled on a pair of jeans and a company polo shirt.

I made it down the front steps and joined him just as he closed the back of the SUV. I put my hand on his back.

When he turned, his eyes were hard, his face expressionless. He'd never looked at me like that. "Alice, don't." He stepped away.

Stung, I dropped my hand to my side. "Charles was just trying to get a rise out of you by bringing up the bite. He made it sound like I enjoyed it, but it wasn't like that at all."

"This isn't about him biting you." He walked around to the other side of the SUV, putting the vehicle between us and the house to keep our conversation private. "I'm disgusted at him for that, not at you."

"Then why—?"

"Because I asked you not to use yourself as bait for Kent Stevens, and the first thing you did as soon as I was out of the picture was do exactly that." He was furious with me, his words clipped and angry. "You very nearly died. You had two bullet wounds. The Vampire Court manipulated you into risking your life. They kept Vaughan safe while you walked around with a target on your back. They knew you'd eventually volunteer to draw him out because that's the sort of person you are."

"The plan to catch him was my idea," I argued.

"Stop defending them," he said harshly. "Damn it, Alice, can't you see when you're being used by those bloodsuckers? They don't care if you live or die. You're nothing but an asset to them, except for Vaughan, who still thinks he has a shot with you if he's just patient enough. Even then you're just a meal and a prize to him, something he wants to add to his collection."

"He doesn't have a shot with me and never will. He can plot and scheme all he wants; it won't get him anywhere."

"This isn't about you and Vaughan. It's about you keeping ledgers."

I blinked. "You lost me."

He paced, too angry to stand still. "You said you had to get Stevens out of the way so you could focus on helping me, but I think you did it for the same basic reason you sacrificed yourself to destroy the *Kasten* and almost died taking out the West-Addison harnad. You may have burned the ledger of things you think you owe me for, but you've got another ledger, a much bigger one, and it's full of the things you did before you moved here. You're trying to offset that list of sins by saving everyone and taking out as many bad guys as you can, no matter what it costs you or those who care about you. You've put Malcolm and me through so much in these past few months, and I don't think you even think about that at all unless we bring it up."

Sean came back to stand in front of me again. "I don't know what's in that ledger. You won't tell me and I'm not going to beg you to reveal your secrets. What I *do* know is that you'll do anything to try to balance the scales, running yourself into the ground and almost dying over and over, and it's still not enough. I don't know if it will *ever* be enough, and as much as I care about you, I don't think I can keep doing this."

"What are you saying?" I didn't even recognize my own voice.

He rubbed his face with both hands. When he looked back at me, his eyes were hollow. "I'm saying I need some time."

If he'd punched me in the gut, it wouldn't have hurt half as much. "Sean, please."

He gripped my hand and his eyes searched my face. "If you could go back to yesterday and do it all again, knowing now how I'd feel about it, would you do the same thing? Would you put yourself in the line of fire to catch Stevens? Would you die to get the cuff off me?"

I couldn't lie to him. "Yes, I would, because there was no other way."

He let go of my hand. "I know. You'll throw yourself on every grenade because you think you're the only one who can and maybe walk away from it. But the thing about just barely surviving every time is that you're not the only one who gets hurt."

My chest ached like someone was standing on it. "Don't do this. We...I..."

"Go home and rest," he told me gently. "Do you want to give the cuff back your client so you can get your bonus?"

In that moment, I couldn't have cared less about Esther Aldridge or her damned bonus. "No. The cuffs are too dangerous to just let them be bought and sold by people who have no idea what they are. No one should have those cuffs. Patrick was right; power like that only ever ends up destroying everyone and everything around it."

"Then I'll make sure they disappear forever." He took a couple of steps back. The physical distance between us was only a few feet, but it felt like miles. "Do you need a ride home?"

"No." I didn't know *what* I needed, but I could get myself home. After that, I had no idea what I would do.

Of all the possible outcomes I had foreseen, Sean asking me to go home without him had never been one of them. I'd predicted he'd be angry, but not that I would push him to his breaking point.

I'd been worried my secrets would be the thing he couldn't live with. I'd never considered that it would be my willingness to risk my life. Maybe I should have seen it when he reacted so angrily to my initial suggestion about using myself as bait the night we were staking out John Doe's motel room, but I hadn't.

For all my planning and dealing, I'd never even thought about how he would react to shifting back to his human form next to my dead body, or how the members of the pack would feel after sharing his pain and grief over my death. Like a vampire—like my grandfather—I'd thought the ends justified the means. Maybe I shared more attributes with Charles and Moses than I'd ever been willing to admit, even to myself.

I wanted to beg. I wanted to rage. I wanted to punch him, then kiss him and hold him and never let him go.

Instead, I got in my car and went home.

CHAPTER 23

Thanks to exhaustion and a glass of Scotch, I managed to sleep until almost noon, when Aaron Riddell woke me with a phone call and a request for an update.

I told him the cuff had been bought by a mage who'd accidentally destroyed it while attempting to intensify the spellwork, but that I could deliver the mirror and cup either to his office or Esther's home. I was too emotionally drained to feel any pang of conscience for lying to him.

He checked with Esther, then called back a few minutes later to say he would be sending a courier over to pick up the items and deliver a check if I'd e-mail my invoice to his assistant. According to Aaron, Esther was unhappy that I'd failed to recover the cuff, but grateful that I'd found the other two items. She'd offered to add a small bonus anyway, despite my only partial success. Aaron advised me to accept graciously, so I did.

I put Sean's toiletries in a bin under the sink so I didn't have to look at them and took a long shower. My emotions were all over the place. I was hurt, sad, confused, and angry in turns. I was deeply hurt that Sean had sent me away, but most of my anger was directed at myself. He'd been so patient and understanding for so long, waiting for me to realize how my actions hurt the people who cared about me, but he'd finally reached the end of his rope. I should have apologized the second I came to and saw the pain I'd caused, but instead I'd acted like it was all business as usual.

Maybe my life with my grandfather was partially to blame for my difficulty in understanding and accounting for other people's feelings. I'd certainly never learned empathy from him, and caring about others was a vulnerability I couldn't afford back then. But I'd been away from the cabal for five years now, and this wasn't the first time Malcolm and Sean had called me out for hurting them with my actions. I couldn't blame Moses for this, as much as I wished I could. No, this one was on me.

After my shower, I sat on my bed in my bathrobe, my hair wrapped in a towel, and finalized my invoice for Esther while Rogue snoozed over by the window. The bill was a nice chunk of change, but I couldn't feel anything close to happy about it. I e-mailed the paperwork to Aaron's assistant and said I'd have the items ready for pick-up within the hour.

I dried my hair and dressed, then put Sean's clothes in a box in the closet. I had no idea what the protocol was for what to do with his things. Should I mail them to his house? Offer to drop them off? Keep them in hopes that we'd forgive each other and fix what I'd broken?

I wiped my eyes, picked up my laptop, and opened my bedroom door to find Malcolm waiting in the hallway. "Hey, Alice," he said somberly.

I'd told him what happened when I got home, over Scotch on my back porch. I could tell he wasn't surprised by Sean's reaction to what I'd done.

To make matters worse, my last thoughts before I fell asleep were that if I'd wronged Sean so badly, I'd done the same to my ghost.

"I'm sorry for everything, Malcolm," I said, leaning against my bedroom doorway. "I'm sorry for every time I didn't think about how much you worried about me, or about how me putting myself in danger affected you. I don't even know how many times I've done that."

"About ten times in the past week alone," he said half-jokingly, but his light tone was forced.

He grew serious. "The thing is, I don't think you have any idea how to let people care about you. We made some progress on that recently, but the bigger problem is that you don't put much value on your own life. Just because *you're* cavalier about it doesn't mean other people are too. Your life isn't just a tool you can use to solve problems and neither is your death, but that's how you act."

I wished I could tell him that I'd been raised to think of myself as literally a tool and a weapon and not as having inherent value beyond my usefulness, but I wasn't ready to reveal that about myself.

Besides, I was beginning to understand that I didn't listen enough when Malcolm talked, so I shut up and listened.

When I said nothing, he went on. "It hurts us when you don't seem to notice how much we worry about you or you brush us off when we express concern. I'm sure this is all a result of what you went through before you came here, but it makes it hard to be around you sometimes. Feeling you die and then you acting like it was no big deal was the last straw for Sean."

"Did you talk to him?"

He nodded. "After you fell asleep, I went to check on him and we talked for a bit. I'm sorry, but as much as I hate what happened between you, I can't blame him for feeling the way he does."

"Neither can I."

"You don't?"

I shrugged wearily and rubbed my eyes. "Everything you both said to me is true. I don't know how to fix this about myself, but I do know I screwed up. I can't turn back time and do it over, and though I owe Sean an apology for not thinking more about his feelings, I'm not sorry for what I did with the cuff or that I helped get Stevens even though he didn't want me to."

"Yeah, he's pretty angry about the Stevens situation." He made a face. "He cares about you a lot, Alice. Maybe you should give him a call and tell him what you just told me about realizing you messed up."

"He told me he needed time. I'm no expert in this sort of thing, but I'm pretty sure that meant more than eight hours." I headed downstairs with Malcolm following as Rogue ran ahead of us to stand by the back door. "In the meantime, I've got plenty of stuff to do to keep me busy."

"Like what?"

"Clean up all that spellwork in the basement, for starters. Aaron will be sending a courier over in a bit to drop off a check from Esther and pick up the mirror and the cup, so I need to get those boxed up. Then I'm going shopping for new living room furniture. Maybe some new patio furniture too, if I can find some that I like."

"Well, that does sound like a full day," Malcolm said, watching me with narrowed eyes. "And then what?"

"Then I'll find more stuff to do." I let Rogue out into the backyard and headed for the kitchen to make coffee. "Oh, hey—there's something I meant to ask you the other day, but I forgot. When I was checking you for more of those hidden retrieval spells, I found the spell that links us together. I think there's a condition that will break the spell. Do you know what it is?"

He looked bemused and shook his head. "No, I have no idea. I would tell you if I did."

I sighed. "I guess that'll stay a mystery for now. Come on—let's go to the basement and get to cleaning."

THAT NIGHT, I was on my back porch in shorts and a T-shirt, drinking Scotch and relaxing on one of my new chaise lounges, when the perimeter wards tingled. I didn't bother to get up; if it was who I thought it was, my visitors knew where to find me.

The back gate creaked open and closed. Charles appeared out of the darkness, wearing a dark gray suit. I didn't see anyone with him, but either Bryan or Adri was somewhere close by, watching us.

The garden rustled ominously when he came into view. Charles paused to study the plants, then turned to me with raised eyebrows. "Fascinating. Your garden recently consumed an entire human body, and yet it seems interested in eating me as well."

I sipped my whisky and set the glass down on the table. "It likes blood—the more powerful, the better. I'm sure it would find you to be quite a delicacy. Strange to be the food for a change, isn't it?"

"You must share your gardening tips with me."

"Why, what are you thinking about growing? A conscience?"

He chuckled and climbed the steps to where I was reclining. "You have new furniture."

"You're very observant." I gestured at the second chaise lounge. "Take a load off."

He unbuttoned his suit jacket and settled into the lounge, crossing his ankles. "Surprisingly comfortable." He glanced at the table between us, where a second, unused glass waited next to the bottle of Dalwhinnie. "Did you anticipate my arrival?"

"Let's just say I had a feeling you'd be coming around. Help yourself."

As he poured himself two fingers of Scotch, I toyed with my glass. "I finally had a few minutes today to do a bit of reading on vampire objects of power, particularly the Tepes stone you purchased at the auction. You've got a tiger by the tail, don't you?"

He sipped his whisky. "It would seem so, yes."

"And you don't think it's going to turn around and bite you?"

"Perhaps I believe it is better I should have possession of this tiger than someone like Vincent Barclay or one of his associates. But I did not come here to discuss the stone." He studied me. "Are you recovered from last night's unpleasantness?"

"Still recovering." I shrugged. "I get dizzy if I stand up too fast and I have a weird headache. I'm sure it will pass."

Charles rested his glass on his thigh and watched the plants in my garden swaying back and forth. "I have heard a rumor that your sacrifice was not as well-received as it might have been and you were sent away."

Of course he'd heard about what happened between Sean and me. "Did you come here to gloat?"

"No."

Oddly, I believed him.

He glanced at me. "Your hurt weighs heavily on me. I can no longer share my thoughts with you, but I sense the pain this rejection has caused you. I do not understand the cause of the wolf's decision to end your relationship, especially so soon after you saved his life at great personal cost."

I didn't bother explaining that requesting time apart wasn't the same as an outright breakup. "He appreciated what I did, but not how I did it."

"He objected to how you obtained the second cuff?"

"He objected to how I died and didn't apologize when I woke up."

He frowned and tilted his head. "You should have apologized for dying?"

"Yep." I sipped my whisky.

"If this is a joke, I do not understand the humor in it."

"It's pretty damn far from a joke." My voice was bitter. "If you didn't come here to gloat, why are you here?"

He rotated the glass in his hands, watching the reflection of the moonlight in the amber liquid. "I have been preoccupied with the question of how you survived and how you severed our connection so thoroughly. I believe I have uncovered the explanation for how it was accomplished."

"Oh, yeah? What's that?"

"You did not do it yourself."

When I didn't reply, he said, "I understand you went to North-bourne and requested an audience with Valas after you left my home. Approximately one hour later, you departed in your vehicle, seemingly alone. Not long after your departure, a Court-owned limousine left the estate. It returned to Northbourne an hour later and unloaded its passenger via a private entrance."

He put his glass on the table and turned to face me, sitting up with his feet on the concrete. "I must conclude that you went to the Hastingses' home with Valas. She not only assisted you in reaching Maclin, but she also caused both your death and your return to life. It was Valas who severed our connection. Was it at your request?"

If I denied that Valas had been involved, Charles would sense my deception, so I went with evasion. "The Court can't interfere in a pack matter; you said so yourself."

His eyes went silver. He caught my wrist and held it. "You have placed yourself in Valas's debt. I can think of no greater folly than what you have done. She is no kind benefactor."

"And *you* are?" I pulled my arm from his grip. "If I made a deal, it was worth it to save Sean. It didn't turn out exactly how I planned, but he's alive and that's what matters."

"Did you tell Maclin about your agreement with Valas?"

Blood magic spooled around my hands as my eyes grew warm and glowed. "If you breathe a word of this to anyone, especially Sean, I will kill you. And now you know that I don't make idle threats."

"Tell me the terms of your agreement with Valas. I will assist you in renegotiating the deal if I can."

"The terms of our agreement are confidential. I'm courting trouble even by having this discussion with you." I drained the last of my whisky. "If you'd told me about the second cuff from the begin-ning, maybe none of this would have happened. I'm not saying you're to blame because I made my own choices, but I wouldn't have ended up in Valas's audience chamber last night if it hadn't been for your games."

Charles said nothing for several long moments. His face was

blank. I couldn't tell if he felt bad about what he'd done, or if he was merely trying to work out what kind of deal I might have struck with the head of the Vamp Court.

When he spoke, I decided it had been the latter. "If Valas severed the connection between us, it was because she did not want me to interfere with her plans. Perhaps she did not wish you to be able to call to me for help." His eyes widened. "Or perhaps...Alice, if you fail to meet your obligations to Valas, is the price your life?"

I said nothing.

He tried to take my face in his hands, but I knocked them away. "You are mad," he said roughly. "She means to turn you. Whatever you have agreed to do in return for her assistance, she will ensure that you fail so you will become a vampire of her line. It would not be the first time she has done such a thing." His eyes glowed in anger. "Why did you not tell me that you intended to go to her? I would have found another way to save the wolf."

"Yes, I'm sure you would have done that out of the goodness of your heart," I scoffed.

"Perhaps not, but I would not have tricked you into making a deal that would cost you your life."

"So you say now." I shook my head. "What's done is done, Charles. We've all made our beds and now we get to lie in them. I won't forget that you kept the second cuff a secret or that you tried to torpedo my relationship by telling Sean about my reaction to your bite."

"I spoke out of jealousy and anger. I am not proud of what I said." He leaned forward. "Allow me to drink from you again and reinstate our link."

Infuriated, I rose. "You are the most shameless—"

He stood and caught my wrist again. "Not for my benefit; for yours," he snapped. "Without our link, you will not be able to call on me to help you. Now you cannot rely on Maclin or his pack to protect you. You have only your ghost and his powers are limited. How will you protect yourself if you are alone?"

"The same way I always have. Let go of me."

He released my arm. "I will not let you face Valas alone."

"You don't seem to understand that you don't get a say in what I do. I've said it before and I'll say it again: I am not yours to protect, and I sure as hell don't need you to *let* me do anything. Now, please leave."

He studied me. "Very well, but should you need assistance, you know how to reach me." He drank the remainder of his whisky and set the glass on the table. "Maclin is a fool to send you away. You were willing to give your life to save his, and he behaves as though he has been wronged. If you had made such a sacrifice for me, all that I have and all of eternity would be yours."

There was little point trying to explain Sean's point of view to Charles. He had even less capacity for empathy than me. "Good night, Charles."

He met my eyes. I read in them his intent to say something in confidence. Since we could no longer share our thoughts, I reluctantly presented my cheek for a good-night kiss.

He brushed his cool lips along my jaw. "Good night, Alice." With his mouth near my ear, he breathed words so softly that I barely heard them. "She is not invincible. Should you need to know how to defeat her, you have only to ask." He took two steps back, then turned to cross my porch and walk down the steps. He joined Bryan, who had appeared, as usual, out of the shadows.

I watched as they crossed my backyard. Halfway to the gate, Charles glanced back. I leaned against the porch railing and gave him a slight nod. He nodded back and they disappeared around the corner of the house. The gate didn't creak, but a few moments later I felt the wards tingle as they left my property.

No doubt Charles's information would come with a price, but it was a good option to keep in my back pocket for when Valas tried to turn our deal against me. That she would was inevitable, but maybe I'd have a few surprises in store for her when she did.

SEVERAL DAYS PASSED with no word from Sean. Workmen sent by Charles came to repair the hole in the wall he'd made the night Fortune was killed. I deposited Esther's check, took delivery of my new living room furniture, deep-cleaned the house room by room, punched the heavy bag for at least an hour each day, created wards for my informant Phil, and utterly failed to not think about Sean every damn minute.

In the meantime, the city was eerily quiet. There hadn't been any more magic attacks since the one that damaged the Heights the day Sean and I had visited Walsh & Quinn to get the mirror. The feds and the mayor were still demanding answers and accountability for the attacks on Darius Bell's cabal, but no one had been charged or even arrested. I assumed Catherine was trying to track Bell down and once she found him, all bets were off. Moses had to be apoplectic that she'd failed to kill him. My grandfather was not renowned for his patience. If she didn't deliver Bell's body soon, she risked being recalled to Baltimore to face Moses's wrath in person.

On the fourth day, I got a call from a woman who wanted wards around the new home she'd just bought with her fiancé. The property backed up to a cemetery and she worried that ghosts and other spirits would haunt the house. That project kept me busy and distracted for the rest of that day and most of the next. The only downside was that Malcolm couldn't help with the wards—ghost-proof wards meant no ghost assistant.

Once the project was complete, I went out and had drinks with Arkady at a dive bar. She listened sympathetically to my tale of woe and bought me shots while I talked about Sean. We both got drunk and sang karaoke. She chose a Stevie Nicks song and sounded pretty great. I went with "Heartache Tonight" by the Eagles.

We had so much fun that we decided to come back the following week. We also made plans to visit her favorite gun range over the weekend and maybe have brunch after. I had no idea how to do the "bestie" thing, but thought maybe I was getting the hang of it.

When I got home that night, Malcolm was out "doing ghost stuff," as he called wandering around the city. The house was dark and quiet. I sat in the living room with the lights off, curled up on my new sofa.

I looked up when Rogue whined, thinking he was at the back door asking to be let into the yard. Instead, he sat in the foyer, staring at the leash on the hook by the front door. It wasn't hard to figure out what was upsetting him.

"He's not coming over tonight," I told the dog. I rose and headed for the stairs. "Come on. Let's go to bed."

Reluctantly, Rogue followed me upstairs and lay in his bed by the window while I washed my face and brushed my teeth. When I crawled into bed, he came over and put his chin on the mattress.

We generally didn't let the dog up onto the bed, but what the hell. I patted the bed. "Come on up, fur-face."

Rogue jumped up onto the bed and immediately settled down on the side closest to the bathroom, the side that still smelled like Sean.

I sat on my side of the bed for a while, listening to the dog's light snore and wondering what Sean was doing right now. Once or twice I started to reach for my phone, but I stopped myself from calling. He'd asked me for time. I didn't know if that meant days or weeks or forever, but I'd give him at least a little more time before I tried calling him.

Finally, I went downstairs, leaving Rogue on the bed still asleep. I poured myself a glass of my best whisky, got the last two chocolate chip cookies out of the package I'd bought the day before, grabbed a dog biscuit from the box in the pantry, and took it all back upstairs.

I sat cross-legged on the bed and poked the dog's nose with the biscuit. "Hey, fur-face. Wake up."

Rogue sat up and took the biscuit, eyeing me suspiciously. He was normally not allowed to eat anything on the bed and it took some encouragement to get him to start gnawing on his treat.

I ate the cookies and drank my whisky and watched Rogue eat. When he was done, he curled up with his back against Sean's pillow and closed his eyes.

"Happy birthday to me," I said to the dog. He was already snoring again.

I put my empty glass on the nightstand and pulled the covers up to my chin.

HOURS LATER, something roused me from a sound sleep.

Groggy, I tried to figure out if I'd heard something. Rogue was asleep in the bed next to me, though, and if it had been a noise in the house he would have woken up.

I was just about to turn over and go back to sleep when I sensed Malcolm cross the house wards as he jumped into one of the crystals in the basement.

Less than a second later, he appeared next to my bed. "Alice!" he shouted frantically. "Alice, Alice, wake up! Everything's on fire!"

I was out of bed in a flash, wide awake, my heart thundering in my ears. "The house is on fire?"

"No, the *city* is on fire!" He pointed at my bedroom windows.

I ran to the curtains and flung them open. In the distance, I saw an orange glow in the direction of downtown. It sure as hell wasn't sunrise at four in the morning. "Oh my God," I breathed. "What happened?"

"There was another magic shockwave. Did you feel it?"

"Something woke me up just before you jumped home. That must have been the wave."

I went to my dresser, pulling my tank top off over my head.

Malcolm quickly turned away, but I was in too much of a hurry to care about modesty right now. I put on a bra and a T-shirt and a pair of jeans. I grabbed my socks, boots, and phone, and ran downstairs.

"Did you see what happened?" I asked as I sat on the couch and put my boots on.

"I couldn't get too close, but I saw a woman standing on a rooftop right smack in the center of the fire. She was holding something that looked like a gold ring and it seemed to be focusing the fire."

A ring was bad news; the most powerful magical objects were circles because they channeled power, like the circles in my basement.

My fumbling fingers pulled up the zipper on the second boot. "What did she look like?"

"Um, dark clothes, red hair? In her forties or fifties, maybe?"

"Catherine," I breathed.

Malcolm stopped flitting and hovered in front of me. "Do you know who she is?"

Oops. "You remember what Cyro said about John Doe trying to get weapons for Catherine Atwood, Moses Murphy's daughter? I bet it's her."

I finished putting on my boots and went to the front closet for a black hoodie sweatshirt. I grabbed my keys on the way out the door.

"What are you going to do? Alice, wait." Malcolm followed me down the sidewalk toward my car. "Alice!"

"She'll burn the whole city down if it means killing Darius Bell," I said as I got to my car. "Let's go, Malcolm. We have to stop her."

"We have to—*what?* Alice, damn it, she's a high-level fire mage with some kind of mega-weapon, and we're one mage and one ghost!"

"*Get in the car, Malcolm!*" I slammed my door closed, turned my key in the ignition, and hit the gas just as Malcolm appeared in the passenger seat area.

"You remember how I said it sucks when I try to warn you about doing dangerous stuff and you ignore me?" He crossed his arms and glared at me. "This is exactly what I was talking about. This right here."

I backed onto the street, shifted gears, and floored it in the direction of the fire. "I know. I apologize in advance for what I'm about to do."

"Oh, God, she apologized," Malcolm muttered. "Now I *know* this is going to end badly."

CHAPTER 24

A LOCAL RADIO STATION REPORTED THAT THE FIRE WAS CONSUMING approximately four blocks just west of downtown. Luckily, many of the structures involved were office buildings with few people at work in the middle of the night, but the fire was threatening to spread to nearby apartment buildings. A dozen fire crews were on scene, attempting to contain the blaze, but the fire was far too intense.

As I drove, Malcolm told me Catherine was on the roof of a building that overlooked a luxury condo. There was a good chance she'd tracked Bell to that condo and had used whatever weapon she'd obtained to create a perimeter of fire before torching the condo itself. Or maybe she was waiting for him to try to escape along with everyone else and target him then. Either way, many people were going to die horribly unless I could figure out a way to stop her.

I picked up my cell phone, scrolled through my recent calls, and dialed a number from the list. I left it in the holder and turned on the speaker so I could keep both hands on the wheel.

The phone rang once before an electronic voice answered. "This is Cyro."

I exhaled. "Cyro, it's Alice Worth. I'm sorry to bother—"

"You're heading downtown toward the fire. What do you need?"

I had no idea how he was tracking my movements—maybe my phone? Or was there a tracking device on my car? Damn it, something else I'd have to worry about later. "I'm sure what I'm asking for is out of my price range, but how much would it cost for you to shut down all the surveillance cameras you can around the scene? I'm going to try to do something about the fire and I don't want to be seen."

I heard keys clicking rapidly in the background. "This one's on the house, unless you die trying to save the city, in which case I'll subtract my fee from your bank account."

I blinked. "Okay. I guess I can live with that—or not, as the case may be. What's a good vantage point close to Ground Zero? I need a rooftop with a good view of the fire, preferably somewhere without people around."

As Cyro searched for an appropriate destination, I thought about what Sean and Malcolm had said about facing danger on my own and how my decisions affected the people who cared about me.

I muted my call with Cyro and glanced over at Malcolm. "We're doing this together, all right? Team effort. Nobody's going Lone Ranger."

"The Lone Ranger had Tonto," Malcolm pointed out.

"Shut up. You know what I mean."

"Yeah, I know what you mean. Way to show personal growth."

I rolled my eyes and unmuted my phone.

"There's a six-story private parking garage about a block north of the fire," Cyro said. "It's at the corner of Twenty-third and Burgess Avenue. I'll cut the cameras and raise the gate for you."

"Holy shit," Malcolm muttered. "Who *is* this guy?"

I took a deep breath. "Thank you, Cyro. If this goes sideways, I want you to know how much I've appreciated your help."

"Just try not to die," he said. "I'd like more interesting projects in the future."

"I'll certainly do my best to survive." I hesitated. "Do you have eyes on the cause of the fire?"

"Yes. It's Catherine Atwood, Moses Murphy's daughter. She's on the roof of an office building next door to the parking garage with some kind of magical object. I'm running a search on it, but I don't have any information yet about what it is or where she got it. Anything else?"

"Yeah, one more thing. If I don't make it out, will you arrange to get my car out of the garage and back to my house?"

"I can do that. I thought you were going to ask me to clear your browser history."

That made me laugh, despite the fear and adrenaline coursing through my veins. "Thanks, Cyro. I gotta go."

"Good luck." The call ended.

"So, do you have a plan or are we just winging it like usual?" Malcolm asked as I turned onto Twenty-third. Ahead of us, the fire raged against the night sky.

"I'm thinking." I hit a dip going too fast and the car's bumper scraped. I winced. "We won't be able to get close enough to her to take out that weapon, so we need options for containing the fire."

"Neither of us has fire magic," Malcolm pointed out. "I have water and you have air and we both have earth magic, but I don't know how that's going to help."

"We'll come up with something." I spotted the garage entrance and slowed to turn. Sure enough, the gate was up.

The garage belonged to one of the office buildings and it was almost completely empty in the middle of the night. I parked on the first level, jumped from the car, and ran for the stairs with Malcolm right behind me. My eyes burned from the heavy smoke and the garage echoed with the deafening sound of a dozen sirens.

By the time I made it to the third floor, I had to pull myself up the stairs using the handrail. "I need to do more cardio," I panted.

Malcolm snorted. "Or maybe the fact that you died a couple of days ago and haven't fully recovered from that yet has something to do with it."

"Maybe." I focused on breathing and making my legs keep climbing the steps.

When I reached the top of the stairs, my legs felt like they were made of rubber and I was gasping for air. I emerged onto the rooftop parking deck and took a moment to bend over and put my hands on my knees, sucking in air and swearing under my breath.

"Alice?"

An unexpected—but very familiar—voice made me jump and look up. I gaped at the sight of Sean, wearing a dark jacket and jeans, striding toward me across the parking deck. He didn't look angry or even surprised to see me. My heart skipped a beat and it had nothing to do with physical exertion.

"What are you doing here?" I asked, trying to catch my breath.

"Karen's brother Patrick lives in that condo with his girlfriend," he told me, joining me at the top of the stairs. "I came to see if I could help get people out, but there's no way through the fire. Cyro called me and suggested I come up here to meet you and get a bird's-eye view."

I set my worries about where we stood aside to focus on the deadly problem in front of us. "Malcolm's with me," I told him, since he couldn't see the ghost.

Sean and Malcolm exchanged greetings as I half-dragged my leaden legs across the parking deck to the waist-high concrete ledge.

We were upwind and a full block away from the blaze, but even at this distance the heat and smoke were nearly unbearable. I counted eight buildings completely engulfed in flames, forming a perimeter around a twelve-story condo. Emergency vehicles packed the nearby streets, filling the sky with red and blue flashing lights. Fire trucks aimed a dozen jets of water at the burning buildings, but they weren't making any headway. The magic-enhanced fires were just too massive.

I moved to the far end of the parking deck and finally spotted

Catherine on the roof of an adjacent building. She faced the fire, holding the gold ring Malcolm had described. I couldn't be sure from this distance, but it looked very much like the ring I'd seen bought at the auction. Somehow it had made its way into Catherine's hands, presumably after we'd had Kendall's stash of stolen weapons and artifacts seized by SPEMA.

At the moment, the weapon was not in use; she'd apparently used it to start the blaze by focusing her fire magic at the targeted buildings.

"What do you know about this?" Sean asked me.

"Cyro says that's Catherine Atwood, Moses Murphy's daughter. My guess is she found out Darius Bell is holed up in that condo and she's trying to flush him out."

"By burning all these buildings down and killing everyone?" His anger prickled on my skin.

"She doesn't care. Moses probably told her to take Bell out or else."

Catherine set the ring at her feet and raised her arms. The fire responded by surging in the buildings closest to the condo. Several thundering crashes indicated that floors were collapsing in those buildings. The fires grew and licked at the exterior walls of the condo. I could see people in the windows and more trying to escape through the various street-level doors, only to be driven back by the fire.

A police helicopter approached us. I ducked my head to avoid being photographed as it flew overhead.

"Oh, shit," Malcolm breathed.

I looked up just in time to see Catherine send a plume of fire toward the helicopter. It avoided the flames and accelerated away, circling at a safe distance as the fire grew and spread.

"Well, that explains why all the news helicopters are keeping their distance," Malcolm said.

"She's going to burn everyone in that condo alive," Sean said grimly.

"No, she's not," I stated. "We won't let her."

Despite how certain I sounded, I wasn't sure what we could do. Neither Malcolm nor I could control fire. We both had earth magic, but that wouldn't help. I had air magic, but even if I tapped a ley line to boost my power I wouldn't be able to do anything but fan the flames more. Malcolm's water magic wouldn't be enough to pull the river this far and we'd flood the city in the attempt. My blood magic could do nothing from this distance without a focus.

Lightning flashed on the horizon. There was a rainstorm north of us, but it was too far away and moving in the wrong direction—not that a storm that small would do much against a fire this size, anyway. But if it were bigger, and it turned south...

"I have an idea," I said to Malcolm. I pointed.

He frowned at the storm and then at me. "I don't get it."

"We need to bring that storm here."

"What are you suggesting? That we do a rain dance?"

"No. I've got air magic. You've got water magic. We just need to work together."

He shook his head. "Water magic can make a storm stronger, but I'm not powerful enough to do it. I know you're strong, but even you can't move a storm against the wind."

"I can if I pull energy from the two ley lines that intersect here."

"Even if you *could* do that, that little bit of rain isn't enough to put this fire out."

"I can make the storm big and strong enough. All you have to do is share my body and let me use your magic."

"*Are you insane?*" He flitted back and forth so quickly that I couldn't track him with my eyes. "Are you out of your damn mind? You can't summon a thunderstorm!"

"Yes, I can," I said calmly. "I've done it before. Not for a while, but I've done it. I just need your water magic."

He stopped directly in front of me. "There's no way in hell I'm going to do this. Just touching me makes your hands turn blue. If I share your body, you'll freeze to death in minutes."

"I only need a few minutes. The storm isn't that far away. It's the only—"

"I swear to God, Alice, don't you dare say it's the only way!" he yelled. "It is *not* the only way!"

"Then give me another idea," I begged. "Name anything else we can do to save the people in that condo and in these other buildings."

Malcolm crossed his arms. "We can't save everyone every time. Some things are just beyond what anyone can do."

"This isn't beyond what I can do. I've done it before. Granted, not by sharing my body with a ghost, but I've used a ghost with water magic in a focus to summon a storm."

"A ghost in a focus?" He hovered right in front of me, his eyes dark with fury. "So you've used ghosts trapped in crystals, just like the ghost Kendall was using in that statue?"

"Not by choice," I snapped. "You know I used to belong to a cabal. Do you think I did it because I *wanted* to? You know me, Malcolm. You don't believe for one minute that I did it by choice."

Sean's attention was still on the fire, but he glanced at me when I mentioned the cabal. He didn't look surprised, however. No doubt he'd already surmised that I'd once belonged to one; few high-level mages escaped their clutches, and he'd probably picked up enough clues over the past few months to figure it out. The scars on my back showed I'd been tortured by a blood mage, as was common with cabal mages who refused to obey orders. I'd basically just confirmed what he already knew.

"No, I don't believe you did it by choice," Malcolm said grimly. "I know you only did it because you had to. But you don't have to do this. This isn't a grenade you have to fall on."

"This is different. This one *is* my grenade to fall on. This time it's not just me trying to balance the scales. It's personal."

"In what way is this personal?" Malcolm asked.

I couldn't very well tell him that was my aunt over there burning the city down. "One of Sean's pack members is in there, along with probably a hundred other people. Isn't that enough?"

"If I share your body, it will freeze you from the inside out. I refuse to help you kill yourself."

"I'm not asking you to kill me. I'm just asking you to let me use your water magic long enough to summon that storm. You can jump out of me before I get to the point where we have to worry about me freezing to death."

Sean had been watching Catherine and listening to us argue. He turned to me, his expression grim. I thought he was going to side with Malcolm, but instead he said, "Let's do it. What can I do to help?"

Malcolm gaped at him. "You're not serious. After everything you said about her falling on grenades, you're going to ask her to do this?"

"She says she can do it." Sean met my eyes. I saw worry and anger, but I also saw his confidence in me.

"I can do this," I told him. "I can save Patrick and the other people in the condo, and I can do it without dying." Tentatively, I reached out and took his hand.

He lifted it to his lips and pressed a kiss to my knuckles. "Then let's save them."

Malcolm swore. "The second you start getting too cold, I'm jumping out, whether it's done or not," he warned me.

"Agreed. Hurry." I squeezed Sean's hand, then let go and stepped back.

Malcolm muttered something I couldn't hear, braced himself, and dove straight at me.

I'd never shared my body with a ghost before. It felt like being dunked in a frozen lake. The shock drove me to my knees. I cried out involuntarily as his non-corporeal form moved under my skin. He settled into my body and my temperature began to drop. The chill was uncomfortable, but not yet debilitating or dangerous.

Sean crouched in front of me. "Are you okay?"

"I'm okay," I said shakily. "This feels really, really weird."

You're telling me, Malcolm said in my head. *Let's do this before you freeze to death.*

Sean helped me to my feet just as a gust of wind blew a thick cloud of smoke in our direction. I coughed and blinked away tears. "I'll be focused on the magic and the storm," I told him. "Keep us safe."

"Always." He squeezed my hands and flinched. "You're already getting cold."

"I know. I need to hurry." I hesitated, then added, "When this is over, I'd like to talk."

"When this is over, I'd like to listen." He let go of my hands. "Bring the thunder, Miss Magic."

I gave him a small smile, turned to face the storm, and closed my eyes.

Malcolm's magic pulsed though me. The unfamiliar sensation of water tugged at my awareness. I'd always had an affinity to the earth and air because of my own magic, but now I could feel the water the fire crews were using to fight the blaze. The sensation was wonderful, like standing in a cool stream.

With Malcolm's water magic now part of me, I sensed the far-off thunderstorm. It was too far away for me to summon, however. I needed a power boost.

Now the ley lines, Malcolm said in my head. *Be careful.*

Brace yourself, I told him.

I'd certainly never imagined that I'd need the lines to fight my aunt or save the city from fire. By doing so I risked outing myself, but it appeared I had little choice unless I was willing to let everyone in that condo, including Patrick, burn to death.

I sensed the ley line energy pulsing on the edge of my senses. We weren't far from their intersection; only a mile or so. I took several deep breaths and grabbed the lines.

Everything went white. For a moment, I thought my chest might explode at the sheer force of the power I was conducting. I gasped for air and fought to contain the energy. Pain seared every nerve and I set my jaw to keep from crying out.

You're getting cold, Malcolm said. I couldn't feel anything but the ley-line power and pain, so his words were a surprise. *And the condo just caught fire, so you've got to hurry.*

Okay. Here goes, I told him.

I let the water and air magic rise until it filled me and danced on my skin. The cool blue and white energy of the storm crackled on the edge of my senses, pulling at me like a magnet. I used the ley line power to enhance our magic, raised my arms, and pulled the storm toward us.

With so much power behind it, our magic brought the storm faster than I'd thought possible. The air changed and became heavy as the rain approached the city. I pushed Malcolm's water magic into the storm and used my enhanced air magic to build it to near-hurricane strength.

"Here it comes," Sean warned me.

The storm arrived with a roar. The wall of wind and rain pushed me back several steps and nearly knocked me over. Sean wrapped his arms around me and braced me, planting his feet and pushing back against the force of the wind.

The rain was so heavy that I thought I might drown standing up in it. The wind made Sean stagger but he stayed on his feet.

I forced my eyes open. I was soaked to my skin, but my hoodie kept enough of the rain out of my eyes that I could see. Despite the power of the magic that created the fires, the deluge began to drown the flames in the buildings around us.

Down at street level, the fire crews took advantage of breaks in the wall of fire surrounding the condo to move people to safety away from the blaze. Residents emerged from various doors and ran to the first responders.

Suddenly, Sean dove to the pavement and covered my body with his as a fireball passed over us. Catherine had spotted us and attacked.

He rolled us behind the concrete barrier along the edge of the roof. Another fireball, this one much larger, blasted over our heads.

"How is she using fire in this rain?" Sean shouted over the roar of the storm.

I was now shivering violently. "It's m-m-magic."

You're getting too cold, Malcolm said in my head. *I'm jumping out.*

No, wait, I told him. *I need your magic still. The storm will dissipate if I let up, and without water magic I can't defend us against Catherine's fire.*

You agreed that I would get out of your body when you started to get too cold, he snapped. *That's the only reason I said I'd do this.*

Just one more minute. I promise I won't—

A fireball arced over the concrete wall and landed right on top of us. Sean snarled and rolled us into a deep puddle to try to put out the flames, but it was fire magic, not normal fire. Stop, drop, and roll would do us no good.

I used Malcolm's water magic to smother the flames. Our clothes were half-burned and my skin was angry red in places. I couldn't feel the pain yet because I was so cold.

"Are you all right?" Sean asked. His arms and back were burned where he'd been trying to shield me. Some of the burns looked like they might be second-degree. It had to be excruciating, but as always, his concern was for me.

It was seeing him hurt that flipped the switch inside me. I hadn't come down here to confront Catherine directly; my goal was to save the people in the condo and the other buildings around us. But she'd hurt Sean, and I'd be damned if that bitch was going to get away with it.

"G-g-get m-m-me up," I said, my teeth chattering. "St-stay b-b-b-behind me and d-don't let her s-see your f-face."

Sean didn't argue. Malcolm, however, did. As Sean lifted me to my feet, the ghost demanded, *What are you doing? She's got fire, Alice!*

Wait 'til you see what I've got, I told him.

With Sean behind me, holding me up as the rain pounded us and the wind roared across the top deck of the parking garage, I looked over at the building next to ours.

Catherine stood facing us, soaked to the skin and struggling against the wind and rain. I could see her fury even from thirty feet away. Orange flames danced on her hands and arms. She looked so much like Moses that bile rose in my throat.

She bent down to pick up the magical weapon at her feet. At this distance, it would turn us both to ash in an instant.

Sean braced himself, his arms tightening around me. "Get behind me," he growled in my ear.

"No, *you* stay behind *me*." *Go to hell, Catherine*, I thought, and raised my arms toward the sky.

My air magic, enhanced by the ley lines, arced through the rain. I seized the power of the storm itself—not the rain, but the charged particles in the air—and the energy was like grabbing a third ley line. The surge of pure power and pain made me scream.

What the f— Malcolm began.

I formed the power into a bolt and brought it down on Catherine's head with all my might and magic. A brilliant flash of white blinded me and a deafening thunderclap shook the parking garage.

Sean dropped us to the pavement again, but this time I didn't even feel the impact when we hit the concrete. I was numb from cold and drained of magic. I landed in a heap and stayed down, too dazed to move or react.

With no more air or water magic to use, I let go of the ley lines. The sudden loss of power and absence of pain made me feel hollow, like a husk with nothing inside.

Nothing inside me but a ghost, anyway.

You conjured lightning, Malcolm said in awe. *I've never seen anyone...Alice?*

I couldn't respond, not even a thought. I was too cold, too drained, too exhausted.

Malcolm swore. I felt a strange popping sensation and realized he'd jumped from my body.

"Alice?" Sean asked. I vaguely sensed him brushing wet hair back from my face. "Jesus, she's blue. Malcolm?"

"Yeah, I'm here," Malcolm said tersely. "She's got severe hypothermia. We need to get her warmed up and into dry clothes before she dies of exposure."

Sean picked me up and ran. I nestled my face against his chest, breathing in his scent as we crossed the parking deck to the stairs.

The rain was gentle now. The storm would fade soon. I hoped it had done enough that the firefighters could put the fires out without too much trouble. In any case, by bringing the storm, I'd done what I could to save the people in the condo. The rest would be up to others; I had nothing left to give.

As he rushed down the steps, I heard Sean ask Malcolm, "Did she just do what I think she did?"

"Yep. She fried someone with a bolt of lightning." A pause. "It was awesome."

"Did you know she could do that?"

"Nope, but it doesn't surprise me. If anyone could smite someone with lightning, it would be Alice."

We reached the bottom of the stairs. "Alice, can you hear me?" Sean asked.

I was shivering so hard that I could barely speak. "C-cold," I managed to say.

He squeezed me tightly against his chest. "I'm taking you to my house to get you warmed up. Hang on."

I mumbled something unintelligible. He carried me to my car and laid me down in the back seat. He disappeared for a few moments and returned with a blanket I assumed he'd gotten from his truck. He removed my boots, ripped off my soaked clothes, and wrapped me in some kind of blanket that smelled like dirt and grass. Maybe a picnic blanket? Did werewolves go on picnics?

"Yes, we do," Sean said. I hadn't realized I'd spoken out loud. He kissed my forehead. "Werewolves like picnics a lot. Rest now. I've got you."

Werewolves liked picnics. Who would have thunk it? Smiling, I faded out.

CHAPTER 25

STRANGE SENSATIONS AND SOUNDS PULLED ME FROM MY REST. I THOUGHT AT first that hands were caressing my body, but somehow I knew that wasn't what was happening. I was miserably cold, deeper than my bones, all the way down to my core. I couldn't even remember what it felt like to be warm. My heartbeat was a slow *lub-dub* in my chest.

The soft noises became recognizable as water sloshing. The sensation of caresses was actually the water tugging at the traces of magic left behind by Malcolm. I realized I was submerged in water, my body against someone I instinctively recognized as Sean even before I detected the scent of forest. He was in the water with me, holding me against his body, my head tucked under his chin as I shivered. I couldn't open my eyes, but I sensed a lot of bare skin between us.

"Alice, are you awake?" Sean asked. His voice echoed, like we were in a bathroom.

I tried to speak. "Ssss..."

He squeezed me. "We're at my house, in a tub full of hot water. I'm trying to warm you up but you still feel like a block of ice."

I tried again. "Sssss...Sean."

He moved a little and I heard the water running. "I've never been more thankful for my tankless water heater and soaker tub. We've been in here over an hour."

"Rrrrr...wrinkly," I said.

He shook with laughter. "My Alice."

My heart soared. "Your Alice," I agreed.

The water shut off and he wrapped his arms around me again. "Malcolm went back to the fire scene to keep an eye on things. Patrick and his girlfriend are fine, but they'll have to find another place to live. The condo took heavy damage from the fire. There were some injuries, but everyone got out of the condo alive and casualties in the other buildings were minimal, thanks to you." He kissed my hair.

I sensed he was holding something back. "What else?" I murmured.

"A stringer got some footage of us on the roof of the parking garage. The quality is terrible because of the storm, but the local and national news channels picked it up. I doubt there's any chance of us being identified, but the video does show you controlling the storm. Thankfully, the recording cuts out before the end."

I was too cold to feel much of anything about that unwelcome news. I'd known there was a chance I'd out myself, but not trying to help was never an option. At least the video hadn't shown me taking out Catherine with the lightning.

"Worth the risk," I said softly.

"The only person who got any kind of look at us was Catherine Atwood, and I doubt she's in any condition to talk about what she saw." He cupped my head with his hand and held me close. "I've heard that air mages could summon lightning, but I've never seen anyone do it before."

It wasn't really summoning—more like conjuring or conducting—but I was too tired to explain the difference. Here I was, reunited with Sean after several days of wishing desperately for a chance to fix things between us, and I didn't have the strength to talk. I snuggled deeper against his chest and made a little unhappy sound.

He tightened his arms around me. "Is there nothing else I can do? Malcolm healed your burns but he said healing spells wouldn't help with hypothermia." He took a deep breath. "Could Vaughan heal you?"

I could only imagine what asking that had cost him. "Don't want his help." My voice was faint, but firm. "Just hold me, please."

"That I can do." He settled deeper into the water so it covered me up to my chin. "I know you said you wanted to talk and I told you I wanted to listen, and I do, but I have something I need to tell you. Maybe this isn't the time and maybe I'm a bastard to say it when you're in this condition, but I'm going to anyway."

My stomach flip-flopped. His tone was strange. I wasn't sure what he was going to say, and I feared very much that I wouldn't like it.

"I've been doing a lot of thinking these last couple of days. There's a lot about you I don't know; too much, to be honest, but here's what I *do* know. I know you're not the Alice Worth who was the daughter of Henry and Laura Worth of Chicago. I know you're powerful and dangerous and that you're on the run from someone who means you harm. I also know you're the most selfless and brave person I have ever met, and you'll never stop saving the world. And I know that I love you, not in spite of all that, but because of it."

I'd feared he would figure out that I wasn't who I said I was. I'd also known he loved me and it was only a matter of time before he said the words out loud. I expected to feel panicky on both counts, like I wanted to run for the hills and never look back.

Instead, what I felt was...relief. And happiness.

My reaction startled me so much that I didn't notice I was slipping away again until my hand slid across his chest and splashed into the water.

"Alice?" he asked worriedly. "I said, I love you."

Just before I drifted off, I smiled and whispered, "I know."

I woke up in the middle of a pile of werewolves.

Five of them, to be exact. Two were gray, one was solid black, one was brown with black and dark brown markings, and the fifth was gray and white. None of them was Sean, but as I blinked blearily and focused on my surroundings, I found that we were all lying on a king-sized mattress on the floor in one of the spare bedrooms in his house.

I was wearing long-sleeved flannel pajamas over what felt like thermal long underwear and two pairs of thick socks, and I was wedged between two very large wolves weighing about two hundred pounds each. Miraculously, I was no longer freezing. I'd thought I'd never be warm again.

When I pushed myself up onto my elbows and moved to relieve a cramp in one leg, all of the wolves raised their heads. The larger of the gray wolves stared at me, as if daring me to move. I froze.

Sean appeared in the doorway, wearing a green button-up shirt and jeans. "You're safe with them, Alice."

I eyed the gray wolf. "I know, but she doesn't seem like she wants me going anywhere."

He came over to the side of the bed. "That's Nan's wolf, and no, she doesn't. When she saw the shape you were in, I got an earful about taking better care of you. And she's been giving me dirty looks every time I come in here to check on you."

In fact, the wolf was giving him one now, presumably for not telling me to lie down and go back to sleep. I'd seldom seen such disapproval on a wolf's face. I giggled before I could stop myself.

"How do you feel?" He leaned over to touch my face. "You're still a little cold."

"I feel good," I assured him. "I'm hungry, actually. I bet a pot of coffee and a hot breakfast would fix me right up."

He chuckled. "When you ask for food and coffee, then I know you're on the mend."

I rubbed my eyes and looked out the window. It was a bright and sunny afternoon, but I had no idea how much time had passed since we'd gotten to Sean's house. "So, how long was I out?"

"It's almost five o'clock. It's been about eleven hours since you put the fire out."

Well, that wasn't so bad. I'd expected it to be at least the next day. I felt low on magic, but plenty rested.

I looked at the werewolves piled on the bed around me. "Thank you so much for this," I said a little awkwardly, wondering how much their wolves would even understand me. "Thanks for taking care of me. I—" I broke off. I'd been about to say that I owed them, but that didn't seem like the right thing to say. Instead, I said, "I don't think I've ever slept better than I did with all of you on this bed."

Sean smiled. "I wasn't sure how you'd react to finding yourself up to your ears in werewolves, but I needed to keep you safe and warm and this seemed the best way to do that. Besides, Nan wouldn't take no for an answer, and I learned long ago to take her advice on such things."

Smart man. "Who else is here?"

"The other gray wolf is Felicia. The black wolf is David, her brother. The brown is Patrick, and the gray and white wolf is Karen."

One by one, the wolves got to their feet and stretched. Each carefully nuzzled my face with theirs before trotting out of the room, presumably to shift back to their human forms and give us some time to talk.

When we were alone, Sean shut the bedroom door and helped me to my feet and off the mattress. When we were standing on the hardwood floor, he took my face in his hands and kissed me very thoroughly.

I rested my forehead on his chest and let his familiar scent envelop me. "Where's Malcolm?" I asked.

"Back at your place. He said he didn't want the other wolves to sense him, and he wanted to keep an eye on the house."

"Any news?"

"Some. Should I fill you in over omelets and coffee?"

His guarded tone made me think that it wasn't good news. "You'd better just tell me now."

"Darius Bell survived the fire, so that's a plus for those of us who don't want Moses Murphy taking over the city. Bell's organization is crippled, but not giving up. Just before noon, there was an attack on Murphy's compound near Baltimore. The building sustained some damage and there were a few casualties, but none of them were Murphy."

I was disappointed but not surprised. It would be difficult or nearly impossible to take Moses out when he was in his compound, but I supposed Bell was angry enough to make an attempt, even if all it accomplished was to make the point that he was willing and able to take the fight to Moses.

"Hopefully he'll have better luck next time," I said. "What else?"

Sean took out his phone and handed it to me. The screen showed a still image from the video of us on the roof of the parking garage. We were little more than two small, dark, faceless figures in the pouring rain, recorded from a rooftop several buildings away. There was no way anyone would be able to identify us from that image.

Then I noticed the headline. "Oh, you have *got* to be kidding me. 'Storm Girl'?"

He frowned and took the phone back to look at the picture. "What?"

"They're calling me Storm Girl," I fumed. "Maybe the hoodie made me look young. I'm a high-level mage and a licensed private investigator. I'm on a first-name basis with five of the nine members of the Vampire Court. I'm *thirty years old*, for crying out loud. Storm *Girl?*"

Sean's mouth twitched. "And?"

I crossed my arms. "Damn it, I should at least be Storm Woman."

He couldn't contain himself anymore and burst out laughing. I scowled and he kissed my forehead, still chuckling. "It's a terrible superhero name," he admitted. "We need to come up with something better."

My scowl deepened. "I don't want a superhero name. I'm not a superhero, or even a hero."

"You are most definitely a hero, but we'll save that debate for another day. I've got one more piece of news." He took a deep breath. "I got a call from Cyro about an hour ago. A jet belonging to Moses Murphy took off from a private airport this morning headed for Baltimore. Cyro managed to get surveillance footage from the hangar showing them loading Catherine Atwood onto the plane. She was in bad shape, but it looks like she survived somehow."

I went cold all over—much colder than when I'd shared my body with Malcolm. Next to Moses himself arriving in the city, Catherine being alive was the worst news I could have gotten. Actually, it might be worse than finding out my grandfather was here. She'd gotten a glimpse of me up on the roof, and if she recognized me as the woman she'd encountered at 1792, there was a chance she'd be able to figure out who I was. Even if she didn't make that connection, she still might be able to track me down if she got a good enough look at me.

I must not have hit her directly with the lightning. It was nearly impossible to hit a target that small with a lightning strike; unlike a bolt of magic, which I could aim, lightning was an imprecise weapon. Even if I'd missed, though, Catherine had been standing in ankle-deep rainwater, a perfect conductor for the electricity in the lightning. She should have been fried to a crisp. I wondered if she'd been using some kind of protection spells, or if she'd just gotten lucky. Either way, it was not what I wanted to hear, not by a long shot.

There was always the chance she'd die from her injuries, hopefully without having a chance to tell anyone about who or what she'd seen on the rooftop. I couldn't very well bank on that, though. I had to assume I was now in imminent danger of discovery.

What surprised me most about my reaction to the news was that I didn't immediately want to run. Even six months ago, that would have been my first thought. Instead, I was angry that Catherine and Moses were threats to the life I had built here. Maybe defiance had overpowered my fear because I'd just summoned a thunderstorm and reminded myself of how powerful I was. Maybe it was because I had allies who I believed would have my back if I had to fight, or because I had so much more to fight for now. Maybe it was because Sean had told me he loved me—an important moment that I hadn't even had a chance to really process yet. Maybe it was all of the above. Instead of mentally lacing up my shoes to run, I sensed myself digging in my heels.

Sean startled me by picking me up around the waist and kissing me fiercely. When he put me down, I was breathless. "What was that for?" I asked.

"For deciding to stay and fight instead of cut and run."

I frowned at him. "You don't know what's going on in my head."

He grinned. "Oh yes, I do. I've seen that stubborn look in your eyes a hundred times. Plus, you just smote someone with lightning. A woman who does that isn't the type to turn tail and run, not when she has so many good reasons to stay."

"The last time we spoke, at Jack's house, you said you didn't think you could do this." I gestured between us. "I have to ask: what changed your mind?"

"I didn't so much change my mind as come to terms with what I already knew." He wrapped his arms around me and rested his chin on top of my head. "What I figured out was that it didn't matter if I thought I couldn't do this; the fact is that I *have* to. You are part of my soul. I had so many people around me wondering if you were strong enough to be my partner that I didn't think to ask if I was strong enough to be *yours*. It's me who needs to be stronger, not you."

When I started to object, he moved so he could see my face, his eyes softly golden. "I've always told myself that I wanted a partner and a mate who would stand beside me and who would fight with and for my pack, but I don't think I ever really understood what that meant until now. The night I met you at Hawthorne's, you sat across the booth from me and stared me down. It was your fearlessness that drew me to you as much as anything else. You are exactly what I'd wished and waited for, and I almost blew it because I didn't know how to deal with your power, your courage, and your need to protect others. You face your enemies as though you were the alpha of a pack. You are fierce and you'll fight until you have nothing left. I don't know how, but you can even use shifter magic. Your strength knows no bounds."

He squeezed my hand. "The other members of the pack already recognize your strength. I shouldn't have advised you not to look Jack in the eye. Your place is at my side, within the pack hierarchy—not outside it. Like an alpha, you will never stop trying to save people, even if it means endangering yourself. It's as much a part of you as your magic. The minute I figured out that I had to stop trying to force you to be someone else, the answers fell into place, and I knew I should never have sent you home the other night without talking everything through."

"So why didn't you come over or call me once you'd figured all this out?" I demanded.

He smiled ruefully. "I had that epiphany all of forty-five minutes before Patrick called to say he and Amanda were trapped in their apartment and their entire neighborhood was on fire."

"Speaking of epiphanies..." I took a deep breath. "I apologize for not thinking about how you and the pack would feel about me dying. I'm not sorry that I did it and I'd do it again, but not without leaving a note telling you what was going on, or at least apologizing when I woke up."

"Both of those would have been good choices," he said mildly.

Might as well tell him the rest of what I'd figured out during our time apart. "I know it comes across like I'm cavalier about my life, but I'm really not. The only reason I did what I did was that I knew I'd make it back. But I *was* cavalier about your feelings, and for that I am truly sorry."

He wrapped me in his arms again. "Thank you for saying that. On the way to my house from the parking garage, Malcolm let me know that you and he had talked about some of this already."

"That meddling ghost," I muttered.

He chuckled. "More like matchmaking ghost. He doesn't like seeing you unhappy, and I think he was afraid that one or both of us would bungle this conversation." He squeezed me gently. "I don't believe in giving ultimatums, but here's what I need from you going forward. Remember your life has value and Malcolm and I care very much that you stay alive. Things that hurt you hurt us. I'm not asking you not to throw yourself on any more grenades, but before you do, remember you are loved and you don't have to face anything by yourself ever again. That includes whoever you're running from."

"I'm not running anymore. If they come looking for me, I'll be waiting."

"And I'll be waiting too, right by your side." He kissed my temple. "You still haven't brought up what I said to you in the tub, right before you passed out again. Nice *Star Wars* reference, by the way."

"What *Star Wars* reference?"

Sean made a choking sound.

I laughed. "I'm kidding. Yes, I quoted *Star Wars*. Well, *The Empire Strikes Back*, actually."

He heaved a sigh of relief. "That was going to be a deal-breaker for me, Alice. I can take a lot of things in stride, but missing obvious *Star Wars* references is just more than anyone can take." He tipped my chin up. "I love you."

"I might be too broken to love you back," I admitted. That could have been the most honest thing I'd ever said to him.

"I know that's what you believe, but I know you well enough to know you're not as broken as you think. In any case, I don't need you to say the words to know how you feel. I see it in your eyes and I feel it when you're near me. That's worth more to me than words."

"Then let me put a couple of cards on the table." I took a deep breath. "You saw me use shifter magic at Jack's house. I don't have any answers for how that might be possible, unless it's related to what I learned from Esther's magic mirror the other day."

He waited while I struggled to force the words out.

Finally, I cleared my throat and continued. "The mirror showed me something that might have taken place when I was about six or seven. I overheard my parents talking. It's possible the man I thought was my father wasn't really my biological father. If it's true, then maybe that has something to do with my ability to use shifter magic and the way I relate to the members of your pack. Maybe my real... real father was a shifter, or had shifter blood."

He held me tightly. "That's a hell of lot to process by yourself, and I know it was hard to tell me about it. I'm glad that you did. What are you going to do about it, now that you know?"

"I don't know. If the memory is real, all I have is a first name. The situation is really complicated. I'm going to have to think about what I want to do, if anything. If I start nosing around, I'm not sure what I'll find. I might be putting him at risk just by looking."

"I think you're right to think about it before you make any decisions. There's no rush."

Some of the tension went out of my shoulders. Sean's reassurance had come to mean something to me.

That left one more card to put on the table. It was even harder to put down than the first one, so I spoke quickly, before I had a chance to talk myself out of it. "You said you know I'm not the same Alice Worth who grew up in Chicago. You're right."

Sean stilled.

"That's who I am now, but once upon a time I used to be someone else, someone who got away from a cabal and needed a new identity and a new life. I had a chance to become Alice Worth, so that's what I did. I've been Alice for more than five years. I *am* Alice."

"And the first Alice Worth?" he asked, his voice quiet.

"Dead. I didn't kill her," I added quickly. "I had nothing to do with her death except be in a position to take advantage of it. That sounds cold, I know, but I was desperate to escape my old life." I took a deep, shaky breath. "I'm not ready to talk about that other life, not yet, but I'm getting there. I have no right to ask you to give me more time on that, but that's what I'm asking for."

I didn't breathe until he answered. "Take as much time as you need until you're ready to tell me," Sean said. I almost sagged in relief. He held me close and nuzzled my hair. "I can wait to hear the rest of the story because I know who you are, even if I don't know who you were before."

"Can I tell you something?" I asked suddenly.

"Of course."

"Yesterday was my birthday, my real birthday. I turned thirty yesterday." I blurted it out in a rush.

"Oh, Alice." He kissed me hard, his hands on my face. When he moved back, he looked stricken. "I am so sorry. I should have been there with you. Did Malcolm know?"

I shook my head. "Nobody knew. Well, except Rogue. We celebrated my birthday on the bed with cookies and a dog biscuit."

"Cookie *and* dog biscuit crumbs in the bed." Sean shook his head with feigned disgust. He grew serious again. "We'll have another celebration, you and I. A real date for once, with dinner and a movie, or whatever else you'd like to do. We'll have a cake and ice cream too."

"I don't need any of that. One thirtieth birthday was enough, thank you very much. But I'll tell you what I *do* want."

"Tell me."

"I want to go to the pack's cookout that's coming up in a couple of days." I took a deep breath. "And I want to go with you to the Bahamas."

His grin made my stomach flutter. "When do you want to go?"

"As soon as you can get the time off. I got paid for finding Esther's cup and mirror, so it will be my treat."

He eyed me. "We'll split it, fifty-fifty."

I relented. "Fine. Don't forget that you said you'd bring me all the umbrella drinks I wanted, whenever I wanted them. And food. And you have to put sunscreen on my back and shake the sand out of my shoes."

"Your wish is my command, my lady," he said. "Now, let's go downstairs so I can fix you some breakfast. Your stomach is growling so loudly that I'm sure Nan can hear it from the living room, and I'm going to catch hell if I don't feed you soon. Do you want to change first?"

I shook my head. "I'm enjoying being warm. I like the jammies. Whose are they?"

"Felicia's, I think. Nan brought them." He took my hand. "She's going to fuss over you until it drives you crazy, so just be prepared."

I smiled up at him. "I'm okay with that."

He raised my hand to his lips, kissed my knuckles, and opened the bedroom door.

HOW MANY HAMBURGERS *can* a pack of werewolves eat? I lost count at fifty, so the world may never know.

By ten o'clock, most of the food was gone and the pack was gathered around the bonfire, talking and laughing and drinking beer while the kids ran through Cole and Karen's backyard chasing each other in some version of tag that involved climbing trees.

I'd socialized before and during dinner, but even with Sean at my side to make sure I didn't get too crowded, it became overwhelming and I had to take refuge on our picnic blanket on the edge of the clearing. I'd worried that my retreat would come across as unfriendly or aloof, but everyone was good-natured about it.

Everyone but Jack, Delia, and Caleb, that was.

I wasn't sure if Sean had warned them not to talk to me or if they chose to avoid me on their own, but the three of them stayed as far from me as they could get from the moment they arrived. Jack and Delia ignored me altogether, but Caleb glared at me throughout the evening. I didn't let it bother me and had a good time talking and laughing with Nan, Felicia, Karen, Cole, and the others.

The older couple I'd seen at Jack's house were Eddie and his wife Thea. They seemed lukewarm toward me; Sean told me that like Jack and Delia, they wanted him to find a shifter mate.

The other pack member I hadn't met yet because he wasn't at Jack's that night was John, who came to the cookout with his husband Brandon and their three kids. John and Brandon warmed up quickly and we chatted all through dinner. All in all, I felt very welcomed by most of the pack, so Jack and Delia's indifference and Caleb's animosity meant little to me other than it irritated Sean.

Sean left the group by the fire and joined me on the blanket. He took a bottle of beer from our cooler and settled in next to me, his leg against mine. "Hey," he said, bumping me with his shoulder. "Are you warm enough?"

"Yep." Despite the warm summer evening, I wore a sweatshirt over a T-shirt and jeans with thick socks and boots and held a tumbler of hot tea. I was still not fully recovered, but with enough layers and a hot werewolf by my side—wink, wink—I felt plenty toasty.

I leaned against him and smiled as the kids ran past us, headed for the trees. "Don't they ever get tired?"

"They'll crash hard before too long. Even shifter kids run out of steam eventually." He took a drink. "Do you remember having that much energy?"

I shook my head. "No, but I'm sure I did at some point. I'm old now, though, so I'm just going to sit here and drink my tea."

"Hey, watch it," he said with mock outrage. "I'm a decade older than you."

"That's why you're over here with me. This is the seniors section."

He kissed me hard. "Seniors," he scoffed, reaching for his beer. "Hardly."

We watched the others while I rested my head on his shoulder and he put his arm around me. Finally, he asked, "Did you have fun tonight?"

"I really did. I'm sorry I had to leave the group."

"It's all right. You handled everything even better than I thought you would. I know these things aren't easy for someone who's used to being on her own." He ran his nose along my hairline. "I did let them know that you'll need some time to adjust to hanging around a big group."

"I figured you did. Thank you."

I noticed that Jack and Delia were standing together with Caleb on one side of the fire. As Jack and Caleb talked, Delia watched us with narrowed eyes.

"Jack and Delia aren't going to accept me," I said quietly. "I don't know about Eddie and Thea either."

"They *will* accept you. They might not like you, but they will accept you." Sean's voice was firm.

I thought about telling him what Malcolm had overheard Jack say to Delia about getting rid of me, but decided against it. No need to stir up trouble unless it looked like Jack might actually be trying to follow through on the threat.

"By the way, I bought our plane tickets to Nassau," Sean said. "And I found us a deal on a little cabana with its own private beach."

"When do we leave?"

He checked his phone. "In nine hours."

My mouth fell open. "Sean Maclin, when am I supposed to pack?"

"All you need is a swimsuit, a toothbrush, and your passport.

We're leaving everything else behind." His voice was firm. He was obviously referring to more than just clothes and toiletries.

We'd been unable to find out anything more about Catherine's condition; even Cyro couldn't get any information other than she'd been taken to Moses's compound. Malcolm and I had been on high alert for the past several days, watching for anything or anyone suspicious, but everything seemed normal.

In the meantime, the city was obsessed with identifying "Storm Girl" and the mysterious man with her. Darius Bell even offered a substantial reward for information. His attorney released a statement claiming Bell wanted to reward the woman who'd saved him and dozens of others from the fire, but I knew better. Bell wanted a powerful mage on his side in the war against Moses. He might not be the butcher Moses was, but he was still the head of his cabal and he would be every bit as ruthless as my grandfather. He'd had Malcolm tortured to death and recalled all of his bound ghosts, killing dozens of mages in the process. I harbored no illusions that I would be any better off as his prisoner than if Moses got me.

And then there was my agreement with Valas...

"Hey." Sean kissed my temple. "Don't let it get too dark in there, Miss Magic. Think about sunshine and umbrella drinks and crystal-blue Caribbean water. Can't you almost smell the sea?"

I closed my eyes and nestled my head against his chest, my nose filled with the scent of forest. "Paradise, here we come."

EPILOGUE

"Can you *believe* this place?"

I looked up from my umbrella drink as a tall black woman with a halo of curls slid onto the barstool next to me. She wore a teal bikini with a wrap tied around her hips and oversized sunglasses.

She grinned at me and signaled to the bartender. "Give me one of those," she said, pointing to my drink.

The bartender gave her a smile and began mixing her drink.

"What are you drinking, anyway?" she asked me, peering at the coconut on the bar in front of me.

"It's rum punch, and it's the best rum punch on the island."

"I love rum punch." She pushed her sunglasses up onto her head. "I'm Ree."

"Alice. Are you from the States?"

"Yep, California."

"Me too. What city?"

"San Francisco area." She took her drink from the bartender and handed him a twenty from a little pouch around her neck. "Keep the change," she told him.

We drank for a bit. I gazed through the palm trees at the ocean and marveled that there could be so many different shades of blue all in one place.

"Hey, I love your bracelet," she said.

I smiled self-consciously. "Thank you."

On our first day on the island, Sean had given me a bracelet made of tiny seashells. I told him I didn't want anything for my birthday. He informed me that it was an "I love you" present. I said I didn't think that was a real thing people did, but he insisted it was. The bracelet was the first gift I'd ever allowed him to give me, and I was trying not to be weirded out about it.

"What brings you to the Bahamas?" I asked as I finished my drink and signaled for another.

"I just had to get away." Ree nursed her drink. "Work has been absolutely insane lately. I'm so busy that I hardly ever get to take a vacation. Then yesterday I decided either I had to take a break or I'd go bonkers, so I booked a flight and *voilà!*" She used her coconut to gesture around us at the palm trees, beach, and sea. "Here I am, in paradise."

"What kind of work do you do?"

"I'm in IT. Yeah, I know, I'm a nerd." She laughed. "Computers and networks and stuff like that. Super boring. What do you do?"

"I'm an administrative assistant." That was my go-to answer when strangers asked what I did. Telling people I was a private investigator usually resulted in a million nosy questions and I just wanted to enjoy the sunshine and my rum punch.

"Sounds about as interesting as my job. You here by yourself?"

"No. My boyfriend had to make a phone call, so he went to our room for a few minutes. He'll be back soon."

"He left you here by yourself?" she teased. "He must trust you not to get into any trouble."

"I'm not sure what kind of trouble I could get into around here, unless it involved falling out of a palm tree or stepping on a sea urchin."

"Hey, you never know," Ree pointed out. "Some people can find trouble anywhere."

"Not me. I stay far away from trouble." I managed to say it with a straight face. I took my new drink from the bartender.

"How long are you here for?" my drinking companion asked. She placed her empty coconut back on the bar and shook her head when the bartender asked if she wanted another.

"Four more days. It's been heavenly to just get away." In fact, I was starting to wonder why on earth I would want to ever go back, despite the dangers of spiny sea urchins and having sand in places I didn't know you could get sand.

"Oh, I agree." Ree put her sunglasses back on. "Having a getaway is crucial, especially when life spins out of control. Hey, is that your boyfriend?" She pointed over my shoulder.

I turned. Sean waved as he headed for the little bar where I'd parked myself while he'd gone to make his daily phone call to the office. He wore a brightly colored shirt, left unbuttoned, and board shorts. He'd managed to turn dark brown in just the three days we'd been here. I couldn't help but notice how many stares he got from other women as he strode across the sand.

I watched him approach and decided we needed to return to our cabana so we could get back to what we'd been doing for most of the past three days.

When Sean joined me at the bar, he gave me a sizzling kiss that sent liquid heat rushing through me. He inhaled and his eyes went golden. "You know how much I love how you look in that bikini," he murmured, his lips near my ear. "But I love how you look even more without it."

Oh, we *definitely* needed to get back to the cabana.

I didn't want to be rude, so I turned back to where Ree had been standing to introduce Sean, but she'd vanished. Huh. Well, I *had* been ogling him for much longer than was necessary. She probably got bored and left.

"How were the drinks?" Sean asked, nuzzling my neck.

I shivered at the feeling of his breath on my sun-warmed skin. "Really great. Rum punch might be my new favorite beverage. Next to Scotch, of course."

"I think I'll order one to take back." He moved away to get the bartender's attention.

I slid down off my barstool and reached for my drink. A small folded piece of paper was tucked under the coconut.

The outside flap had a little drawing of a bottle with a skull and crossbones on the label and a long-stemmed rose.

With a frown, I opened the note. Inside was a short message, written in a neat, feminine hand. *Catherine is awake. If you need help, call me.*

Beside that message was a single word—the name of a woman everyone thought had been killed five years ago in an accident at Moses Murphy's cabal headquarters. It was a name I hadn't used since the night I fled the compound and left that life behind.

I stood frozen in shock, the note crumpled in my hand, my heart pounding so hard that I was sure everyone on the island could hear it.

Bottle of poison. A rose. Cyanide Rose. Cyro.

I looked around but saw no sign of Ree. Her empty coconut remained on the bar, but the straw was gone. She'd taken it with her. No DNA left behind.

Sean joined me, a coconut in each hand and a big grin on his face. "I figured we both needed one for the walk back." His smile faded. "Everything all right?"

"Fine." I forced a smile and took the coconut he was offering, the note hidden in my other hand. "Thank you. I was just thinking I could really use a drink."

He laughed and put his arm around my waist as we headed down the path that led to our cabana. I finished my drink before we got halfway there and left the empty coconut on another of the hotel's many bars.

The note I tore into tiny pieces and flushed down the toilet when

I got back to the cabana. I washed my face at the sink and stared at myself in the mirror. My eyes looked shadowed.

Having a getaway is crucial, she'd said.

Catherine is awake.

If you need help, call me.

I heard Sean's voice in my head. *Remember you are loved and you don't have to face anything by yourself ever again.*

"Alice?" Sean called through the door. "You okay?"

I dried my face and opened the door. "I'm fine," I assured him. "Too much rum punch. Race you to the hammock!" I took off running down the hall.

With a laugh, he gave chase. I let him catch me before we got to the door.

We never did make it out to the hammock.

THE END

SNEAK PEEK: HEART OF STONE

I ran through the trees, moving as quickly and quietly as I could. Small twigs and branches I couldn't see in the dark whipped across my face, leaving scratches that stung mercilessly.

Behind me, sirens blared and bright lights swept across my path, searching for targets. I thought of the snipers on the walls of the compound and my back itched. I expected to hear shots and feel an impact at any second. I ran faster.

I chanted swear words in my head as I ducked under branches and dodged the searchlights. *Where the hell is Arkady?*

I had little time to worry about my partner's fate. Dark figures moved in the trees to my right, heading in my direction. I veered left, hoping to find cover and a chance to regroup while I came up with a strategy for avoiding capture.

I stole a glance at my watch. Only a little over an hour until sunrise. Dawn meant safety and hopefully escape. I'd survived this long—surely I could make it just one more hour.

A twig snapped behind me. I dropped to my stomach in the mud and held perfectly still as stealthy footsteps passed less than ten feet away. I held my breath as they went by, my heart pounding in my ears.

I waited until my pursuer was out of earshot before I belly-crawled through the mud to hide behind a downed tree and catch my breath.

If Arkady was still out here, she'd be headed in the same direction I was going, hoping to either meet up with me or reach a secure position to wait it out until our rescue arrived. I heard shouting back in the direction of the compound, but I couldn't tell what they said. If those shouts meant she'd been captured...well, I'd have to deal with that later. Either way, I couldn't stay where I was. I needed to keep moving.

I listened hard but heard only the usual chorus of nighttime insects, rustling leaves, and branches creaking in the wind. I moved to a crouch and peeked over the top of the tree trunk.

Nothing.

I rose and grimaced at the mud covering the front of my long-sleeved black tee, borrowed BDU pants, and combat boots. I'd actually thought I looked fairly badass and had a little bit of Arkady-style swagger, but that was before we'd tripped some kind of perimeter alarm near the compound, given away our position, and had to split up to avoid capture. And before I'd had to crawl through the mud.

I swung my legs one at a time over the downed tree and continued heading east. As an earth mage, my affinity to the land meant my internal compass was stronger than most. Heavy cloud cover meant lack of moonlight with which to see or navigate, but I knew which way was east. With any luck, I'd make it to the rendezvous, find Arkady waiting there, and get the hell out of Dodge.

Just as I thought that, the earth literally fell out from under me.

One second my boots were on firm if muddy ground, and the next I was falling. It happened so quickly I didn't have a chance to do more than gasp.

My body landed in what felt like rope webbing. That broke my fall, but then the webbing gave way. I fell about four more feet and landed face-down in—of course—more mud. The impact knocked the wind out of me and left me stunned, unsure of what had just happened or where I'd ended up.

I raised my head, spat out a mouthful of mud and leaves, and found myself in a pit about the size of two graves, six feet wide by ten feet long and ten feet deep.

And I was not alone.

Arkady Woodall, my new best friend and the person I wanted to kill most in the world right now, grinned at me and picked leaves out of her hair. She sat with her back against the side of the pit, and she —almost unbelievably—was covered with more mud than I was. "Hey, Alice. Are you having fun?"

"Am I having *fun?*" I hissed, pushing myself up on all fours with a grimace. I spat out something slimy I didn't look at too closely. "I have mud in my boots, mud in my bra, and mud in my...never mind. No, I am *not having fun!*"

She laughed. "Liar."

I flipped her off and pushed muddy hair back from my face. "When I said I'd do a girls' weekend with you, this is definitely *not* what I thought we'd be doing. A two-day intensive survival camp? *Really?*"

She rolled her eyes and pulled a twig out of her hair. "What did you think we'd be doing, champagne brunch, mani/pedis, and seaweed wraps? You know me well enough to know I wasn't taking us for a spa weekend. And hey, look at this." She wiped some of the mud off her face and held up her hand. "People pay hundreds of dollars for mud treatments at spas, and it was included here at no extra cost."

"This mud smells like something died in it, Arkady."

"That probably makes it even better for your skin."

I didn't know whether to laugh or cry, so I made a sound that was a little of both. "I'm so tired. And cold. And thirsty. And I smell like... God, I don't even want to know what I smell like." I looked up at the top of the pit. "How long are they going to leave us in here?"

"They'll come get us at dawn."

I groaned. I was getting perilously close to whining. "That's almost an hour from now! Why not just come get us? We lost. We surrender. We're dead. Why make us suffer more?"

"You signed off on the rules, same as me." She settled in more comfortably. "Just think of it as more time for us to bond."

"I think I've already bonded with you as much as I want to for one weekend. We bunked together last night and we had to use the communal showers in the locker room, remember?"

"Oh, yeah." She grinned again. "That was fun. It's like being at summer camp, right?"

I'd never been to a summer camp. Activities like that weren't an option when you were a prisoner of your grandfather's crime syndicate from ages four through twenty-four. I'd rarely gone beyond the walls of his compound for months at a time, much less spent weeks away at camp, doing whatever it was non-mage kids got to do at such places.

"Yeah, just like summer camp," I said after a moment. "So, how many times have you made it to the extraction point without getting caught?"

"Twice."

"Out of how many attempts?"

She rested her forearms on her knees. "I've lost count. They change it up every time—different traps, different patrol routes, different objectives. It's never the same challenge twice. That's why I like it. If I could beat it, I wouldn't get better. I'm here to improve my skills, not to win."

"I don't see why the two should be mutually exclusive," I grumbled. "Or why we have to stay in this pit until sunrise."

"They'll actually probably come get us sooner than that. The last time, it was only about twenty minutes before they got me out."

"The *last* time? How many times have you fallen into one of these?"

She frowned at me. "That's not the point, Alice."

"So, a couple of times."

"Four times," she muttered.

I laughed.

Arkady made a *pfffft* sound. "Hey, you think this is bad, you should try getting caught in a snare and dangling upside down ten feet off the ground by one ankle. Then you *really* want them to come get you quickly."

"I don't remember that from the orientation."

"Yeah, they discontinued that one. Something about too much risk of head injury and the insurance company was going to cancel their coverage."

"Insurance companies are such killjoys," I said dryly. "Head trauma, spine injuries, blah blah blah."

"No kidding." She looked completely at ease sitting in a mud pit in the deep woods. "So, how are things between you and Sean since you guys got back from the Bahamas?"

"It's been good," I said, smiling despite how cold and gross and miserable I felt. "Really good. This two-day getaway with you is the longest we've gone without seeing each other since we got back." And I missed him more than I'd ever admit to anyone. I'd had a hard time falling asleep last night without him next to me, even as exhausted as I'd been after nearly twenty hours of running around trying to evade capture by the camp's employees.

"You two thinking about maybe moving in together?"

I shook my head. "We haven't talked about it."

Sean had hinted once or twice about the possibility, but I'd ducked the conversation. I saw no way for him to move into my home, which was much smaller than his, and the thought of members of his pack coming and going from my house all the time, invading my space, made me almost break out in hives.

At the same time, I couldn't just move in with him; my basement was a heavily warded fortress that had taken nearly five years to create, and giving that up didn't seem like an option. Particularly not when recent events made it likely I might be found by my grandfather and I'd need all the protection I could get.

Arkady distracted me with another question. "And things with the pack? Better?"

My smile faded. "About the same."

"Is Sean's beta still giving you trouble?"

I shrugged. "I've only seen Jack once since we got back. We crossed paths outside Maclin Security one day when I met Sean for lunch, and he just ignored me. I've heard he pretends I don't exist and doesn't say anything if the subject comes up in conversation with other pack members. It's pretty obvious he and his wife Delia still strongly disapprove of Sean and me being together, but Sean warned him to keep his opinions of me to himself, so that's probably why he hasn't been bad-mouthing me."

"But the rest of the pack likes you, right?"

"Most of them. There are some others who also think Sean should date a shifter, but none of them are as angry about it as Jack and Delia." I made a face. "And Caleb."

"Caleb's the kid who got bitten a couple of months ago and is having a hard time controlling himself?"

"Yeah. He moved in with Jack and Delia so they could keep an eye on him, and they're just three little Alice-hating peas in a pod. I'll be seeing them all later today. There's a birthday party for one of the pack and everyone's getting together to celebrate." I decided to change the subject. "And how are things between you and Matthias?"

She waggled her hand in a so-so gesture. "Okay, I guess. I'm still hurting over Fortune. Matthias is being gentlemanly about it."

Arkady's lover Fortune had been an enforcer for Charles Vaughan of the Vampire Court. He'd been killed about a month ago during an attempt on Charles's life. She'd been instrumental in the death of the man who killed him and that had helped, but it would take her some time to heal.

I was glad to hear that Matthias, who was also a Court enforcer, was patient and supportive. It didn't surprise me, though. The man practically worshiped the ground beneath her combat boots.

"So you two haven't...?" I asked.

She gave me a wry smile. "We've fooled around some, but I'm still not at a point where it feels like the right time. It's not that I feel like I'd be betraying Fortune, but..." She shrugged.

"It's okay. I get it. Matthias can wait until you're ready."

She grinned. "Damn right he can. I'm worth waiting for."

Footsteps crunched on the ground above us. I looked up to see four well-muscled men standing at the edge of the pit. Their haircuts and the way they stood said former Army. Two of them had paintball rifles slung over their shoulders. They were either the snipers or part of the patrols who'd hunted us for the better part of two days. I couldn't help but glare balefully from where I sat at the bottom of the pit.

"Hey, Joe," Arkady said casually, as if we'd just run into some old friends in a bar. She draped her arms over her knees. "How's it hangin'?"

"Still lower than my ex's new husband." The man in the center of the group regarded us with his hands on his hips. "You ready to get out of there?"

"Nah." She settled back against the wall of the pit. "We were right in the middle of some serious girl talk. Could you give us another ten, fifteen minutes?"

"Shut up, Arkady. Yes, we are ready to get out of here." I lurched to my feet on tired legs and almost fell over when my boots sank into the mud. "Do you have a ladder?"

The end of a rope dropped into the pit beside me. I stared at it, a little nonplussed.

Grinning, Arkady got to her feet. "You're getting soft, Joe. A rope? Last time I had to scramble up the dirt wall while you yelled insults."

Joe gripped the other end of the rope with both hands. His biceps strained the fabric of his T-shirt. "Your new friend doesn't look strong enough to get out of there without help." He flicked the rope at me. "Let's go, princess. Grab the rope and I'll haul you up."

My eyes narrowed. "Hey, Arkady? You want to get out of this pit without their help?"

She put her hands on her hips and studied me. "What are you thinking?"

"I'm thinking G.I. Joe Junior up there can kiss my ass." I crouched, stuck my hands into the mud, and started spooling earth magic. "You ready to go for a ride?"

She didn't ask for an explanation, just planted her feet shoulder-width apart and braced herself. "Okay, let's blow this popsicle stand."

"What'cha doing, princess?" Joe called. "Grab the rope. We got stuff to do."

"I'll show you princess," I muttered and pushed earth magic into the ground.

The earth trembled beneath us. The men stumbled back from the edge of the pit, cursing as the rumbling grew in volume.

In a burst of bright green earth magic, the ground heaved us up as though we were surfers riding a wave made of dirt instead of water. Arkady whooped and laughed as we shot upward in a spray of mud, rotten leaves, and twigs. The wave deposited us on the ground next to the pit and dumped a hundred gallons of smelly mud on Joe and the others, covering them from head to toe in muck. They stared at us, dumbfounded, blinking like muddy owls.

"Oops," I said insincerely, as the magic faded and the ground went still.

Arkady brushed leaves off her shoulder and gave Joe her biggest smile. "Guess we didn't need your help after all."

She turned to me and gestured at the lights of the compound. "Matthias is due to pick us up in forty minutes. Let's hit the showers and get the hell out of here."

And so we did.

Acknowledgments

Every time I sit down to write the acknowledgments for an Alice Worth book, I'm always amazed and humbled by how many people I need to thank. If it takes a village to raise a child, it requires a small army to make a book.

First, all my thanks to my longtime editor Heather McCorkle for her continued support, guidance, and patience through all of the stages of the writing process: drafting, revising, drinking, revising, editing, more drinking, more revising, some crying...wait, where was I? Oh, yes, and then copyediting!

A mountain of gratitude to my faithful *Heart of Ice* beta readers: Dr. Marie Guthrie, Dr. Adrienne Foreman, Dr. Robert James, Amy Hopper, Shannon Butler, and Dr. Kimberly Dodson.

A special thank you to Sgt. Richard Hass, U.S. Army Combat Engineer, for saving me from relying on Groupons and YouTube videos for information on things that go bang and boom; to Jennifer White, who rules the boxing gym when she isn't busy saving the world; and to Dr. Rick Moberly for medical advising.

When the going gets tough, the tough call on their friends to talk it through, and I owe many friends for their help during the writing and revising process. Thank you Dr. Jeff Stumpo, Dr. Trey Jansen, and Adrianne Treinies for helping me through the rough patches. I'd also like to thank Christine Rice, Jen Bauer-Krueger, J.C. Krueger, Jennifer Miller, Stacey Kelley, Neda Benitez, Rachel Ballantine, and Dr. Nicholas Lawrence for always being there when I need a laugh, a shoulder, a smile, a friend, or a kick in the butt. And of course a huge thank you to Bridget and Jennifer at The Full Cup, my second home, where I can usually be found at a table by the window, chugging coffee and writing.

As always, all my love and thanks to my wonderful and encouraging family: my mother, my sister Susan, my brother-in-law Josh, my sweet nephew Madden, and my lovely and brilliant cousins Antoinette and Felicia. I'd especially like to express my love and gratitude to Steve and Sheran Herrin for welcoming me as part of their family, and to my awesome cousin Tom Snowe for a whole list of things, but most importantly for making sure I didn't miss my chance to make some important family connections this year.

And because I saved the best for last, thank you to my wonderful husband Bill for his seemingly never-ending patience and support. You make loving fun.

About the Author

Lisa Edmonds was born and raised in Kansas. A graduate of Buhler High School, she studied English and forensic criminology at Wichita State University. After acquiring her Bachelor's degree, she considered a career in law enforcement as a behavioral analyst before earning a Master's in English from Wichita State and then a Ph.D. in English from Texas A&M University.

For ten years, she was an associate professor of English at a college in Texas, where she taught a variety of writing and literature courses.

Now a full-time author, she shares a cute Victorian-style home called The Storybook House with her husband and their pets, and enjoys writing, reading, traveling, spoiling her niece and nephew, and singing karaoke.

Don't miss new releases and announcements. Visit LisaEdmonds.com to follow Lisa across all platforms.